Airdrie
Marigold Library System
MAR 0 7 2019

D0042111

House Arrest

Also by Mike Lawson

The Inside Ring

The Second Perimeter

House Rules

House Secrets

House Justice

House Divided

House Blood

House Odds

House Reckoning

House Rivals

House Revenge

House Witness

Rosarito Beach

Viking Bay

K Street

House Arrest

MIKE LAWSON

Atlantic Monthly Press
New York

Airdrie Public Library
111 - 304 Main Street S
Airdrie, Alberta T4B 3C3

Copyright © 2019 by Mike Lawson

All rights reserved. No part of this book may be reproduced in any form or by any electronic or mechanical means, including information storage and retrieval systems, without permission in writing from the publisher, except by a reviewer, who may quote brief passages in a review. Scanning, uploading, and electronic distribution of this book or the facilitation of such without the permission of the publisher is prohibited. Please purchase only authorized electronic editions, and do not participate in or encourage electronic piracy of copyrighted materials. Your support of the author's rights is appreciated. Any member of educational institutions wishing to photocopy part or all of the work for classroom use, or anthology, should send inquiries to Grove/Atlantic, Inc., 154 West 14th Street, New York, NY 10011, or permissions@groveatlantic.com.

FIRST EDITION

Published simultaneously in Canada
Printed in the United States of America

First Grove Atlantic edition: February 2019

This book was set in 12-pt. Garamond Premier Pro
by Alpha Design & Composition of Pittsfield, NH.

Library of Congress Cataloging-in-Publication data is available for this title.

ISBN: 978-0-8021-2930-7
eISBN: 978-0-8021-4702-8

Atlantic Monthly Press
an imprint of Grove Atlantic
154 West 14th Street
New York, NY 10011

Distributed by Publishers Group West

www.groveatlantic.com

19 20 21 22   10 9 8 7 6 5 4 3 2 1

For Gail

Author's Note

I completed this book in May 2018. The 2018 midterm elections—the elections that would determine which American political party would control the U.S. House of Representatives—were to be held in November 2018, six months after I finished the book. If you keep reading, you'll see that the outcome of the 2018 midterms has a significant impact on the future of Joe DeMarco, and at the time I finished the book, I had no idea what the outcome would be.

—Mike Lawson

1

The killer knew the location of every surveillance camera in the Capitol.

He was dressed in a dark blue uniform: a blue baseball cap, a dark blue short-sleeved shirt, and matching pants with cargo pockets. An equipment belt held a holstered .40-caliber Glock, zip ties that could be used as handcuffs, an extendable metal baton, and a canister of pepper spray. On his feet were black combat boots. On his hands were thin, black leather gloves.

The rotunda was dimly lit because of the hour, and as the killer walked he followed a route he'd practiced many times, staying against the walls, taking advantage of shadows. Nonetheless, three cameras captured his image, but as he passed into camera range he would turn his head, placing his big hands over his face, the bill of the baseball cap further obscuring his features. The cameras, however, did record a blue-and-white insignia patch on his right sleeve.

He ascended a marble staircase, and on the third floor he again kept his head lowered, so the bill of the cap and his hands blocked his face from a hallway camera. Once he was past the camera, he quickened his pace until he reached the main door to the politician's suite of offices. Before he opened the door, he unholstered the Glock, pulled a silencer from a pocket, and screwed the silencer into the barrel of the weapon.

The door was not locked. The politician most likely locked it when he left for the day, but there was no reason to lock it when he was there. What did he have to fear? He was in one of the most well-protected buildings in the United States.

The killer walked into the suite, holding the gun down at the side of his leg. He passed several small offices and desks in open areas where secretaries, aides, and interns usually sat. Because of the hour, he'd been hoping the politician's staff had left for the day; most of them usually left by seven or eight, unless there was something extraordinary going on. If any of them hadn't left, he'd have been forced to kill them too, which he really didn't want to do.

The politician he'd come to kill was seated behind the desk in his office. There were a Virginia state flag and an American flag in floor stands behind the desk, photographs of party leaders on the wall, and on his desk, a photo of his late wife. A smiling portrait of the fool who was now president was prominently displayed.

The politician wore a white shirt, the sleeves rolled up, and a blue-and-red-striped tie loosened at the collar. He was holding a phone to his right ear, and the killer heard him say, "Kathy, if you don't get on board with this—"

At that moment the politician saw the killer standing in the doorway but didn't see the gun he was holding next to one leg. He was puzzled by the appearance of the killer, wondering why he had come to his office, but he wasn't concerned or alarmed. Why would he be concerned? The U.S. Capitol Police were there to protect him.

He said into the phone, "Kathy, hang on a minute." Cupping his hand over the phone, he said, "Can I help you, Officer?"

The killer raised his weapon, pointed it at the man's chest, and whispered, "Tell her you'll have to call her back."

"What?"

"You heard me. Do it, or I'll shoot you."

Eyes expanding with fear, the politician said into the phone, "Kathy, I'll have to call you back," and disconnected the call—and the killer shot him in the heart.

The politician slumped back in his chair, dropping the phone on the carpeted floor, and the killer shot him a second time, in the forehead. Blood splattered the wall behind the desk, creating an interesting Rorschach pattern. The politician fell forward after the second shot and ended up, still seated, with his head resting on the blotter on his desk. The blotter slowly turned from green to dark red as the pooling blood from the forehead wound formed a halo around the dead man's head.

The killer didn't bother to pick up the two shell casings ejected from the Glock. He could have, but he didn't. He wasn't worried about leaving evidence behind. He removed the silencer from the gun, put it back in his pocket, and holstered the Glock. He then made his way back through the maze of staff offices, and when he left the suite, he locked the door behind him. If anyone came to see the politician tonight— though it was unlikely, considering the hour—they'd think that he had gone home for the day. His body shouldn't be discovered until the next morning, when his secretary, who was always the first to arrive, came to work. In fact, given that this was a Friday night, it might not be discovered until Monday.

The killer walked down the stairs to the rotunda level, again always mindful of the cameras, then took another staircase to reach the subbasement of the Capitol. In the subbasement, he unlocked a door marked with the letter *E* and a series of numbers. The room he entered was a small closet, and inside it was a gray metal cabinet containing electrical equipment. On the floor of the closet was a gym bag he'd placed there hours ago.

Now he would wait an hour and hope that was enough time.

The waiting didn't bother the killer; he'd spent a lifetime standing around waiting.

The hour passed, and he took out his cell phone and made a call. He let the phone he was calling ring five times but hung up before an answering machine could pick up.

He left the electrical equipment closet, taking the gym bag with him, and walked down the hall to an office that had the words *Counsel Pro Tem for Liaison Affairs* written in flaking gold paint on the frosted-glass window of the mahogany-stained door. The phone the killer had called before he left the closet belonged to the man who occupied the office, and he'd called to verify that the man was no longer there.

He unlocked the door with a key he'd had made a month ago. The office was small and practically barren. There was an old and battered wooden desk, a wooden chair behind the desk that could swivel and tilt backward, and another, plain wooden chair—a visitor's chair—in front of the desk. On the desk was a phone connected to an answering machine and a laptop computer. The only other items in the room were a four-drawer gray metal file cabinet and a coatrack near the door. Hanging on the coatrack were a tan London Fog trench coat and a battered L. L. Bean Scottish-tweed rain hat.

The killer didn't turn on the lights in the office. Moving quickly, he removed his equipment belt and stripped down to his underwear; he didn't remove the gloves he was wearing or the ball cap. He took his cell phone out of a pocket and placed it in the gym bag. He left the silencer in the pocket of the pants he'd been wearing. Now, attired in only his ball cap, his underwear, black socks, and thin black gloves, he removed a flashlight from the gym bag, one small enough to hold between his teeth. He also removed a screwdriver.

The killer took the visitor's chair and placed it beneath a ventilation grille in the ceiling. He unscrewed the four screws holding the grille in place, set the grille on the floor, and put the pants, shirt, boots, and equipment belt holding the Glock he'd used inside the ventilation duct. Before he placed the boots in the duct, he removed inserts that had made him an inch taller. He didn't, however, put in the ball cap he was wearing. He left the cap on his head.

Next, he removed the black leather gloves and put them on the desk, and from the gym bag he took latex gloves, the kind surgeons wear. He donned the latex gloves and pulled from the gym bag a baseball cap identical to the one he was wearing. He made sure the two long, dark hairs he'd placed inside the cap were still there, and then put the ball cap and the leather gloves inside the ventilation duct and screwed the grille back into place. After he finished inserting the screws, he used the screwdriver to scratch the ventilation grille, making bright white marks in the metal, as if the screwdriver had slipped several times while he was threading in the fasteners.

He put the visitor's chair back where it had been originally and placed the screwdriver inside the center drawer of the desk. He removed his own clothes and boots from the gym bag next—clothes that appeared to be identical to those he'd been wearing—and got dressed. He also put on an equipment belt that was in the gym bag; the belt too appeared to be identical to the one he'd placed in the ventilation duct and included a holstered .40-caliber Glock. After he was dressed, he stood without moving for about sixty seconds, mentally reviewing everything he'd done, trying to think of anything he'd forgotten. He decided he was good; the entire operation had gone precisely as planned. He was pleased—and frankly somewhat surprised—that he was so calm.

The killer had never killed before.

He opened the office door and peeked down the hall. It was empty, as he'd expected at eleven thirty at night. He walked back to the electrical closet, holding the now mostly empty gym bag, and stepped back inside. Then he realized he *had* forgotten something and laughed out loud. He took off his cap, removed the wig from his bald head, and placed the wig in the gym bag. That would have been a hell of a mistake, if someone had spotted him with a full head of hair.

Now he had hours to wait, but that was okay. It'd give him plenty of time to think of the things he could do with the money he'd earned.

———◆◆◆———

The dead politician was discovered by his secretary at seven o'clock the following morning.

The politician's name was Lyle Canton. He was the House majority whip.

His killer was arrested thirty-eight hours later.

2

The J. Edgar Hoover Building, headquarters for the Federal Bureau of Investigation, is less than a mile from the U.S. Capitol. Ten minutes after the body of Congressman Lyle Canton was found, six FBI agents arrived in a black Chevy Suburban SUV, blue and red grille lights flashing. While the agent in charge went to look at the body and take over control of the crime scene from the Capitol Police, another agent commandeered a conference room that would be used as a temporary command center.

The Capitol had been locked down by the Capitol Police before the FBI arrived, but now an announcement was made telling everyone who wasn't law enforcement to gather in the rotunda. It was still early morning, and a Saturday, but there were about twenty civilians in the building. The Capitol Police checked each person's credentials, patted him or her down for weapons, and searched all backpacks and purses. Then all twenty people were moved into a conference room and told they'd have to remain there until they were interviewed by the FBI. One of the people turned out to be the chief of staff of the Senate majority leader. He was dressed in casual clothes and had stopped by the Capitol only to pick up something from his office on the way to his daughter's soccer game. He told the Capitol cops who his boss was and demanded to be released immediately. An unimpressed cop, not adequately trained on how to address his betters, told him to sit down and shut up.

More Capitol Police were called in—over a hundred of them—to assist the FBI in searching the building and to make sure no one was lurking in a closet with an AR-15. As the Capitol has about six hundred rooms, it took several hours to complete the search.

At the time, it never occurred to the FBI that the killer could be a Capitol cop.

By noon there were over forty FBI agents and crime-scene technicians at the Capitol, all of them wearing blue windbreakers with *FBI* on the back in yellow letters. The Speaker of the House and the Senate majority leader had been informed that no business would be conducted in the Capitol for the rest of the weekend—not that much business was ever conducted there anyway, even during the workweek.

———————◆◆◆———————

The agent in charge of the investigation was a man named Russell Peyton, a twenty-five-year veteran of the bureau. J. Edgar Hoover may have been a pudgy cross-dresser, but Peyton was the type of agent Hoover had almost always hired: tall, slim, white, male, Protestant, and married. At the age of fifty-two, Peyton was in better shape than most men half his age because, unless a case prevented him from doing so, he jogged five miles every day. He suspected that with this case he wouldn't be jogging—or for that matter sleeping much—until the killer was apprehended.

The director of the FBI had told Peyton, "I'll need updates every four hours because the president told me he wants updates every four hours."

The FBI director was a man named Ronald Erby. He'd been in charge of the bureau for only a few months, since the president had fired his predecessor for reasons that people were now writing books about.

Erby was a lawyer who had spent some time in law enforcement prior to his appointment, but he was best known for his political acumen and his unwavering loyalty to the president—which was the main reason he was now the director.

Erby and Peyton both knew that the president had liked Lyle Canton—Canton had been a lapdog for the president during his campaign—but a lot of Republicans didn't care for Canton because of his abrasive personality. As for the Democrats, it would be literally impossible to find a Democrat inside the Beltway who didn't despise the man. Nonetheless, and regardless of Canton's popularity—or lack thereof—it was unacceptable to have one of the leaders of the Republican Party assassinated. At noon the president was going to stand in the Rose Garden and make a speech praising Canton for his service to the nation and promise that everything that could be done would be done to bring his killer to justice—and Director Erby wanted some answers by then.

Based on the last call Canton had made—to Texas congresswoman Kathy Thomas—and the time of death as estimated by the FBI's pathologist, Peyton knew the congressman had been killed sometime between 10:13 p.m. on Friday and approximately 4:00 the following morning. Peyton's agents went to work compiling a list of everyone who had been in the Capitol during those hours. They interviewed the Capitol cops who'd been on duty and started looking at video footage obtained from the many cameras in and around the building. An elite team of crime-scene technicians dusted Canton's office for fingerprints, took photos, and vacuumed carpets for trace evidence. The two shell casings found in Canton's office were the first pieces of evidence they bagged.

Peyton learned Lyle Canton had a reputation for working long hours, but the specific reason he'd been in his office at ten o'clock on a Friday night was that he'd been doing his job: whipping up support for a bill that would go to the floor for a vote in a week—a bill that many Republicans didn't like. In other words, Canton had been twisting the

MIKE LAWSON

arms of reluctant Republicans like Congresswoman Thomas to make sure they didn't stray from the herd.

About four hours after the body had been found, Peyton held a meeting in the commandeered conference room with four of his senior agents. Peyton had been getting periodic updates, but he wanted his senior people to have the whole picture and to make sure he had the latest news, so he could brief his boss and his boss could brief the president.

"Jack, you go first," Peyton said to one of the agents.

Jack said, "The big thing is, we're ninety-nine percent certain we've got the killer on video. He's either a Capitol cop or somebody disguised as one. But we don't have a clear image of his face."

One of the other agents said, "You're shittin' me. That means the shooter could still be in the building. He could have—"

Peyton held up a hand for silence and said, "Go on, Jack."

Jack went on. "This guy knew where every camera was, and he kept his head turned away or placed his hands over his face when he was in camera range. And he was wearing gloves, which is another reason we're pretty sure he's the killer. Why would a guy be wearing gloves this time of year?" It was late June. "Anyway, we can see him on a camera walking up the stairs leading to Canton's office. About two minutes before Canton made his last phone call, which he made at ten thirteen p.m., we got him walking down the hall toward Canton's office. Three minutes after Canton's last call, he walked back up the hall. This means that Canton was most likely killed at about ten fifteen. We can tell from the video footage that the killer is white, about five eleven, and weighs around one eighty. The techs will get us more precise measurements. He's wearing one of those ball caps the guards here wear, but you can see he has dark hair. He doesn't have a limp or anything else that's distinctive about the way he moves."

"How many people were in the building when Canton was killed?" Peyton asked.

"Forty-three," Jack said.

10

"That's all?" Peyton said.

"It was a Friday night, and with the weekend coming there just weren't that many folks working late. At the time of the killing there were twenty-four cops guarding the entrances and patrolling the grounds. There were four aides in various offices researching sh-, stuff for their bosses. There was an IT guy trying to fix a computer, eight janitors who were on the Senate side vacuuming and cleaning toilets, two gals making copies of some bill that was about five thousand pages long, and one guy trying to fix the sound system in one of the hearing rooms."

Jack paused and smiled slightly. "In addition to all those folks, the House minority whip, Conrad English, was in his office with a twenty-two-year-old intern who works for a congresswoman. They were just a few doors away from Canton's office but didn't see or hear anything. One of the Capitol cops said there's a rumor going around that English, who's married, and the intern spend a *lot* of late nights together and probably didn't hear anything because—"

Peyton said, "I don't want to hear any nonsense like that unless it bears on the murder."

"Yes, sir," Jack said. "Last, there was a lawyer down in the subbasement, some guy named DeMarco. He got here at nine forty-five and left about fifty minutes later. So that's a total of forty-three people. And even though we now know the killing happened about ten fifteen, we're interviewing everyone who was in the building between eight p.m. and seven this morning. So far no one has reported seeing anything useful, like a Capitol cop walking around wearing gloves."

"How do you know who was here during those hours?" Peyton asked.

"During normal working hours, people who have the right badge can just walk in and out of the building. They have to pass through the metal detectors and go past the guards, of course, but they're not logged in and out. For some reason—maybe just to keep the guards awake—after eight p.m. everybody going in and out, even if they have the right ID, is logged. We haven't finished looking at the cameras near the entrances yet, but we will, then we'll confirm that everybody who entered after eight is on the log."

Peyton said, "We need to know exactly where every security guard was at about ten."

Jack said, "I realize that, boss. We're building a matrix showing everyone's location at that time, then confirming their locations through interviews and video footage."

Two hours later, Jack came back to Peyton and said, "We've got something interesting. As you know, the shooter was wearing what appears to be a Capitol cop's uniform, but we took a close look at the patch on his right sleeve. It's not an exact duplicate of the insignia patch the Capitol Police wear. I mean, it's the correct colors—blue and white—shows the Capitol building, and has 1828 on it, but—"

"What's the 1828 mean?" Peyton asked.

"That's the year the Capitol Police were founded. Anyway, the image of the Capitol and the oak-leaf cluster on the patch are slightly different in a number of small ways. What I'm saying is, the patch appears to be a fake the shooter had made, but it's not an exact duplicate of a real insignia patch. We're getting the names of companies that could have made the patch, but it's going to be a long list and will include companies in China, Vietnam, and Bangladesh. As for the uniform the guy was wearing—blue shirt, dark blue cargo pants—you can buy those clothes anywhere. Same with the stuff on the equipment belt, the zip ties, the baton, the Mace. You can buy all that commercially and online. But if we can find the shirt with the patch on it, that'll be a significant piece of evidence."

<hr>

Peyton called Ronald Erby and gave the director another update.

"I've told the head of the Capitol Police that I want all his people polygraphed," Peyton said.

"Can he do that?" Erby asked. "I mean, without his cops raising a stink and getting union reps and lawyers involved?"

"Yeah. His people agree to periodic polygraph testing as well as drug testing when they sign on. And naturally anyone who refuses becomes an instant suspect. I've also told him I want to see the personnel files on all his cops, including ID photos."

"How many people does he have?" the director asked.

"About thirteen hundred, but we'll immediately weed out anyone who's not white or male or who doesn't meet the physical description of the killer. But I seriously doubt it was a Capitol cop who killed Canton. For one thing, a cop wouldn't have to make a fake insignia patch for his shirt.

"I also don't think this was terrorist-related, and we should tell this to the media at the next press conference, just to calm everyone down. A terrorist most likely would have killed several people, not just one guy, and some organization would have taken credit for the killing. It's also hard to imagine that some politician did this. I mean, the Democrats hated Canton, but I can't imagine a politician actually murdering him."

"Yeah, but the man went out of his way to make enemies," the director said.

What the director meant was that Canton was the designated hatchet man for the Republican majority in the House. The Republican Speaker of the House wished to be viewed as a reasonable man who could work with those on the other side of the aisle and he tried his best not to poke the Democrats too rudely in the eye with a sharp stick. He left that job to Lyle Canton. Canton was the one who made brash statements to the media castigating the Democrats for their opposition to every Republican-sponsored bill. And Canton didn't choose his words carefully when he accused Democratic Party leaders of being responsible for every malady affecting the country. So the Democrats hated the man, particularly the Democratic minority leader, John Mahoney, who was usually Canton's primary target.

"The last time I can think of that one American politician shot another," Peyton told the director, "was when Burr killed Hamilton. These guys assassinate people with money and lies, not bullets. A more likely possibility is that some nut could have taken offense at something Canton was doing—like maybe this bill he was working on last night—but this doesn't feel like a nut to me. A nut would have walked up to Canton at some event and started spraying bullets, like the guy who shot Giffords."

He meant Congresswoman Gabrielle Giffords, who had been shot in the head in an assassination attempt near Tucson in 2011. In addition to Giffords, twelve other people had been wounded, and six were killed.

"This was planned well in advance," Peyton told Erby. "The shooter got a uniform, made up his own Capitol Police insignia patch, and he knew where every camera was on the route to Canton's office. He had to have spent days, if not weeks, planning this, so this was done by someone who spent a lot of time in the building."

"Like a Capitol cop," Erby said.

"But if it was a Capitol cop," Peyton countered, "why make a fake patch?"

Peyton continued. "I think this was personal, and not politically motivated. Canton was an abrasive asshole, and I suspect he stepped on a lot of people to get to where he is today. Maybe he destroyed someone's reputation. Maybe he crushed someone's career. We're going to have to take a hard look at his personal life and his past to find people who had some reason to kill him."

"I assume you're going through all his hate mail," the director said.

"Yeah, everything he got in the last year," Peyton said. "The Secret Service had already investigated the people who sent them before he was killed, and they didn't see any serious threats, but we're going back over everything. So far no one has popped out that looks promising, but we're still digging."

"You seem to be ignoring the most obvious suspect, Russ," the director said.

"I'm not ignoring him, boss," Peyton said. "I just haven't figured out what I'm going to do about him."

"Do you know where Sebastian Spear was when this happened?"

"Yeah. He was in China, and he's still there. According to his PR person, he's been there almost a week at a conference that was scheduled two months ago. But that means nothing. With his money, Spear could have hired the best pro in the business, and if everything that's been written about him and Canton is true, he had a better motive than anyone I can think of for killing Canton."

"You're going to have to tread carefully with Spear," the director said. "The guy's a politically connected billionaire."

"I know," Peyton said. "And right now I don't have anything to justify getting a warrant to look at his finances or his phone records or anything else. I could go to China to question to him but I think that would be a complete waste of time unless I can find something that actually ties him to Canton's death."

"So what are you going to do?" the director asked.

"I'm going to talk to the reporter who broke the story about Spear's affair with Canton's wife. She seems to know more about it than anyone else."

3

Four months earlier, Jean Canton—the wife of Congressman Lyle Canton—had been killed in a car accident. Her blood alcohol level was three times the legal limit when she lost control of her Audi and crashed into a hundred-year-old oak tree. She was pronounced dead at the scene.

It was raining the day they buried Jean at a cemetery in Vienna, Virginia. She was interred in a family plot that contained several of Lyle Canton's ancestors, including his father, the former senator Eric Canton. Many of the people attending the burial service saw a man wearing a black trench coat and blue jeans standing on a knoll about fifty yards from the grave site. The man's head was bare, and his dark hair was matted down from the rain, but he appeared oblivious to the elements. He hadn't shaved in several days and was leaning against a tree, taking sips from a pint bottle as he watched the service. The people who saw him thought he was some pitiful street person who had wandered accidentally into the cemetery, but as Jean Canton's coffin was being lowered into the ground, he staggered down the hill toward the grave, pushed his way through the crowd of mourners, and headed for Lyle Canton.

Accompanying Canton, because of his congressional rank, were two U.S. Capitol policemen dressed in suits. They immediately moved to stop the drunk. As they grabbed him, the man shouted: "You son of a bitch. You killed her. And I'm going to kill you. I swear to God I will."

The two Capitol cops hustled the lunatic away from the grave site. Threatening to kill a member of the United States Congress is a felony. The man was handcuffed and placed in the back of a Vienna Police patrol car. (The Vienna Police had led the funeral procession from the church to the cemetery and had provided traffic control along the way.) Canton's bodyguards needed to stay with Canton, so they told the Vienna cops to toss the drunk into a cell and that someone would be out to interview him later and decide whether charges would be filed.

Only two people at Jean Canton's funeral recognized the man; had he been wearing his trademark glasses and not been so disheveled, maybe others would have. One of those who recognized him was Lyle Canton. The other was a woman who had gone to high school with both Jean and Lyle Canton. Her name was Libby Baker, and she was now a reporter for the *Richmond Times-Dispatch*. Libby hadn't been close friends with either Lyle or Jean, but she'd lied to her editor, convinced him that she knew them both well, and asked to be allowed to write an article about them: what they'd been like when they were young; the tragedy of Jean Canton's passing at such an early age; the fact that widower Canton would now be one of the most eligible bachelors in Washington.

But when Libby Baker recognized the man who'd threatened Canton . . . Well, now she *really* had something to write about.

Before leaving the cemetery, Canton told his security detail to hold the drunk until he'd departed and then let him go. The senior Capitol cop told him that they couldn't do that. He said they needed to identify the man and make sure he didn't pose a real threat to the congressman and other politicians. At this point Canton got pissy. He said he knew who the man was, knew he was harmless, and to let him go. But the head of his security detail—who despised Canton because he was an overbearing bully—stood his ground.

"Sorry, Congressman, but I can't do that," he said again, and then stood there stone-faced as Canton berated him.

While Canton was tongue-lashing his security guys, Libby Baker walked over to the police car where the drunk was sitting in the back seat, his head down, sobbing. She quickly took two photos of the prisoner with her cell phone. She wondered what the cops would do when they learned that the man they were holding was Sebastian Spear, one of the wealthiest men in northern Virginia.

A week later, Libby Baker published an article claiming that Sebastian Spear had been having an affair with Lyle Canton's wife, and the night Jean Canton had died she'd been on her way to see Spear to tell him she was leaving her husband. Sebastian Spear—who was never charged for threatening Canton—refused to comment on the article. Congressman Canton did make a comment. He said that had he been a private citizen, he would have sued Ms. Baker and her paper. "I'm absolutely disgusted," Canton said, "that the *Times-Dispatch* would print a pack of lies attempting to soil the good name and reputation of my late wife. And that's all I'm going to say on this sordid subject."

The real reason Canton didn't file a lawsuit was that the claims in Libby Baker's article were true.

4

Peyton told one of his agents to get him Libby Baker's unlisted cell-phone number. Five minutes later he had it.

"This is FBI Special Agent Russell Peyton," he said, when Baker answered her phone.

"What?" she said. "How did you get my number?"

Peyton almost laughed. "As I said, Ms. Baker, I work for the FBI, and I'm investigating Congressman Canton's murder. I'd like to speak to you about the article you wrote about Jean Canton and Sebastian Spear."

"I'm not going to divulge my sources," Baker said.

Again, Peyton almost laughed. Who did the woman think she was? Bob Woodward? "I'm not interested in your sources, Ms. Baker. I just want to talk to you, as you may have information that might assist me in my investigation."

"Is Sebastian Spear a suspect?" Baker asked.

Peyton didn't bother to say that Spear was obviously a suspect as he'd publicly threatened to kill Lyle Canton. Instead he said, "I'd like you to come to Washington so I can speak to you in person. To speed things up, I'll have a helicopter pick you up in Richmond."

Peyton knew what Baker was now thinking. Here was a chance for her to get inside the investigation. No way in hell was she not going to come to Washington and talk to him. Not to mention, she'd probably never taken a ride in a government chopper.

"Where do I meet the helicopter?" Baker said.

———————◆◆◆———————

Libby Baker was a short, plump woman with brassy blond hair, an impressive bosom, and sharp brown eyes—eyes that tried to take in every detail of Peyton's command center. With her stout figure and her head swiveling, her eyes darting from papers on the conference table to the writing on a whiteboard on one side of the room, she reminded Peyton of a pouter pigeon, searching for bread crumbs to snatch off the ground.

Peyton took her to an office down the hall from the conference room/command center. He offered her a bottle of water, then took a seat behind a desk that belonged to some congressman's aide who'd been ejected from the office.

"I'd like you to talk to me about the article you wrote about the Cantons and Sebastian Spear," Peyton said.

"Did you read my story?" Baker asked.

"I read it quickly online while I was waiting for you," Peyton said, "but I didn't read it at the time it was published. Whether or not Mrs. Canton had an affair with Mr. Spear was of no interest to the Federal Bureau of Investigation until Congressman Canton was killed."

"So you are saying that Sebastian is a suspect," Baker said.

"Ms. Baker, anything said here today is off the record."

"I won't agree to that," Baker said.

"If you don't agree, then I'll terminate this discussion and have someone drive you back to Richmond." *No more helicopter rides for you, honey.* "On the other hand, if you're cooperative, I'm willing to give you a preview of the press conference that I'll be holding this evening, and your paper will have a two-hour lead on the story."

"Will give you me an exclusive if you arrest someone?"

"No," Peyton said emphatically. "Now are we off the record or not?"

Peyton again knew exactly what Libby Baker was thinking: an off-the-record conversation with the FBI was better than no conversation at all, and there was no way she could pass up getting a two-hour jump on the other reporters. Peyton had been playing the media for years, and he'd played against much stronger opponents than Libby Baker.

"Yeah, all right. We're off the record," Baker said. "For now, anyway."

"Good. Now to answer your question, Sebastian Spear is not a suspect at this time. He was in China when Congressman Canton was killed."

"That doesn't mean *anything*," Baker said. "With his money—"

"That's true," Peyton said. "But right now we have nothing to indicate that Mr. Spear conspired with or paid someone to kill Congressman Canton."

Sebastian Spear was chairman of the board and CEO of Spear Industries, a publicly traded company that specialized in the manufacture and installation of almost anything having to do with the generation and transmission of electricity. It operated internationally, and anywhere in the world where a hydroelectric dam or a power distribution system was being built or upgraded, there was a good possibility that Spear Industries was the lead contractor. Sebastian Spear's father had founded the company, and Sebastian had taken over at the age of thirty, when his father was diagnosed with Parkinson's disease. His net worth was estimated to be about three billion dollars.

To get things rolling, Peyton said, "I understand that you went to high school with Spear and the Cantons. Is that true?"

"Yeah, and elementary school," Baker said. "My family had money back then, and I lived in McLean, where Sebastian Spear, Lyle Canton, and Jean Mitchell all lived. My father managed to drink and gamble away his fortune, but I guess you're not interested in that."

"I'm not," Peyton said.

"Anyway, we all went to the same private schools in McLean. Sebastian's family was the richest, of course. And as I'm sure you know, Lyle Canton's father was Senator Eric Canton. The senator died the same year Lyle was elected to the House. Jean Mitchell's father was a professor at George Mason, and her mother wrote children's books. She was quite successful. I'll bet if you have kids, your wife read to them from Mary Mitchell's books."

Peyton smiled slightly. "She did, actually."

Libby Baker began her story: "Sebastian Spear probably fell in love with Jean Mitchell when he was twelve years old."

The tale Baker told was as old as teenage love, older than Romeo and Juliet.

Sebastian Spear was a studious, dorky kid as a teenager. Jean Mitchell was pretty and shy. They began dating in freshman year of high school, and Sebastian took Jean to every dance, every party, every football game. Everyone who knew them was certain they'd get married eventually. And while Sebastian and Jean were totally committed to each other, Lyle Canton played the field. He was a handsome, athletic kid—not a good student like Sebastian or Jean—and he dated cheerleaders and young ladies of questionable virtue. The three all went to college at the University of Virginia, Sebastian majoring in electrical engineering, Jean Mitchell in creative writing, and Lyle studying for an eventual law degree—but spending most of his time partying with his fraternity brothers.

Baker said, "Sebastian's dad had wanted him to go to MIT because it's a more prestigious engineering school than UVA, but Sebastian went to Virginia because that's where Jean went. And what happened is that he basically lost Jean because of engineering."

"I don't understand what you mean by that," Peyton said.

"I mean electrical engineering is an academic ballbuster, and he was taking courses like calculus and differential equations and had to study his ass off. And while he was cramming for exams, he wasn't spending much time with his girlfriend.

"The other thing was, in high school Jean was this skinny, awkward, wallflower type, but she blossomed in college. She grew into a beautiful woman, and Lyle Canton finally took an interest in her. He was charming and handsome and funny, and he just swept her off her feet.

"And I'll tell you another thing," Baker said, "although I'm just guessing about this. I think, even back in college, Lyle probably figured that Jean Mitchell would make the perfect politician's wife. Anyway, sophomore year at UVA, Jean broke up with Sebastian and started going out with Lyle."

Baker took a sip from the bottle of water Peyton had given her. "Now here's the interesting part, and three of my sources confirmed this. When Jean broke up with him, Sebastian had a nervous breakdown. He'd been in love with her since puberty, and when she started dating Lyle, he stopped going to classes and started drinking and began stalking her all over the campus. Two people told me that they were convinced he was going to commit suicide. Eventually, someone told his parents what was going on, and his mother came down and got him, and the next year, after he spent some time with a therapist, he was attending MIT. And three years later, Lyle Canton married Jean Mitchell and stayed married to her for the next twenty years. So what I'm saying is, Sebastian had a good reason to hate Lyle even before he killed Jean."

Peyton said, "What do you mean by that, Ms. Baker? Jean Canton died in a car accident."

"That may be true, but Sebastian believed it was Lyle's fault she got drunk that night and ran her car off the road. And that's basically what he said at her funeral."

Peyton had no idea how Baker could know what Spear was thinking or whether it was Canton's fault that his wife got drunk the night she died, but didn't say this. Instead he said, "Tell me about the affair between Sebastian Spear and Jean Canton. Your article said it began three months before her death."

"It did. Sebastian never got over Jean and—"

"How could you possibly know that?" Peyton asked.

"Well, for one thing, he never married. And I've seen photos of some of the women he's dated, and all of them looked like they could have been Jean's twin sister. He probably broke up with them when he finally figured out that none of them were ever going to *be* Jean Canton."

Peyton hated dealing with people who mixed facts, gossip, and speculation all into the same narrative without making a distinction. "What about the affair?" Peyton said.

"During the twenty years Lyle and Jean were married, Sebastian never contacted Jean. Ever. She was the one who took the initiative by attending a charity event at the Smithsonian just to see him. At this point, her marriage to Canton was dead and—"

Peyton had had enough. "Ms. Baker, please. How could you know all this? How could you know that Spear never contacted Jean Canton for twenty years? How could you know about the state of the Cantons' marriage?"

"I told you I'm not going to name sources, but one of them was extremely close to Jean. She was her confidante, and they spoke almost daily. This person hated Lyle because of the way he treated Jean, and that's why she agreed to speak to me. She was hoping my article would destroy his political career."

Peyton would look at Jean Canton's phone records later and find out whom she spoke to on an almost daily basis. To Baker, he said, "Okay. I'll assume for now that your information's accurate. You were saying that Jean's marriage to Lyle was dead. Why was that?"

Baker said, "Because he treated her horribly. He was abusive and—"

"Abusive? Physically abusive?"

"No. He never hit her, or anything like that. He couldn't afford the political consequences of her walking around with a black eye. He mentally abused her. He emotionally abused her. He wanted Jean to be his political partner, to give speeches when he was campaigning, to wheedle money out of potential donors, but Jean was terrible at that sort of thing. She was an introvert. She wasn't comfortable speaking in public and didn't have the, the *guile* for raising money. He was constantly telling her she was useless.

"And Lyle wanted children. But that wasn't because he really wanted kids. He wanted a campaign poster of him posing with his beautiful wife and two beautiful children. You can't talk about family values if you don't have a family. But Jean couldn't get pregnant, and he made her life a living hell for years, with fertility clinics and in vitro fertilization and all that shit. He refused to adopt, and when he finally gave up on her giving him children after three miscarriages, he beat her over the head with that, too."

"I see," Peyton said.

"Jean wanted to become a writer, like her mother, and Lyle crushed those dreams as well. He told her she wrote like an addled teenager and that she'd never be published. He refused to use any of his contacts to help her get an agent. I think he was afraid she was going to eclipse him in some way if she became successful, or he was afraid her writing might embarrass him politically. Whatever the case, he did everything he could to discourage her, and she stopped writing."

Baker shook her head. "In public, that prick was always holding her hand and giving her all these lovey-dovey looks, but in private he was an absolute bastard to her—always putting her down, constantly criticizing her. And because of the way he treated her, she became an alcoholic. You'd never know it to look at her, but she was one of those women who would start hitting the wine bottle about noon every day, and by seven or eight at night she'd be completely stewed. And that's usually when she talked to my source, in the evening, when she was drunk and crying about the way Canton treated her."

"So why didn't she divorce him?" Peyton asked.

"I have no idea. Some women stay in abusive relationships their entire lives. Whatever the case, one day Jean found out that Sebastian was attending this Smithsonian event, and she went to see him, and their affair began that night. They went to the bar in the Mandarin Oriental and talked for two hours, and when Jean asked him to get them a room, he did. If he used a credit card to check in, I'm sure you can confirm that. Anyway, he'd been in love with Jean all his life, and after twenty years they were finally back together again. After that first night, they met two or three times a week, usually at his home in McLean. I know they once spent a weekend together in Hilton Head."

"Wasn't Mrs. Canton worried about being recognized?"

"Apparently not," Baker said. "And it's not like she was a public figure. She didn't campaign with her husband much and she never appeared on talk shows. I mean, you know what the president's wife looks like and maybe the vice president's, but I'll bet you wouldn't recognize the wife of the Speaker of the House, much less the wife of the majority whip."

That was true, Peyton thought. He didn't think he'd be able to recognize the wife of any congressman. Well, there was that one congressman from California who had married a woman who'd once posed in *Playboy*, but other than her—

"The night Jean died," Baker said, "she called my source. She was drunk. She and Lyle had attended a dinner party with people Lyle was trying to impress, and apparently Jean didn't comport herself appropriately. When they got home, he started into his usual rant about how useless she was to him politically, but that night she fought back. She told him she hated him and was leaving him. When she called my source, she was in her car on her way to be with a man who loved her unconditionally." Baker closed her eyes briefly, as if mourning the tragedy of Jean Canton's death. "That day at her funeral when Sebastian said it was Lyle's fault that she died, he was absolutely right. Lyle may not have literally killed her, but he drove her to do what she did."

Peyton didn't agree. Jean Canton was responsible for her own behavior, and it wasn't her husband's fault that she'd decided to drive drunk and make phone calls while driving.

"I couldn't get Sebastian to talk to me," Baker said, "but a week after Jean died, there was a board meeting that he would have normally chaired. I asked one of the people who attended how he behaved at the meeting, and he told me that Sebastian didn't show up. He hadn't been to work since Jean died and nobody had been able to reach him. He was obviously in mourning. Jean's funeral was a week after that board meeting and you know what happened there, how Sebastian showed up drunk and tried to attack Lyle. So you may claim that Sebastian isn't a suspect, but I think when he said he was going to kill Lyle, he meant it. I'll bet you anything that he hired some . . . some *hit man* to do it."

"Jean Canton's funeral was almost four months ago," Peyton said. "Why would he wait so long to kill Lyle?"

"I don't know. Maybe he was trying to figure out a way to do it where he wouldn't get caught. Maybe it took him a while to hire a killer. Now it's your turn, Mr. FBI. What are you going to say at the press conference?"

"I'm going to say that we have evidence—video footage—that someone wearing the uniform of a U.S. Capitol policeman may have killed Congressman Canton."

"My God," Baker said, and started scribbling in a notebook.

"Cameras in the Capitol show this person walking toward Canton's office at the time of the murder. He is five feet eleven inches tall, has dark hair, and weighs approximately one hundred and eighty pounds. We're following up a number of leads at this time."

"Such as?"

"I'm not going to divulge those details, but we do have leads we're following."

Peyton meant such things as trying to figure out who made the fake insignia patch and where the killer purchased a uniform, but he wasn't going to tell the media that.

"I'll also say that we're planning to polygraph-test Capitol Police employees, but so far have no direct evidence that a Capitol policeman was involved and believe that Canton's killer may have been an imposter."

"An imposter? Why do you think that?"

"I can't tell you at this time."

"What are you going to say when one of the reporters at the press conference asks if Sebastian Spear is a suspect?"

"I'm going to say what I've already told you. That Sebastian Spear is not a suspect at this time and that he was in China at the time of the murder. Now can I have someone drive you back to Richmond, Ms. Baker?"

"Nah, that's okay. I'm gonna stick around for a few days to see how things progress."

5

———◆◆◆———

Peyton had an agent take a look at Jean Canton's phone records to see whom she called almost daily. It turned out to be her younger sister, which made Peyton think that Libby Baker's information on the state of the Cantons' marriage and Jean Canton's affair with Spear was most likely correct. He would have someone interview the sister later.

Peyton called his boss and relayed what he'd learned from Libby Baker and went over what he planned to say at the next press conference.

"So Sebastian Spear is still your primary suspect," Director Erby said.

"Yeah, and I still don't have anything to connect him to the crime."

The director said, "I can understand Spear hating Canton, but do you think he would actually pay to have someone killed?"

Peyton thought the question was stupid, but was tactful enough not to say so. Instead, he said, "I don't know, sir. We'll just have to see where the evidence leads us."

The Sebastian Spear that Libby Baker had known in high school— the fragile kid who became suicidal and had a nervous breakdown when his girlfriend broke up with him—was not the man that Spear appeared to be today, at least not according to everything Peyton had read.

Spear was an intensely private man, and he didn't give interviews or appear on talk shows. He never spoke to the media personally; he let his company spokesperson and his lawyers do all the talking. But according to articles that had been written about him in *Forbes* and the *Wall Street Journal*, Spear was a ruthless businessman who cared only about the bottom line and would do anything to best the competition. Some of things he had done to beat his rivals were not only unethical but also illegal—or so his rivals' lawyers claimed. No one to date, however, had ever won a major legal battle against Spear's lawyers.

But did his ruthlessness as a businessman mean he'd actually kill another human being? There was no way for Peyton to know—and he wasn't going to base his decisions on secondhand reports of someone's character.

The character of Sebastian Spear, however, was about to become irrelevant.

The press conference went the way those things normally go. Peyton had realized a long time ago that members of the media—particularly the television media—weren't really interested in simply reporting the facts. They wanted a story to entertain and titillate the viewers. The TV types also wanted to be part of the story—as if the news was a Broadway play in which they had strong supporting roles.

A female reporter from Fox—a woman who'd been the runner-up in a Miss America contest and who, Peyton suspected, had a brain the size of a cashew—asked Peyton whether Sebastian Spear was a suspect, as he'd threatened the congressman at his wife's funeral.

Peyton said he was not.

When the same reporter asked if it was possible that Spear had hired a killer, Peyton pointed at another reporter whose hand was in the air.

The Fox reporter gave the camera a pouty look with her perfect, pouty lips: *Can you believe he just ignored me?*

When asked whether Canton's murder could have been politically motivated, perhaps having to do with the bill he was working on the night he died, Peyton said, "We have no idea what the motive was at this point. We're exploring all possibilities."

Another TV reporter, a man who was a walking advertisement for the benefits of plastic surgery, asked: "How could a person posing as a member of the U.S. Capitol Police gain access to the building?"

Peyton said, "Well, since he was dressed in the uniform of a Capitol cop, he could have simply walked in." He didn't add, *you dummy.*

At the end of the press conference, Peyton looked into the cameras and said that the bureau had established a hotline, and anyone with information related to the congressman's death was encouraged to call. He said the FBI was also offering a half-million-dollar reward for information that would lead to a conviction.

The FBI hotline was flooded with calls.

One caller said that Barack Obama had formed a squad of Muslim assassins after leaving office and was bumping off Republicans he found particularly annoying. Another said she saw a man who went by the street name of Hammer lurking near the Capitol around the time Canton was killed. She said she knew Hammer to be a stone-cold killer. When asked how she knew Hammer, she said she used to be married to the asshole.

But not all the callers were crazy. One suggested that the FBI investigate a former Canton aide whom Canton had fired during his last campaign and then blacklisted from getting another job in politics. The FBI followed up on that call.

Another man, calling from a cell phone with a blocked number, said: "You need to take a hard look at a guy named Joe DeMarco. Check out who his father was and who he works for, and you'll see what I mean."

That call interested the FBI because a Joe DeMarco had been in the Capitol at the time Canton was killed.

6

At the time the call came into the FBI hotline, an FBI agent had already interviewed Joe DeMarco. He had been interviewed less than three hours after the congressman's body had been found.

The agent who interviewed him was a young woman named Alice Berman, and she'd gone to DeMarco's home to question him, because DeMarco had not come to work the morning Canton's body was discovered. This didn't surprise Berman. For one thing, it was Saturday. Plus, she figured that DeMarco had probably heard about Canton's death on the news and learned that the Capitol was locked down.

DeMarco lived on P Street in Georgetown in a narrow two-story town house of white-painted brick. The grass needed mowing, and the shrubs needed trimming—but DeMarco didn't appear to care. When Berman arrived at his place, the garage door was open, and DeMarco was placing a golf bag and golf shoes in the trunk of his car. He was wearing a faded red golf shirt, knee-length beige shorts, and flip-flops.

Berman introduced herself and said she'd come to interview him because he'd been in the Capitol at the time Congressman Canton was killed—and DeMarco had appeared genuinely surprised to hear this. He said, "I heard about Canton a couple of hours ago on the radio, but I had no idea it happened when I was in the building."

Berman thought DeMarco was a good-looking man: muscular build, thick dark hair combed straight back, blue eyes, a prominent nose, a cleft in a big square chin. He seemed relaxed and friendly when he spoke to her, but she sensed something hard about the guy—an edge that was difficult to define—and she imagined he could be intimidating when he chose to be. It didn't occur to Berman until later, after she'd been subconsciously influenced by what she subsequently learned about DeMarco's father, that DeMarco looked like someone who could have played the part of a Mafia hood in a movie, like one of the guys Tony Soprano sent to break the legs of a deadbeat who owed him money.

"Did you know Congressman Canton?" Berman asked.

"No," DeMarco said. "I knew who he was, of course, but I never met the man or ever spoke to him."

"Did you see anything unusual last night?"

"Like what?" DeMarco said.

Berman almost said, *Like a guy with a gun walking around*—but didn't. She said, "Did you see anyone in the building who struck you as odd in any way? Someone you didn't recognize, someone who seemed out of place. Did you hear anything unusual?"

At the time Berman asked this question, she wasn't aware that FBI agents examining video footage had concluded that the killer was dressed as a Capitol cop.

"No," DeMarco said. "My office is in the basement. Well, actually, the subbasement, and I was in it the whole time I was there last night. Canton's office is up on the third floor, and I never went near there."

Berman said, "Why did you go to your office last night? Logs maintained by the Capitol police show you arrived at nine forty-five and left approximately fifty minutes later."

Berman noticed that DeMarco hesitated briefly before he answered. He said, "I had dinner last night on Capitol Hill. Afterward—"

"Where did you have dinner?"

"At 701."

This was a restaurant at 701 Pennsylvania Avenue, close to the Capitol.

"After dinner, I decided to stop by my office and pick up a novel I'd been reading. Also a gym bag full of clothes that were overdue for washing, but mostly I went to get the novel, which I wanted to finish."

"It took you almost an hour to pick up a book?" Berman said.

Another brief hesitation. "No. When I got to my office I decided to review something I'd been working on, and, you know, time passed."

Berman had the sense that DeMarco was making up the story as he was going along. But why would the guy lie?

"Did you have dinner alone?" she asked.

DeMarco said, "No. I had a date."

"And you interrupted your date to go pick up a book?"

"No, it wasn't like that. It was a first date. We had dinner, and afterward I caught a cab for her, and she went home." He smiled and said, "You know how first dates go."

Berman did. She'd had a lot of first dates that hadn't gone the way she'd hoped.

DeMarco said, "So since I was near my office and had nothing better to do for the rest of the night, I went to pick up the novel. Then, like I told you, I got caught up in some work stuff and lost track of the time."

"What was your date's name?" Berman said.

"Do you really need to know that?" DeMarco said.

"Yes. This is a murder investigation. We need to know everything. Is there some reason you're reluctant to tell me the woman's name?"

"Her name is Carol Hansen."

"What's Carol's phone number?"

DeMarco shook his head—as if Berman were being silly—but pulled out his cell phone and read off a number.

Berman concluded the interview not long after that. DeMarco bothered her because she'd sensed that he wasn't being completely truthful or was holding something back. On the other hand, when he'd said that he didn't know Canton and had never spoken to the man, it had sounded as if he was telling the truth.

It wasn't long before Berman learned that DeMarco had lied his ass off.

***

Because she'd interviewed DeMarco the day before, Peyton assigned Alice Berman to follow up on the hotline call. Four hours later, Berman knocked on the door to Peyton's temporary office and said, "Boss, I need to have a word with you."

Peyton liked Berman. She was a bright young woman, twenty-nine years old, who'd been an Arlington County cop before being hired by the bureau. She had a degree in criminal justice, a good record as a cop, and had made a name for herself with Arlington County when she went undercover to bust a guy selling illegally modified AR-15s to yokels. She was tall and athletic—she'd played volleyball in college—and good-looking in a wholesome, healthy, girl-next-door sort of way. She was also able to deflect sexual advances from male agents without getting all bent out of shape, which Peyton *really* appreciated.

He gestured her to a chair in front of his desk.

"This guy, DeMarco, is interesting," Berman said.

"Why's that?" Peyton said.

"Well, to start with, he looks like the killer." By now Berman had seen the video footage of the primary suspect. "He's five eleven, has dark hair, and weighs one eighty according to his driver's license. Second, he works down in the subbasement, and from the cameras that tracked the killer, the killer might have come from the subbasement. DeMarco's worked in this building for a long time, and he'd know where all the cameras are if he made the effort to locate them. But the interesting thing, and like the guy said who called the hotline, is his father and who DeMarco works for, although that's not exactly clear."

"It's not clear who he works for? How could it not be clear?"

"Boss, I've spent the last four hours trying to get a handle on DeMarco. According to his personnel file he's an independent counsel who serves members of Congress on an ad hoc basis."

"An ad hoc basis? What does that mean?"

"I have no idea. And on his office door it says he's 'Counsel Pro Tem for Liaison Affairs,' and I don't know what that means either. So I started talking to people. I began with the House Office of General Counsel, figuring if he was a lawyer they'd know him, but they've never heard of the guy and don't have a clue what he does. I looked at the congressional staff directory. He's not on anyone's staff. I went back to his personnel file and saw a note in the file that said any questions regarding his position should be directed to a Beverly Rawlins over at the Office of Personnel Management. The note was dated and over a decade old.

"Rawlins is now retired but I tracked her down in Florida, and when I mentioned DeMarco's name, she said, 'Oh, yeah, that guy. I always knew there was something fishy about him.' When I asked what she meant, she told me that years ago she'd been assigned to do a personnel review, looking for positions that could be trimmed to reduce the budget, and she came across DeMarco. Just like me, she couldn't figure out what he did or whom he worked for. Well, she started poking around and gets a call from John Mahoney, who was Speaker of the House at the time. It blew her away that Mahoney would call her personally. Anyway, Mahoney told her to back off on DeMarco and not to screw with his position. He said DeMarco was on a special assignment for him and he didn't want anything to interfere with what he was doing. When Rawlins complained to her boss about Mahoney, her boss told her to back off too, saying that he wasn't about to get into a wrestling match with the Speaker of the House over a single GS-13 position."

"Huh. That *is* a bit strange," Peyton said. "Although I'll bet you there are all kinds of people employed by Congress that have special relationships with somebody. Nepotism is alive and well, Berman. Is DeMarco related to Mahoney?"

"No, sir. I'll get to DeMarco's relatives later. Anyway, after talking to Rawlins, I headed up to Mahoney's office and—"

"*You* talked to John Mahoney?"

"No, sir. I figured talking to the minority leader of the House was above my pay grade."

"Good decision, Berman."

"I showed DeMarco's picture to a couple of people on Mahoney's staff, including Mahoney's head secretary. The secretary turned all frosty on me and said any questions regarding personnel who were not members of Mahoney's staff should be directed to OPM. But this other woman, she said, 'Oh, yeah, I know Joe. He's a hunk. I tried to hook him up with my sister but he never called her.' I asked her, 'What does he do?' and she said she didn't know, that he was sort of mysterious—those were her words, *sort of mysterious*—but she'd seen him several times going in and out of Mahoney's office."

Berman leaned back in her chair and said, "So, boss, I don't know what this guy does. All I know is that he has some connection to Mahoney. I also don't understand why the hotline caller would say to check out who DeMarco works for. I mean, since I can't figure out who he works for and since nobody else seems to know, how would the caller know who he works for?"

Peyton glanced at his watch—he needed to give the director an update in half an hour—and Berman wasn't telling him anything that appeared to be useful. He said, "What's the story on his father?"

Berman laughed. "You won't believe this. His father was a guy named Gino DeMarco. He died right after Joe DeMarco graduated from law school. Anyway, Gino was an honest-to-God hit man for the old Italian mob up in New York."

"Really," Peyton said.

"Yes, sir. I talked to our organized crime guys and the OC guys in NYPD, and as far as anyone knows, Joe DeMarco has never had anything to do with the mob up there. He has a cousin in Queens who's a fence, but other than that, he has no known connection to the mob." Berman laughed again. "His cousin, by the way, married DeMarco's one and only ex-wife after she and DeMarco got divorced. I have no idea what the story behind that is."

"Is there any reason to believe that the Mafia had anything to do with Canton's death?" Peyton asked. "For example, was he working on legislation that might have affected organized crime in some way?"

"I talked to Norton—"

Norton was the agent that Peyton had assigned to look at pending legislation that might provide some motive for killing Canton.

"—and he said there was nothing organized crime- or Mafia-related on Canton's agenda and hadn't been for the last four years. I mean, no speeches on the subject, no bills he was sponsoring, nothing like that."

"Do you have a suggestion as to how we should proceed with Mr. DeMarco, Berman?"

"Yes, sir. But just one more thing. I interviewed DeMarco yesterday, and I think he lied to me."

"About what?"

"When I asked him why he was in the Capitol at ten on a Friday night, he gave me this story about stopping by to pick up a book he was reading. The story just sounded off to me. Anyway, to answer your question, I want to search his office. He's not here today, which isn't surprising since it's Sunday, but people I talked to who work on his floor said he doesn't spend much time in his office anyway. Which again makes you wonder what he really does. So I want to search his office mainly because I think he may have lied to me, but I don't think I have enough for a warrant."

"You don't need a warrant," Peyton said. "This is a public building and the owner of the building, namely the U.S. Government, has given us permission to search it."

"Good. I'd also like to take a look at his phone records and bank accounts. If his phone records show a connection to Sebastian Spear, then—"

"That will require a warrant, Berman, and it doesn't sound to me like you have enough for one. But go see what the lawyers say. Maybe the hotline call plus DeMarco's physical similarity to the killer will be enough. While you're waiting to hear back from the lawyers, do the office search. It can't hurt."

7

An hour later, Berman walked back into Peyton's office. The front of her white blouse was streaked with dirt.

"Sir, you need to come with me. I found something."

Berman's smart brown eyes were shining like spotlights.

Peyton followed Berman to the subbasement, passing a workroom the maintenance people used and a room containing an emergency diesel generator. The heavy hitters were clearly not housed on this floor. As Berman had told him, on the frosted glass of DeMarco's office door were the words *Counsel Pro Tem for Liaison Affairs*. Peyton still had no idea what they could possibly mean.

DeMarco's office was unimpressive. Peyton had a toolshed in his backyard that was larger. There were a desk that had probably been purchased when Jimmy Carter was president, two old wooden chairs, and a single gray metal, four-drawer file cabinet. All the file drawers were open and the only thing in the cabinet was a lone bottle of Hennessy cognac.

"Did you take anything out of the file cabinet?" Peyton asked.

"No, sir," Berman said. "That bottle was the only thing in it. You'll also notice there is no paperwork in here related to congressional business. No bills currently working their way through the House, no legal briefings on laws being proposed, no reports from organizations like the Congressional Budget Office. The only paperwork in here is two copies of the *Washington Post* and five copies of *Golf Digest*, which makes me wonder what DeMarco was supposedly working on for fifty minutes the night Canton was killed."

Peyton gestured at the computer. "Maybe he was using the computer."

"Maybe," Berman said. "It's password-protected, so I don't know. I'm going to need tech help to get into it and, I'm guessing, a warrant. And after you've seen what I found, a warrant won't be a problem."

"So what did you find?" Peyton asked.

Berman pointed at the ceiling, and Peyton could see a hole where a ventilation grille had been. The grille was leaning against a wall. Berman pulled over DeMarco's visitor's chair and said, "I noticed there were scratch marks on the grille near the screws, and they looked new, the metal all shiny and bright, so I removed the grille. Sir, if you wouldn't mind, stand on the chair and look inside the duct, but don't touch anything."

Peyton did as Berman instructed, and inside the duct he saw what appeared to be the uniform of a U.S. Capitol cop. On top of the uniform was a cop's equipment belt including a holstered Glock.

"Who the hell is this guy?" Peyton muttered.

<hr />

The impressive machinery of the Federal Bureau of Investigation went into high gear.

Forensic specialists photographed the uniform and gun in place and then carefully removed them from the ventilation duct. The clothes— dark blue pants, a dark blue short-sleeved shirt, boots, a police equipment belt, and a dark blue ball cap—appeared to be identical to what the Capitol Police wore. The technicians immediately confirmed—no microscope required—that the Capitol Police insignia patch on the shirt matched the fake patch captured by the security cameras.

As for the Glock, it appeared to have been fired recently, and the magazine, which could hold seventeen bullets, contained only fifteen. The gun barrel was machined to accept a silencer, which was later found in one of the pockets of the uniform pants. Everything was placed into evidence bags—gently, so that fingerprints and potential DNA were not disturbed. One of the technicians noticed two longish dark hairs inside the ball cap, stuck in the sweatband, and she made sure the hairs were not dislodged when she bagged the cap.

The uniform and the weapon, DeMarco's computer, everything in DeMarco's desk, and even the ventilation grille were then whisked off to the FBI's lab in Quantico, Virginia, for further examination.

For a case like this, Department of Justice lawyers and a friendly federal judge were always on standby, and it took less than half an hour to get the warrants needed to invade DeMarco's life: warrants to search his home, computers, phone records, financial records, safe-deposit boxes. About the only thing the warrants didn't permit was a body-cavity search, but that could be accomplished without a warrant after DeMarco was arrested.

It took one phone call to Verizon and less than ten minutes to find DeMarco based on his cell-phone location. He was at the Westfields Golf Club, a public course in Fairfax County, Virginia. Eight agents were dispatched to throw a net around him. At the golf course, two agents removed their suit jackets and ties, and rented clubs and a cart. The kid in the pro shop found it odd that two men in white shirts, nice pants, and dress shoes had decided to play golf but didn't say anything. He figured it was a couple of guys on a business trip who'd decided to goof off instead of working. And anyway, all golfers were nuts.

The agents found DeMarco on the eleventh green. He was playing by himself. Through binoculars, an agent watched him miss a three-foot putt, then look skyward, as if asking God how that could have possibly happened. The agent notified Peyton they had DeMarco in sight, but Peyton dispatched a helicopter to hover over the golf course, and the pilot was directed to stick with DeMarco when he left the course. Peyton didn't want his agents losing DeMarco thanks to a traffic jam or a badly timed light.

About the time DeMarco was teeing off on the thirteenth hole, Peyton was informed that the gun found in DeMarco's office had been used to kill Canton. Marks on the shell casings found in Canton's office confirmed this. The autopsy on Canton had not yet been completed, but Peyton was sure that after the pathologist removed the slugs from the body, there would be no doubt that the weapon used to kill Canton was the one found in DeMarco's office.

By the time DeMarco reached the tee box for the sixteenth hole, FBI accountants had already taken a peek at his finances. DeMarco had a simple and unimpressive financial life. His latest tax return showed no stocks, no bonds, no income from any source other than his government job. He had no real estate other than his Georgetown home, and he was still paying the mortgage on that. His checking account balance was approximately $3,000 and rarely got higher than that amount. His savings account showed a balance of $121,000—but the day before Lyle Canton was killed, the balance had been only $21,000. A hundred thousand dollars had been wire-transferred into the account the day the congressman was killed.

The FBI accountants—men and women who spent most of their time tracking money going to terrorists—easily traced the wire transfer to an account in the Cayman Islands, but that's where the trail ended. The Cayman bank refused to cooperate in identifying the account holder. So Peyton told the Treasury Department and the State Department to threaten the bank and the Cayman government with anything they could think of. He doubted they'd have much luck, but he had to try.

About the time DeMarco was searching for his ball in the rough near the seventeenth fairway, the lab at Quantico reported that the equipment and clothes worn by the killer were amazingly free of trace evidence. There was gunshot residue on the front of the shirt, but there were no fingerprints on anything: belt buckle, buttons, boots, and so forth. One might have concluded that the clothing had never been worn if not for two strands of dark hair found in the ball cap. A technician said that he would be able to make a DNA match off one of the hairs as soon as he had something or someone to match it to. DeMarco's DNA was not in any federal or state database.

Peyton called the senior agent watching DeMarco and told him to look for an opportunity to get a DNA sample. The agent said, "I think I can do that right now. He's in the clubhouse having a beer, bullshitting with a couple of old codgers. I'll get in there and get the beer bottle when he finishes."

Thirty minutes later the agent called Peyton back and said, "Okay. I got two beer bottles DeMarco drank from and half a hot dog he threw in the trash. One of my guys is on his way to Quantico with them."

In the time it took for DeMarco to drive from the golf course to his home in Georgetown—followed by agents in four different cars and a helicopter in the sky overhead—the Quantico lab had reported that a preliminary DNA test showed that the hair found in the ball cap matched the DNA taken from DeMarco's half-eaten hot dog. A more comprehensive DNA test would be performed later, but the odds right now were already about a billion to one that the hairs in the cap belonged to Joe DeMarco.

8

─────◆─────

Peyton called FBI director Erby. He'd been keeping Erby informed ever since they found the uniform in the vent duct in DeMarco's office. He assumed the director was keeping the president informed and hoped that there was nobody else in the loop. Peyton's fourteen-year-old daughter could keep a secret better than the White House.

After Peyton told the director about all the evidence they'd accumulated, he said, "I'm going to arrest DeMarco in the next hour, and we'll tear his house apart at that time."

"But why did he do it?" the director asked.

"Well, one reason could be the hundred thousand someone wired into his savings account," Peyton said.

"But why him?" the director said. "His old man may have been a professional killer, but he's not. Or least it doesn't sound like he is based on what you told me earlier."

"Another reason could be he did it for John Mahoney. Mahoney might have even paid him the hundred grand," Peyton said. "But that seems pretty far-fetched. It's no secret that Mahoney hated Canton, but it's hard to imagine him paying to have the guy killed."

Anyone who watched the news was aware of the animosity between John Mahoney and Lyle Canton. The two men—usually standing in the hallways of the Capitol—would hurl sharp verbal spears at each other while the cameras rolled. Each accused the other of being a liar and a hypocrite; of twisting statistics and polling data to misrepresent the facts; of supporting economic policies that were destroying the economy and crushing the dreams of the poor and the middle class. Canton delighted in saying that Mahoney, because of his age, was out of touch with reality and living in the past. Mahoney, a veteran, delighted in pointing out that Canton was a hawk who'd never had the guts to serve in the military but didn't hesitate to send other people's children off to war. After these exchanges, the Republican Speaker of the House would usually appear and say, basically, "Now, boys, let's play nice and try to work together. Although I must say that I agree with Congressman Canton when it comes to—"

The war of words between Canton and Mahoney reached a new low point the Sunday before Canton was killed. Chuck Todd had invited both men to appear on *Meet the Press* to discuss the bill that Canton had been working on the night he died—a bill that the Democrats unanimously opposed. (The Republicans could have proposed a bill proclaiming that kittens were cute, and the Democrats would have been unanimously opposed.) Mahoney had shown up on the set after a breakfast meeting where he'd consumed several Bloody Marys and was even less careful choosing his words than he normally was—and normally he wasn't all that careful. So at one point, after Canton accused Mahoney of deliberately misleading the American people on one aspect of the bill, Mahoney said he wasn't misleading anyone, that the facts were clear. Which was when Canton said, "Congressman, how can you sit there and lie like that?" Mahoney leaped to his feet and said, "How dare you call me a liar, you little—"

The next word was bleeped out, and Chuck Todd refused to say later what the word had been, but lip-readers hired by Fox were pretty sure it had been *cocksucker*. Todd broke for a commercial so the staff could clip the microphone back onto Mahoney's lapel; the mic had torn loose when he'd stood so abruptly. When the show resumed, Mahoney was still steaming but managed to make it through the remainder of the interview without any more swearing at Canton.

Director Erby said, "Or maybe Mahoney didn't pay him, but what if someone who had a hundred grand to spare paid DeMarco to kill Canton to get Canton off Mahoney's back?"

Growing weary of playing "what if" with his boss, Peyton said, "Sir, it doesn't matter why DeMarco did it. We don't need a motive to prove he killed Canton. We have all the evidence we need for a conviction. The fact that he became a hundred grand richer the day Canton was killed may not be proof that he was paid to kill him, but it will certainly give the jury another reason to conclude he's guilty. Anyway, unless you object, I'm going to go arrest him."

———◆———

Peyton made a few phone calls, telling his people to saddle up. It was time to put Mr. DeMarco in handcuffs. Right now, according to the agents watching him, DeMarco was at home, standing in his kitchen, making dinner for himself. He was visible through the kitchen window. As Peyton was putting on a bulletproof vest, Berman walked into his office. She was still wearing the same blouse she'd soiled when she'd searched DeMarco's office.

"I just learned something interesting," Berman said. "When I asked DeMarco what he was doing in the Capitol at ten on a Friday night, he said he'd had a date with a woman, and when they finished dinner, he'd sent her home in a cab, like the date had been a bust. But I called his date to confirm his story, and she told me they were having a great time, when DeMarco suddenly gets a text message and says he has to leave immediately."

"Okay," Peyton said. "But I don't understand what the big deal is."

"Well, first DeMarco lied to me about why he went to his office, just like I suspected. But that's not the big thing. I just finished looking at DeMarco's phone records, and the text he received when he was at dinner came from John Mahoney's cell phone. And that's not all. At ten thirty, like fifteen minutes after Canton was killed, DeMarco called Mahoney's cell phone, then he left the Capitol a few minutes later."

"Do we know what the text message said?"

"No, not yet, but it just strikes me as odd that DeMarco and Mahoney were communicating with each other right before and after Canton was killed. I'd love to get my hands on DeMarco's phone. The text message might still be on it."

"Well, your wish might come true, Berman," Peyton said. "I'm on my way to arrest DeMarco. You wanna come with me?"

"Hell, yes," Berman said.

———◆———

Peyton and Berman drove together from the Capitol to Georgetown, stopping a block from DeMarco's house, where a dozen agents were waiting. The agents were dressed in full body armor, including helmets with face shields, and they were armed with a combination of M16s, semiautomatic pistols, shotguns, flash-bang grenades, and tear-gas grenade launchers. They were as pumped up as an NFL team about to play in the Super Bowl.

"Okay," Peyton said to the group, "everybody take a deep breath and take it down a notch. We're going to surround the house, and then I'm going to call him and tell him to come out with his hands up. If he doesn't, or if he starts firing at us, then you can go all commando on him."

9

DeMarco was preparing spaghetti and meatballs, and he was preparing enough to last him several days. Being a bachelor, he often did this when he cooked: made a batch of whatever he was cooking—fried chicken, beef stew, pot roast—so he wouldn't have to cook again for two or three days. And he was making his spaghetti dinner the easy way.

His mother was an incredible cook, and although she was Irish, she specialized in Italian cuisine, mainly because she'd married an Italian, DeMarco's late father. When his mom made spaghetti and meatballs, she bought handmade pasta from a place in Queens and made her sauce and meatballs from scratch. The sauce started out with a couple of cans of crushed tomatoes and a little tomato paste, then she started tossing things into the pot: eggplant, fresh herbs, a little onion, a little sugar, and so on. The meatballs were made by combining two pounds of hamburger with eggs, Parmesan cheese, bread crumbs, and spices she refused to divulge even to her own sister. She then formed the meatballs into perfect spheres, identical in size, seared them in a frying pan to seal in the juices, and then let them simmer in the sauce for three hours.

DeMarco's way was much simpler. He bought a box of spaghetti, two jars of Newman's Own marinara sauce, and a package of twenty-four frozen, already-cooked meatballs; dumped the meatballs into the sauce—and thirty minutes later he was ready to open a bottle of red wine and sit down to dinner. He had to admit that his mom's pasta tasted better than his, but his was edible.

As he waited for the spaghetti water to boil, DeMarco watched the news on the small TV in his kitchen. The lead story was still the killing of Lyle Canton. It sounded as if the only thing the FBI knew—or was telling the public—was that it appeared as if a man dressed as a Capitol cop may have killed Canton. That had to have taken balls, DeMarco thought, to kill the man while real Capitol cops were roaming all over the building.

DeMarco had never met Canton personally nor had any dealings with him and didn't really have a strong opinion about the man—other than that he was a typical, worthless politician. DeMarco sincerely believed that there was no institution in America more useless than Congress. The executive branch and the judicial branch at least functioned. Maybe they didn't function well, but they did *something*. Taxes were collected, at least most of them; the mail was delivered, at least most of the time; federal cops and spies and soldiers did their jobs. And the Supreme Court at least *decided* cases, even if all the decisions were five to four. But Congress, made up of two political parties that couldn't agree on the time of day and did nothing but throw stones at each other, never seemed to do anything truly meaningful about anything that truly mattered. Congress was Kabuki theater as far as DeMarco was concerned, and men like Lyle Canton and John Mahoney were no more than actors giving endless monologues about the evils of the other party—and the play just went on and on and on.

DeMarco had always gotten a kick out of Mahoney and Canton going at it, each accusing the other of being the reason the country was such a mess. And although Mahoney had hated Canton, DeMarco had never thought that Canton was really any different from Mahoney when it came to doing his job. He couldn't believe it when Mahoney, following Canton's death, said to the press with a straight face, "It's well known that Congressman Canton and I had our differences, but I always admired him for his patriotism and his dedication." In private, Mahoney had always called Canton a scheming little motherfucker— pretty much what he'd said on *Meet the Press*.

DeMarco had been shocked to learn that he'd been in the Capitol at the time Canton was apparently killed. He was even more shocked when that good-looking female FBI agent had asked why he'd been there and whether he'd seen anything that might shed some light on Canton's death. He was a little concerned that he'd lied to the agent— lying to the FBI is a crime called obstruction of justice—but he wasn't too concerned. It wasn't like he'd committed a *real* crime—he'd told a small fib—and he hadn't seen anything that could help find Canton's killer.

As he'd told the agent, he'd been having dinner at 701 with a woman named Carol Hansen. Carol was a lobbyist in a town that had about a hundred thousand lobbyists, and she was quite attractive: long dark hair, gray eyes, and a noteworthy figure. DeMarco had met her at Clyde's, a Georgetown watering hole within walking distance of his house.

On the night Canton died—just as he and Carol were finishing dinner, DeMarco wondering whether she might invite him in for coffee when he dropped her off at her apartment—Mahoney sent him a text message. It said: *Go to your office immediately. Be there in fifteen minutes.* DeMarco had assumed that the text meant that *Mahoney* would be there in fifteen minutes. The odd thing about the text was that Mahoney never went to DeMarco's office; he always ordered DeMarco to come to him. But the oddest thing was Mahoney sending him a text in the first place. In all the years he'd worked for Mahoney—even after Mahoney finally learned how to use a smartphone—Mahoney had *never* sent him a text. Not ever. Mahoney always called and bellowed at him over the phone, and the reason Mahoney didn't text was the same reason he hardly ever used e-mail. As he'd told DeMarco several times, "They can't subpoena air."

At any rate, after he got the text he apologized profusely to Carol, put her in a cab, and walked over to the Capitol, cursing Mahoney every step of the way.

When he got to the Capitol, however, Mahoney never showed up. DeMarco waited almost an hour and finally called Mahoney to ask him where he was, and the way Mahoney answered the phone, he sounded as if he'd been sleeping. He also sounded drunk, although Mahoney being drunk was not unusual; Mahoney was an alcoholic. He asked why in the hell DeMarco was calling him after ten at night and said that he'd never sent DeMarco a text message. All DeMarco could surmise was that Mahoney had sent the message to him by mistake—but he was still puzzled because, again, to the best of his knowledge, Mahoney didn't send text messages.

But when the FBI agent had asked him what he'd been doing in the Capitol when Canton was killed, he'd lied. He told her that he'd been there to pick up a book he'd left in his office—the first excuse that popped into his head. He did this only because he didn't want the bureau bugging Mahoney. He figured there was no way the FBI would know about the text—not unless they got a warrant—and why would they get a warrant? Mahoney texting him had no bearing on Canton's murder. Still, it made him nervous, lying to the bureau.

Just as he had this thought, his cell phone rang.

He didn't recognize the number, just that it had a 202 area code. He thought for a moment about ignoring the call, then answered it, saying, "Hello. This is Joe."

"This is Special Agent Russell Peyton, Mr. DeMarco. FBI. I'm standing outside your house with a dozen other agents, all of them armed. I'm here to arrest you for the murder of Congressman Lyle Canton."

"What!" DeMarco said.

"Look out your front window, DeMarco."

DeMarco left the kitchen and walked to his living room—and when he looked out the front window he saw the street lit up like the national

Christmas tree, with all the blue and red lights coming from the grilles and dashboards and roof racks of SUVs. Headlights were aimed at his front door.

"What the hell's going on?" DeMarco said.

"Your house is surrounded, DeMarco. If you fire a weapon at us, we will return fire and blow your house into kindling with automatic weapons."

"This is nuts!" DeMarco said. "I didn't have anything to do with Canton's death. I didn't even know the man."

"Mr. DeMarco, if you don't come out of the house immediately with your hands on top of your head, we're going to fire tear gas into your house and fight our way in. I don't want to have to kill you. So come out the front door with your hands on your head. If you're carrying a weapon, we'll—"

"I don't have a fucking weapon!" DeMarco screamed. "I don't own a weapon."

"Mr. DeMarco, are you going to surrender peacefully?"

DeMarco hesitated, not knowing what to say. The whole situation was insane. How could they possibly think he had anything to do with Canton's death?

"Mr. DeMarco—"

"Yeah," DeMarco said. "I'm coming out. But I'm telling you, this is fucked up."

DeMarco put his phone in his pocket and opened his front door slowly. He stood for a moment in the doorway, his hands above his shoulders, palms facing outward so they could see that he didn't have a weapon, and then stepped onto his front porch. He placed his hands on his head, as Peyton had instructed, turned in a circle so they could see he didn't have a gun in the back of his pants, and began to walk down the sidewalk toward the cars that were blinding him with their headlights.

Peyton yelled, "Get down on the ground, DeMarco."

"Fuck you," DeMarco said. "You can see that I'm not armed. I'm not getting on the ground."

"Get down on the ground," Peyton said.

"Fuck you," DeMarco said again. "What are you going to do? Shoot me if I don't?"

Two agents in body armor and holding M16s stepped out in front of the SUVs, taking up positions where they had clear shots at him. A third agent—the same female agent who'd questioned him—walked directly toward him, pointing a pistol at him. She held the pistol in a two-handed grip, and it was aimed at his face. He figured she'd shoot him right between the eyes if he so much as twitched.

When she was about five feet from him, she said, "Turn around and place your hands behind your back."

DeMarco did, and she holstered her weapon and handcuffed him.

DeMarco said, "I'm telling you, you're making a big mistake. I didn't have anything to do with—"

"You have the right to remain silent," the agent said. "You have the right to an attorney. If you cannot afford . . ."

10

DeMarco was taken to the Alexandria city jail. He didn't realize it, but that particular jail had been home to several high-profile federal prisoners awaiting trial: CIA spy Harold James Nicholson; the D.C. snipers John Allen Muhammad and Lee Boyd Malvo; John Walker Lindh, an eighteen-year-old American captured fighting for the Taliban in Afghanistan; and Judith Miller, the reporter who'd refused to reveal her sources during the investigation into the outing of CIA agent Valerie Plame. And now Joe DeMarco, the accused killer of Lyle Canton, the House majority whip.

DeMarco was strip-searched, fingerprinted, and photographed, then given flip-flops and an olive green pullover shirt with matching pants held up by an elastic waistband. The pants and shirt resembled hospital scrubs except for the word PRISONER stenciled in white letters on the back of the shirt. While he was being processed in the jail, Agent Peyton stood by watching but never said a word to him. The FBI had made no attempt to question him since his arrest, because DeMarco had said he wouldn't talk to anyone without a lawyer present. Or there could have been another reason the agents didn't question him: maybe they had enough evidence that they didn't need to hear anything he might have to say.

After he was dressed DeMarco told his jailers he wanted to make a phone call to arrange for a lawyer. His jailers—guys dressed in neat white shirts and gray pants—worked for the Alexandria Sheriff's Office, but they looked over at Peyton, and Peyton nodded his approval. The guards took DeMarco over to a wall-mounted phone and stepped back a couple of paces, pretending they were giving him privacy; DeMarco had no doubt the phone was monitored.

DeMarco didn't have a lawyer. The last time he'd hired one had been when he got divorced—and the lawyer he'd hired then had been a moron, and his ex-wife's lawyer had cleaned his clock. He hadn't even used a lawyer when he'd prepared his will. He'd just printed off some online forms, figuring they'd be good enough. Consequently, he didn't call a lawyer; he called the only person who could help him, praying she'd answer her phone. She often ignored phone calls; he just hoped she didn't ignore this call tonight.

She answered the phone saying, "Yes?"—which was the way she usually answered the phone.

"Emma, it's Joe. I've been arrested for murdering Lyle Canton. I'm at the Alexandria city jail. I need a lawyer."

His statement was greeted by several seconds of silence, before Emma said, "Okay." Then she hung up.

DeMarco thought: *She could have at least* acted *surprised that I've been accused of murder.*

———— ◆ ————

After the phone call, two burly deputies led DeMarco to a six-by-ten-foot box that contained a cot and a stainless-steel toilet. There was no window in the room, and the door was solid steel except for a small sliding panel that could be opened so his jailers could peer in to see if he'd slashed his wrists or hanged himself. The cot was bolted to the floor and had a mattress less than two inches thick, a single sheet that was more gray than white, and a pillow that was like a sack filled with rags. Down the hall from him was a lunatic who howled something incomprehensible about every ten minutes.

DeMarco stood for a moment in the center of the room, then lay down on the cot and placed his forearm over his eyes.

He was scared out of his mind.

One thing he knew about the FBI was that the bureau didn't go off half-cocked. The FBI would investigate for months, and sometimes years, before making an arrest, and they didn't make the arrest until they were about 100 percent certain that they had enough evidence to support a conviction. But what evidence could they possibly have to make them think that he was Canton's killer? He was pretty sure they wouldn't have arrested him just for lying about getting a text message from Mahoney.

An hour after he was placed in the cell, the door opened. It was the same two jailers who'd placed him in the cell. One of them said, "Your lawyer's here. Come with us."

He thought they would handcuff him or put manacles on his ankles, but they didn't. Walking beside him, they led him to an interview room, opened the door, and let him in. Inside the room, sitting at a small table that was bolted to the floor, was a woman in her fifties.

The woman was slim, had short dark hair, a longish nose, and a wide mouth. She was wearing a dark blue suit. She was attractive yet at the same time had a face that said she didn't take crap from anyone. The only thing on the table in front of her was a yellow legal tablet, and nothing was written on it.

"Close the door when you leave," she said to the jailers, and they did.

"Sit down, Joe," she said, and he took a seat across from her. "My name's Janet Evans. I'm a friend of Emma's. Regarding my credentials, I've practiced criminal law for twenty-five years, fifteen years as a federal prosecutor. I was an assistant U.S. attorney. For the last ten years, I've been a partner in a D.C. firm."

"Okay," DeMarco said. "But you don't have to convince me that you're competent. Emma wouldn't have sent you if you weren't. About your fee—"

"Don't worry about my fee. At least not now."

But DeMarco *was* worried about her fee. She would probably charge a minimum of a hundred grand to defend him against a murder charge—and he didn't have a hundred grand. But as she'd said, this wasn't the time to sweat the small stuff—like going bankrupt. If she couldn't get him acquitted, bankruptcy would be the least of his problems.

"Have you talked to the FBI at all since your arrest?" Evans said.

"No. The only thing I said to them was that I wanted a lawyer."

"Good."

"But I have no idea why they arrested me. They didn't tell me anything."

"I've seen the arrest warrant, Joe. They have a strong case."

"What! How the hell could they possibly have a strong case? I didn't kill Canton. The only thing that connects me to his death is that I was in the Capitol around the time he was murdered."

"They have more than that, Joe. A lot more."

Evans laid out the case against him. There was video footage showing a man of his height and weight, and with his hair coloring, walking to Canton's office. The man was wearing what appeared to be the uniform of a U.S. Capitol policeman, but the uniform had an insignia patch that was not an exact match to the real patches worn by the Capitol cops. The killer had apparently had the patch made to match the rest of the uniform he was wearing, but the patch wasn't perfect. The kicker was that the uniform the killer wore, including the gun and silencer used to kill Canton, was found inside a ventilation duct in DeMarco's locked office.

"You gotta be shittin' me," DeMarco said.

Evans went on. Ballistics tests had already confirmed that the gun was the one used to kill Canton. The most damning piece of evidence was that inside the cap the killer had apparently worn were two strands of hair, and preliminary DNA testing proved that one of the hairs was DeMarco's.

After she said this, DeMarco said, "How the hell could that be?"

She didn't answer the question. She just kept driving the stake deeper into his heart.

"Furthermore, a hundred thousand dollars was wired into your savings account the day of the murder. The money came from an account in the Cayman Islands."

DeMarco, now looking as if he'd been hit between the eyes with an ax handle, said, "The last time I checked my account balance was three weeks ago when I got a statement from the bank. There was only about twenty grand in my account."

As if he hadn't spoken, Evans said, "Then there's the fact that you lied to the FBI about why you were in your office."

Before DeMarco could ask how the FBI knew he'd lied, Evans said, "They obtained a warrant to look at your phone records and saw you'd received a text from a cell phone belonging to John Mahoney. Then, after Canton was murdered, you placed a call to Mahoney. The FBI doesn't know what was said on that phone call, but they know what the text message said. It said, 'Go to your office immediately. Be there in fifteen minutes.' They think the call you made to Mahoney might have been to tell him that Canton was dead."

"I'm telling you that I didn't kill Canton. The only reason I didn't tell the FBI about the text from Mahoney was because I didn't want them bugging him. And the reason I called him was that when he didn't show up, I called to ask him why. That's when Mahoney told me he never texted me. And how does the FBI know what the text said?"

"After they arrested you, they looked at your phone. You didn't delete the text from Mahoney."

Well, shit!

"Is there anything else?" *What else could there possibly be?*

"No. Or at least not that I know of."

"Will I be granted bail?"

"No, you will not," Evans said, the statement sounding like a door being slammed shut. "I will argue for bail, but considering who the victim was and the evidence against you, I'm positive you won't be granted bail."

DeMarco leaned back in his chair and closed his eyes. He was fucked.

He opened his eyes and said, "You've probably heard clients say this before, but I'm being framed. I didn't kill Canton."

"Joe, I'm your lawyer. You don't need to convince me of your innocence."

"Yeah, I do. Because I didn't do this, and you have to believe that I didn't. And if I'm not granted bail, I'm not going to be able to find out who's done this to me. I need someone to start investigating to see who set me up."

"Someone is already investigating, Joe."

She meant Emma.

That was the only good news DeMarco had heard since meeting his new lawyer.

The following day DeMarco was arraigned at the U.S. District Court on Constitution Avenue in D.C. He wasn't granted bail. After the arraignment, he was returned to the Alexandria city jail to await trial for the first-degree murder of U.S. congressman Lyle Canton.

11

John Mahoney was in his office drinking coffee laced with bourbon. He'd been shocked by Canton's death but wasn't shedding any tears for the man. He'd despised Canton. What had shocked him was that somebody had had the audacity to kill a United States congressman in the Capitol. What had shocked him even more was DeMarco being arrested for Canton's murder. Canton was a devious prick, and the fact that somebody had killed him at least made sense, but there was no way that DeMarco had killed the guy.

Mahoney didn't know what to do about DeMarco, however. He'd always kept his relationship with DeMarco very low-key, if not exactly secret. He wasn't about to step into the limelight and publicly defend him. If he did, then he'd have to explain his connection to DeMarco and the sorts of things DeMarco sometimes did for him, and he wasn't about to do that. But he had to do something. He couldn't let DeMarco go to jail for a crime he was positive he hadn't committed, no matter what the evidence might show.

The phone on his desk rang. It was Mavis, his secretary. Like him, Mavis had known DeMarco for years and was also stunned by his arrest. She wasn't, however, totally convinced he was innocent—and that was because she knew about some of the things he'd done for Mahoney in the past.

"There's an FBI agent here to see you, Congressman. A Special Agent Russell Peyton."

Shit. "Send him in."

Mahoney had met many FBI agents during his time in Washington. Some were white, some were black; some were male, some were female; some were short and some were tall—but they were basically all the same. He was convinced they had some sort of human cookie cutter over at the Hoover Building that stamped them out. Like Peyton, they were usually in good shape. Like Peyton, the men almost always wore their hair short and dressed in conservative suits and ties. But it wasn't their appearance that made them similar; it was their *attitude.* They were always polite and formal when dealing with the public, but beneath a thin veneer of civility was a core of arrogance. They made it clear, without ever saying so, that they were members of the most powerful federal law enforcement organization in the land, and if they were out to get you . . . Well, they'd get you.

Mahoney pointed Peyton to a chair in front of his desk. He noticed that Peyton barely glanced at the photos on the wall behind him, photos of Mahoney posing with presidents and generals and athletes and movie stars. If Peyton was impressed that John Mahoney was a former Speaker of the House, currently the House minority leader, and arguably the most powerful Democrat on Capitol Hill, he didn't show it. Mahoney knew the man would be respectful—but not the least deferential. Fuckin' FBI.

"What can I do for you, Agent?" Mahoney asked.

"I was hoping you'd be able to help me with a couple of things, sir. I'm trying to figure out who Joe DeMarco is. We've looked at his personnel file, and it's amazingly, well, *skimpy* is the only word I can think of. About all it says is that he's an independent counsel who serves members of the House. As you can imagine, we've asked a lot of people about DeMarco. Representatives and their staffs, Capitol policemen, administrative personnel in this building, and no one we've spoken to seems to know what his job really is or who he works for. However, a few people we've talked to say they think he works for you. They've seen him with you or going in and out of your office. Can you explain your relationship to DeMarco, sir?"

"Sure," Mahoney said, as if there were no big mystery whatsoever when it came to DeMarco. "He doesn't work for me, at least not directly, and he's not a member of my staff. It's like his personnel file says. He's a freelance lawyer the members call upon from time to time."

What Mahoney had just said wasn't exactly a lie. Other members of the House, as well as a few other people Mahoney knew, had used DeMarco's services in the past—but on those occasions, Mahoney had *lent* DeMarco to those people. DeMarco was *his* guy.

"Called upon to do what?" Peyton asked. "Can you be more specific?"

Mahoney was on rocky ground here. He wasn't about to tell Peyton that DeMarco was the one he sent to pick up cash from folks who didn't want to be identified as contributors. Some legal nitpickers might conclude that the money DeMarco collected should be called *bribes* and not campaign contributions. And Mahoney could definitely not go into detail about some of the assignments he'd given DeMarco, assignments in which DeMarco had sometimes strayed over the thin, meandering line separating legal acts from criminal ones.

Mahoney said, "DeMarco's kind of a troubleshooter who just comes in handy when there's something going on that my staff can't handle. Like a few months ago. There was this old lady up in Boston, one of my constituents, who was being screwed over by some developer. I asked DeMarco to look into that because I was running for reelection at the time, and my staff was completely tied up with the campaign."

Mahoney didn't tell Peyton that the developer ended up dead, killed by a Mexican drug cartel, and that DeMarco had had a hand it that.

"Another time," Mahoney said, "a buddy of mine, a guy I served with in Vietnam, called me because his granddaughter was getting death threats. She'd learned a bunch of state politicians out in North Dakota were being bribed by a big energy company. I asked DeMarco to look into that one because the guy was a friend and because I didn't want my staff traipsing off to North Dakota."

That was another case where he couldn't talk about what DeMarco had *really* done. He'd helped Mahoney's war buddy get away with murder—a justified murder but still a murder.

Mahoney concluded with: "So, like I said, he's done a few small jobs for me, but I don't really know him all that well, not on a personal level."

When Mahoney said this, he couldn't help recalling the Last Supper story in the Bible, the part where Jesus tells Peter that before the cock crows he'll deny three times that he knew him—which old Pete did. Not that DeMarco was Jesus Christ or Mahoney Saint Peter. At the moment, he felt like Judas.

So, feeling guilty, Mahoney added: "But I can tell you that he seems like a good guy, and I have a hard time believing he killed Canton. What motive would he have?"

Instead of answering the question, Peyton said, "Sir, why did you send a text message to DeMarco the night Congressman Canton was killed?"

Mahoney barely remembered DeMarco calling him the night Canton had died, talking about some text message. He'd been so drunk that he'd passed out on the couch when he got home after having dinner with a couple of guys from Boston, and when he got the phone call, he'd said that he didn't know what DeMarco was talking about because he really hadn't known.

"Agent, I never sent DeMarco a text message," Mahoney said. "In fact, I've never sent a text message to anyone in my life. When I have something to say to people, I call them. And they always answer or call me back." He said this to remind Peyton that he wasn't some ordinary schmuck impressed by a guy with a badge.

"Congressman, we've seen the text. It was on DeMarco's phone, which we examined after we arrested him. And we know it came from your phone."

"Goddamnit, Peyton, I'm telling you I never sent him a text." Mahoney was now truly alarmed and was making no attempt to hide the fact. "What did this text say?"

Peyton hesitated. "It said, 'Go to your office immediately. Be there in fifteen minutes.'"

"And what time did I send this text that I never sent?"

Peyton again hesitated, as if he were being asked to divulge classified information. "It was sent at nine thirty p.m. And about an hour later, DeMarco called you. Or I should say, he called the number that's registered to your cell phone."

"Well, I never sent that message, and as for DeMarco calling me. . . . Look, this is a little embarrassing, but the night Canton was killed I had dinner over at Old Ebbitt's, and I had a lot to drink. My driver took me home right after the dinner, like maybe nine or so. I don't remember the exact time. That night, after I got home, DeMarco called and asked me why I texted him. I was asleep when he called, and he woke me up and my brain was barely working. Anyway, I told him the same thing I'm telling you, that I didn't send him a text and I didn't know what he was talking about."

"I see," Peyton said. But his tone of voice said, *Sounds like bullshit to me*—which pissed Mahoney off.

"Peyton, I'm telling you for the last time. I didn't send that text. I don't text. You need to seriously look into the possibility that someone hacked my phone."

Peyton stared at him for a moment—as though he was eyeballing some lying scumbag criminal—before saying, "We'll do that, sir."

Mahoney didn't believe him.

"And what motive would DeMarco have for killing Canton?" Mahoney asked for the second time.

This time Peyton answered the question. "Congressman, a hundred thousand dollars was transferred from a bank in the Caymans to DeMarco's savings account the day Canton was killed. We don't know who sent the money yet—I'm sure we'll find out eventually—but it appears as if DeMarco was paid to kill Canton."

Mahoney shook his big head. "I think DeMarco's being framed for Canton's murder."

"I suppose that's possible, sir, but in the twenty-five years I've been with the bureau I'm not aware of a single case where someone was framed for a crime. That only happens in movies."

Mahoney almost said, *Well, if it was a perfect frame, you wouldn't have heard about it.* But he could see he'd be wasting his breath. Peyton had already made up his mind that DeMarco was guilty.

Peyton rose and said, "Thank you for your time, Congressman."

After Peyton left, Mahoney added two fingers of bourbon to his coffee cup. Before Peyton's visit, he'd been worried about DeMarco—but now he was worried about himself. It was as if the FBI was trying to connect him to Canton's death. His animosity toward Canton was public knowledge, so a case could be made that he had a motive for wanting Canton killed. And the FBI now knew that DeMarco had done a couple of jobs for him, because he'd just helpfully told Peyton about those jobs. So why not a murder? Then they had the damn text message supposedly from him to DeMarco, but even worse was the call DeMarco had made right after Canton was killed—like maybe a call that said, "I took care of the guy, boss." The hundred grand that the FBI had traced to the Cayman bank was another potential problem. If someone could hack into his phone and make it look as if he'd texted DeMarco, maybe the hacker could make it look as if he—John Mahoney—had sent the money from the Caymans to DeMarco's account.

DeMarco needed to be found innocent, or he might not be the only one going to prison. And even if Mahoney himself didn't go to jail, this was the sort of scandal that would hang over him politically for years, with people always wondering if he'd paid to have Canton killed. He had no doubt whatsoever that any information the FBI had would be leaked to the media.

He had to get someone looking into this mess, and he could think of only one person for the job. He called her but got her voice mail. He said, "Hey, you need to call me back. Right away. It's about DeMarco."

He thought she'd call him back, because she liked DeMarco, but with her you could never be sure. She was so goddamn ornery and independent. Not to mention condescending and sanctimonious, when it came to him.

Mahoney sat for a moment, brooding, and something else occurred to him. There was one thing he could do for DeMarco; he owed him that much at least.

He called Mavis and said, "I need you to set up a meeting for me."

The IHOP on the Jeff Davis Highway is about a mile from Ronald Reagan National Airport. Bob Anderson, sheriff of Alexandria, hurried into the restaurant, flustered because he was fifteen minutes late, thanks to a traffic accident he hadn't been able to get around, even using lights and a siren. The road had been blocked like a clogged artery until the police could bring in a tow truck big enough to yank a bus out of the way.

Anderson had been told to dress in civilian clothes, and he'd opted for a suit, considering whom he was about to meet. But at first he didn't see the man. He'd never met John Mahoney, but he knew what he looked like: a big guy, only five eleven but broad across the back and butt, a shock of pure white hair, and bright blue eyes. Maybe Mahoney was late, too.

He had no idea why Mahoney wanted to see him, but when a guy with Mahoney's political clout calls and says he wants a meeting, you don't ask questions and you don't refuse—not if you're a Democrat. And Bob Anderson was a Democrat—he was serving his second term as sheriff and would probably run for a third term—so he wasn't about to ignore Mahoney. He just hoped Mahoney hadn't gotten there before him and then left because he was late.

A man in a booth near the back of the restaurant, wearing a red Nationals baseball cap and a gray sweatshirt, raised his hand. It was Mahoney. Thank God.

Anderson rushed over to Mahoney's table, and as he sat, he said, "I'm sorry I'm late, Congressman, there was a wreck on—"

"Don't worry about it. Thanks for taking the time to see me, Sheriff."

"Uh, sure, yeah, I was happy to. It's an honor to meet you, sir."

He noticed Mahoney didn't seem very friendly, in fact he looked pretty serious, like something was bugging him—and Bob Anderson sure as hell hoped he wasn't the cause of Mahoney's annoyance.

"You got a guy in your jail named Joe DeMarco," Mahoney said.

"Yes, sir." DeMarco was the biggest name in his jail at the moment.

"I've never been in prison myself," Mahoney said, "but you hear stories. Guys getting beat up, shanked, raped. That sort of thing."

"I run a good jail, Congressman."

"I'm sure you do, Bob. But I wanted to let you know something. If anything bad happens to DeMarco while he's in your jail, I'm going to crucify you. You won't be running for a third term; you won't even finish your current term. And you won't be able to get a job anywhere in law enforcement. Hell, you might not be able to get any job at all."

Before Anderson could say anything, Mahoney said, "On the other hand, if DeMarco stays safe and healthy until his trial, I'm a guy who can help you. You're a young man. What are you, about forty-five?"

"Forty-two, sir."

"Then you might have political ambitions beyond being sheriff, and I can help you if you do. And if you want a third term, I know some guys who will contribute to your campaign and give you some advice

69

to make sure you win. So, are we clear, Bob? I can be the best friend you've ever had, or I can be your worst nightmare."

Anderson swallowed as if he was trying to get a baseball down his throat. "Yes, sir, we're clear," he said.

"Good," Mahoney said. He rose from the table, gave Anderson a friendly pat on the shoulder, and said, "And this meeting never happened, Bob."

12

Gravelly Point Park is on the Virginia side of the Potomac River, just off the George Washington Memorial Parkway. The main attraction of the park is that you can lie back on the grass and watch the planes taking off from Reagan National Airport. That is, they take off right over your head, folding up their wheels as they pass over you, and it's a rush, particularly at night and if you are drunk or high, to have a 747 blowing by two hundred feet above you.

About the time Mahoney was threatening the Alexandria sheriff, two men were meeting for the first time in the park. They were sitting at a picnic table across from each other, and they made an odd couple. An observer's initial impression might be a parolee meeting with his parole officer.

One of the men was Bill Brayden, a rather ordinary-looking white man wearing a suit and tie. He was fifty-four years old, clean-shaven, and had receding dark hair and a small potbelly. He was head of security for Spear Industries.

His companion, Hector Montoya, was the exact opposite of ordinary. He was thirty-two years old, his head was shaved, and he had a soul patch beneath his thin lower lip. He was wearing loose-fitting blue jeans, yellow Timberland work boots, and a sleeveless T-shirt.

The most striking thing about Hector was his tattoos, which covered every inch of his body that Brayden could see: his arms, his hands, and the part of his chest visible above the top of the T-shirt were all covered with ink. Two blue snakes coiled around Montoya's throat, the heads of the snakes meeting near his Adam's apple, their mouths open, fangs dripping venom. On his arms were tattoos of skulls, red devils, nude women, wolves and tigers, and other animals that came purely from the tattoo artist's imagination. Below his collarbone, in elaborate script, were the words *Mara Salvatrucha*. On the back of his neck, in heavy dark blue, was *MS-13*. He even had tattoos on his face: there were two lightning bolts near his right eye and three teardrops at the bottom of his left eye. According to urban legend, the teardrops indicated the number of people he'd killed.

Mara Salvatrucha, or MS-13, is an international criminal gang that originated in Los Angeles and spread like a noxious weed through the Americas—North, South, and Central. It is involved in trafficking people, drugs, and weapons, and its members often serve as enforcers for Mexican drug cartels. Almost all MS-13 gangbangers are heavily tattooed, often with tattoos covering the entire face. (Compared with some, Hector Montoya's face was practically a blank canvas.) There are estimated to be fifty thousand members worldwide and over ten thousand in the United States. MS-13 also had a strong presence in almost every prison in the country—which was the reason Bill Brayden was meeting with Hector.

Brayden had encountered MS-13 a few times while working for Sebastian Spear. In countries like Mexico, Honduras, and El Salvador, he quickly learned that the most pragmatic way to provide protection for Spear's personnel—to keep them from being robbed, kidnapped, raped, and murdered—was to simply pay off the local criminals. As a result of his past dealings with the gang, he knew an MS-13 "executive" in Honduras. It was the Honduran who had provided Brayden with an introduction to Hector Montoya, the current leader of MS-13 in northern Virginia.

Brayden placed a paper bag on the picnic table, then sat there looking at Hector, saying nothing. He was thinking that Hector's appearance hardly inspired confidence.

Finally Hector, tired of being stared at, said, "I don't have all day, man. You wanna get to it? Guzman said you'd pay good money for something you wanted taken care of."

Guzman was the Honduran.

"There's twenty-five thousand in the bag," Brayden said.

"Okay," Hector said. "That'll get you something. So what do you want?"

"There's a man named Joe DeMarco in the Alexandria city jail," Brayden said. "Do you know who I'm talking about?"

"I watch the news," Montoya said.

"I want DeMarco dead," Brayden said.

13

Sebastian Spear headed toward his office, and as he walked past her desk, Evelyn said, "Good morning, Sebastian." She was the only one in the company who called him by his first name. "Your schedule for today is on your desk. Your first appointment is at nine."

He didn't respond; he didn't even glance over at her. She might as well have been a potted plant. He entered his office, closing the door behind him. Sebastian Spear had never been one to waste time chatting with his secretary but he used to at least say good morning to her and ask how she was doing.

Evelyn's attitude toward him had always been somewhat maternal because she had known him since he was a child, and he, in turn, although he wasn't overtly affectionate, wasn't as brusque and business-like with her as he was with everyone else in the company. But after Jean Canton died—

Each day when Evelyn Walker came to work she was surprised that she still had a job. For one thing, she was almost seventy years old. But the main thing was that she didn't do much more than sit at her desk all day and occasionally answer the phone. She didn't type Sebastian's letters; all his correspondence was prepared by his lawyers or one of the vice presidents. She didn't file papers, because everything was stored on

74

the company's servers. She rarely set up meetings for him or arranged his travel plans, because those things were also mostly handled by the VPs. The paper schedule she placed on his desk every morning was totally unnecessary, as it was also on his computer and all he had to do was tap a key to see it.

Evelyn suspected the only reason she was still employed was that Sebastian's father had most likely made him promise not to fire her, but as soon as her social security maxed out she planned to quit. Not only was the job boring, but being around Sebastian now . . . it was like working for a corpse.

She'd been hired by George Spear, Sebastian's father, when she was in her twenties, and she imagined she'd gotten the job because of the way she'd looked. She'd been a knockout when she was young. She'd even had a brief affair with George—back when she still had a waist. George Spear had been a rogue and a womanizer and a cutthroat businessman, but he'd been a *human being*, not a moneymaking robot like his son. He'd been fond of his employees—genuinely cared about them and enjoyed their company. When George was running the business, there'd been Christmas parties and picnics and outings to sporting events.

Sebastian was completely different. Not only was he not the least bit sociable—Evelyn could have accepted that; some people just aren't outgoing or gregarious—but Sebastian truly didn't seem to give a damn about the people who worked for him. As far as he was concerned, the thirty thousand he employed worldwide were nothing more than numbers on a spreadsheet. If it was more profitable to move a thousand jobs to India, he never appeared to give any thought whatsoever to what would happen to the thousand people who lost their jobs in America. All he seemed to care about was next quarter's dividend.

But Evelyn knew, even if no one else who worked for him did, that he hadn't always been this way. As a boy he'd seemed normal enough, although he'd been what the kids these days would call a nerd. When he was young and his father would bring him to work, he drove the engineers crazy with all his questions. Yeah, he'd been a bit goofy as a kid, but he'd been a *nice* kid.

His personality changed drastically by the time he became an adult, and Evelyn knew the reason, because she'd been sleeping with George at the time. Jean Mitchell, his high school sweetheart—who later married Lyle Canton—broke up with him in college, and Sebastian had a nervous breakdown. George said that if Sebastian's mother hadn't intervened, he was convinced that his son would have committed suicide. And Evelyn could understand, even if George couldn't, how the awkward young teenager she'd known might go off the deep end after losing the love of his life. What she couldn't understand, however, was the person he turned into.

When he came to work for George after graduating from MIT, the sweet kid she'd known had morphed into this intense, brooding creature, lurking in his father's shadow, watching silently as he learned the business. Then, when he took over the company after his father became ill and had to retire—and when George was no longer there to restrain him—Sebastian immediately stripped away any part of the company he considered inefficient and went after the competition as if he were a combatant engaged in some sort of financial blood sport. Somehow losing Jean to Canton had hardened him in ways Evelyn couldn't understand. Any compassion he'd once felt for others had vanished.

Sebastian had also taken an interest in other competitive activities after he took over the company. He hired a personal coach and began to play tennis, becoming good enough to play with the best amateurs in the region. Evelyn had watched him in a match once, and he was absolutely *savage* when he played. He drove a race car for a brief period, winning several races, destroying several cars, and firing members of his pit crew for any error that added seconds to the clock. He took karate and earned a black belt or something. But the thing was, he didn't seem to take any real pleasure from these activities, as he pursued them in the same grim, winning-is-everything fashion in which he conducted his business.

Seven months ago, however, his personality had abruptly changed, if only for a short time. For a brief, three-month period, he was the happiest Evelyn could ever remember seeing him. He became, if not exactly sociable, at least more friendly and approachable. One day he even brought her flowers; it was her birthday, but she was so shocked she was rendered speechless. At the time this transformation in him took place, she had no idea what could have caused it—then she found out, at the same time as the rest of the world, when it was reported after Jean Canton's fatal car accident that Sebastian had been having an affair with her.

Evelyn couldn't believe how hard Jean's death had hit him. First, he missed two weeks of work, never once checking in to see how things were going, which for him was unheard of. And after he returned to work . . . It was as if he'd lost all interest in the only thing he'd ever really cared about, his company. He'd spend hours alone in his office, refusing to see people who needed to see him. He wouldn't take phone calls from people he always took calls from and never returned their calls. He began to miss meetings he normally would have attended. He would show up for work some days unshaven, his clothes looking as if he'd slept in them. Evelyn had seen people devastated by the death of a loved one, but she'd never seen anyone affected as badly as poor Sebastian. It was as if he were disappearing inside himself.

Oh, well, what could she do?

She had just flipped open the novel she planned to spend the next eight hours reading when Bill Brayden entered the office. "I need to see him," Brayden said.

She didn't much like Brayden. He was polite enough and was never rude to her, but there was something sinister about him. He reminded her of those SS officers you see in World War II movies, the ones always hunting down the beautiful heroines who were members of the French resistance.

Evelyn glanced at the phone on her desk and said, "He's not on the phone and doesn't have anything scheduled until nine. Just go on in. I'm sure he'll be *delighted* to see you." That was a joke, but Brayden obviously didn't get it.

Headquarters for Spear Industries was a twenty-one-story glass tower in Reston, Virginia. From Sebastian Spear's penthouse office, you could see the cars going by on the Dulles Airport access road and the lush fairways of the Reston National Golf Course—although Spear rarely took in the view. He might as well have worked in a cave, as his attention was usually totally focused on the Bloomberg terminal or the two computer monitors on his desk.

On one side of Spear's office was an old-fashioned draftsman's table—it had belonged to his father—and rolled out on the table were schematics for some future project. In front of his glass-topped desk were two uncomfortable stainless-steel and leather chairs, but as meetings with Spear rarely lasted long, the chairs' inhumane design didn't much matter.

When Bill Brayden walked into the room, he was surprised to see his boss standing and looking out a south-facing floor-to-ceiling window. Sebastian Spear was a tall, slender man with narrow shoulders that tended to make his head seem larger than it actually was. His face was pale, as for the last four months he'd spent very little time outdoors. He wore black horn-rimmed glasses—the same style he'd worn since high school. When he was younger the glasses had made him look like a nerdy Bill Gates wannabe. Now they seemed perfectly suited to him, somehow even fashionable.

Spear didn't turn to look at Brayden, even though he must have heard him open and close the office door. Brayden waited a moment for Spear to face him, and when he didn't, he said, "I believe everything regarding Canton will soon be resolved."

What he meant was that DeMarco would soon cease to pose any risk whatsoever.

Brayden waited, staring at Spear's back, for Spear to say something—like *Thank you, Bill* or *You did a great job, Bill*—but he didn't. He just stood there, apparently mesmerized by whatever he was looking at on the other side of the glass. After a moment of uncomfortable silence, Brayden said, "I'll, uh, keep you apprised of any developments." When Spear still didn't respond, Brayden shook his head and left.

Fucking Spear. What a whack job.

***

Sebastian had expected to feel different. He'd expected to feel something . . . *more.*

When Canton was killed, he'd been in China, at a symposium, listening to a so-called expert talk about the current state of China's power grid and the need for expansion. He didn't even know why he'd attended the symposium in the first place, because once he arrived he realized he had no interest in anything anyone had to say. He'd been bored and began scrolling through his iPad, and that's when he saw the headline that Lyle Canton had been shot inside the Capitol.

He'd left the auditorium, walked outside, staring down at the headline, waiting for it to hit him: a spike of elation, a surge of vindictive joy, a sense of triumph because the only man he'd ever hated was gone. But nothing happened. He didn't feel anything. The empty, hollowness in his chest that had been there since Jean's death remained. She was gone—and nothing would ever fill the void.

After Jean had dumped him in college for Canton, he'd spiraled downward into a deep depression, shattered by grief and loss and betrayal. Had it not been for his mother, he was certain he would have killed himself. She brought in the psychiatrist from Cambridge, and he'd helped somewhat—or at least the drugs had helped—but it was mostly his mother, who spent hours comforting him, sometimes just sitting next to him, holding his hand. She'd understood, even if no one else had, that Jean hadn't been a passing teenage infatuation. Sebastian had been in love with Jean longer than many people stayed married, and when she left him for Canton, it was no different from a man losing his spouse. Only his mother understood this.

It was his father, however, who changed him into the man he became. His father couldn't see the point of wallowing in grief over a single woman, not when you're only twenty years old. His father's attitude had been that there were a million women out there, and Sebastian just needed to get back on his horse and start riding again. His father was wrong about that. The world may have been filled with women, but there had been only one for him. When it came to Jean, the expression *soul mate* wasn't a cliché.

But there was one thing his father had been right about. His father pointed out, in his typical macho, callous fashion, that the reason Sebastian had lost Jean was that he hadn't been willing to fight for her. He'd let Lyle Canton steal her, as if she'd been a car and Sebastian had carelessly left the keys in the ignition. His father had said that real men don't let other men steal things from them.

It was from that point forward that Sebastian had decided he would never lose again, or if he did, it wouldn't be because he backed away from a fight. People thought his business tactics had to do with making money but they really didn't. He had all the money he would ever need. What drove him was that he'd vowed that he would never be beaten again because of being weak or disengaged or unwilling to do whatever it took to keep what was his.

He couldn't believe it the night Jean walked up to him at the Smithsonian event. He hadn't seen her in over twenty years—he'd deliberately avoided looking for photos of her online and refused to read anything written about her by the press—but there she was, in the flesh, and he'd been amazed at how little she'd changed since college. He was so stunned to see her that he wasn't able to speak. Nor was he able to move. He knew he should turn and walk away to show his contempt for her, but he didn't. He couldn't. He was fixed to the spot as if the past and her beauty had nailed his feet to the floor. Then she said, "I'm sorry for what I did to you, Sebastian. I've been sorry for twenty years. Can we talk? Please?"

And talk they did, although she did most of the talking: about the regrets she had for marrying Canton, about the way he treated her, about how she knew her life would have been completely different if she'd stayed with Sebastian. When she took his hand and said she wanted him to get them a room—as if one night could make up for all those lost years—he did so without hesitation.

After his affair with Jean began, Sebastian could feel the change in himself. It was as if his heart had been a dormant seed and her renewed love for him had caused it to sprout and grow. For the three short months they were together, he'd felt like a kid again, happy in a way he couldn't remember being happy since high school. He would find himself smiling for no apparent reason. He took delight in simple, beautiful things, like children laughing and the way the world smelled new again after it rained. But after her death—after Canton killed her—his heart shriveled and died, and he knew there would be no second resurrection.

Following her death he again spiraled out of control, just as he had when she broke up with him in college: drinking until he passed out, unable to sleep, fantasizing for hours about the way things could have been, sometimes crying so hard he couldn't breathe. He broke every mirror in his house one morning, because every time he saw himself he experienced a nauseating, overwhelming sense of self-loathing for his failure to save her from Canton. Then he'd made a complete ass of himself by showing up drunk at her funeral and threatening to kill Canton, after which he was tossed into a cell like some pathetic maniac, which he truly had been that day. He hadn't gone to the cemetery to confront Canton; he'd gone to say good-bye to Jean. He'd planned to wait until Canton had left the cemetery and then go stand by her grave and say how sorry he was for having failed her. But when he saw that son of a bitch pretending to weep for her—

After he was questioned by the Capitol Police and then released without being charged, he'd returned home and searched his house until he found his grandfather's gun, a .38 revolver that neither he nor his father had ever fired. He started to walk out the door, the gun in his hand, intending to hunt Canton down and kill him. He stopped with his hand on the doorknob. The logical, barely functioning side of his brain knew his chances of succeeding were practically nil and that he'd most likely be killed himself. Which led to: *Why not kill myself?* He knew he'd never be content again or experience love or true happiness again. But then he thought, *No!* If he killed himself, Canton would *win*, and he couldn't allow Canton to win.

He could just see Canton marrying some other woman like Jean, some woman he could trot out like a puppet onto the political stage. And who knew where Canton might end up? Becoming president of the United States was not outside the realm of possibility; he certainly might become the next Speaker of the House, which would make him second in line for the presidency.

At that moment—the moment when he thought of the possibility of Canton becoming president—it was as if someone had doused him with a bucket of ice water. He showered and shaved for the first time in days, took a pill, and slept for twelve hours. When he woke up, he dressed in one of his conservative suits and went to his office, trying to act as if the past two weeks had never happened. The first thing he did when he reached his office, however, was summon Bill Brayden, and the only thing he said to Brayden was, "I want Lyle Canton gone."

And that's all he'd said.

Brayden had worked for him for a long time. He didn't need to be told anything more.

But now Sebastian realized that killing Canton hadn't given him the sense of satisfaction that he'd expected and once again felt the despair wash over him. Nothing had changed. Nothing would fill the void.

What really was the point of going on?

14

After Bill Brayden retired from the air force, he was hired as the deputy to Spear Industries' head of security, a man named McDonald, a former D.C. Metro detective. In less than a year, Brayden was managing Spear's security operations—in other words, he was doing McDonald's job. He hired and fired security personnel, updated equipment as needed, and developed and executed plans for protecting Spear Industries' assets. The only thing he didn't do was run a small group called Special Security Operations. When he asked McDonald what SSO did, he was told, "Don't worry about it."

Now "Special Security Operations" might sound like an outfit composed of elite soldiers, like Delta Force guys. It wasn't. SSO consisted of a couple of tight-lipped lawyers and two cynical ex-cops, one from Chicago and one from Philly.

One day McDonald called Brayden into his office. McDonald had been absent from work quite a bit before that meeting, and Brayden knew that he had had his prostate removed and there'd been some complications. McDonald, a notoriously unsentimental man, told Brayden, without any preamble: "I'm dying. Fucking cancer. I'm going to stick around here for about a month to teach you the ropes, then I'm gone."

After he got over the shock of McDonald's pronouncement, he wondered what McDonald meant by "teaching him the ropes," because as near as Brayden could tell he was already running Spear Industries' security division—except for the guys in Special Ops. And that's when he learned what Special Ops did.

McDonald explained that in some countries corruption was so rampant that the only way Spear Industries prevailed was by figuring out whom to bribe and then bribing them. And in these countries, you didn't even have to be very subtle about it. You'd drop by the office of the government minister whose palm had to be greased and basically say, "So how much do we have to pay you to get the contract?" In other places, including the United States, a more oblique approach was required. Contributions were made to political campaigns; a local official would be the beneficiary of a first-class European vacation; a visiting congressman would have a sexual experience borrowed from *Fifty Shades of Grey*.

Special Operations also did what McDonald called "opposition research"—which meant learning everything it could about rival corporations so it could exploit any weaknesses. When government contracts were involved—federal, state, or municipal—Special Ops would do what it could to find out what other companies were bidding so Spear could come in just under their bids, or it would bribe the guy in charge of reviewing the bids.

McDonald said, "We don't do anything our competition isn't also doing. We're just better at it." When Brayden asked, "Isn't some of this stuff illegal?" McDonald said, "Yeah, and if you got a problem with that, you should quit."

Brayden didn't quit.

McDonald explained to him that the trickiest part of his job often wasn't the opposition. The trickiest part was Sebastian Spear. "I started under Spear's old man," McDonald said, "and George knew exactly what I was doing, and sometimes he'd be directly involved in the planning.

Well, Sebastian doesn't work that way. He's way too cagey. He makes sure that he's at least a step or two removed from anything me and my guys are doing, so if someone lands in the shit it won't be him. Every once in a while, I might have to brief him on something to make sure he knows what I'm doing, and he won't say a word. It's like he's making sure he's never on record for approving anything. And when he wants you to do something, he'll be so fucking cryptic it might take you a day or two to figure out what the hell he wants.

"Like one time he calls me to his office and says: 'Dobson.' I say, 'Dobson?' And he says, 'Yes, Dobson. That'll be all.' It took me two days to figure out that Dobson was this activist who was about to screw up a job in Oregon and that he wanted Dobson to go away."

"What did you do?" Brayden asked.

"You don't need to know that," McDonald said. "The other thing— and it's the only reason I've been doing this job as long as I have—is that when me and my guys pull off something that's, well, let's say *extraordinary*, we get a bonus. The bonus I get every year can be two or three times my salary when things go right. Spear might be a heartless prick, but he rewards a job well done."

Bill Brayden knew that when it came to Lyle Canton, the bonus he would get this year would be unprecedented.

Bill Brayden's office was on the second floor of the building; the only view he had was of the parking lot. He could have had an office on one of the upper floors with the other VPs and the lawyers, but he liked his office where it was. The computers that controlled the security system for the building—cameras, motion detectors, the system that permitted him to lock down the building and electronically monitor when doors were opened and closed—were all on the second floor. The two men who supervised the security guards at the Virginia location and at other locations around the world were in offices thirty feet from his, so Brayden could easily yank their chains when so inclined. In the office next to him was Nick Fox, his cybersecurity expert. Nick Fox was also the newest and brightest member of Special Ops.

Nick Fox's real name, by the way, was Nikita Pavlovich Orlov.

As head of security, Brayden was responsible for protecting facilities, personnel, and information. In some of the places where Spear worked—places like Africa and Central and South America—this wasn't a matter of a couple of overweight rent-a-cops patrolling the premises. He had a core group of elite personnel, all of them trained to kill by Uncle Sam, and when he needed more manpower for jobs overseas, he contracted with companies that supplied mercenaries. In some areas—like Mexico and South America—kidnapping was a cottage industry, and it was Brayden's job to make sure his employer didn't have to pay millions to ransom back his own personnel. Theft was also a major problem in some backwater countries. People who made a few dollars a month were willing to risk their lives stealing the materials Spear used, particularly the copper used in distribution systems. Last, under Brayden's umbrella was cybersecurity. Cyberattacks could be devastating to the bottom line, and Brayden was responsible for preventing them—and Nikita "Nikki" Orlov was his pit bull, the prettiest pit bull you've ever seen.

Brayden had met Nikki in Russia. Spear Industries had won a $350 million contract to accomplish various upgrades on the hydroelectric stations on the Volga River. Contrary to the way things happened in the United States and other parts of the world, Spear Industries did not get the contract for being the lowest bidder. In fact, it was the highest bidder, because Sebastian Spear and Bill Brayden understood the way government contracts worked in Russia—and the Russians knew that they understood.

To keep the math simple, a $100 million contract in Russia was actually a $75 million contract, because $10 million went to the oligarch who operated the power company—a guy who was a good friend of Vladimir Putin—and $10 million reportedly went to Putin. The other $5 million went to various local functionaries, including members of the Russian mafia, to keep the necessary wheels greased and prevent production "inefficiencies." In other words, the money flowed from the Russian government to the contractor, who then kicked back 25 percent to Putin, his cronies, and various other criminals.

While in Russia, however, Spear's computer systems—systems vital to engineers and financial managers—crashed a dozen times, bringing work to a complete standstill. Brayden flew in experts from the States, who told him the system was being hacked, but they weren't smart enough to stop the hacker. Then one day, with Brayden standing there, watching the so-called experts frantically trying to build an electronic wall around Spear's computers, the hacker crashed the system again. It was as if he knew Brayden was there and was just rubbing Brayden's nose in what he was doing.

That evening, a frustrated Bill Brayden was sitting alone at a table in the bar of the Hotel Alpina. The Alpina, in Brayden's opinion, had as much charm as a Russian winter, but it was the best hotel available in Zhigulyovsk, a city on the banks of the Volga and near one of the hydroelectric stations being modified. He was drinking vodka. What else would one drink in Russia?

A strikingly handsome man in his twenties took a seat at Brayden's table. The man's dark hair was gelled into little rock-star spikes, and he was wearing a vintage Grateful Dead T-shirt and stonewashed jeans mass-produced with holes in the knees. His eyes were as blue as the sky in Montana.

"Go sit somewhere else," Brayden said in English. He wasn't a particularly sociable person to begin with, and he certainly wasn't in the mood for company that night.

"I am the one who fucks up your computers," the young man said. His English was excellent, although he had a noticeable accent. Then he had the balls to stick out his hand for Brayden to shake. "My name is Nikki."

Brayden ignored the outstretched hand. "So how much do you want?"

Brayden actually wasn't all that displeased; paying off the hacker—a guy who was obviously smarter than his guys—was the simplest and cheapest solution to his current problem.

"I don't want money," Nikki said. "I want a job with your company. In America. And I need your help to leave Russia." He paused, then added, "Before I'm killed."

Brayden told the bartender to bring Nikki a glass and poured from the bottle of Zyr on his table. In this part of Russia, you were expected to buy a bottle rather than run the bartender ragged bringing you drinks.

Brayden learned that Nikita Pavlovich Orlov had been born into a middle-class family and had aced every math test he'd been given since the age of four. He graduated at eighteen from the Moscow Institute of Physics and Technology—the Russian equivalent of MIT—with master's degrees in mathematics and computer science. "I'm a genius," Nikki said. He wasn't bragging; he was simply stating a fact.

Then he went to work for the GRU, the Russian foreign intelligence agency.

"Cyber warfare?" Brayden said.

"I don't know if I'd call it *warfare*," Nikki said. "I'm a lover, not a fighter." He smiled before adding, "Which is why I need to leave Russia."

Nikki explained. He said he couldn't resist women, and few could resist him. Considering how good-looking the guy was, Brayden could believe this. Nikki's problem was that he was caught in bed with the wife of a GRU general—a man in his sixties who had married a twenty-four-year-old model/actress/hooker from Saint Petersburg.

"He beat Galina so badly she's going to need plastic surgery, and he said he was going to kill me. And this isn't a man who makes idle threats.

A month ago I returned to my apartment, and two GRU thugs were waiting for me. It was just luck that I got away, and I've been in hiding ever since. I can't get on a plane or train because they'll catch me."

Nikki said he left Moscow with nothing more than his laptop—which in Nikki's case meant he left with a complete set of cyber burglary tools. He'd been tickling money out of ATMs and living off stolen credit card numbers since fleeing Moscow. Screwing up Spear Industries' computers was his idea of a job application.

He said, "I know you use charter planes to bring equipment into Russia and figured you could get me out of the country on one. After I get to the United States, I won't have a problem creating an identity."

When Brayden didn't respond, Nikki said, "I can be very valuable to you. I can protect your computers from, well, from people like me. And if your competitors—and your government—have information you need, I can get the information."

So Brayden hired Nikki Orlov, who became Nick Fox.

Sending a text message from John Mahoney's cell phone to DeMarco's phone, and moving a hundred thousand dollars from an untraceable source into DeMarco's bank account, was, for Nikki Orlov, literally child's play. He could have done those things when he was sixteen.

15

The Hay-Adams Hotel was constructed in 1928. It's an Italian Renaissance–style building made of white granite and fronted by Doric columns and a sculptured frieze with rosettes and triglyphs. It's impressive, in other words, and suitable for the nation's capital. It's also one of the most famous hotels in the world, because it's a short walk across Lafayette Square from the White House, and folks visiting the president often stay at the Hay-Adams.

The hotel bar is cleverly named Off the Record. It's a dimly lighted room—ideal for hatching conspiracies—and has a reddish glow thanks to high-backed red-cloth-covered benches along one wall, overstuffed red chairs, and a hardwood floor and bar stained mahogany red. On the walls are amusing caricatures of past and present occupants of the Oval Office. That is, the bar's patrons find them amusing. The presidents, not so much.

Emma was drinking a Grey Goose martini at a corner table beneath a cartoon of George W. Bush, the man's ears drawn large enough to make flight seem possible. She was a regal-looking woman, with patrician features and blue eyes as pale and cold as chips of Arctic ice. She was dressed in a black Armani suit. She could afford Armani. She was tall, had short, expensively styled blond-gray hair, and was slim because she ran in marathons. She was disdainful of golf—DeMarco's favorite pastime—as she considered it to be the aerobic equivalent of sitting in a recliner eating potato chips.

Emma could see two senators at a table near hers, one a Democrat, the other a Republican, who railed at each other on political talk shows but appeared to be having a great time getting drunk together. Seated at the bar was a *Washington Post* reporter assigned to the White House press corps and known to have a severe drinking problem; he was typing furiously on a laptop with two fingers, stopping frequently to lower the level in the glass near his right elbow. Emma wondered how long it would be before he spilled his drink onto his laptop. Also present were a man and a woman, the man wearing a suit, the woman a black cocktail dress that clung to her rather generous figure. Emma knew the couple were military: the man an admiral, the woman an air force colonel and a Pentagon spokesperson who appeared frequently on the news. She also knew they were married—but not to each other. The Hay-Adams bar was a great place to people-watch.

The man Emma was waiting for rushed into the bar, twenty minutes late. She wasn't surprised or annoyed that he was late; with his job, he was probably running late most of the day. He was in his mid-forties, and his dark hair had thinned considerably since Emma had last seen him. When Emma knew him as an army lieutenant he'd been slim and muscular; now he was at least thirty pounds overweight, most likely because the only exercise he got was picking up the phone to scream at someone. His name was James Foster. He was the president's latest chief of staff. (The president went through chiefs the way a wood chipper disposed of tree limbs.)

"I apologize for being so late, ma'am," he said.

Emma laughed. "James, you're the president's chief of staff. I'm no longer a *ma'am* to you. Call me Emma."

"Well, if that's an order, ma'am, I'll follow it," Foster said, but he smiled.

"I need a favor, James," Emma said.

"Anything," Foster said.

"Don't say that until you've heard what I want."

"The answer will still be the same, Emma. Anything."

———————◆◆◆———————

Emma had spent her career working for the Defense Intelligence Agency. At the DIA she'd been a spy, a handler of spies, and an intelligence analyst. Almost everything she'd done during her thirty-year career would stay classified for another fifty years, because she'd done the sort of things the Joint Chiefs wanted done but hadn't really wanted to know about.

James Foster had also worked briefly for the DIA. He was a West Point alumnus, one who had graduated near the top of his class. After giving back to the army the obligatory five years to repay the service for his expensive education, he had resigned his commission to do what he really loved: politics. The first time Emma had met him, however, Foster had been a newly minted first lieutenant assigned to the Defense Attaché System, an arm of the DIA. Defense Attachés, similar to members of the CIA, operate out of U.S. embassies around the world.

On August 7, 1998, two truck bombs exploded simultaneously at the United States embassies in Dar es Salaam, Tanzania; and Nairobi, Kenya, killing two hundred people, mostly non-Americans. The attack was the work of the Egyptian Islamic Jihad, which had connections to Osama bin Laden and al-Qaeda. The masterminds behind the attack were two Egyptians, Fazul Abdullah Mohammed and Abdullah Ahmed Abdullah—and the U.S. government wanted their heads.

Two months after the bombings, young Lieutenant James Foster was approached in a café by an Egyptian professor of literature who taught at Cairo University. He knew Foster was assigned to the U.S. embassy, and he may even have known that Foster was DIA. The professor said he knew that one of the embassy attackers, Abdullah Ahmed Abdullah, would be in Cairo in two days to visit his dying mother.

The United States *pounced* on this information. President Clinton wanted Abdullah captured, and he didn't trust the Egyptians to make the arrest. Elite soldiers from the Joint Special Operations Command were flown secretly to Cairo. The professor who'd provided the information was quickly vetted and determined to have no connection to al-Qaeda or the Egyptian Islamic Jihad. Young Lieutenant Foster, however, said that he wasn't sure the professor should be trusted. The man simply didn't smell right to him. But a couple of army generals and the president's national security adviser told the lieutenant to sit down and shut up. Smarter guys than him had done the background checks on the professor.

It turned out that the professor's tip was a setup, and one American soldier was killed when the U.S. team raided Abdullah's mother's empty house. The remaining soldiers, one of them wounded, picked up their dead comrade and beat a hasty retreat from Cairo. The Egyptian government—maybe thanks to the same professor—learned about the raid and the gun battle that had taken place in its capital city and was naturally outraged.

The president ended up with egg all over his face, and he wasn't in the best of moods anyway, because at the time he was also dealing with the Monica Lewinsky scandal. Consequently, Clinton wanted someone's head on a platter—and the army decided that the head that should be proffered was that of Lieutenant James Foster. Discussions began regarding whether Foster should be court-martialed for his incompetence; he was, after all, the man who had passed on the professor's bogus tip and was therefore responsible for the dead soldier and a diplomatic nightmare. He would certainly be drummed out of the army with a dishonorable discharge. Foster's dreams of a brilliant career in politics were about to end before they ever started.

Well, Emma wouldn't allow it. She went toe-to-toe with generals and the president's national security adviser. She told them—which they already knew—that Foster had expressed concerns about trusting the professor. Emma wasn't a person anyone told to sit down and shut up, and at that point in her career, she knew where all the bodies were buried. She said she'd go public with the entire debacle—classified material be damned—before she'd allow young James Foster to become the designated scapegoat.

Emma made more enemies—as if she hadn't had enough already—but she eventually won. The army ultimately wrote a report spreading around the blame without really identifying anyone as being singularly responsible. Clinton, at this point, didn't care—he was worried about being impeached—and James Foster finished his brief army career and vectored into politics.

James Foster owed Emma.

***

"I want to be on the inside of the FBI's investigation into Lyle Canton's murder," Emma said.

"I don't understand," Foster said.

"The FBI has arrested the wrong man, James. Joe DeMarco didn't kill Canton."

"Do you know DeMarco?"

"Yes. I can't tell you how I know him but I've known him for years. And he once saved my life. Actually, he saved it twice."

"The evidence against him is overwhelming."

"I don't care. DeMarco didn't do it."

Foster was silent for a moment. He knew Emma was rarely wrong. In fact, he couldn't remember her *ever* being wrong.

"Exactly what do you want?"

"I want to see all the evidence the FBI has, and I want them to under-stand that if I ask them for something, they're to give it to me."

"They won't agree to that."

"Which is why I'm talking to you. They'll agree to whatever you direct them to do. Tell them that the president wants one of his people—namely me—looking over their shoulder because of the politi-cal significance of Canton's murder."

"Man, they are not going to like that at all," Foster said.

"Well, there's an old army expression that covers these situations, James." She paused and then said, "Tough shit."

———◆◆◆———

James Foster had wanted to be a politician. After he gave the army the active-duty years he owed for West Point, he set his sights on becoming the U.S. congressman from his district in Colorado. He soon learned, however, that he didn't really have what it took to be the guy up front. He wasn't charming; he wasn't good in front of a camera; he didn't have the patience to put up with all the bullshit a candidate had to tolerate to get elected. He found out after his first failed campaign that where he belonged was *behind* the guy running for office.

Foster excelled at the backroom deal. He developed the strategies that got people elected. He knew how to leak things to the press in such a way that they never came back to bite him on the ass. And he could twist arms as arms had never been twisted before. He was an outstanding presidential chief of staff.

When he told the director of the FBI that Emma was to be allowed inside the investigation into Canton's murder, Foster listened for about two minutes to all the reasons the FBI wasn't comfortable with that—then basically told the director what Emma had said: *Tough shit.*

16

"Who is this damn woman?" Peyton asked, when Director Erby told him that Emma was being assigned by the White House to look over Peyton's shoulder.

Erby said, "All I know is that she's ex-DIA. She worked for them for about thirty years. The president's chief is also ex-DIA, and I'm guessing that's how he knows her. I tried to get her personnel file and ran into a brick wall at the Pentagon. Since I figured we didn't have time to get into a pissing contest with the Joint Chiefs over classified files, I asked friends at IRS and Homeland what they could tell me about her. My guy at the IRS said she's quite wealthy—she inherited some money when her folks died—and the rest she earned through investments. She hasn't been employed since leaving the DIA, but according to Homeland, her passport shows she's traveled to places people don't usually go on vacation, places like Iran, Palestine, and Syria. The thing is, she went to these places during periods when the State Department said Americans shouldn't go there, and her travel history made me wonder if she could be moonlighting for the DIA even though she's supposedly retired. Whatever the case, we're stuck with her."

"Well, I don't like this at all," Peyton said. "How do we know she won't talk to the press?"

Peyton was really thinking that this was the sort of thing that happens when the FBI director was a political appointee who didn't have the balls to tell the White House to blow its orders up its ass.

"Foster assures me she would never do that. I've also told Foster that if she leaks anything or impedes the investigation in any way, we'll give her the boot."

Yeah, right. "Does she know DeMarco? Did he work with her when she was at the Pentagon? Is he a friend?"

"I don't know that she has any history with DeMarco. DeMarco was never in the military, and she travels in completely different social circles from him. Oh, she's gay by the way, not that that's relevant. Foster says the only reason he wants her involved is that he wants an independent, politically unbiased source following the investigation, particularly now that he knows that Mahoney might have some connection to DeMarco."

"That's an insult to the bureau," Peyton said. "We *are* a politically unbiased source."

"Hey, Russ, what can I tell you? The president's hatchet man wants her in, so she's in. And anyway, what harm can she do?"

Peyton was in his office in the Hoover Building when he met Foster's watchdog. After DeMarco's arrest, the FBI had cleared out of the Capitol, allowing Congress to get back to doing whatever it is it does. The two-day interruption caused by the FBI's investigation unsurprisingly had no apparent impact on the smooth running of the nation.

Peyton's first impression when she walked into his office was that she was a striking-looking woman and a woman who, he sensed immediately, was used to being in charge. He could also tell, before they exchanged more than a dozen words, that she wasn't the type to be intimidated by a senior member of the most powerful law enforcement organization in the world. He noticed that she was wearing two badges on lanyards around her neck: One badge was similar to his, and gave her unlimited access to the Hoover Building and the FBI lab at Quantico. The other badge gave her unlimited access to the Capitol. How in the hell had she managed to get those credentials? Foster, he guessed.

Peyton said, "Please sit down Ms.—"

"Call me Emma," she said. "And thank you for agreeing to meet with me."

"I wasn't given a choice," Peyton said.

"And I was just being polite," Emma said.

Peyton couldn't help smiling. "So, what can I do for you? The president's chief indicated that you would be, I guess, overseeing my investigation. Would you like one of my agents to give you a briefing on where things stand?"

"No," Emma said. "I want to see the raw evidence myself without anyone playing middleman. Based on what's been reported in the paper, I know you have video footage of Canton's killer, ballistic evidence, DNA evidence, and so forth. I want to see everything, and after I do, maybe we'll sit down and talk some more."

"You understand that if you leak anything to the media—"

"I won't be speaking to the media at all. I never have and never will."

The way she said this, Peyton had the distinct impression that she had as much disdain for the jackals as he did.

Peyton called Agent Berman and told her to come to his office. While they were waiting for her, Peyton explained that Alice Berman was the agent who had discovered the clothes and the murder weapon in DeMarco's office.

Two minutes later, Berman arrived and Peyton said to her, "This is Emma. She's an independent observer assigned by the White House, and she's to be allowed to see whatever we have on the Canton case.

Evidence, field reports, information obtained by warrants, the whole nine yards. You're her escort."

"Excuse me, sir?" Berman said, clearly shocked that an outsider would be granted such access into an ongoing investigation.

"You heard me, Berman. Show her everything. Nothing, of course, is to leave the building, and she's not allowed to make copies of anything. And you will stay with her at all times."

Peyton thought Emma might push back on the directive not to make copies or to having Berman bird-dogging her, but she didn't. She stood and said to Berman, "Lead the way, Agent."

For the next six hours, Emma examined the mountain of information collected by the FBI. It was astounding what fifty field agents and technicians could accumulate in a forty-eight-hour period.

She looked at the video footage of the man in the Capitol Police uniform walking toward Canton's office. She read through more than three hundred interviews agents conducted with people in the Capitol, including a number of interviews in which FBI agents asked people what they knew about DeMarco. She looked at photos of the uniform worn by the killer and close-ups of the fake Capitol Police insignia patch on the uniform. She examined the records related to the text message John Mahoney had sent to DeMarco, phone records proving DeMarco had called Mahoney, and the banking transaction sending a hundred thousand dollars to DeMarco's savings account. She smiled slightly when she learned that the bureau had obtained DeMarco's DNA from a hot dog he'd half-eaten at a golf course. Where else would he be on a Sunday but at a golf course? For that matter, if it had been a Monday he might have been there just as well.

She reviewed a memo that Peyton had prepared in which he summarized a meeting with the Richmond reporter who'd exposed Sebastian Spear's affair with Canton's wife. Another memo, prepared by an FBI profiler, concluded that the killer was intelligent, well organized, familiar with the Capitol's security systems, and most likely not a terrorist or some nut who had acted impulsively. One thick file identified people who had sent threatening-sounding e-mails to Canton but also contained the reasons the Secret Service did not think these people should be added to a watch list or further investigated. In other words, the hate e-mails appeared to be from people just blowing off steam, ranting about Canton's politics. The FBI had reviewed about half the e-mail senders and crossed them off its likely suspect list but hadn't looked at the others after DeMarco was arrested.

She asked to see the photographs of DeMarco's office taken at the time the bureau searched it. In one photo she saw what she was looking for: on the coatrack in DeMarco's office were a trench coat and a flat woolen cap, the cap DeMarco would wear when it rained. DeMarco had stopped using umbrellas years ago because he always lost them. The hat was important.

The whole time Emma was reviewing the evidence, Berman sat there, clearly bored to death. At one point Emma said to Berman, "Agent, would you mind getting me a bottle of water and a sandwich, preferably one not containing meat. A tuna or egg salad sandwich would be perfect."

Berman hesitated.

Emma said, "Agent, there is no copy machine in this room. And if you want, before I leave today, you can search me to make sure I haven't taken anything."

Berman said, "I'll go get your sandwich, ma'am, as long as you agree not to leave the room while I'm gone."

"I agree," Emma said, smiling slightly. She liked that Berman was a young woman who took her job seriously.

As soon as Berman left the room, Emma pulled an object from the inside pocket of her jacket, an object that appeared to be a ballpoint pen—and that functioned as a ballpoint pen—and took photos of several documents, primarily those related to Mahoney's text message and the banking transactions and the fake Capitol Police patch. She had an excellent memory but didn't want to rely on it.

She ate the egg salad sandwich Berman brought her—it was awful—and continued to look at the evidence for two more hours. She then asked Berman to escort her back to Peyton's office.

Peyton was sitting behind his desk, talking on the phone with someone. Emma concluded it was his wife when he said, "I have to go now, honey, but I should be home early tonight, no later than seven."

He hung up the phone and said to Emma, "Well?"

She said, "You have an impressive circumstantial case against DeMarco."

"I'm delighted you think so," Peyton said, making no attempt to keep the sarcasm out of his tone. "And I wouldn't call it circumstantial."

Emma couldn't tell Peyton that she knew DeMarco wasn't the killer because she knew DeMarco. If she admitted knowing DeMarco, Peyton would think she was biased and would certainly insist that James Foster remove her from the case. Instead of saying why she knew DeMarco was innocent, she said, "Yes, the evidence is circumstantial. The fact that the gun and the clothes the killer used were found in his office doesn't mean that DeMarco hid them there."

"The hair found in the ball cap proves DeMarco wore the cap," Peyton countered.

"No, it doesn't," Emma said. "There's a rain hat in DeMarco's office clearly visible in the photos your people took. Hypothetically, and as I'm sure DeMarco's attorney will argue, the killer could have taken hairs from DeMarco's rain hat and placed them in the baseball cap."

"What about the money transferred into DeMarco's bank account?" Peyton said.

As Emma had no answer to Peyton's question, she asked a question of her own: "Agent Peyton, have you considered the possibility that someone may be trying to frame DeMarco for Canton's murder?"

"You know, John Mahoney said the same thing, and I'll tell you what I told him. In my twenty-five years in the bureau, I've never heard of a single person being framed for a crime."

"Well, how would you have heard?" Emma said. "If the frame was perfect, an innocent man would be sent to jail and no one would ever know."

"Yeah, but I've never even heard of a *botched* frame. Nor can I remember a defense attorney ever making a plausible argument in court that a client was framed. Mistaken identity, yes. Framed, no. People are framed in movies."

When Emma didn't immediately respond, Peyton said, "Let me ask you something, Emma. If a smart, rich person like you wanted someone dead, why would you do something as complicated as framing someone for the murder? Killing the guy yourself in some clever way would be simpler. Or if you couldn't do it yourself, why not just hire a sniper to shoot the guy?"

"I'll tell you why," Emma said, "and the reason is you."

"Me?" Peyton said.

"Yes. If the person I wanted to kill was a U.S. congressman, I would know that the FBI would assign a man like you to the case, along with a hundred other agents, and you wouldn't give up until you caught me. But if I framed someone and if you caught the person I framed immediately—which you did in the case of DeMarco—then I might get away with the murder because you'd no longer be hunting for me."

Peyton frowned. "Does that mean you're going to tell Foster that I *should* be hunting for someone other than DeMarco?"

"No. I'm going to tell Mr. Foster that you've done an outstanding job proving that DeMarco is guilty. But I have one question and one request."

"Okay," Peyton said, relieved that Emma didn't intend to go running to Foster with a complaint.

"Early in your investigation, consideration was being given to polygraph-testing the Capitol cops. Were any polygraph tests ever administered?"

"No. After we arrested DeMarco, there didn't appear to be any reason to do that. And at this point, I don't want to ask the Capitol Police to polygraph thirteen hundred people, as it will cause them a lot of employee aggravation, and they'll spend hundreds of man-hours doing something that distracts them from their mission. Are you saying that we should polygraph them?"

"No. I just wondered if any testing had been done."

"What was the second thing?" Peyton said. "The request?"

"I saw that you asked for and received an electronic copy of the personnel files of everyone working for the Capitol Police. I'd like a copy of that information, and I want to take it with me so I can go through it at my leisure."

"Why?" Peyton said.

"Why not?" Emma said. "I can ask the president's chief of staff to obtain the information for me directly from the Capitol Police, but since you already have it, it'd be simpler if you cooperated and provided it. It would be a shame if I had to bother someone as busy as Mr. Foster."

She could tell that Peyton didn't want to give her anything, but she could also imagine what he was thinking: if she was wasting her time looking at the personnel records of thirteen hundred people, she wouldn't be bugging him or meddling in his investigation.

"Fine. I'll have Berman make you a copy of the file we got from the Capitol cops."

As she was leaving the Hoover Building, Emma called a man named Neil.

17

Considering some of the things he had done for Mahoney over the years, it was surprising that up till now DeMarco had spent only one day in jail. He'd been tossed into a cell by a corrupt redneck sheriff in some southern backwater, but Mahoney had landed on state politicians like an eight-hundred-pound gorilla and managed to get him sprung in a day. And in the southern jail, he'd been the only occupant, spent his time bullshitting pleasantly with the Barney Fife deputy on duty, and caught up on his sleep. The experience hadn't been much different from spending the day in a not-so-comfortable motel room, and his primary emotion had been boredom—as opposed to abject fear.

By comparison, the Alexandria city jail was like the waiting room to hell—hell being the federal prison where he would end up if convicted. The jail was crowded; it had been designed to hold x number of occupants and was now holding three or four times x. There was a monkey-house odor to the place; it was noisy with men talking loudly and constantly, and it seemed as if someone was always screaming. Jails are a convenient place to park the mentally ill, and DeMarco suspected the screamers were nuts off their meds.

Since his arrival, the only thing DeMarco could think about—other than the fact that he might be convicted of Lyle Canton's murder—was every prison movie he'd ever seen, and Hollywood directors seemed to be fairly consistent in their portrayal of prison life. He knew, therefore, that prisons were filled with violent, frustrated people with little to zero impulse control—thus the odds of being beaten to a pulp were fairly high. All it took was inadvertently crossing some invisible line in the sand or looking for too long into the eyes of a psychopath, and some guy who had spent most of his adult life lifting jailhouse weights would use his head for a punching bag.

Then there was the possibility of sexual assault, and DeMarco couldn't get out of his head the scene in *The Shawshank Redemption* where an innocent Tim Robbins finds himself in a storeroom, backed into a corner by three sadistic deviants, and the next thing you hear is Morgan Freeman's mellow voice saying, "I'd like to tell you that Andy fought them off but . . ."

After a sleepless night, thanks to anxiety and the screaming maniac down the hall, DeMarco was led to the cafeteria by a silent guard. He wondered if today he'd be put into a cell with other inmates. He suspected not. He knew, even if most of the other inmates probably didn't, that he was a celebrity—the man who'd killed Lyle Canton—and he doubted the head jailer wanted the publicity he'd get if DeMarco was mauled or molested before his trial.

He shuffled forward in the serving line. He didn't feel like eating but knew it would be unwise to pass up a meal. He needed to keep his strength up—back to the storeroom scene in *The Shawshank Redemption*. He observed that the men sitting in the cafeteria were, most likely of their own volition, racially segregated. Blacks sat with blacks, Hispanics with Hispanics; white guys with too many tattoos ate with other tattooed white guys. He knew his chances of surviving in prison would increase if he joined a gang. He wasn't yet ready, however, to join the Aryan Brotherhood and get a swastika tattooed on his forehead—but it was early days.

He collected his breakfast from servers who never looked at him as they slapped food onto his tray: something yellow and runny that might have been scrambled eggs, burned bacon, two dry pieces of toast, and a little cup of fruit. (It was the fruit cup that some guy built like a Redskins linebacker would pluck off his tray to see if DeMarco was willing to fight to the death for sliced peaches—and, of course, he'd have to fight. According to Spielberg, Scorsese, and others of their ilk, he couldn't show weakness or he'd end up being someone's boy toy for the remainder of his stay.)

He looked for a place to sit, not knowing jailhouse cafeteria etiquette. If he sat down with the white guys, the black and brown guys would all assume he was a racist. Conversely, if he sat with the black guys, (a) that might provoke a fight because they didn't like white guys, and (b) all the white guys would mark him as a someone who didn't know whose side he was supposed to be on. Then he noticed a table full of old guys, a mixed white, brown, and black group. Yeah, they looked like the perfect breakfast companions. He began walking toward the old guys' table, when a man came up next to him and said, "You sit with me."

The man speaking was *enormous*: at least six foot eight and weighing in at about 270 pounds. He had a shaved head, a face that hadn't been shaved in a couple of days, biceps the size of cantaloupes, and a tattoo of an eight-pointed star on each side of his neck—like a pair of markers for the place where the bolt should be inserted. DeMarco's first thought was: *Oh, fuck me.*

Seeing DeMarco's face, the guy said, "Relax. I've been told to make sure nothing happens to you."

"What?" DeMarco said.

"Just follow me."

So DeMarco did, having no idea what the guy was talking about and at the same time not wanting to provoke a man the size of the Chrysler Building.

They walked up to a table where four slender, vaguely effeminate Hispanic men were sitting together. They'd finished their breakfast and were bullshitting in Spanish. DeMarco's new friend said, "You little bitches are done eating. Go." The little bitches looked at him, looked at each other for a moment, then picked up their trays and left.

DeMarco and the behemoth sat down, and the behemoth said, "The warden told me to make sure that no one fucks with you while you're here."

"Why would the warden do that?"

"I don't know and I don't care. For some reason, he wants you protected."

DeMarco's immediate thought was: *Mahoney.* Mahoney got to the warden and told him to make sure that DeMarco didn't become Shawshank Andy.

"What do you get out of this?" DeMarco asked.

"What do you care?"

"I don't. I'm just curious."

"This is not a good place to be curious. They've put me in the cell next to yours, and from now on, when you leave your cell, I go with you."

That sounded fine to DeMarco, especially the part about the guy not being put in the *same* cell with him. He didn't want his cell becoming the Alexandria jail honeymoon suite.

"What's your name?" DeMarco asked.

"Lazlo."

"Lazlo?"

"Yeah, my parents were from Bosnia. You got a problem with that?"

"No, no," DeMarco said.

Lazlo didn't have an accent, so DeMarco assumed he had been in the United States for a long time or was born here. Not that he was going to ask.

Lazlo said, "Eat your breakfast. Oh, can I have the fruit cup?"

"Help yourself," DeMarco said.

18

Emma could tell that Neil had not been happy to hear from her.

He'd been at home, playing in a high-stakes video game against three competitors located in London, Tehran, and Tokyo. Emma thought it absurd that a man Neil's age should waste his time on such an adolescent pastime but supposed it was no worse than DeMarco wasting his time playing golf. Men were essentially useless creatures. Women really needed to find a way to have children without a sperm donor.

However, unhappy or not, when Emma called him from the Hoover Building and told him to be in his office in half an hour, Neil agreed. Of course he agreed. It was only thanks to Emma that Neil was currently not residing in a federal penitentiary. He owed her, and he knew it. And he was afraid of her.

Neil's office was on the fourth floor of a four-story building in Washington, D.C., on the banks of the Potomac River. He had a view of the Pentagon. If the people in the Pentagon had any idea of the number of times Neil had breached their databases they would have ordered a drone strike on his building. Neil owned the building, by the way. He may have been lazy, but he was a genius and he charged clients an exorbitant amount for his services.

As for Neil's profession, he called himself an information broker. What this meant was that if you wanted to know something about a person or an organization, and if that information was stored in a computer, Neil could most likely obtain it for you. He had the ability to slither through most firewalls, but these days he often didn't need to do that. Now it was much easier for him to pay folks he'd met over the years who had access to the data he needed, such as people who worked at banks and telecommunications companies and law enforcement agencies. Neil honestly didn't consider that what he did was criminal; it wasn't as if he was stealing money intended for orphans. Neil, like DeMarco, had his own unique interpretation of ethical conduct.

Neil was seated behind his desk when Emma arrived at his office. He was an overweight white man in his forties who dressed most often in Hawaiian shirts and baggy shorts, no matter the season. He persisted in tying what remained of his thinning blond hair into a short ponytail that hung to his collar. His office was like the command deck of the Starship *Enterprise*, filled with computer equipment and a zillion little blinking lights.

"I suppose this is about DeMarco," he said.

"Yes," Emma said. "We're going to prove he's innocent."

"It doesn't sound like he's innocent. Based on what I've read, the case against him looks pretty solid."

"Neil, do you seriously believe that DeMarco killed Lyle Canton?"

"No, but maybe for a hundred grand . . ."

"He wouldn't have killed him for a million. And you know it."

———◆◆◆———

Emma had met DeMarco more than a decade ago when, as she'd told James Foster, he'd saved her life. DeMarco hadn't done anything overtly heroic; he'd simply been in the right place at the wrong time. The day it happened, Emma had just disembarked from a plane returning from Iran, knowing that two men from the Iranian secret police had been on the plane with her. As she walked through baggage claim, with the men not far behind her, she noticed a woman walking up to them and handing one of them a canvas shopping bag. Emma suspected there were weapons in the bag.

The Iranians wanted a flash drive she was carrying. They also wanted her dead because of what she'd learned in Iran. They were in fact so desperate to kill her that she thought they might shoot her right there in baggage claim. Not bothering to collect her luggage, Emma stepped outside the terminal, looked for a cab, and saw a car idling at the curb, right in front of the door. She got into the car and told the driver, "Drive or we're both going to be killed."

The driver, a puzzled Joe DeMarco, who had been waiting for a friend, said, "What? Who are you?"

Emma screamed, "Go!"—and at that moment DeMarco saw two pissed-off-looking guys burst out of the terminal, one of them pointing at Emma. The other reached into a bag, and DeMarco saw what he thought looked like an Uzi coming out of the bag. So DeMarco, not knowing what the hell was going on, stepped on the gas—and the two guys piled into another car that had also been waiting at the curb. Not long after that, DeMarco was flying down the Memorial Parkway at about a hundred miles an hour while a guy in a car behind him was firing a machine gun at him.

And that had been DeMarco's introduction to Emma.

Over the years that had passed since then, he'd found out a little—but not much—about who Emma was and about her career in the DIA, and he came to her sometimes for help, particularly when he needed information from the Pentagon or some local spy shop.

Emma's feelings toward DeMarco had always been ambivalent. One strike against him was that he worked for John Mahoney—a man as corrupt as any politician who'd ever occupied an office on Capitol

Hill. She also knew that DeMarco was Mahoney's bagman and the guy Mahoney used whenever there was some sort of skullduggery to be performed.

DeMarco's work ethic—or lack thereof—was a second strike against him. DeMarco was lazy and unambitious, the type of man who gives civil servants a bad name. He did the minimum required of him, had no real interest in his job, and did it only because one day he'd get a pension. And although he didn't like working for Mahoney, he had never made any real effort to find another job. The only reason he had a job with Mahoney in the first place was because his godmother, a woman who'd once had an affair with Mahoney, had blackmailed Mahoney into hiring him.

Emma suspected that DeMarco's idea of the perfect job would be managing a golf course. He'd be able to play every day, schmooze and drink with the other golfers, and have affairs with the lady golfers. Had DeMarco ever worked for her when she was with the DIA she undoubtedly would have fired him.

On the other hand, DeMarco was bright and likable, and when he took an interest in an assignment he could be as tricky and stubborn as he had to be to get results. The other thing was that when Emma helped DeMarco, it wasn't always just because she owed him. She'd helped him several times when—as odd as it might sound—DeMarco had actually been on the side of the angels. The first case on which she'd assisted him had involved a Secret Service agent who appeared to be conspiring to kill the president. On another case, DeMarco had unwittingly stumbled into a nest of Chinese spies, and Emma had *wanted* to be part of that one. And that had been the second time DeMarco saved her life.

The upshot of all this was that Emma most often acted toward DeMarco the way an older sister would act toward an annoying younger brother—one who frequently needed a sharp kick in the ass. She'd force him to do the ethical thing as opposed to the expedient thing. She'd do her best to make sure that if he didn't stay on the right side of the law he at least didn't do any real harm when he stepped over the line.

And one thing she was sure of was that DeMarco would never murder a man for political reasons or for money.

Joe DeMarco was hardly a saint—but he wasn't his father.

"So, what do you want me to do?" Neil asked. He knew that whatever Emma wanted, he was going to do it, whether he liked it or not.

"Before we get to that, I'm going to tell you everything the FBI has." Emma then gave him a succinct synopsis of what she'd learned in the last six hours at the Hoover Building. When she finished, Neil said, "Sounds to me like DeMarco's ass is cooked."

Emma ignored that comment; she was in no mood for pessimism. She said, "Now, here's what we're going to do. First, we're going to make an assumption. We know that the person who killed Canton had to have access to the Capitol. He knew where all the security cameras were. He had to be able to get into DeMarco's office to plant the evidence found in the ventilation grille. He had to be able to get a gun past the metal detectors. Last, he had to spend a *lot* of time in the Capitol planning and arranging everything. This wasn't a crime committed on the spur of the moment; it took days, if not weeks, of preparation. Taking all those factors into account, and since we know DeMarco didn't do it, we're going to assume that the person who killed Canton was in fact a real Capitol cop."

"Okay," Neil said, his tone saying, *Well, if you say so.*

"I like a Capitol cop for the killer because in addition to having unlimited access to the building and knowing about the cameras, he'd also be familiar with all the other security measures, such as where the guards are during their shifts, when they tour the building, and so forth. And after Canton was killed, a real cop would be able to blend in with all the other cops running around searching for the killer. If he was seen in the Capitol either before or after the shooting, he wouldn't stand out in any way; he'd blend in like the furniture."

Neil said, "There are a lot of other people who know the Capitol, including about six hundred politicians and all the people who work for them. Then you have contractors—like the guy who was fixing that senator's computer the night Canton was killed—who also know the building pretty well and would have a legitimate reason for spending a lot of time there."

"That's true," Emma said, "but we're going to start with the Capitol cops because they're the most logical group of suspects."

"What about the fake insignia patch?" Neil said. "A real cop wouldn't need a fake patch."

Emma said, "I believe the fake patch was calculated misdirection. The killer had an imperfect patch made knowing it would be picked up by the cameras and therefore make the FBI think it was someone *other* than a real Capitol cop."

Neil countered with, "Or if the killer wasn't a Capitol cop, he had the fake patch made so he could pretend to be a cop."

"No," Emma said emphatically. "It's Occam's razor. It would have been easier for a real cop to get a fake patch than it would have been for a fake Capitol cop to commit the crime."

Before Neil could debate the issue further, Emma handed him a flash drive. "That contains the personnel files of the thirteen hundred people employed by the Capitol police. I want you to eliminate anyone who isn't a white male approximately DeMarco's weight and height. Then what I want you to do is see if any of those people have any connection to Sebastian Spear or Spear Industries. Just as a Capitol cop is the most likely person to be the killer, Spear is a logical suspect for hiring someone to murder Canton. But the FBI is not investigating Spear, because all the evidence points to DeMarco and Mahoney."

"But Spear can't be the only person on the planet who might have wanted Canton dead," Neil said.

"Probably not," Emma said. "But he was at the top of the FBI's list until DeMarco was dropped into their lap, and so now he's at the top of *my* list. So I want you to look for connections to Spear."

"Okay," Neil said, "I can write a program to—"

"After you've done that, I want you to see if anyone employed by Spear has the sort of skills you do."

"Skills to do what?"

"If Mahoney isn't lying—and, for once, I don't think he is—then someone hacked his phone to send a text message to DeMarco. So I want to know if someone connected to Spear could have done that."

"I already know who Spear would use," Neil said.

"You do?" Emma said, although she wasn't completely surprised. Almost all of Neil's friends were people like him: people who spent almost all their waking hours with their fingers on a keyboard, people who wandered the Dark Net in the wee hours looking for excitement, people who thought that hacking into a private server was the best game ever invented.

"Yeah," Neil said. "His name is Nikki Orlov, but he calls himself Nick Fox."

Neil explained how he knew Orlov—he explained in his long-winded, meandering way, making Emma just want to scream. When she'd worked for the DIA, she'd demanded that her people brief her concisely, quickly getting to the point—but she knew screaming at Neil wouldn't shorten the story.

Neil said that about five years earlier, a mid-level Russian computer guy named Dmitri Sokolov, who'd worked for the GRU, had defected to the United States. After the NSA, the CIA, and the FBI had squeezed him dry, a process that took over a year, Dmitri settled in the D.C. area, found a job on the Geek Squad at Best Buy, and eventually got into gamer circles, which is where Neil met him.

Neil said, "Dmitri's a good guy, and I like him, but the truth is that when it comes to computers, he's pretty mediocre. I mean, he's probably a Geek Squad superstar, but he doesn't have the skills of a top-notch cyber operative, and I imagine he didn't know anything that the FBI and NSA didn't already know about the Russians. If he had known something, the Russians would have whacked him before the FBI ever got their hands on him."

"What does this have to do with—"

"I'm getting there," Neil said.

Two years ago, Neil had attended a trade show in Las Vegas along with about a hundred thousand other people. He'd gone with Dmitri and another man so they could split the cost of a room. Neil was a tight-wad. The trade show was one where Apple and Microsoft and Google showed off all the new, whiz-bang toys they were developing, and nerds from all over the globe flocked to Vegas like Muslims to Mecca. One night, while Neil and Dmitri were having a drink in one of the casinos, a handsome young guy walked into the lounge accompanied by a statuesque blonde who looked like a Vegas showgirl. When Dmitri saw the man, he said, "Jesus Christ, it's him. He's alive."

After recovering from the shock of seeing a ghost, Dmitri told Neil that the man's name was Nikita Orlov. When Dmitri had defected to the United States, he said, Orlov had already been working for the GRU, though just a teenager. The guy was a genius and basically a Green Beret when it came to cyber warfare. Dmitri said, "Nikki Orlov is the best the Russians have. Or did have."

"What's he doing here?" Neil asked.

Dmitri said the better question was: *What's he doing alive?* Dmitri had kept in touch with friends back in Russia after he defected—via encrypted e-mails—and he'd heard that Orlov had disappeared because he'd screwed the wife of some Russian general. "The guy was a legendary pussy hound," Dmitri said. "But all my friends over there said he'd disappeared, and they figured he was probably dead. And if the GRU knew he was here in the United States, they'd definitely kill him. He knows so much about the Russian cyber program that they couldn't afford to let him live."

"So what was he doing in Vegas?" Emma asked.

"I don't know," Neil said. "Maybe he figured he was safe. It was a huge convention, and the chance of bumping into someone from the Russian government was small. But he was taking a big risk, because I know the Russians had some of their top people there. Every spy shop in the world had people there."

"But how do you know he works for Sebastian Spear?" Emma asked.

Neil said he saw Orlov—minus the showgirl—the next day at one of the booths in the convention hall, bugging a vendor with questions the vendor wasn't smart enough to answer. Neil sidled over near him to see his badge. Attendees were given badges after they paid their fee so they could wander the convention hall; the badge had the person's name on it as well as a company name if he or she was representing a company. Orlov's badge said his name was Nick Fox and he worked for Spear Industries.

"For Christ's sake, Neil," Emma said. "Why didn't you report this to someone?"

"Report what to who?" Neil said.

"Don't be obtuse. If you knew the man was a Russian who'd been engaged in cyber operations against the United States, you should have told the FBI."

"Emma, I don't talk to the FBI. You know that. Plus, for all I knew, he could have been a defector like Dmitri and the FBI already knew about him. Maybe that's why he felt safe going to the convention."

Emma felt like smacking Neil on the back of his ponytailed head, but decided to drop the subject—for now. She needed to focus on freeing

DeMarco. "We'll get back to Orlov later," she said. "Right now, I want you to concentrate on the Capitol cops."

"Okay. I'll start on it first thing in the morning."

"No. You'll start tonight. I'll come back here tomorrow morning, and by then I expect some answers."

Neil put his head down on his desk and groaned.

19

DeMarco was starting to realize that the worst things about prison—provided that Lazlo continued to be his bodyguard—were going to be boredom, lack of privacy, the constant background noise, and, of course, the food. And DeMarco's lawyer had told him he was going to be in the jail for at least a year before he went to trial.

"A year?" DeMarco had said.

"And if necessary I'll delay the trial even longer," his lawyer had said. Seeing the expression on DeMarco's face, she added, "Emma and I need all the time we can get to prove you're innocent. If we fail, the year you spend in this jail is going to seem like summer camp in the Poconos compared with the federal prison where you'll spend the rest of your life."

His lawyer was not an uplifting person.

After breakfast, he took a shower as Lazlo stood nearby—looking for threats and not at DeMarco's nubile form—and the experience was no worse than showering in a high school locker room. Nobody was being sodomized; no one was jerking off; no one's blood was running down the shower drain. Entertainment was provided by two guys who were going on and on about a woman named Chantelle, whom they'd both been married to and who they agreed was a stone-cold, avaricious, lying, cheating bitch with the body of a *Playboy* centerfold.

After the shower, Lazlo escorted DeMarco to the jail library. He needed something to occupy his mind other than wondering what Emma could be doing to save him. On the way to the library, Lazlo walked slightly behind him, his massive head swiveling, assessing potential risks. The men they encountered on the way stepped aside for Lazlo and didn't make eye contact—with one exception. They met a black guy in a hallway who was just as big as Lazlo, and he and Lazlo eye-fucked each other for a moment, then they both nodded, and the black guy went on his way. The experience made DeMarco think of two bull elephants meeting on a jungle path and silently agreeing that they'd do battle some other day.

DeMarco returned to his cell with four novels. Lazlo told the guard—he didn't ask him—to lock DeMarco's cell, and DeMarco spent the afternoon taking a nap he didn't need and reading a novel about an alcoholic English girl who spent her days looking out the window of a train.

He walked to the cafeteria for dinner, feeling lethargic after having done nothing but lie on his back most of the day. Tomorrow he'd start doing push-ups; that's what guys in prison movies did. Lazlo, a man of few words—or no words—said nothing as they walked. They'd just joined the serving line when a fight involving a long-haired white guy who looked like a Hell's Angels prototype and a tall, lanky Hispanic guy started at the other end of the cafeteria. Another couple of guys joined the fight, prisoners formed a cheering ring around the combatants, and guards surged toward the mayhem—and DeMarco heard Lazlo say, "Watch your ass."

Four stocky, heavily tattooed Hispanic guys were running toward him and Lazlo as everyone else headed toward the fight. All four had knives in their hands—real knives, not homemade prison shanks—and the knives had serrated four- or five-inch blades. Three of the men went for Lazlo. He hit one with a massive fist, probably breaking every bone in the man's face, but one of the other little guys jabbed him in the side.

Lazlo backhanded the man who'd stabbed him, knocking him onto his back, but as he did so the third guy came at him from the other side and stabbed him in the stomach. And that was the last thing DeMarco saw regarding Lazlo because by then he was fighting for his own life.

While his three buddies were attempting to take out DeMarco's over-size bodyguard, the fourth attacker came at DeMarco. So DeMarco took the tray he was holding and swatted the man hard in the face just as he was jabbing his knife at DeMarco's heart. Fortunately, DeMarco's arms were longer than his opponent's, and the blade didn't touch DeMarco's chest. The man staggered backward, blood pouring from his broken nose, but he recovered quickly.

The man was incredibly fast, like a good featherweight boxer. He feinted to his left, and DeMarco swung the tray at the point where he'd expected the man's face to be—and hit nothing but air as the guy came under his arm and thrust the knife. DeMarco had just enough time to twist sideways, and the blade, instead of piercing his stomach, penetrated his side, just above his waist.

And then it was over. A guard came up behind DeMarco's attacker and hit him in the head with a baton. Two of Lazlo's attackers were now on the ground, and both appeared to be unconscious, but the third man was circling Lazlo, still jabbing at him with his knife, when he was hit with Taser darts. He dropped the knife, danced for a moment like a spastic puppet as the current surged through him, and collapsed to the ground. Lazlo dropped to a sitting position on the floor, his back against the serving counter. DeMarco didn't know how many times Lazlo had been stabbed, but the lower half of his shirt—front and back—was soaked with blood. DeMarco stood there breathing heavily, holding his hand over the bleeding wound in his side.

He figured the whole attack had taken less than a minute, and it was just dumb luck that guards coming into the cafeteria to help break up the fight at the other end of the room had seen Lazlo and him being swarmed by knife-wielding assassins.

20

Mahoney heard about the attack on DeMarco via CNN. Some weasel guard at the jail had leaked the story.

"The alleged killer of Congressman Lyle Canton, Joseph DeMarco, was stabbed yesterday at the Alexandria city jail by another inmate," the newscaster said. "He's expected to survive but—"

Mahoney shut off the television and yelled to his secretary, "Mavis, get me that asshole sheriff who runs the Alexandria jail on the phone right now."

Mahoney was in a horrible mood because he was being hounded relentlessly by the media. It had been leaked to the press by unnamed sources—meaning the FBI—that Mahoney frequently met with DeMarco and might be DeMarco's boss. Furthermore, Mahoney had been questioned by the FBI. The reporters didn't mind spreading speculation and rumors, but they did do their best to find a few facts. They spoke to DeMarco's neighbors in Georgetown and people who occupied offices on the same floor of the Capitol, trying to find out exactly what DeMarco did and what his connection to Mahoney might be—and learned nothing. Those they talked to all basically said that DeMarco was a nice guy but they had no idea what he did or whom he worked for.

So every time Mahoney stepped outside his office, some reporter would thrust a microphone into his face: "Would the Congressman care to comment on his relationship to Joe DeMarco?" *No, the Congressman wouldn't care to comment, and you can shove that microphone up your narrow ass.*

All Mahoney's refusal to comment did was whip the media into a feeding frenzy, and every time he turned on CNN there was some self-proclaimed expert talking about Mahoney's hostile relationship with Lyle Canton. Clip after clip was played showing Mahoney and Canton calling each other names. As for DeMarco, he was discussed mostly in the form of questions as opposed to declarative sentences: *Who is Joe DeMarco? What exactly does he do at the Capitol? Why is it that he's a lawyer but has never practiced law and isn't employed by a specific politician or organization in the legislative branch? Why has he been seen so often meeting with John Mahoney when he's not a member of Mahoney's staff? How did a man whose father worked for the Italian mob get a job inside the Capitol?*

As a result of all these unanswered questions—and in the absence of any facts—DeMarco morphed into a political bogeyman, the Phantom of the Capitol. Comparisons were made to people like G. Gordon Liddy and the Watergate burglars who went around doing shady deeds for dirty politicians. With all the imaginary dots connecting Mahoney to DeMarco, the newscasters wondered aloud if it was possible— even though there was no evidence showing this to be the case—that DeMarco could have been acting on John Mahoney's behalf when he killed Canton. The word *allegedly* was used a lot.

When Bob Anderson—the man Mahoney had ordered to make sure that DeMarco stayed safe in prison—came on the line, Mahoney unleashed all the pent-up anger he was feeling toward the media onto the sheriff. He screamed, "What did I fuckin' tell you was going to happen to you if anything happened to DeMarco?"

"Congressman, I—"

"What the hell happened?"

Sheriff Anderson explained that in addition to telling his guards to look out for DeMarco, he'd assigned one of the biggest, meanest, most lethal cons in the jail to be DeMarco's personal bodyguard, figuring no one would go near DeMarco with this guy watching over him.

"So what happened?" Mahoney screamed again.

Anderson said that for reasons he didn't understand, MS-13 had staged a coordinated, well-planned-out attack on DeMarco. "They started a fight in part of the cafeteria, and while the guards were trying to break up the fight, four guys attacked DeMarco and his bodyguard. And they had knives, combat knives like Navy SEALs use. I don't know how they got those into the prison." He quickly added, "But, by God, I'm gonna find out."

"What DeMarco's condition?" Mahoney asked.

"He's okay. He got a slice on his left side, but no organs were hit, and he didn't bleed all that much. The doc put a few staples in him, gave him some painkillers, and he's back in his cell. And there's a guard standing outside his cell. But Lazlo isn't doing too well."

"Who's Lazlo?"

"The inmate I had protecting DeMarco. He's in the hospital, knife wounds in one kidney and his liver. They think he's going to make it, but—"

"I don't give a shit about him," Mahoney said. "Why did these MS-13 guys attack DeMarco?"

"I don't know. He wasn't in the jail long enough to piss them off, and as near as I can tell, he never had any contact with them."

"Well, did you *ask* them why they did it?" Mahoney said.

"One of them is in a coma, and one's larynx was crushed and he can't speak. The other two guys won't say a thing. MS-13 guys never talk."

"So drag 'em into a room and beat the truth out of them."

"I'm going to pretend you never said that, Congressman."

Mahoney took a breath. "What are you going to do to protect DeMarco from now on?"

"I'm going to keep him in his cell twenty-four hours a day, and I'll have a guard standing outside his cell. I'll have his meals brought to him so he won't have to go to the cafeteria. Other than that—"

"I'm telling you, Sheriff, if anything else happens to him, I'm not only going to get you fired, I'm going to destroy your life. You got it?"

"Yes, sir."

Mahoney slammed down the phone and then wondered: *Why in the hell would a bunch of gangbangers try to kill DeMarco?* Since he couldn't think of a reason, he called Emma.

21

Emma woke up at six and went for a three-mile run. She liked to run along the Potomac, but this morning she ran through the neighborhood where she lived, which happened to be McLean, Virginia, the same wealthy Washington suburb where Jean (Mitchell) Canton, Lyle Canton, and Sebastian Spear had been raised and where Spear still lived.

She jogged past Spear's residence, slowing her pace slightly. For the home of a billionaire, it wasn't all that impressive. It wasn't a castle. The house sat on a well-tended acre filled with trees, flowering plants, and a manicured lawn, and was surrounded by an eight-foot brick wall. A twelve-foot-wide black wrought-iron gate barred the driveway. She could see a security camera over the front door and imagined there were other cameras and security measures she couldn't see, but she didn't see armed guards or patrolling Dobermans.

Emma returned home, showered, and had oatmeal for breakfast. Her home wasn't as grand as Spear's, nor was it enclosed by a protective wall, but had she any desire to sell, it would go for about two million. The house was silent, which pleased her enormously, although she felt somewhat guilty that she felt this way.

Christine, her roommate/lover, played cello for the National Symphony Orchestra. She was also a member of a string quartet, and the quartet was currently on a ten-city tour—and frankly Emma was glad it was. She loved Christine but was happy to be spending a month alone and to have some time to herself. She also liked that music wasn't coming through the twenty or so speakers around the house. When Christine was home, music was always playing. It would usually be soft, classical pieces, which Emma didn't mind so much, but Christine's taste was eclectic. Sometimes the house would be practically vibrating with old rock and roll, gospel songs, reggae, or even hip-hop—which made Emma want to jam chopsticks into her ears.

She dressed in a lightweight gray blazer, jeans, a dark gray polo shirt, and running shoes. She was just leaving to go see what Neil had learned when the phone rang. It was Mahoney. The last time Emma had spoken to him was when he'd called her right after DeMarco was arrested and asked her to help.

"DeMarco was stabbed last night at the jail," Mahoney said.

Emma inhaled sharply. "Is he alive?"

"Yeah. It was just a flesh wound. He was stabbed through a love handle."

"Who tried to kill him?"

"Four MS-13 bangers."

"Do you know why?"

"No. The sheriff said DeMarco hadn't been in there long enough to irritate MS-13. So maybe it was just a typical jailhouse thing. He looked at the wrong guy the wrong way, didn't show proper respect, whatever. In prison it doesn't take much to end up with a shank in your back."

"Have you talked to DeMarco?" Emma asked.

"No," Mahoney said. He didn't bother to add that there was no way he was going to talk to DeMarco with all the media flak he was already catching because of him.

"I'll go see him today," Emma said. "But we need to do something to make sure he's not killed in there."

"I've already told the sheriff who runs the place that I'm gonna have his balls if anything happens to Joe. He's got him in a cell by himself, being guarded twenty-four hours a day."

"That may not be good enough," Emma said. "What do you think would happen if DeMarco was killed right now?"

"I don't know what you mean."

"What I mean is that the investigation into who killed Lyle Canton would end with DeMarco's death. Right now the FBI has stopped investigating Canton's murder because they're sure they have the killer, and the only thing they're currently doing is getting ready to present all their evidence at DeMarco's trial. But if DeMarco dies, there will be no trial. Which means there will be no opportunity to present a defense that someone else killed Canton. So what I'm saying is that it's possible that the attack on him was arranged by the people who framed him, and they'll probably try again."

Neil looked like a man who'd spent the entire night staring at a computer monitor: bloodshot eyes, stubble on his chin, jittery from too many caffeine-spiked energy drinks. There was a pizza box on a table near his workstation, and the office reeked of pizza—and of Neil.

Emma took a seat across from him and said, "Well?"

"Of the thirteen hundred people employed by the U.S. Capitol Police, four hundred and twenty-three white guys bear a physical resemblance to DeMarco, which isn't surprising. DeMarco's a pretty average white guy, five eleven, a hundred and eighty pounds. But there's one man who's approximately his size and who has, I guess you'd say, an indirect connection to Sebastian Spear."

"What do you mean by *indirect*?"

"I mean there is no one employed by the Capitol cops related to Spear or who ever worked for his company or went to the same schools with him or anything like that. The connection is via his head of security, a guy named Bill Brayden."

Neil picked up a crust of cold pizza and popped it into his mouth—making Emma wince—before continuing. "Brayden is a retired air force colonel. He spent most of his career as a security officer."

Emma knew that air force security officers were responsible for protecting the planes, facilities, weapons, and personnel at air force bases all over the planet. They were also responsible for law enforcement on those bases. The officers were highly qualified and carefully selected, and when they were assigned to bases in places like Afghanistan and Iraq, the job was dangerous.

"The guy I found," Neil said, "is named John Lynch. He was also in air force security, but he wasn't a colonel like Brayden. He was a corporal and served as an MP."

Which Emma knew meant Lynch spent his time in the service mostly as a gate guard or arresting drunks. But she wasn't surprised that he'd been hired by the Capitol Police. The Capitol Police would give hiring preference to veterans, and particularly veterans with prior experience in security work.

"And right before Brayden retired from the air force, he commanded the Eleventh Security Forces Group at Andrews, and Lynch was in the Eleventh at the same time. But that's all I got, that Lynch was a grunt and Brayden was his commanding officer for a year or so. Brayden may not have even known the guy when they served together."

"Is Lynch the only Capitol cop who served in the air force?" Emma asked.

"No. There were more than a dozen. But they were black or female. One guy was six foot eight. Another six foot four. One guy DeMarco's size works full-time as a bean counter in the Capitol Police office on D Street. Another guy, only two inches taller than DeMarco, is in charge of the guards assigned to the Library of Congress, not the Capitol. Emma, you told me to look for cops with some connection to Spear, and Lynch is the only one I could find."

"What does Lynch do at the Capitol?" Emma asked.

"He's just a guard. Perimeter guard, entrance guard, that sort of thing. Basically doing the same thing he did in the air force. He's received weapons training, anti-terrorist training, knows what to do in a lockdown situation, but it's the same training every other guard gets. He started as a GS-3, and five years later he's a GS-5 and still guarding the doors. He's not an overachiever."

Neil tapped his keyboard and a photo of Lynch appeared on the monitor closest to Emma.

"He doesn't look *anything* like DeMarco," Emma said.

Lynch was ten years younger than DeMarco and had a porcine nose, thin lips, and brown eyes. He was also almost completely bald, and what little hair he had left was dark like DeMarco's but shaved close to his skull. He was one inch shorter than DeMarco and five pounds heavier.

"How did you connect him to Brayden in the first place?" Emma asked.

"Spear Industries' website identified the company VPs, and there was a brief bio for each of them, which is where I learned that Brayden was an ex–air force security officer. Then, when I started looking at the Capitol cops' personnel files, I came across the fact that Lynch was also ex–air force."

"Well, I need more, a lot more. I have someone at the Pentagon who can peek into Brayden's and Lynch's military files. I want you to start digging deeper into their lives as civilians."

"Jesus, Emma, I've been up all night. I need some sleep."

She looked at him—actually she glared at him—but she had to admit that he didn't look good. "Fine," she said. "Go lie down on the couch in your office and sleep for a couple of hours, then get back to work."

Neil opened his mouth to say that he needed more than two hours, but Emma said, "Neil, Joe was almost killed yesterday. He was stabbed. We have to get him out of that jail as soon as possible."

22

Emma returned to her car, where she sat for a moment, tapping her fingernails on the steering wheel.

All she felt sure of was her first assumption—that the killer had been a Capitol cop. But as for Lynch being the killer, the only thing that made him a possible suspect was that he and Bill Brayden had both had jobs in air force security at the same time. That was all she had. And although Spear was a likely suspect for murdering Canton, someone else could have conspired with a Capitol cop to kill Canton. For that matter, it was possible that a Capitol cop could have some motive of his own for killing Canton. And when it came to John Lynch and Bill Brayden, she didn't know if they even knew each other, let alone if they would be willing to commit murder. Whatever the case, the Spear-Brayden-Lynch connection was all she had, so she'd run with it until she hit a wall or something else occurred to her.

Before starting the car, Emma made a call to a woman named Latisha Thomson. Latisha was a civilian, a GS-14-level employee, who managed a group in the Pentagon dealing with procurement, stocking, and disbursement of spare parts for army field equipment, like tanks and personnel carriers and cannons. But when Emma met her, Latisha had been a twenty-two-year-old GS-3 civil servant who had two kids, ages two and three, and had been one of several secretaries who worked for her. Latisha had had only a high school degree but was extremely bright and doing her best to improve herself. At the same time, she was timid and had no self-confidence.

One day, Latisha showed up for work with a black eye. Emma asked her what had happened, and Latisha muttered something about a cabinet door. Emma thought, *Bullshit*, but didn't say anything. A week later, Emma noticed that Latisha had a split lip and was moving as if her ribs might be bruised or broken.

Emma called Latisha into her office and bluntly asked, "Who's using you for a punching bag?" The answer, not surprisingly, was Latisha's ex-husband, Clayton. She'd divorced Clayton a year ago, but he'd get drunk, show up at her place, scream at her, smack her around, and take the cash she had in her purse. Sometimes he'd rape her. She'd gotten a restraining order, which did nothing to stop him. She'd even had him arrested, and after Clayton was released from jail, he came back and slapped her around again, asking how she could be such a bitch to do this to the father of her children. She told Emma she was thinking about moving out of the state. If she didn't move, she was afraid Clayton was going to kill her.

That night Emma and two Delta Force soldiers followed Clayton from his job at a car wash to a bar. The soldiers were both about six foot three and could bench-press 350 pounds. Clayton was a small, wiry man, about five seven, and Emma thought he just *looked* stupid.

Clayton left the bar three hours later, and before he could get into his car to drive drunk to wherever he was going, Emma parked a van next to him and the soldiers, wearing ski masks, manhandled him into the back of the van. Inside the van, they gagged him with duct tape, placed a hood over his head, and handcuffed him. Half an hour later, they walked him onto a twenty-two-foot sportfishing boat moored at a marina on the Potomac River. Emma steered the boat into the middle of the river, a couple of miles downstream of the Lincoln Memorial.

It was a cold night in January, snowing lightly, and Emma figured the water temperature was about forty degrees.

Emma motioned to the soldiers, and they took the hood off Clayton's head, ripped the duct tape off his mouth, and undid the handcuffs. Then they yanked off the ski jacket he was wearing, sat him down on the gunwale on the port side of the boat, and loomed over him, still wearing their masks. Clayton was terrified—who wouldn't be?—and his eyes seemed to be about the size of hard-boiled eggs.

He said, "Who are you? Why the fuck you doing this?"

Emma, who was not wearing a mask or disguised in any way, said, "Clayton, your wife works for me. She's an extremely valuable member of my staff."

"Latisha?" He said this as if he couldn't imagine his ex being valuable to anyone.

"Yes, Latisha. I can't have her showing up at work looking like she's gone ten rounds with a middleweight. Or in your case, a lightweight. So in the interest of national security—"

"National security?"

"Yes. In the interest of national security, a decision has been made that you have to go. We discussed—"

"Who's 'we'?"

"Senior people in the Pentagon. Like I said, Latisha's important. What I started to say was that we discussed having you arrested again, but because you're stupid and you're a drunk, we decided that wouldn't do any good, and you'd just keep beating Latisha up."

"I don't get it. What are you saying?"

"I'm saying you have to go, Clayton."

She placed a hand in the middle of his chest, shoved, and Clayton went backward off the boat. The water sucked the breath right out of him, so cold it almost stopped his heart.

Clayton screamed, "I can't swim! I can't swim!"

"I know," Emma said. "Why do you think we threw you in the river?"

While trying to keep his head above water, Clayton started flapping his arms, trying to do what he'd seen swimmers do to stay afloat. Before his head went under a second time, Emma threw him a life preserver attached to a rope. He grabbed it, and the Deltas helped him back on board.

He lay on the deck, choking, and when he was finally able to speak, he said, "I swear. I won't bother her no more."

"Sorry, it's too late for that. And I don't believe you," Emma said. "The reason we pulled you out was I forgot to remove your wallet. Silly me. The river's running hard, and I imagine your body will end up in Chesapeake Bay and eventually be eaten by sharks, but in case you're found, I don't want them to ID you. That'll just cause complications."

"Wha-, what?" Clayton said, his teeth chattering.

"Get his wallet," Emma said. One of the soldiers did, and Emma said, "Good. Now chuck him back in the water." The soldiers did.

Clayton started screaming again, and slapping at the water, and somehow he made it over to the stern of the boat and grabbed onto the swim step. "Don't kill me. I'll leave her alone."

Emma said, "I don't believe you, Clayton." To the Deltas she said, "Pry him loose and throw him farther away from the boat."

"No. You can't do this. I swear to God, I won't go near her again."

Emma pretended to think this over and said, "All right. But if you do, if you do anything to her or your children, I'm going to find you, and the next time I'm going to attached a block of concrete to your feet before I throw you in. Do you understand?"

"Yeah, I understand. I swear to God I won't—"

"Shut up," Emma said.

They hauled Clayton out of the water, gave him a blanket so he didn't die of hypothermia, and dropped him off at the marina. Before they let him go, Emma looked into his wallet to make sure he had enough cash to catch a cab back to his car. The last thing Emma said to him was, "I will come for you, Clayton, if you don't behave yourself."

Latisha went on to get degrees in accounting and business administration and then began hopping from one job to another within the Department of Defense until she reached the position she held today. Her children were both college graduates, one a dentist, the other a CPA. Clayton, who never contacted Latisha again, ironically died by drowning five years after Emma pushed him into the Potomac. One night he drank too much, passed out, and landed facedown in a pothole that contained no more than three inches of water. God's a prankster.

So when Emma called Latisha's Pentagon office and said she needed something, Latisha, without hesitation, said, "Just name it."

Emma said, "I want you to take a look at the personnel records of a retired air force colonel named William Brayden. He commanded the Eleventh Security Forces Group at Andrews toward the end of his career, and he's now head of corporate security at a company called Spear Industries. I also want you to look at the file of a noncom named John Lynch, who was in the Eleventh when Brayden was the CO."

"Am I looking for anything in particular?" Latisha asked.

"I just need to get a handle on these people. What kind of airmen were they? Did they have discipline problems? Did they leave the service because of some kind of scandal or legal issue? In other words, I'm trying to find out if there's anything in their history that would lead you to think that either of them could be a bad actor."

"What kind of bad actor?"

"The kind who would commit murder."

"Oh," Latisha said.

Emma knew that with the jobs Latisha had held at the Pentagon for the past twenty years, she wouldn't have any problem getting access to a couple of personnel files. And Latisha never asked why Emma wanted the information.

Had Emma asked Latisha to donate a kidney, Latisha would have performed the surgery on herself.

23

Emma was allowed to meet with DeMarco in the same conference room where he'd met with his lawyer. Unbeknownst to DeMarco, the guards had received an epic ass-chewing from the sheriff, who told them that a lot of people were going to be fired if DeMarco so much as bruised a toe while in their custody. It was for this reason that the guards decided it would be better if Emma met DeMarco in the conference room and not in any area where there might be prisoners walking about with toothbrush handles sharpened into lethal spikes.

Emma was already seated when DeMarco entered the room, and she saw him wince as he sat down and his hand move unconsciously toward the wound on his left side.

"How are you doing?" Emma asked.

"Couldn't be better," DeMarco said. "Got a roof over my head, three hot meals a day, and scintillating companionship. What more could a man ask for?"

DeMarco's attempt at humor couldn't disguise the stress he was under. His skin was so taut it looked as if his face would crack if he smiled.

"Do you have any idea why those men attacked you?"

"No. I haven't been in here long enough to make any enemies. The only inmate I've spoken to since I've been here is Lazlo."

"Who's Lazlo?"

DeMarco explained that Lazlo was an inmate the size of LeBron James who'd been assigned by the warden to protect him, and if it hadn't been for Lazlo he'd most likely be dead. "He was almost killed," he concluded. "I need to find out how he's doing."

Emma said, "I think whoever framed you may have orchestrated the attack on you yesterday. And they might try again."

She told him the same thing she'd told Mahoney: that if DeMarco died, any investigation into Lyle Canton's death would come to an abrupt halt and whoever framed him would get away with murder.

"I'm sure it's not pleasant staying in a cell twenty-four hours a day," Emma said, "but stay there. Don't allow the guards to take you out to the exercise area, the infirmary, or anywhere else. When the doctor needs to check your wound, insist that he come to you."

"I'm not in a position to insist on much of anything," DeMarco said.

"Yeah, you are. Mahoney has told the guy who runs this zoo that if anything happens to you . . . Well, I'm sure Mahoney made his point."

"Is Mahoney catching a lot of flak because of me?"

"Yes, and who cares. You worry about yourself. And don't trust the guards, either. The person who may have framed you is rich enough to buy any guard in this place."

"What! What are you saying? You think you know who set me up? Who is it?"

"Not here. This room could be monitored. And I'm not sure I'm right, and I don't have any evidence to prove it. The main reason I came here today is to tell you to stay vigilant and don't give up hope."

"Well, right now, the only thing I can be is hopeful," DeMarco said.

Emma rose to leave, and DeMarco said, "Hey, but there are a couple of things you could get me."

"What's that?"

"A miniature rock ax and a poster of Raquel Welch."

"Raquel Welch?"

"Yeah. Didn't you ever see *The Shawshank Redemption*?"

"You're an idiot, DeMarco."

24

Emma had just parked near Neil's office when Latisha called her.

Latisha said, "Bill Brayden was a good officer. He advanced steadily and rapidly through the ranks, received outstanding personnel evaluations from his superiors, and got commendations for doing his job well."

"Then why wasn't he promoted to general?" Emma asked.

"The air force was downsizing about the time he retired. They didn't need as many generals, and he just didn't make the cut. It didn't help that he spent his career doing security work. That's not a glamour job in the air force. It ain't like flying F-16s. But he wasn't passed over for doing something stupid. At least there's nothing stupid on his record.

"I talked to one guy who knew him. He was Brayden's deputy when Brayden was stationed in Iraq. He told me that Brayden drove his people hard, was very ambitious, and wouldn't allow anything to prevent him from completing an assignment. But he said Brayden was a good guy, treated people fairly, and took the heat as the guy in charge if something went wrong."

"What about his personal life?"

"Married once, got divorced, been single a dozen years. He doesn't have kids."

"What about Lynch?" Emma asked.

"Lynch was a screwup. Mediocre and sometimes below-average personnel evaluations. The highest rank he ever held was E4, then he was busted back to E3 for falling asleep on guard duty when the base where he was stationed was on alert. There were comments in his file about having a poor attitude, sloppy work habits, and being disrespectful to his superiors. And he was court-martialed once but never convicted of a crime."

"Why was he court-martialed?"

"For allegedly stealing ten laptops. The laptops were old ones being replaced by newer ones, and the old ones were supposed to be destroyed so some civilian didn't end up with classified information. But he wasn't convicted—the files I looked at didn't say why—and a year later he was given an honorable discharge."

Which made Emma wonder how well the Capitol Police vetted their personnel, but then if all Lynch did was guard the doors, he wouldn't have been subjected to the vetting performed for a Top Secret security clearance. She imagined the background checks performed for low-ranking personnel not given sensitive duties were most likely limited to record checks, which would have shown that Lynch had been honorably discharged and had no felony convictions. And who knows? Maybe after the court-martial he cleaned up his act, and someone gave him a good letter of recommendation. Or maybe he knew someone on the Capitol force who helped him get the job. Whatever the case, the fact that he was court-martialed and found innocent apparently wasn't a reason for the Capitol Police not to hire him.

"When was he court-martialed?" Emma asked Latisha.

"The same time Bill Brayden was CO of the Eleventh at Andrews."

"Now that's interesting," Emma said.

"And speaking of Brayden," Latisha said, "there is one more thing. I did an Internet search because I was curious about him. A few years ago, Spear Industries did a job in Colombia, upgrading equipment on La Esmeralda Dam on the Batá River. This one Colombian activist, a guy named Manuel Concha, claimed that Spear Industries bribed people in the Colombian Ministry of Mines and Energy to get the contract, and Spear awarded a local transportation subcontract to a company owned by one of the drug cartels. There was a big brouhaha in the Colombian media, lawsuits were filed, and so forth. Then Manuel Concha, the guy who started the whole fracas, disappeared, and folks claimed that the cartel killed him because of the noise he was making about them."

"What does this have to do with Brayden?"

"According to Manuel Concha, Brayden was Spear Industries' bagman. He was the guy who bribed the bureaucrats, and he was the one responsible for the cartel's trucking company getting the contract."

"Huh," Emma said.

Latisha said, "The thing is, Emma, Spear Industries operates in some pretty rough places, places in South America and Africa where there's so much corruption that bribery is just one of the costs of doing business. If Manuel Concha was right about what Brayden did in Colombia, maybe he's Spear's go-to guy when it comes to stuff like that. Brayden may have been squeaky-clean in the air force, but when he went to work for Sebastian Spear, he had to learn how to play a different game to be successful. I'm just sayin.'"

25

This time Bill Brayden met Hector Montoya in the parking lot of a Catholic church in Fairfax, the lot empty on a hot weekday afternoon. Hector was leaning against the fender of a bright orange Trans Am equipped with a spoiler, and Brayden wondered if the money he'd given Hector for killing DeMarco had financed the car. Hector was shirtless, the tattoos covering his torso on full display, and Brayden couldn't help thinking: *The Illustrated Man.*

Brayden got out of his car, slamming the door, but before he could chastise Hector for failing to kill DeMarco, Montoya said, "Yeah, yeah, I know. My guys fucked up. Sorry about that."

Sorry about that?

"Can you get another shot at him?" Brayden asked.

"Maybe, but it's not gonna be easy," Hector said. "They're keeping him in a cell twenty-four hours a day, and there's a guard stationed outside his door."

"So what are you saying? Can it be done or not?"

"I don't know. I need to talk to my main guy in there. Let me do that, and if it's doable, we'll do it. If not, I'll let you know and return half the money you gave me."

"I don't give a damn about the money," Brayden said. "And I'm willing to give you more if necessary to get the job done. Like if you have to bribe someone."

And Brayden meant that. Spear could afford to pay whatever it cost, and considering the stakes—namely the possibility of him and Spear going to jail—money was absolutely not a concern.

Four hours later, Hector Montoya texted Brayden: *It's doable.*

Brayden was happy to see Hector's response—and was surprised that he hadn't asked for more money. You can just never tell about people. Hector may have been a tattooed gangbanger and a murderer, but he apparently had some sort of skewed moral code.

26

Neil looked somewhat better now than the last time Emma had seen him. If not exactly bright-eyed and bushy-tailed, he was at least functioning. She wondered if in addition to sleeping for a couple of hours he'd popped a pill or two.

"Go," Emma said, meaning for Neil to get on with telling her whatever he'd learned about Lynch and Brayden.

Neil tapped a keyboard and one of the monitors on his desk flickered to life.

"Financially, Lynch is barely keeping his head above water. He was married for eight years, has two young kids, and his wife divorced him for physical and emotional abuse not long after he got out of the air force. She got everything in the divorce. The house, all the money they had in savings, the one car they had at the time, and she gets three-fifths of his government salary for alimony and child support. He now lives in a one-bedroom rat hole in Alexandria, and he's still paying off a loan on a used Ford Focus he bought four years ago."

"Did you look at his phone records?" Emma asked.

"Of course. The only phone he has is a cell phone—no landline— and he never called or received a call from Bill Brayden or Sebastian

Spear. That is, he was never called by any number registered to Brayden, Spear, or Spear Industries."

"Bank accounts?"

"He's got three hundred bucks in a savings account. I guess that's his rainy-day stash, and God help him if it pours. His government check is automatically deposited into his checking account, then three-fifths of it is automatically redeposited into his ex-wife's checking account. Lynch's own checking account is usually overdrawn by the time he gets his next paycheck."

"Brayden?" Emma said.

"William Brayden went to work for Spear right after retiring from the air force. He was initially hired as the deputy to Spear's head of corporate security, then a couple of years later became the head guy. Based on his tax returns—and by the way, I owe a guy at the IRS a grand for this information—he makes an outstanding salary, but it varies between two fifty and five hundred K. I don't know why it varies so much, and five hundred thousand seems excessive for a security honcho.

"The other thing about Brayden is he's made the news a couple of times and not in a good way. Spear Industries was doing a job in Colombia, and a guy named Manuel Concha claimed that he bribed—"

"I already know about the Colombia job and Concha. What else?" Emma said.

"In Nigeria something similar happened. Spear Industries was accused of bribing a government official, and Brayden was named in a lawsuit, but nothing ever came of it. He also testified once before a House committee. Some congressman got pissed off because a company in his district didn't get a job that was awarded to Spear, and he accused Spear of rigging the bid. Spear was called to testify, but instead of Spear showing up, Brayden came with a couple of lawyers. I don't know how Spear could ignore a congressional subpoena, but he did, and the investigation went nowhere. So what I'm saying is that Brayden might do a few things for Spear that cross the line, but killing a U.S. congressman is a big step up from bribing a corrupt African bureaucrat."

Emma held up a hand and said, "Be quiet, Neil. I need to think."

Emma closed her eyes.

She had a theory: that Sebastian Spear, who hated Lyle Canton because he blamed Lyle for Jean Canton's death, decided to kill Canton, just as he said he would at Jean's funeral. So Spear's fixer, Bill Brayden, hired John Lynch—a man of questionable character, living barely above the poverty line—to kill Canton and frame DeMarco for Canton's murder. And they probably planned in advance to kill DeMarco right after he was arrested, ending the likelihood that the FBI would hunt for another suspect.

But why did they decide to frame *DeMarco*? Why him of all people?

The answer to this question was that they didn't *start* with DeMarco. They didn't pick DeMarco as the "framee" and then look for a killer who matched his appearance. They started with the killer, who may or may not have been John Lynch. Emma figured the big advantage they had when it came to finding a person to frame was Russian cyberwarfare expert Nikki Orlov.

In 2014, the Chinese hacked into OPM personnel files and obtained information on about four million federal employees, most of whom had security clearances. Why the Chinese did this, and what they did with the information they stole, was never determined. What the Chinese did in 2014, however, was pertinent because Emma imagined that Nikki Orlov could have done the same thing: hacked into OPM's files looking for someone about John Lynch's size who had unlimited access to the Capitol. He would have ended up with a list of several hundred people—and then it was just a matter of selecting one of them.

Emma could imagine Spear/Brayden/Orlov looking at congress-men and their aides and probably finding several candidates who had some personal reason for disliking Canton. They may have considered people with criminal records, like maybe one of the Capitol's janitors or maybe a lobbyist with a shady past who spent a lot of time in the Capi-tol. Ultimately, they settled on DeMarco, this mysterious lawyer who dwelled in the subbasement and was the son of a Mafia killer. They also learned that DeMarco was in some way connected to Mahoney, and given how much Mahoney hated Canton, that would have provided another reason for picking DeMarco. How they found the connection between Mahoney and DeMarco wasn't clear. Maybe Orlov had looked at DeMarco's and Mahoney's phone records. Whatever the case, and most likely after a considerable amount of research, they decided that of all the white guys who worked in the Capitol, DeMarco was the perfect patsy.

Another thing Emma could now understand was why Lyle Can-ton was killed four months after Jean Canton died. Spear may have hated Canton and probably wanted him dead as soon as possible, but it would have taken a long time to plan the murder and locate the person to frame.

Emma opened her eyes.

Yes, she had a logical and plausible theory.

What she didn't have was one shred of evidence to support it.

27

Emma told Special Agent Russell Peyton—who she could tell had been hoping never to see her again—that she wanted to take another look at the surveillance videos showing the killer approaching Canton's office. When Peyton asked her why, she said, "I'm just curious about something."

With Agent Alice Berman again watching her, Emma looked at the videos to see if the killer was recognizable as John Lynch. She wasn't concerned about the fact that Lynch was an inch shorter than DeMarco and bald. Lifts in his shoes and a wig would have been all he needed to solve those small problems. But whoever had killed Canton had been able to disguise his features adequately by hiding beneath a baseball cap and placing his hands over his face and turning his head away from the cameras at strategic moments.

She noticed in looking at the videos a second time that there was a *choreographed* quality to the killer's movements. She could imagine him rehearsing in a gymnasium, counting his steps as he practiced the moves to hide his features from the cameras—as if someone had placed footprints on a dance floor, so he'd know precisely when to turn. And again she was certain that framing DeMarco had taken a long time to plan—and the planning had been perfect, in that, so far, she'd been unable to identify the killer as John Lynch. In one photo, it appeared as if the killer had a double chin—DeMarco didn't, Lynch did—but Emma had to wonder if she was seeing things that weren't there because she knew DeMarco was innocent. After wasting an hour studying the videos, she thanked Peyton and left, ignoring him when he asked if she'd be back again.

Emma decided, standing on the street in front of the Hoover Building, virtually on the FBI's doorstep, that she was going to commit a crime.

A small crime, but a crime nonetheless.

Her grand theory—built solely on logic and the lack of alternative suspects—was that Lynch and Orlov were connected with Canton's death and the framing of DeMarco. The problem remained, however, that she still had no evidence that they'd done anything illegal or conspired in any way. According to Neil, there were no records of Lynch communicating with Orlov, Spear, or Brayden. Lynch's fingerprints had not been found on the gun or the uniform the FBI had found in DeMarco's office. From the videos that she'd just looked at for a second time, it wasn't clear that Lynch could have been the killer instead of DeMarco.

But there had to be *something*. For DeMarco's sake, there had to be.

One possibility was to see if Neil could somehow prove that Orlov had hacked Mahoney's phone to send the text message to DeMarco. Or maybe Neil could prove that Orlov had raided personnel files to identify DeMarco as the person to frame. But she doubted that Neil would be successful. Orlov wouldn't have left a bread-crumb trail for Neil to follow, because Orlov was a genius.

John Lynch, on the other hand, was not a genius.

So Emma decided that she was going to do something the FBI couldn't do without a warrant: she was going to search John Lynch's apartment to see if she could find any evidence connecting him to Canton's murder. Maybe she'd find paperwork related to the fake insignia patch, like a sketch used to make the patch. Maybe a copy of Canton's schedule, which a security guard would have no reason to have. Maybe a receipt for the gun used to kill Canton or the clothes the killer had worn. Maybe a key to DeMarco's office or anything at all related to DeMarco.

Yeah, maybe. But not likely.

If her theory was right—that extremely bright people like Spear and Orlov had developed the plan to frame DeMarco—she doubted that they would have overlooked any detail.

But she was still going to break into Lynch's apartment. What else could she do?

———◆◆◆———

Before driving to Lynch's place in Alexandria, Emma went home to get a few things she would need. She then called the general number for the Capitol Police, saying she worked for a collection agency and needed to speak to Lynch. She was informed, rather rudely, that Lynch was on duty at one of the entrances and unable to come to the phone. Which confirmed what Emma had wanted to know: that Lynch was at the Capitol and most likely wouldn't be home until the end of his shift.

Lynch's apartment building, located in one of the poorest neighborhoods in Alexandria, was a three-story redbrick structure with peeling hunter-green trim. Steel bars covered the windows on the first-floor units. The front door to the apartment building didn't lock, and Emma could see marks where someone had used a tool to force the door open. She figured that management had grown tired of fixing the door and left it to the tenants to protect their own apartments.

She took the stairs to Lynch's unit on the second floor and immediately saw that his door had two locks—a main lock and a deadbolt lock—but neither posed a problem. She pulled a small leather case from the back pocket of her jeans and took out the appropriate picks. Lock picking had not been part of her DIA training; Emma had hired a tutor.

The interior of Lynch's apartment was what she'd expected: a small, poorly kept space filled with much-abused secondhand furniture. The dishes from Lynch's breakfast were in the sink, and a greasy frying pan was on the stove. There was no dishwasher in the kitchen, and the stove and refrigerator were a quarter century old. Clothes and newspapers were strewn about the living room, and on the kitchen table was a pile of unopened mail.

There were only two closets in the place, one near the front door and one in the bedroom. The closet near the front door contained coats and jackets and hats, a suitcase, and an upright vacuum cleaner that she suspected was used infrequently. On the shelf in the closet were half a dozen unlabeled boxes. The small bedroom closet was filled to capacity with clothes, shoes, and boots, including three uniforms for a Capitol cop.

As small as the apartment was, however, Emma knew it was going to take her at least two hours to search it thoroughly. She put on a pair of thin plastic gloves and got to work. The primary purpose of the gloves was not to prevent leaving fingerprints but to keep her hands clean while she was searching a dusty, grimy living space.

Lynch didn't have a computer in the apartment—he probably couldn't afford either a computer or Internet service—so there were no computer files to look at. He didn't even have a desk. He kept recently paid bills, bank statements, and his auto insurance policy in a cardboard box on the floor near his television set. There were no papers in the box, however, that pointed to any involvement in Canton's murder—like a convenient brochure from a company that made insignia patches.

She checked the pockets of all the clothes in both closets. She looked inside every shoe and boot. She removed every box on the closet shelves to examine its contents. She flipped through magazines, including Lynch's porn magazines, to make sure there was nothing between any of the pages. She looked inside every cereal box and every pot and pan in the kitchen cabinets. She removed the lid on the toilet tank. She probed sofa cushions and Lynch's mattress to see if anything might be sewn inside. She lay facedown, holding her breath to avoid a dust bunny attack, and searched beneath the bed. She looked through the garbage in the garbage can beneath the kitchen sink.

In the cabinet under Lynch's kitchen sink, partially hidden by a bucket containing dishwashing soap and other cleaning products, she found a steel, fireproof lockbox. The box wasn't locked, however. What would be the point? If intruders couldn't open it easily they would just take it with them and open it later, as the box was heavy but small and portable. The main purpose of the box was to protect the papers inside it in case of a fire.

Inside the lockbox, Emma found Lynch's important papers: his birth certificate, his Social Security card, the title for his car, his discharge papers from the air force, and a hundred dollars in cash. She found only one unusual thing: a passport that had been issued to Lynch only two months ago. She doubted that Lynch, who was practically broke, had obtained it because he was planning some exotic foreign holiday. If he'd been involved in Canton's murder, however, he might have decided that having a passport would be prudent in case he needed to leave the country.

She continued searching and noticed a heating grille inserted in the living room floor, which made her think of the evidence planted in the ventilation grille in DeMarco's office. She removed the grille and saw that the duct below the cover went straight down for about four inches and then turned where it was connected to a sheet-metal elbow. She put her arm into the duct and reached beyond the elbow—and her fingers touched something. She grasped the object and pulled it out. It was a phone. A cheap flip phone, most likely a prepaid disposable phone.

Emma smiled—and someone seeing that smile might have been disturbed by it. It was the smile of a predator that had just caught the first scent of its prey.

Why would Lynch have hidden a phone? If he was involved in Canton's murder, the answer was obvious: The people who murdered Canton and framed DeMarco would have needed to communicate with one another to plan and execute such a complicated crime—and they wouldn't have used phones registered to them. They would have used burner phones, like the one she'd just found.

She turned on the phone and looked at the contacts list and recent calls directory. There were no recent calls or text messages—they'd most likely been deleted—and there was only one number in the contacts list. There was no name, however, assigned to the number. Emma wrote down the phone number for Lynch's burner phone and the single number in the contacts list, then placed the phone back in the heating duct.

She glanced at her watch. Almost two hours had passed since she'd begun searching, and she needed to go before Lynch got home from work, but she decided to take one last tour of the apartment to see if there was anyplace else she should look. As she was walking, a thought occurred to her: *If Lynch had been paid to kill Canton, where was the money?* He didn't have a backyard, so it wasn't buried there. It wasn't in his checking or savings account; Neil had peeked into Lynch's accounts, and there was no evidence that he had recently come into money. His banking records had indicated that he didn't have a safe-deposit box, at least not in the same bank where he had his checking account.

It was possible that if Lynch had received any money, it had been electronically deposited in some offshore bank—which was maybe another reason Lynch had obtained a passport: so one day he could fly to that foreign bank to collect his well-earned fee. It seemed to her though, that Lynch, a man who was almost broke, would want at least part of his payment in cash in case he needed to flee. But where would he hide the cash? If he'd buried it someplace or put it in a rented storage locker she'd never find it, and she knew it wasn't in his apartment, as she'd searched everyplace there was to search. She stripped off her gloves, getting ready to leave, when something occurred to her.

She'd found in Lynch's living room a small canvas bag containing tools, the sort of tools an apartment dweller might own: a battery-powered electric drill and drill bits, a hammer, a box cutter, pliers, a set of screwdrivers and wrenches, a plastic container filled with screws of various sizes. In other words, the sort of tools you might use for assembling IKEA furniture or hanging pictures. In that same bag, she'd also found a can of Spackle for patching holes in walls and a small roll of joint tape—the type of tape used for installing wallboard or drywall, to cover the seams. Why would Lynch have joint tape? If for some reason one of the walls in his apartment needed to be repaired, he'd ask his landlord to do it.

She went back and looked at the bag of tools again. In the plastic box containing assorted screws she noticed something she hadn't noticed before: half a dozen two-and-a-half-inch-long blue screws for attaching drywall to studs.

Emma made another tour of Lynch's apartment, this time examining the walls. They were all painted eggshell white, but they probably hadn't been painted in a decade and were now a yellowish color, making her wonder if one of the previous occupants had been a heavy smoker. There were black scuff marks in places where furniture had scraped the walls, and there were two dozen holes in places where pictures had been hung and removed. (Lynch had not hung a single picture.) The walls in the small kitchen were covered with a thin layer of grease, and it was apparent they had never been cleaned, much less repaired or replaced.

She started to leave for the second time when it occurred to her that there were walls she hadn't examined—in the closets. She went back to the bedroom closet and pushed the clothes aside. The closet's back wall—which was about six feet high and four feet wide—was a freshly painted eggshell white. She also noted a few drops of paint on the closet floor.

Emma smiled again: the wolf catching a glimpse of a red hood in the forest.

She put the clothes back where they'd been and left Lynch's apartment. She would be back.

28

Emma sat impatiently, rubbing her forehead, her eyes closed, as Neil prepared to trace the phone call.

She had decided to call the number in the phone she'd found hidden in Lynch's apartment from Neil's office, because Neil would be able to record the call and, more important, would be able to locate the phone. His equipment would give her a street address or GPS coordinates.

Finally, after tinkering with one of his machines for what had seemed an eternity, Neil said, "Okay. All set."

Tapping a keyboard, he entered the number, and the phone being called began to ring. On the fifth ring a man's voice said, "Yes?"

One of Neil's computers responded: "Hi, this is Emily. Are you burdened by credit card debt? If so—"

The person who answered grunted a curse and hung up—but Emma had what she wanted. A monitor on Neil's desk showed a map, and on the map was a pulsing red dot—the location of the phone he'd just called.

"Where is it?" Emma asked.

Neil's fat, nimble fingers danced across the keyboard, and a millisecond later an address appeared. "It's in Spear Industries' headquarters in Reston," he said.

Yes! Emma *finally* had something more than a theory. She had evidence that supported her theory. She now knew that the unregistered phone that John Lynch had hidden extremely well was being used to communicate with somebody at Spear Industries. Whether it was Spear, Brayden, Orlov, or someone else she didn't know—but she knew enough to know that she was on the right track.

Now she wanted to know what was hidden behind the freshly painted wall in John Lynch's closet.

Miguel Rivera had curly black hair streaked with gray and a thick mustache that he was vain about. He was only five foot six but heavily muscled from a lifetime of manual labor.

Miguel was a master craftsman and could do just about anything: plumbing, electrical wiring, masonry, cabinet and countertop installation. Emma had been using him for years for home repairs and remodeling projects, and at six a.m. the day after she'd searched Lynch's apartment, she was sitting with Miguel in his pickup in front of Lynch's apartment building. They were waiting for Lynch to leave for his job at the Capitol; his shift started at seven.

At ten minutes past six, Lynch left his apartment and began walking in the direction of a bus stop. Emma knew that the bus would take him to the Braddock Road Metro station, and from there he would catch the subway to the Capitol. He wouldn't return to his apartment for at least ten hours.

Then they waited for another two hours. Emma wanted the other tenants in the building to head off for work or school or wherever they spent their day. She suspected the building wouldn't be completely empty when she and Miguel went inside, but fewer tenants meant fewer witnesses, which would definitely be better.

As they waited, Emma talked to Miguel, asking after his wife and daughters, what he thought of the Nationals' chances this year, his opinion of the moron who was currently president—just small talk that gave her an opportunity to practice her Spanish, but mostly she was trying to get him to relax. She wasn't successful. He was so nervous he looked ill.

At eight Emma said, "Let's go."

They were both wearing blue coveralls with matching blue baseball caps, looking, Emma hoped, like a small—and legitimate—construction crew. In the back of Miguel's truck were a sheet of drywall, tools for removing and installing drywall, and a can of eggshell-white paint.

Emma carried the tools and the paint, and Miguel carried the sheet of drywall to the door of Lynch's apartment building. Emma held the door open for Miguel, and they proceeded up the stairs to Lynch's apartment, Emma unconsciously humming "Whistle While You Work."

Emma said, "Are you sure you're okay with doing this, Miguel? We haven't done anything illegal yet, and I'm not going to get mad at you if you want to back out."

Miguel didn't want to do *this* at all, but he said, "I'm okay." He didn't look okay; he looked as if he was about to vomit.

Emma had told him that she planned to break into a man's apartment and remove and replace a section of drywall in a closet. And that's all she was planning to do. She wasn't going to steal anything. If they were caught by the police—which she assured him was highly unlikely—they'd be arrested for breaking and entering. If they were caught, Emma said that she would take the blame and swear that she'd told Miguel that she was the owner of the apartment and had tricked him into helping her—but the police most likely wouldn't believe her, and they both might be charged. Since neither of them had a criminal record, and since they'd have the help of Emma's high-priced lawyer, it was unlikely that they'd actually spend any time in jail. Emma had also told Miguel that she'd pay him a thousand dollars for a couple of hours of work, knowing Miguel could use the money. She honestly wasn't concerned about getting him into trouble, but she could see that he was clearly having second thoughts.

Emma once again picked the locks on Lynch's apartment door, while Miguel stood there terrified that one of the other tenants in the building might come down the hall as she was doing so. Once they were inside the apartment, it took five minutes for them to remove the clothes and shoes from Lynch's bedroom closet and another ten minutes for Miguel to remove the wallboard at the back of the closet.

Between the wall studs were stacks of currency wrapped in clear plastic. Miguel gasped when he saw the money; Emma smiled.

Emma peeled back the plastic from one of the stacks of currency, and saw that the bills were in twenty-, fifty-, and hundred-dollar denominations. Had they all been the same denomination she could have calculated how much money Lynch had hidden, but as they were different denominations she couldn't. If she had to guess, however, she would have said that there was between a hundred thousand and two hundred thousand dollars.

Two hours later they were finished, and Lynch's clothes were back in his closet. Miguel had installed a new section of wallboard and painted it. Emma had hauled away the old pieces of wallboard and placed them in Miguel's truck. Emma used Lynch's vacuum cleaner to clean up the closet floor, and Miguel used a hair dryer to more rapidly dry the quick-drying paint he'd applied. The smell of new paint was still evident, but Lynch wouldn't be home for at least another six hours, and they hoped that by then the odor wouldn't be noticeable among the other odors in his dusty, dirty apartment.

Emma didn't know it, but after Miguel dropped her off back at her house, and she'd paid him the money she'd promised, he went to the nearest Catholic church, put a hundred dollars in the poor box, lit ten votive candles, and prayed to Saint Nicholas—the patron saint of repentant thieves.

Emma showered and then made a tomato and cucumber salad for lunch. As she ate, she thought about the money she'd found in Lynch's apartment. There was no way he could have saved a hundred thousand or two hundred thousand dollars, not on his salary, and not with the alimony he was paying his ex-wife. But why had he hidden the money the way he did?

She had a theory, another theory. Lynch was worried that if he was ever investigated for Canton's murder—as unlikely as that possibility now seemed—the FBI would look into his finances. Therefore, he couldn't put the money he'd been paid for killing Canton into a bank account; he had to put it someplace that couldn't be found, yet at the same time a place he'd be able to get to quickly if he had to run. And he'd done an excellent job of hiding the money; had Emma not seen the drywall screws and the joint tape, she never would have found it.

Another thing occurred to her. If Lynch had killed Canton—and she was now almost certain he was involved, not only because of the money but also because of the burner phone she'd found—he would know that he couldn't begin to act like a man who'd suddenly come into a fortune. She imagined his plan was to wait a suitable period, quit the Capitol Police, and then, using his new passport, head off to some sunny place with a low cost of living and enjoy the good life. She also imagined he'd been paid more than the amount she'd found hidden behind the closet wall. Had she been him, she surely would have demanded more than two hundred grand for killing Canton, particularly if the one paying her was a man as wealthy as Sebastian Spear. She suspected he had more money in an offshore account, although at this point, whether he did or not was irrelevant, because Emma now had evidence that she could present to the FBI, evidence that would hopefully get them looking at someone other than DeMarco. Once the FBI was convinced that

Lynch had been involved in Canton's murder, they'd go back over all the security videos and see if they could prove he was at the Capitol when Canton was killed.

The problem she now had, however, was that she wasn't exactly sure how she should tell the FBI about evidence that she'd obtained by illegally searching a man's apartment. As determined as she was to help DeMarco, she'd just as soon not get arrested herself.

She took out her cell phone, planning to call her lawyer to ask for some advice, and noticed her phone was turned off. She'd turned it off before breaking into Lynch's apartment; if her phone had rung or vibrated while she was in there with Miguel, the poor man might have soiled his britches.

She turned on her phone and discovered that she had two voice mails, one from Mahoney and one from DeMarco's lawyer.

Both messages were the same: DeMarco was at Inova Alexandria Hospital.

He was in a coma.

29

The contraband phone in Jesús Díaz's pocket vibrated. He looked at the text, written in Spanish. It said: *He's on his way.*

Jesús was nineteen years old, an illegal immigrant from El Salvador. He was in the Alexandria jail awaiting trial for assaulting his ex-girlfriend's new boyfriend. Following his trial he'd be either deported or sentenced to five years in prison, as he'd almost killed the boyfriend. Deportation seemed more likely. During his eight months in the Alexandria jail, Jesús had been given a choice: join MS-13 or get your ass whipped on a daily basis. He'd opted to join.

Jesús worked in the jail kitchen; you didn't have to graduate from a culinary school to scrub pots and pans. The text message he'd just received meant that the guard who would bring DeMarco his lunch was on his way to the cafeteria.

Jesús walked over to the serving line and up to one of the servers, a black guy who was about ninety years old. Okay, he wasn't that old, but he was fuckin' old. He told the old guy, "I'm taking your place for the next ten minutes." The old guy looked as if he was about to object, then was smart enough to realize it wasn't worth it—which was most likely why he'd lived as long as he had.

The guard, a mean prick named Donovan who delighted in using his baton on the inmates, walked into the cafeteria at that moment, came up to the serving line, and pushed aside the prisoners waiting in line. He said to Jesús, "Make me up a tray."

"Sure thing, boss," Jesús said.

Jesús grabbed a tray, put two slices of meat loaf on it, green beans, a mound of instant mashed potatoes slathered with instant brown gravy, and a piece of dry, white cake with chocolate frosting. As he was putting the food on the tray, another MS-13 member—a kid named Angel Gómez, awaiting his trial for robbing a bodega—walked up to Donovan, tapped him on the back, and said, "I wanna register a complaint."

Donovan spun around and said, "Did you just touch me?"

"Hey, there's a guy," Angel said. "He's some kind of homo, and last night—"

"I don't give a shit what he did to you. You ever put a hand on me again—"

"Hey, man, I'm sorry, but this guy—"

"Back off, you little shit. Right now."

While Angel was distracting Donovan, Jesús took a small vial out of a pocket and poured the liquid in the vial over everything on DeMarco's lunch tray except the cake. The cake might look funny if the frosting was wet. He palmed the vial and said to Donovan, "Hey, boss, your tray is ready."

Donovan took the tray from Jesús, brushed past Angel with a contemptuous sneer, and walked away.

The thing that saved DeMarco's life was the unappetizing nature of the food. The meat loaf tasted as if the hamburger had been mixed with sawdust, the mashed potatoes were cold, the green beans soggy. The only edible item was the piece of cake. He took two bites of the meat loaf, one forkful of mashed potatoes, ate about three green beans, and then had dessert.

Five minutes later, he was having a hard time breathing—it felt as if a python was wrapped around his throat—and he couldn't seem to get any air into his lungs. He staggered over to the door, his face turning red, and began beating on the door with his fist. He tried to yell but couldn't.

The guard standing outside his cell slid back the peephole panel and looked in, wondering what the fuckin' guy was doing, pounding on the door. So far DeMarco hadn't been a problem inmate. At first he couldn't see DeMarco, then he saw his legs. He was on the floor, his legs were twitching, and he was making a weird, choking sound. The guard opened the door, took one look at DeMarco's purple face, and screamed into his radio, "This is Moran in isolation. I need a medic! Need a medic now!"

Moran didn't know what to do. He'd been given CPR training but had practiced only once on the CPR dummy. He screamed into his radio again, "Goddamnit, get a medic here!" He dropped to his knees, trying to remember what he'd been taught, and pushed down on DeMarco's chest three times, then pinched DeMarco's nose and started blowing air into his mouth. Thank God one of the medics got there ten seconds later.

30

Emma didn't bother to wait for the elevator. She ran up the hospital steps to reach the nurses' station in the ICU. She demanded to see DeMarco's doctor immediately, and when a nurse asked her who she was, she said she was DeMarco's older sister. Then, realizing that a prison inmate might not be the hospital's highest priority, Emma added that if her precious baby brother didn't receive the best medical care available, the hospital was going to see the largest malpractice suit it had ever seen.

A doctor was quickly brought over to talk to her.

The doctor, a brusque man with an Indian accent—and a physician's typical air of arrogance—informed her that it appeared as if DeMarco had been poisoned and that he was doing all that could be done when a person has ingested some unknown toxin. He said he was waiting for toxicology results to determine which poison had been used, and assured her that DeMarco's legal status would have no bearing whatsoever on the care he received. Emma doubted that.

"What's his condition?" Emma asked.

"He's stable, currently in a medically induced coma, and on a ventilator," the doctor said.

"I want to see him," Emma said.

"Like I said, he's in a coma."

"And like I said, I want to see him."

The doctor led her to DeMarco's room. Outside his door was a guard from the Alexandria jail. The man was sitting in a chair, both chins on his chest, obviously sleeping. Emma would deal with him shortly.

DeMarco was in bed, connected to machines monitoring his vital signs. Emma couldn't see much of his face, because of the ventilator. What she could see was not encouraging: his eyes were closed, his chest was barely rising and falling, and his face was the color of cigarette ash. One of his ankles was shackled to the bed.

Emma was not an overly emotional person. Nonetheless, she took one of DeMarco's big hands—the hand was cold and damp—and said, "You're going to be all right, Joe. I promise."

Turning to the doctor, she said, "He has health insurance but if you need to do something not covered by his policy, call me. I have money." She asked for something to write on, the doctor gave her a prescription pad, and she wrote down her name and phone number. The doctor didn't ask why her last name wasn't DeMarco, and if he had asked she would have said it was her ex-husband's name.

Emma left DeMarco's room and walked over to the sleeping guard. A metal name tag on his chest said his name was Donovan. Emma pulled back her right hand and slapped Donovan hard on the side of his head, knocking off the baseball cap he was wearing.

Donovan awoke, saying, "Wha-, wha-, what the fuck."

Emma screamed, "Stay awake! Your job is to protect the man in that room. If I catch you sleeping again, I'm not only going to make sure you're fired, I'm going to see that you're prosecuted for criminal negligence."

———————◆◆◆———————

Emma decided that she needed to get someone over to the hospital as fast as possible to protect DeMarco. Considering what had happened to him in jail—not once, but twice—and considering the incompetent guard outside his room, she had no confidence that the people who were supposed to protect him could keep him alive. It was also going to be harder to protect him in a hospital than a jail. There were no armed guards or metal detectors at the hospital's entrances, and anyone could walk in off the street, armed to the teeth, and massacre DeMarco while he was unconscious.

She thought for a moment, then called an ex-soldier named Mike Leary. Mike was former Special Forces, and Emma had worked with him a few times when she was with the DIA. He now ran a company that provided security for relief organizations that sent their employees to dangerous places. She gave Mike the background on DeMarco and told him that someone—she didn't mention Sebastian Spear—wanted DeMarco dead. She also told him that MS-13 had tried to kill DeMarco when he was in jail, and she was worried that the gang might try again in the hospital.

Mike said he'd get two of his best guys over to the hospital immediately.

Emma told him to send his bill to her.

———————— ••◆•• ————————

Emma now knew that it was more urgent than ever that she prove to the FBI that DeMarco was innocent. He wouldn't be safe, no matter where he was, until the bureau arrested the people really responsible for Canton's death. While standing in the lobby of the hospital she thought about what she should do and again decided that she needed legal advice. She called Janet Evans, DeMarco's lawyer—who was also her lawyer—and said they needed to talk immediately. Janet said she'd be happy to talk to her. As Janet billed her time at eight hundred dollars an hour, of course she'd be happy to talk.

When Janet Evans was a federal prosecutor, she'd had a small, windowless office with a cheap government-issue metal desk and mismatched metal file cabinets. Private practice was clearly more rewarding than public service, judging by her cherrywood desk, the Persian rug covering the floor, and the view of the Washington Monument in her current digs.

She offered Emma a cup of coffee made from some costly, exotic bean and said, "So. What's the problem?"

Emma told her how she'd learned that a Capitol cop with a poor military record and no money had once served under Sebastian Spear's head of security, Bill Brayden. Then, really based on not much more than that and Lynch's physical similarity to DeMarco, she'd broken into Lynch's apartment, where she found a pile of cash and a hidden burner phone containing the phone number of someone located at Spear's headquarters.

"You broke into his apartment?" Janet said.

"Yeah, and ripped out and replaced a wall in his closet."

"My God, Emma. Are you insane?"

"The reason I'm here," Emma said, "is that I want your opinion on what the FBI will do when I tell them what I did."

"For one thing, they'll arrest you. And not just for breaking and entering. You interfered in a federal investigation and your interference might, even if you're correct about Lynch, prevent them from convicting him."

Before Emma could object, Janet continued. "Lynch's lawyer will argue that the evidence you found is inadmissible because it was obtained without a warrant. I'm sure you've heard the expression 'fruit of the poisonous tree.' Well, Emma, you're the poisonous tree."

"What I did may have been illegal, but since I was acting as a civilian, as opposed to a member of law enforcement, I don't see why the FBI can't use what I've found. You know, like they'd use evidence obtained from a confidential informant."

Janet said, "Lynch's lawyer will argue that since you were appointed by the president's chief of staff to oversee the FBI's investigation, you weren't acting as a civilian. Moreover, nothing you found proves that Lynch killed Canton or conspired to kill him."

"I realize that," an irritated Emma said. "But I want the FBI to arrest him and squeeze him, and if they squeeze him hard enough, he'll give up whoever he was working with."

"Squeeze him with what?" Janet said. "It's not illegal to hide a phone. Nor is it illegal to hide a large amount of cash the way he did. Considering the area where he lives, his lawyer will argue that hiding his money in such a way was prudent."

"But where did he get the money?"

"Who knows?" Janet said. "Maybe he got lucky in Atlantic City. Wherever he got the money, you can't prove it came from Spear. If I was Lynch's lawyer, I'd advise him to take the Fifth and not say anything if the FBI arrests him. And unless the FBI can prove he did something illegal, they won't have anything they can use to pressure him."

Emma shook her head, not happy with anything she was hearing. "The problem I've got, Janet, is *time*. I have to prove DeMarco is innocent before someone kills him, and the longer it takes, the higher the odds are that someone will succeed."

"If it's time you're worried about, going to the FBI with what you've found certainly won't speed things up. I mean, you know how the FBI works as well as I do, Emma. Let's say that they ignore how you learned about the cell phone and the money, and believe your theory that Lynch conspired to kill Canton. The first thing they'll do is hold a bunch of meetings with DOJ and talk for hours about what to do next. They'll reexamine all the evidence. They'll spend days looking at the surveillance camera videos, trying to figure out where Lynch was when Canton was killed. They'll try to obtain warrants to look at

Lynch's finances and his phone records, which will take more time, and in the end, they might not get the warrants. They'll throw a thirty-man surveillance team around Lynch and watch him for days, or maybe *weeks*, hoping he'll lead them to something or someone. And I can assure you that they won't arrest Lynch and question him until they've done all those things."

Emma let out a sigh. Janet was right. She had to do more to prove DeMarco was innocent—and she had to do it quickly and without the FBI.

At that moment, she noticed the sleek Apple laptop sitting on Janet's desk—and realized that she had an option she hadn't previously considered.

There was another player in this drama, one who could be squeezed and squeezed very hard. And once he was squeezed in the way that Emma had in mind, he'd give up everything.

She decided, however, that she wouldn't tell her lawyer what she had in mind. If Janet had a problem with her ripping out of piece of drywall, she'd *really* have a problem with what Emma was planning to do next.

31

Emma took a seat at a table for two in a restaurant called the Red Sky Steak and Fish House. The reason she was there was not the food. It was instead because the restaurant was in Laurel, Maryland, which is about twelve miles from Fort Meade—home to the NSA.

At exactly seven p.m., Olivia Prescott walked into the restaurant and over to Emma's table. Olivia, like Emma, was obsessive when it came to being punctual.

Emma knew Olivia Prescott from her days at the DIA and had worked with her on a couple of task forces. Olivia had a doctorate in mathematics from Princeton and had begun her career at the NSA working on encryption programs. Olivia's skills, however, went beyond mathematics and code breaking. She was blessed with the Machiavellian cunning to compete in a complex, backstabbing federal bureaucracy, and after thirty years of service was now one of the highest-ranking officials at the agency.

Olivia and Emma had other things in common than being punctual. They were about the same age—Emma wondered whether Olivia was ever going to retire—and both were tall and slender. Both were extremely competent. Both tended to be aloof, had few friends, and weren't particularly sociable. Olivia wasn't gay—or at least Emma didn't think so—but she'd never married. The only odd thing about Olivia—at least Emma thought it odd—was that she dyed her hair platinum blond and styled it in a bob, like a 1920s flapper's, which Emma thought looked absurd on a woman her age.

When Emma had called Olivia after leaving her lawyer's office, she said they needed to talk about a Russian hacker named Nikita Orlov. Olivia didn't recognize Orlov's name but agreed to a meeting because she knew Emma was a serious person and wouldn't have called if it wasn't important—to national security, that is. Emma was also certain that if Neil was right about what Orlov had done when he was in Russia, Olivia's elves at the NSA would know who Orlov was and could provide Olivia with all the information they had on the man before their meeting.

Prescott and Emma both ordered vodka martinis. They didn't bother to toast or touch glasses as friends might do; they didn't chat about what they'd been up to since the last time they'd seen each other. Emma got right to the point.

"Did you check out Nikita Orlov?" Emma asked.

"Yes," Olivia said. "He was a mathematics prodigy who started working at the GRU when he was about eighteen. But we heard that he'd disappeared. One of the CIA's sources said the GRU was hunting for him all over Russia, but we don't know why they were hunting for him. And that's about all we have on the man other than some background data like where he went to school. We don't have a photo of him."

Emma said, "I happen to know that Nikita Orlov was engaged in cyber warfare when he was in Russia. He had to run for his life when he had an affair with a general's wife, and is now alive and well and living in the United States."

"My, my," Olivia said.

Emma went on to explain that a man she knew—she didn't give Olivia Neil's name—was an acquaintance of another Russian defector, named Dmitri Sokolov. She told Olivia how Dmitri had spotted Orlov in Las Vegas at a computer trade show a couple of years ago.

"Do you know where Orlov is right now?" Olivia asked. "I'd like to have a chat with him."

"I thought you might. And yes, I know where he is. He works for an American company. But let me tell you one other thing. I suspect that Nikita is still working for the GRU."

"Why do you think that?" Olivia said.

"Because a man with his intelligence would know that some of the people he worked with in Russia would almost certainly be at the trade show in Vegas. Hackers from North Korea and China and every other country in the world engaged in electronic eavesdropping and cyber warfare go to that sort of event. So I think that Orlov went to Vegas because he knew he'd be safe. He knew that GRU agents wouldn't kill him or snatch him and send him back to Russia."

Emma explained. She suspected—although she had no proof—that the Russians had somehow learned that Orlov had made it to the United States and was working for Sebastian Spear. How they learned this, she didn't know. And although a certain Russian general wanted Orlov dead, saner heads in Moscow prevailed, knowing that Orlov was too valuable to waste, particularly when the only crime he'd committed was diddling a general's young wife. Emma further suspected that when the Russians located Orlov they gave him a choice: a bullet in the head or continuing to work for the GRU in America. (In America, he wouldn't be in the vicinity of the man he'd turned into a cuckold.) She had no idea what sort of work Orlov had been doing since he'd been in the United States—maybe he was preparing to screw up the *next* American election—but she was convinced that no way would Orlov have taken the risk of going to the Vegas conference if the GRU was still hunting for him. So she didn't *really* know whether Orlov was still working for the Russians, but logic told her this had to be the case, and Olivia Prescott agreed with her.

"Which brings me to what I want," Emma said.

"Ah, I should have known this wouldn't be simple," Olivia said.

Emma gave Olivia the background on the death of Congressman Lyle Canton—that is, the background not reported in the newspapers. She explained how she believed that a Capitol cop named John Lynch had killed Canton for Sebastian Spear. She also explained how a hacker had used Mahoney's cell phone to send a text message to DeMarco and put money into DeMarco's bank account, and that she was about 90 percent certain that the person who did those things was Nikita Orlov.

"What I want," Emma said, "is for you to scoop up Orlov, and I'll be with you when you do. Then what I want is for you to threaten him with whatever you can think of to make him talk—such as life in a cage for espionage—and force him to confess that he helped kill Canton."

Emma knew that, unlike the FBI, the NSA wouldn't have a problem doing what she wanted. The FBI was a Boy Scout troop. The NSA was more like . . . well, a motorcycle gang.

"After he confesses to his role in Canton's death," Emma said, "and agrees to testify against everyone involved, I'll have enough to get DeMarco out of jail. And you, of course, will benefit by being able to squeeze everything out of him that he did while he was in Russia and whatever he's been doing lately in the United States."

Olivia smiled. "Emma, I believe another martini is in order."

32

Nikki Orlov was in an excellent mood—but then he almost always was.

Nikki loved living in Washington, D.C. He had a spacious two-bedroom apartment in Georgetown, close to the bars on the M Street strip—bars always filled with lovely lady government workers and co-eds from the nearby universities. He had an up-to-date entertainment system in his apartment, a king-size bed with silk sheets, a closet filled with stylish clothes, and, thanks to a bonus he'd been paid by Bill Brayden, he'd recently purchased a sporty Mazda Miata convertible roadster. Life was grand. He was a lucky man.

As the elevator descended to the parking garage, he thought about the woman he had met last night at the Palm, whom he'd invited to his place for dinner tonight. She was exquisite: long red hair, green eyes, a sprinkling of freckles dusting incredible cheekbones. She also had a magnificent body, which he suspected might not be totally natural, not that he cared. Her only flaw was that she was married.

That seemed to be his curse, to fall in love with married women.

The elevator stopped, and the doors opened. As he walked toward his car, he noticed the white panel van idling near the elevators. The cab of the van had tinted windows, and the cargo bay had no windows at all. There was no logo on the vehicle to indicate ownership, but there was a ladder on the roof, making him think that it probably belonged to a contractor hired to repair something in one of the apartments. Nikki was so grateful for a job where he worked with his brains and not his hands.

He started toward his car. He'd walked only a few paces when the van surged forward and stopped next to him, and two large men jumped out. These brutes were six inches taller than Nikki was and outweighed him by a hundred pounds. They were wearing black ski masks.

They grabbed Nikki before he could run and muscled him into the van. Once he was inside they overpowered him, smothering him with their large bodies, squeezing his arms with their big hands so he couldn't move, and handcuffed him. Then they slapped a strip of duct tape over his mouth and placed a black hood over his head.

A black hood. He's seen photos of terrorists snatched by the CIA: hoods over their heads, wearing orange jumpsuits, taking short, choppy steps as they walked with manacled legs. He figured the guys who had just captured him most likely worked for the CIA—an organization unconstrained by law or morality. Rather like the GRU. The fact that they hadn't simply shot him meant that he was most likely in for a very long and uncomfortable interrogation session. He would explain to them as soon as they took the bag off his head that he had absolutely no secret he wasn't willing to reveal to avoid being tortured.

Less than twenty minutes later the van stopped, and he heard what sounded like a garage door opening. The van pulled forward, stopped again, and the garage door closed. He heard the back door of the van open, and he was pulled from the van. Then, with a man on each side of him holding his arms, he was walked a short distance and shoved down into a chair.

The hood was removed, and he saw that he was inside a large two-car garage. The van took up one bay of the garage. In the other bay was a wooden table, and sitting at the table were two old women. One of the women had short, stylish blond hair streaked with gray, and the other had an unnatural-looking platinum-colored bob. Both women radiated power and confidence.

He wondered for a moment why they were in the garage instead of inside the house, then noticed that the chair he was sitting in was resting on a large plastic sheet. He also noticed the tools attached to a pegboard on one wall—just ordinary tools: hammers, pliers, drills—and realized that those tools could be used for something other than household repairs. *Oh, Jesus.*

The two masked men who had kidnapped him were standing behind him, and the woman with the platinum bob said to the men, "Did you search him?"

"No, not yet," one of them said.

"Well, for Christ's sake. Frisk him and empty his pockets."

One of the masked men jerked Nikki to his feet, patted him down, and pulled everything out of his pockets. He placed Nikki's wallet, his keys, a small box of breath mints, and his cell phone on the table in front of the old women, then shoved Nikki back down into the chair. Almost as an afterthought, he ripped the duct tape off Nikki's mouth, peeling a layer of tender skin off his lips.

The platinum blonde—apparently the person in charge—said to the ski-masked men, "Undo the handcuffs and wait outside."

Now that was insulting! The old women obviously didn't consider him to be a physical threat.

Emma studied Nikita Orlov. He was an extraordinarily good-looking young man, and she could see why women would be attracted to him. His sky-blue eyes were darting from side to side, looking at Emma, then at Olivia, then back at Emma, as if he were watching a tennis match. But neither Emma nor Olivia said anything immediately. They let a few moments pass as they looked at him—as if they were studying a bug trapped in a mason jar—letting the silence increase his nervousness.

"My name is Olivia Prescott," Olivia finally said. "I work for the National Security Agency. My associate's name is unimportant."

"NSA?" Nikki said.

"Yes. I'm sure you've heard of the organization. I'm here to tell you what's going to happen to you if your refuse to cooperate. This is not a negotiation. We know you worked for the GRU in Russia and were engaged in cyber warfare against the United States. We know you entered this country illegally and are using a false identity. We also know that you've continued to work for the GRU while in the United States."

Olivia didn't really know this, but figured Emma was most likely right about Nikita still working for his Russian masters.

"What all this means," Olivia said, "is that you can be sent to prison for thirty years and you'll be incarcerated in a maximum-security federal penitentiary. I'm talking about the kind of place where you spend twenty-three hours a day in a cell by yourself with a surveillance camera watching everything you do. Most people placed in these facilities go insane long before they complete their sentences. So. Do you understand the predicament you're in?"

"Yes. Is there something I can do to, uh, improve my situation?"

Olivia and Emma both displayed thin smiles. Nikki Orlov was clearly a practical young man.

Olivia said, "You're going to tell the NSA everything you did in Russia. Every operation you were engaged in, the people you worked with, the sort of equipment you used. Everything. I imagine debriefing you will take several months. What we do with you after you're debriefed will depend on how cooperative you are and if you tell us anything useful."

"I'll be very cooperative," Nikki said.

"But the first thing you're going to do," Emma said, "is confess to your role in Lyle Canton's death."

Nikki said, "What? I had nothing to do with Congressman Canton's death."

Emma figured that Nikki knew being arrested for espionage was one thing; being an accomplice to killing a United States congressman was something else.

"Yes, you did. I know you did," Emma said. "And if you don't confess to what you did and testify against the people who helped you kill the congressman, then we're back to the scenario where you spend thirty years alone in a concrete box."

For a moment, Emma thought that Nikki was going to deny again that he was involved in Canton's death, but then he closed his eyes briefly, and when he opened them he said, "Okay."

Emma heard the side door to the garage open. She assumed it was the NSA agents who'd brought Nikki to the safe house coming back into the garage for some reason.

When she looked over at the door she saw that she was wrong.

Very wrong.

33

The man and woman who walked into the garage were holding MP-443 Grach pistols equipped with silencers. The woman was short and stocky; the man was built like a Russian weight lifter, fat and strong.

The woman said, "We don't want to kill you, so don't do anything foolish." She spoke English with a strong Russian accent. She then turned to Nikki and said something quickly in Russian. Emma spoke several languages, but Russian was not one of them. Whatever the woman said, Nikki gulped, then stood and took his possessions off the table and put them back in his pockets. The woman said something else in Russian and Nikki walked over and stood behind the weight lifter.

"Do you know who I work for?" Olivia said to the woman.

"No," the woman said. "And I don't care." She pulled several plastic zip ties out of a pocket and while still pointing her pistol at Olivia, walked behind her and said, "Put your hands behind your back." The male Russian was now pointing his weapon at Emma's face. Emma thought the man looked rather dull—the woman was clearly the brains of the operation—and stupid people with guns made her nervous.

The woman used the zip ties to bind Olivia's hands behind her back and then used more zip ties to bind her hands to the chair. She then did the same thing to Emma. After Emma and Olivia were both secure, the male came over, picked up Emma's chair with her sitting in it, and placed her chair so she was back-to-back with Olivia, then bound the two chairs together with more zip ties. Last, the woman took a small roll of duct tape and placed a strip of tape over Emma's mouth. Before she could gag Olivia, Olivia said, "Did you kill my men?"

"No," the woman said. "Tasers. They'll come around in an hour or so."

"I'm going to catch you," Olivia said. "You'll never get out of this country alive."

"Good luck with that," the woman said, the word *luck* sounding like "luke." She pressed the duct tape over Olivia's thin lips.

<hr />

About an hour later, one of Olivia's men staggered into the garage. He was holding a pistol but barely able to walk. He went over to Olivia, took out a pocketknife, freed her, and then freed Emma.

Olivia, looking mad enough to kill, said, "I'll deal with you and your idiot partner later."

Olivia took out her cell phone, punched a button, and said, "This is Prescott. Give me the duty officer. Now!" Emma heard her describe the Russians and Nikki Orlov and issue orders to commence a manhunt. These included checking surveillance cameras, repositioning satellites to hover over Washington, getting agents immediately out to every small airport within a hundred miles. She apparently assumed that the Russians wouldn't fly out of a major airport on a commercial flight. She also instructed the duty officer to begin looking at seaports in Maryland and Virginia for Russian ships. One thing she didn't do was order her man to ask for help from local law enforcement agencies—but then an organization as large as the NSA didn't often need to ask for help.

When she got off the phone, she said to Emma, "I'll find them." Then she said, "How in the hell did they know we had him?"

"They could have been watching him," Emma said. "But more likely, he sent out a distress signal."

"How?"

"He had his cell phone in the side pocket of his sport coat. He could have reached the phone even with his hands cuffed behind his back and sent a signal. Then they used his phone to track him here."

Olivia said, "My men should have removed his phone and disabled it as soon as they captured him. Those two fools are going to be spending the rest of their careers in Somalia."

"You have to find Orlov," Emma said. "If you don't, DeMarco is going to jail for the rest of his life. That is, if he's not murdered first."

"Oh, I'll find him," Olivia said. "And you can take that to the bank." She paused, then said, "Emma, I am *so* embarrassed."

34

Emma had a large backyard at her home in McLean—and she was fanatical about it. There were no weeds in the flower beds; there was no crabgrass in the lawn. Azaleas and rhododendrons were perfectly trimmed; a dazzling variety of lovely, healthy flowers bloomed. She used professional gardeners to maintain the grounds, and over the years the gardeners had eventually—painfully—adjusted to her high standards.

She poured herself an iced tea and took a seat on the patio. Normally, her eyes would roam the yard, sector by sector, looking for any sign of imperfection. Imagine Patton scanning an African plain through binoculars looking for Rommel's tanks. Today, however, after the debacle with Olivia Prescott and the Russians, she was oblivious to her surroundings.

Olivia had sounded certain that she would find Nikita Orlov, and maybe she would. Of the sixteen intelligence agencies in the country, the NSA was the largest and arguably the one with the most brainpower. More important, it had the ability to monitor surveillance cameras, both public and private, and was probably listening—whether legally or not—to every cell-phone conversation in the D.C. area. If NSA eavesdroppers heard someone talking about Orlov and two Russians trying to get out of the country, agents would swoop down on the phone's owner like hawks dropping out of the sky to snatch a rabbit.

Emma, however, was not so confident. The GRU was a formidable adversary, well aware of the NSA's capabilities, and she had no doubt that the Russians had a plan for getting Orlov out of the country that would take the NSA's skills into account.

She couldn't wait for Olivia to find Orlov; she needed to come up with a way to save DeMarco without him.

She called the hospital to check on DeMarco's condition and was told that although he was still unconscious, he appeared to be stable and was improving—but as far as Emma was concerned, this was not necessarily good news.

She called a friend—a retired physician who worked part-time for Doctors Without Borders—and asked for a favor. Her next call was to her lawyer, Janet Evans. She told Janet that the doctor would meet her at the hospital, and their job was to make sure that DeMarco stayed in the hospital as long as possible. Janet was to threaten the hospital with various and sundry lawsuits if he was discharged without Emma's doctor giving his consent—and the doctor would not give his consent even if DeMarco was capable of doing backflips. Emma was convinced that DeMarco was safer in the hospital with Mike Leary's men watching him than he would ever be in the jail.

She called Mike next to see if he had anything to report.

"Yeah," he said. "I was just about to call you."

Mike said that a few minutes before, three Hispanics teenagers got off the elevator on DeMarco's floor, and the two guys Mike had assigned to protect DeMarco saw them coming down the hall. The three kids could have been coming to visit their sick mama—but Mike's guys didn't get that vibe. While the Alexandria jailer assigned to protect DeMarco sat there nodding off, oblivious to the situation, Mike's guys faced the teenagers as they came down the hall—then opened their own jackets to display the large pistols they carried in shoulder holsters. The three teenagers stopped, one of them said something to the other two, and they left the hallway using the nearest staircase instead of the elevator.

Mike said, "I think these kids were MS-13 newbies and someone told them that if they wanted to make their bones, they had to kill DeMarco. They were probably packing automatics and would have mowed down anyone who tried to stop them, but they hadn't expected to run into guys armed and ready like my guys."

"Damn it," Emma muttered. "If you think you need more men to protect DeMarco, assign them. Like I told you, I'll cover the bill."

Mike said, "I've got a better idea than adding more guards."

Emma wasn't sure Mike's plan would work but it was worth a try. At any rate, she'd have to trust him to protect DeMarco until she could figure out a way to prove DeMarco innocent. She needed a plan B.

Well, actually, she needed a plan C.

Plan A had been to get the FBI to arrest Lynch based on what she'd found in his apartment, then get him to flip on his co-conspirators. But her lawyer had convinced her that plan A would take too long and that Emma might be the one arrested.

Plan B had been to get Nikki Orlov, under the threat of going to prison for espionage, to confess that he'd helped frame DeMarco and then to agree to testify against whoever had helped him. Plan B, however, had gone up in flames after Orlov had been taken by the Russians. If Olivia could just find Orlov—

Her phone rang. It was as if God had been eavesdropping on her reverie. It was Olivia calling.

Emma said, "Did you get him?"

Olivia paused. A long pause. "Yeah. In a way," she said.

"What does that mean?"

"We had our machines set for Russian-language speakers, and we picked up a call," Olivia said.

Emma didn't know a lot about the technical aspects of the NSA's eavesdropping programs—even at her clearance level, some things were out of bounds—but she knew that the NSA could program its phone-monitoring computers to listen for certain voices, languages, and key words, like the word *bomb*. And that's what Olivia was saying. They'd been plucking conversations in Russian out of the atmosphere, hoping to get a lead on Orlov.

Olivia continued. "The phone was located near Ocean City, Maryland, in a house on the beach. I think the Russians were planning to send in a fishing trawler—or maybe a submarine—to pick Orlov up. I deployed a team, but when my guys breached the place, the Russian woman who took Orlov shot him in the head before we could stop her. I'm certain she was told that he was too valuable to be captured."

"What happened to the woman?"

"She's dead, too. She didn't give my men any other option. As for the man who helped her snatch Orlov from our safe house, he wasn't at the place in Maryland. So he's in the wind, but I don't care about him. I wanted Orlov, not a couple of Russian gunslingers. I told my guys to give Orlov and the woman a bin Laden funeral."

She meant burial at sea.

Olivia sighed. "I don't know what else to say, Emma, other than this has to be one of the lowest points in my career."

Emma didn't know what to say, either. The best she could come up with was, "Well, I'm grateful that you tried to help, Olivia. One of these days we'll get together and have dinner and commiserate about it." They wouldn't.

Emma was starting to think that the only kind of luck DeMarco had was bad luck, but there was no point dwelling on things out of her control. Back to plan C. There had to be a plan C.

———◆◆◆———

Emma had been drinking iced tea, but after the news she'd received from Olivia, she decided a gin and tonic would be more appropriate. She made one and went back out to sit on her patio to think—and again it was as if God had decided that today was the day to fuck with her. Her nemesis appeared.

Emma didn't think squirrels were cute—they were nothing more than bushy-tailed rodents—but she had no deep-seated animus toward the species in general. But this one particular fat, brown little creature—she *hated*.

One of her neighbors had a walnut tree, and this squirrel, instead of burying the walnuts in her neighbor's yard, as he should have, liked to bury them in Emma's yard. Why, she had no idea. And not only would the little bastard dig up her grass to hide the nuts in the first place, but because he was a particularly stupid squirrel, he wouldn't be able to remember where he'd hidden them and would dig a dozen holes trying to find a nut he'd buried.

Thanks to the mood she was in after talking to Olivia, Emma felt like going into the house and getting one of her guns and blowing the destructive critter's head off. Since she knew she couldn't do that—who knows what bad karma could come from assassinating squirrels—she looked around for something to fling at it. Then, not able to find a suitable projectile close at hand, she had no other option but to stand, clap her hands, and yell, "Hey! You! Get out of my yard."

The squirrel stopped digging and looked at her. Emma could have sworn he *smirked* before he went back to excavating a hole twice as big as he needed to bury a single walnut.

Emma said, "I'm going to get a dog. Do you hear me? Your days are numbered."

She knew she'd never get a dog.

As she stood there, hands on her hips, glaring at the squirrel, smarting with the humiliation of defeat, plan C came to her.

35

Bill Brayden couldn't believe it.

MS-13 had failed three times to kill DeMarco.

This time he met with Hector in a Walmart parking lot. Hector parked his Trans Am so it was facing in the opposite direction from Brayden's car, and by rolling down the driver's-side windows they could talk without getting out of their vehicles.

As might be expected, Hector was embarrassed. He said, "I'm sorry, man. I don't know what to tell you. My guys said they got to the hospital, expecting to see some fat-ass guard from the jail, but there were two other guys there. They looked like pros, like fuckin' Secret Service or something. If they'd tried to take DeMarco out, these guys would have killed them. I mean, you didn't tell me that DeMarco had private security."

"I didn't know he had private security," Brayden said.

"Well, there you go," Hector said, glad he was able to shift some of the blame to Brayden.

"So do you have a plan?" Brayden said.

"The best thing would be to wait until they move him back to the jail."

"That won't work. They'll put him in isolation, they'll have a platoon of guards watching him, and they'll probably have some inmate nobody gives a shit about tasting his food. The sheriff who runs the jail was just put on administrative leave by the governor for failing to protect DeMarco, and the guy they've assigned to replace him won't make the same mistakes. DeMarco will be protected better than the damn president until his trial."

At that moment an overweight, young white woman with a crying, mixed-race little boy passed in front of Hector's car. She was pushing the kid along, her hand squeezing the back of his thin neck, and Hector heard her say, "I'm telling you, Robbie, you don't knock it off, I'm gonna just smack the shit out of you."

Hector thought, *Some women, they shouldn't be allowed to have kids.* Then he smiled.

To Brayden, he said, "I got an idea. And I got the perfect person for the job."

<hr />

Brayden decided he needed to tell Sebastian Spear where things stood, although so far Spear hadn't asked for an update. Spear wasn't known for his patience, but when he had to be patient he could be like a spider, willing to sit forever on the edge of its web waiting for a fly to entangle itself in the sticky mesh. In the four months that it had taken Brayden to set up Canton's murder, Spear had never pushed him and only once had he asked what Brayden was doing, and then it was only a one-word question.

One day after a meeting, two months into the planning phase, while Brayden was still putting all the pieces in place, Spear had pulled him aside and said, "Canton?"

Thinking he wanted a detailed status report, Brayden had said, "Sir, it's complicated, and the reason it's taking so long is because I'm currently—"

Spear had said, "Fine. That'll be all." Apparently, he'd just wanted to know that Brayden was moving forward. He never asked another question, nor, as Brayden discovered, would he ever even thank him for the job he did.

Now, and whether Spear wanted to know or not, Brayden needed to tell him that Nikki Orlov had gone off the grid, and he didn't know whether Orlov posed a danger. If Orlov was simply hiding because he was worried about being caught, that was fine. But if Orlov was talking to someone in law enforcement—well, not so fine.

Brayden also thought he should tell Spear about DeMarco, although DeMarco wasn't as much of a concern as Orlov. The best thing would be for DeMarco to die as soon as possible, before his trial, but even if Hector failed to kill him, it still appeared as if Canton's murder was going to be pinned on the poor bastard.

Brayden was beginning to wonder, however, whether Spear was becoming completely unhinged. Following the two-week meltdown after Jean Canton's death, and after he gave the order to have Canton killed, Spear appeared to return to normal. Well, maybe not exactly normal; he hardly spoke, and he didn't appear to be as engaged in the company as he used to be, which could be attributed to grief, but at least he showed up for work every day. But since Canton had been murdered, Brayden had heard reports of him acting bizarrely. One VP told him that Spear had shown up for a breakfast with a potential multimillion-dollar customer— a white-robed Saudi prince—unshaven, wearing a jogging suit. During the breakfast, he didn't touch his food and then left abruptly, before the Saudi had even finished eating. Another VP had said that Spear was now missing meetings and briefings he normally would have attended, and when he did attend, he often wouldn't say a word. It was as though his body was there, but his mind was on a different planet.

It was a good thing that Spear Industries had a stable of competent VPs.

Brayden walked into Spear's outer office. His ancient secretary was at her desk, just sitting there. Normally she'd be yakking with a friend on the phone or reading a book or painting her nails. Why the woman still had a job, and what she did all day, was a mystery to everyone. But today she was just sitting, almost rigidly, and she looked upset.

"Is he in?" Brayden asked.

"Oh, yeah, he's in," she said. "In fact, he didn't go home last night. I went in this morning to put his schedule on his desk like I always do, and he was lying on his drafting table, his hands on his chest. You know, like someone lying in a *coffin*. I wasn't expecting him to be there, and it just scared the crap out of me when I saw him. Anyway, I asked him if he was all right, if he needed anything, and he didn't move. If I hadn't seen his foot sort of twitch, I would have thought he was dead." Evelyn lowered her voice and said, "Mr. Brayden, he needs help."

Brayden almost said *No shit* but didn't. Instead, he opened the door to Spear's office, wondering if he'd still be lying on the drafting table. He wasn't.

Spear was in the chair behind his desk, looking down at an old .38 revolver, like the type cops carried fifty years ago. The pistol was sitting in the middle of his desk. Behind the revolver, standing up, spaced exactly one inch apart, were five bullets. Brayden was almost certain the revolver could hold six bullets, but because of the way the gun was oriented he couldn't see if there was another bullet in the cylinder.

Was the crazy son of a bitch playing Russian roulette?

Brayden said, "Sir, are you all right?"

Talk about a stupid question.

Spear didn't look at him. He wasn't sure that Spear even knew he was in the room. He just continued to stare at the gun, seemingly fascinated by it, as if it was some alien artifact and he was trying to understand its function.

After standing there for what seemed an eternity, Brayden said, "Sir, why don't I come back later. I can see you're, uh, busy now."

As he was leaving, he thought about telling Spear's secretary that her boss was armed and possibly contemplating suicide but decided not to. Instead he said, "Mr. Spear told me that you should take the rest of the day off."

"Sounds good to me," Evelyn said, and grabbed her purse.

36

Emma was going to need at least two people to help her.

One of the people she could have called on was Neil, but she knew Neil was practically useless unless he was sitting in front of a computer. He wasn't the least bit athletic, he was out of shape—he probably wouldn't be able to walk a mile without collapsing—and she wasn't sure he could even drive a car.

She considered her problem for a couple of moments and then called two women. Both were ex-military—one an ex-marine, the other ex-army. Their names were Pamela Stewart and Shandra Morgan. Both suffered from post-traumatic stress disorder, having been victims of improvised explosive devices, Pamela in Iraq, Shandra in Afghanistan. They'd recovered completely from the physical injuries they'd sustained, but couldn't get over the shock of seeing their friends killed and maimed. They had vivid, recurring flashbacks that were sometimes debilitating. They felt guilty to be alive when their platoon mates had died, even though they knew their guilt was irrational.

Emma had met them at Walter Reed. For the last five years she had been volunteering at the medical center, working with female wounded warriors, in particular women suffering from PTSD. The suicide rate among veterans was skyrocketing—one source reported that as many as twenty veterans committed suicide each *day*—and Emma felt compelled to do something. The veterans would return from war, become addicted to alcohol or painkillers, be unable to hold a job or deal with spouses and family members, and spiral downward like proud birds shot out of the sky. What Emma had been doing was attending support-group meetings, doing her best to help these young women recover and resume normal lives.

Shandra and Pamela, compared with some of the other women, were both doing relatively well. Their flashbacks occurred less often, and they attended AA meetings together and were no longer using alcohol. Both were taking classes at community colleges. Shandra wanted to be a teacher; Pamela was artistic and studying graphic design. But although they were improving, they lacked the confidence they'd had when they first enlisted.

Emma figured a little field exercise would be good for them, the perfect tonic to boost their morale.

———◆———

Emma invited Pamela and Shandra to her home in McLean. She gave them glasses of iced tea, and they took seats at Emma's patio table. Pamela, the artist, was impressed by the beauty of Emma's backyard; Shandra was impressed by the size of it.

Emma told them about DeMarco's case and her conclusion that DeMarco had been framed and that Sebastian Spear, Bill Brayden, and a Capitol cop, John Lynch, were the ones really responsible for Canton's death. She told them that she knew that Lynch had a large amount of money hidden in his apartment and that he'd been communicating via a burner phone with someone at Spear Industries. When Shandra asked how she knew about the money and the phone, Emma said, "I can't tell you that, but I know."

"The problem," Emma said, "is that I need to be able to prove that these men did what I suspect and I need to do it quickly, before they make another attempt on DeMarco's life. Which is where you come in. I need some help."

Emma told them what she had in mind—and both young women instantly perked up. They were thrilled to be asked to help and delighted to see that someone still had faith in them, even if they had little in themselves.

Emma said, "Tomorrow I want you to follow John Lynch." She gave them Lynch's address in Alexandria and told them that Lynch left for work about six a.m. She also gave them photos of Bill Brayden and Sebastian Spear that Neil had found online. "The main thing I want to know is if Lynch meets with either of these men."

The truth was that Emma had no expectation whatsoever that Brayden or Spear would meet with Lynch. She was certain they wouldn't go near Lynch. The other thing was, she didn't really need Pamela and Shandra to follow Lynch. She gave them the job so they could get acclimated to the game and to increase their confidence. She told them to keep the tail loose and that if they lost Lynch it was okay; it was more important that he didn't spot them tailing him.

To which Shandra said, "No way is this a-hole gonna spot us."

"Roger that," Pamela said—and she and Shandra stood up and high-fived, making Emma laugh.

While they were following Lynch, Emma said she planned to follow Bill Brayden. Emma suspected Brayden would be more likely to spot a tail than Lynch, but she didn't say that. And Emma actually needed to follow Brayden because she planned to conduct a small experiment.

The next morning, while Shandra and Pamela were tailing Lynch, Emma was waiting outside Brayden's upscale apartment building in Arlington. The building had an underground parking garage for the tenants, and a metal gate barred the entrance to the garage. Neil had obtained the license plate number of Brayden's car and the make of the car, a 2016 Lexus. At six thirty the parking garage gate rolled up, and a black Lexus left the garage; Brayden was driving.

Brayden stopped at a Starbucks for morning coffee and a breakfast sandwich, then drove to Spear Industries headquarters in Reston. He parked his car in a spot with his name on it but then walked into the building so quickly that Emma wasn't able to do what she wanted.

Emma waited all morning near the parking lot, but Brayden never left the building. At noon, he came out the front entrance and started walking in the direction of a nearby shopping mall.

Before Emma left her car, she attached an earpiece with a microphone to her iPhone, the ear-mic intended for hands-free phone use while driving. In this case, however, she wanted the ear-mic for a reason that had nothing to do with driving. She fell in a block behind Brayden.

Brayden entered the shopping mall and walked to a crowded food court and ordered lunch from a place selling Chinese food. He took a seat at a table for two and began to eat. Emma headed toward a table fifty or sixty feet from him, and on her way to the table, she scooped up a magazine that someone had left.

While Brayden was eating lunch, he pulled out his phone—a standard smartphone with a six- or seven-inch screen—and it looked to Emma as if he was checking his e-mail. Emma noted that he pulled the phone out of the right-hand front pocket of his pants.

Emma placed her phone on the table in front of her and punched in the number she'd found in the phone hidden in John Lynch's ventilation duct. Before she hit the CALL button, she raised the magazine she'd grabbed and held it up so it was concealing the lower half of her face. When she punched CALL, she was too far away to hear a phone vibrating, but Brayden's head snapped up as if he'd received an electrical shock. He reached into his suit coat and pulled out a second phone—a phone identical to the one Emma had found in Lynch's apartment. He looked at the phone for a moment, and finally answered, saying, "Yes?"

Emma had no way to know that the burner phone Brayden was holding was not only the one he used to communicate with John Lynch, but also the phone he used to talk to Hector Montoya. He answered the phone when he saw he was getting a call from the 703 area code, thinking it might be Hector calling.

When Brayden answered, Emma, in a robotic voice, said, "Do you have credit card debt? Are your interest rates too high? If you do—"

She heard Brayden curse, and he hung up.

Up to this point, all Emma knew was that Lynch had called someone located at Spear Industries. But now she had what she needed: proof that John Lynch had been calling Bill Brayden.

But she wanted one more thing.

The next morning, Emma met with Pamela and Shandra at Neil's office to hear what they'd learned after tailing John Lynch and to discuss the next step in Emma's plan. Neil didn't like strangers coming to his office, but he was too afraid of Emma to object.

The young women—both more animated than Emma could ever remember—reported that yesterday morning Lynch had left his apartment, taken a bus to the Braddock Road Metro station in Alexandria, caught the Metro, and got off at the Capitol South station in D.C. He wore civilian clothes during his commute and put on his uniform after he arrived at the Capitol. All day yesterday he had been assigned to the east entrance, the one across from the Library of Congress, and spent the day checking ID badges before folks walked through the metal detector.

"Boring fucking job," Shandra said.

After work, his return trip home was the reverse of his morning commute. Before going home, however, he stopped at a bar called Rusty's, about two blocks from his apartment. He had a couple of beers, ate a hamburger, had a couple more beers, then headed home.

"We got the impression," Pamela said, "that this was his usual routine, to have dinner and a few after-work pops at this bar. The bartender knew him and BSed with him, and he chatted with a couple of the alkies sitting at the bar."

"Very good," Emma said. "Now here's what we're going to do next."

Emma told them her plan, and again they both looked absolutely thrilled to be part of it.

"Neil," Emma said, "what I want you to do is teach these young women how to use a parabolic mic and video camera. After you've given them a briefing on the equipment and practiced here in your office, I want you to go outside and practice on people walking around Georgetown. I'll meet you all back here at sixteen hundred hours."

"What?" Neil said.

"Four o'clock, Neil," Emma said. "Then the girls and I will head over to Alexandria."

Emma's plan was simple: She was going to panic Lynch into running to Brayden and, with the help of Shandra and Pamela, record their meeting. Then, with proof in hand that Lynch and Brayden knew each other, and a recording on which she was sure they would discuss Canton's murder, she would present the evidence to Peyton. If she needed to, she would force Peyton—with some help from the president's chief of staff—to get a warrant to search Lynch's apartment. If Peyton didn't find the money in the wall behind Lynch's closet or the cell phone hidden in the ventilation duct, Emma would give the FBI a few pointers on how to conduct a proper search. The search, plus the recording, would certainly be enough for Peyton to arrest Lynch and force him to confess. And unlike illegally breaking into Lynch's apartment, there was nothing illegal about her recording two men talking in a public place.

Yep, that was her simple plan.

What could possibly go wrong?

37

Anita Ramirez wasn't exactly insane. On the other hand, she wasn't exactly sane either.

She was nineteen—but looked older, thanks to an abnormal amount of wear and tear—and had been dating MS-13 gang members since she was thirteen. Almost all of Anita's past romantic relationships had ended in bloodshed, and her ex-boyfriends were the ones who usually bled.

As near as Hector Montoya could tell, Anita wasn't afraid of anything. She'd been involved in one drive-by shooting, in which MS-13 had retaliated against a Vietnamese gang, and Anita had been one of the shooters, not the driver or a passive passenger. She was suspected—not by the cops but by Hector—of killing a witness who'd testified against her last boyfriend, a man now serving fifteen years in Red Onion State Prison in Pound, Virginia.

Hector met Anita at her mother's house in Fairfax, where Anita was currently living, having been evicted from her last apartment. Anita told her mother to take Anita's two-year-old son—a kid pretty much destined to end up behind bars—into the bedroom. Her mother immediately did so; she was terrified of her daughter.

Hector told Anita what he wanted her to do and how much she'd be paid. Knowing her competitive nature, he pointed out that nine male members of MS-13 had been given the job and all had failed. Was she interested?

"Fuck, yeah," Anita said.

———◆◆◆———

Brian Moore and Steve Chin were the two men Mike Leary had watching DeMarco on the midnight to eight a.m. shift.

When the elevator dinged they both tensed up, then relaxed when they saw it was the little Muslim nurse. The graveyard shift was aptly named, because between midnight and six a.m. the hospital was as quiet as a cemetery, unless one of the patients flatlined. The little Muslim nurse had shown up for the first time yesterday. Except for the blue head scarf, she was dressed like the other female nurses and aides they'd seen, in a floral-patterned top, white pants, and running shoes. Pinned to her top she had a hospital badge that identified her as Louise Anderson, LPN. Anderson wasn't a Muslim-sounding name, and Brian and Steve figured it was her husband's last name. She *was* wearing a wedding ring.

As she'd done the previous night, the Muslim nurse walked down the hall holding a clipboard, entering various rooms along the way—not all the rooms, just some of them—and she stayed inside the rooms for only a couple of minutes. Last night she'd checked on DeMarco, and when she did, Steve had watched her. She'd looked at the clipboard hanging on the end of DeMarco's bed—the one that had the doctors' orders on it—and studied it for a bit. She'd gone over to the box that showed DeMarco's blood pressure, pulse, and temperature, and made sure everything was okay there. She'd checked to make sure the catheter bag was functioning the way it was supposed to and checked the IV bag on the stand to make sure that whatever was dripping into DeMarco was still dripping. When she'd left DeMarco's room she'd smiled shyly at Brian and Steve but didn't speak to them, then she'd headed for a room a couple of doors down the hall.

She did exactly the same thing tonight.

———————

Anita Ramirez figured the hijab was a stroke of brilliance. She knew the men guarding DeMarco might be looking for Mexicans, but a brown-skinned woman wearing a head scarf . . . Well, she didn't look like a Mexican. Or a terrorist, for that matter, not with the clothes she was wearing. She'd bought them after seeing how the nurses at the hospital dressed. She'd taken the ID badge from a white lab coat when the woman wearing it took the coat off in the cafeteria and went up to get her lunch. The fact that the woman had an Anglo-sounding name wasn't a problem after Anita put on her mother's wedding ring.

The problem was, she hadn't yet figured out how to kill DeMarco with the two bodyguards watching. She'd noticed, however, that they hadn't watched her as closely tonight as they had the first night she'd gone into DeMarco's room. They were getting used to her.

38

Emma decided to confront John Lynch in Rusty's, his local watering hole. She figured that in a public place he'd be less likely to do anything stupid—like shoot her.

Rusty's was a typical neighborhood dive, frequented mostly by blue-collar workers and local alcoholics who preferred not to drink alone. There were fifteen stools in front of the bar, six booths with red Naugahyde seats, and three televisions over the bar, muted and permanently set to various ESPN stations. A short-order cook, who was quick and competent, made hamburgers and sandwiches. A balding man with a beer gut and anchor tattoos on his forearms tended the bar.

Lynch had arrived at Rusty's fifteen minutes ago. Shandra was outside Spear Industries' building in Reston waiting for Bill Brayden to appear. Pamela was parked outside the bar and would follow Lynch when he left.

Lynch was seated near the end of the bar, by the door, having his first after-work beer, watching a Nats game playing on one of the TVs over the bar. Emma was struck once again by Lynch's appearance—the bald head, the porcine snout, the close-set eyes—and how clever it had been to frame DeMarco with a man who looked nothing like him. She also noted that Lynch seemed to be a contented man as he sat there sipping his beer, a man without a worry in the world. That would soon change.

Emma took a seat on the barstool next to him, and he looked over at her, clearly wondering why she'd decided to sit there when a dozen other barstools were empty.

The bartender hustled over and asked what Emma wanted. "Nothing for me," she said. "I won't be staying long. But bring John another beer."

"You got it," the bartender said.

Lynch said, "Do I know you?"

Emma said, "Good evening, John. How was your day?"

"My day was fine, but why are you buying me a drink?"

"Wait until the bartender brings your beer and I'll tell you."

The bartender placed another bottle of Bud in front of Lynch, and after he walked away, Lynch said, "So, who are you?"

"I'm the person who's going to make sure that you spend the rest of your natural life in prison."

"What? What in the hell are you talking about?"

Emma decided to tell Lynch the same thing that Olivia Prescott had told Nikki Orlov. She said, "I imagine they'll send you to one of the supermaxes, like the one in Florence, Colorado. I'm sure you've heard of it. You're locked in a cell twenty-three hours a day, the lights are always on, a surveillance camera is always watching you, and nobody speaks to you, not even the guards when they take you into the exercise yard. The average time it takes for someone to go insane is about five years, and you'll be there until you die."

"Goddamnit, what are you talking about?" Lynch said. He was growing agitated and appeared genuinely confused. But unless he'd committed some other crime, he had to know exactly what she was talking about.

"Lower your voice, John. You don't want anyone here to know what you've done."

"I haven't done a damn thing," Lynch said. "And I want to know—"

"Yes, you have, John. You killed Lyle Canton and helped frame Joe DeMarco for his murder."

Lynch stood up, jabbed a finger at Emma's face, and said, "Lady, you're fucking crazy. Get the hell away from me."

The bartender, seeing that Lynch was upset, said, "Everything okay, John?"

"Yeah, everything's fine," Lynch said to the bartender. He obviously didn't want the bartender to hear what they were talking about. It occurred to Emma that had Lynch been a more intelligent man he would have remained calm and let her continue to talk so he could learn more about what she knew. But he *wasn't* an intelligent man; she knew that from his air force file.

He started to say something to Emma—probably to tell her again to get away from him—but before he could, she said, "I've seen the video footage from the Capitol surveillance cameras. You only made one mistake. In one of the shots you can see a portion of the right side of your jaw and your chin, your double chin. The FBI has image-enhancing techniques you can't imagine, and all they need is one small part of your face to build a complete image and then, with a little help from me, they'll match that image to you."

Everything Emma had just said was a lie—but it sounded plausible.

Lynch, still standing, turned and looked over at the door, as if he were expecting FBI agents to walk in at any minute and arrest him. Or maybe he was wondering if he could make it to the door before anyone could stop him. Whatever was going on in his head, he looked as if he was ready to bolt.

"Are you a cop? I want to see some ID."

Emma could see no reason to answer his question, and the last thing she was going to do was identify herself. She said, "John, I'll give you one chance and one chance only. Tell me, right now, who paid you to kill Canton. It's the only way you'll be able to get a deal to reduce your sentence."

Lynch's hands clenched into fists and his eyes narrowed, and Emma wondered if he was thinking about taking a swing at her. He didn't. He hissed, "I'm telling you I don't know what you're talking about and I didn't have a damn thing to do with Canton's murder. You stay the hell away from me." Then he turned and practically ran out of the bar.

Emma had achieved her goal: John Lynch in a state of panic.

39

As soon as Lynch was out the door, Emma turned off the small tape recorder in her shirt pocket—nothing Lynch had said was useful—and called Pamela.

"Do you have him?" she said.

"Yeah, I got him," Pamela said. "He's walking toward his apartment. He's walking so fast he looks like a penguin."

What Emma expected to happen next was that after Lynch got over the shock of his encounter with her, he'd remove the hidden cell phone from the ventilation duct in his apartment and set up a meeting with Brayden. People these days, unless they were complete fools, would never say more than a couple of words on a cell phone, especially if they knew that someone who might be in law enforcement considered them suspects.

Emma also suspected that Brayden must already be nervous because of Nikita Orlov. He obviously hadn't shown up for work since the Russians had snatched him, and Brayden must be going crazy not knowing where Orlov was or why he couldn't reach him. When Lynch called Brayden—and she was sure he would—she was certain that Brayden would want to meet with Lynch.

Emma left the bar and drove over to Lynch's apartment, then went and sat with Pamela in her car to see what Lynch would do next. An hour later, Lynch was still inside his apartment.

———◆◆◆———

Bill Brayden had left Spear Industries about the time Emma confronted Lynch in Rusty's. He was now having dinner in a restaurant halfway between his office and his apartment in Arlington.

Shandra was sitting two tables away, having a Coke, pretending to study the menu.

A waitress had just placed Brayden's dinner in front of him, when Shandra saw him reach into his suit coat and pull out a cell phone. He looked at the screen for a moment, as if he was checking the caller's identity, then answered the phone.

"What are you doing calling me?" This was followed by a second of silence, and then Brayden saying, "Shut the hell up! I'll get back to you." Then, looking angry, Brayden disconnected the call.

Shandra texted Emma: *Someone just called him. He only talked for a second. He looks REALLY pissed.*

Emma texted back: *Good. Stick with him.*

Brayden sat without moving for ten minutes after he got the call, still holding the phone, looking pensive, ignoring his dinner. Finally, he typed a text message, then put the phone back in his pocket.

Shandra texted Emma: *He just sent a text.*

Emma texted back: *Perfect.*

Brayden stood up, tossed two twenties onto the table, and left the restaurant. Shandra waited a moment, then walked to the restaurant's entrance and watched, through a window next to the door, Brayden walk rapidly to his car. As soon as he left the parking lot, she ran to her car and took off after him.

Shandra hadn't felt so alive since Afghanistan.

By midnight, nothing had happened.

Bill Brayden was in his apartment.

Shandra was waiting outside Brayden's apartment, near the exit from the building's parking garage.

John Lynch was in his apartment.

Emma and Pamela were still sitting in Pamela's car, waiting outside Lynch's apartment. They'd run out of things to talk about two hours ago.

Emma had thought that Brayden would have wanted to meet with Lynch that night, but it appeared as if she'd been wrong. She wasn't: five minutes after she had that thought, Lynch walked out of his building and down the street to where his car was parked.

Emma texted Shandra: *Lynch is on the move. What's Brayden doing?*

Shandra texted: *No sign of him. Still in his apartment, I guess.*

Emma waited until Lynch disappeared from sight, then ran to her car, which was parked behind Pamela's, and took off after Lynch with Pamela following her.

Emma wasn't worried about losing Lynch. She doubted that he was the brightest candle in the candelabrum, but if he had any brains at all, he'd be concerned about someone following him to his meeting with Brayden. So what Emma had done that day—while Lynch was at work and while Neil had been teaching Pamela and Shandra how to use a video camera and a parabolic mic—was attach a GPS tracking device to the underside of Lynch's car (something else the FBI would have needed a warrant to do). The tracking device was a magnetic black disk, about the diameter of a fifty-cent piece, and only a quarter of an inch thick. Emma had smeared the top of it with grease and dirt from the underside of Lynch's car, and it looked as if it was part of the car's frame and was almost invisible. What Emma was now doing was looking at a small monitor, one about the size of a Garmin GPS device, suction-cupped to her dashboard. It showed a moving red dot—John Lynch's car.

Lynch made a number of what appeared to be random turns, but he was headed in a generally northwestward direction. Emma caught up with him at one point so she could actually see his car, then dropped back again and continued to track his progress with the GPS monitor. Finally Lynch stopped making arbitrary turns and got on Route 7, going in the direction of Arlington, where Brayden lived.

Emma called Shandra and asked, "What's Brayden doing?"

"Nothing," Shandra said. "No sign of him yet."

Emma once again pulled up close enough to see Lynch's taillights and watched him turn off Route 7 and onto George Mason Drive. Again she wondered if he could be headed to Brayden's apartment in Arlington, but then Lynch turned right on Columbus Drive, drove another couple of blocks, and turned right again, on Chesterfield Road.

Not the way to Brayden's place, Emma thought.

Then Lynch's car—or the red dot representing his car—stopped moving. He'd pulled into a parking lot adjacent to Barcroft Park. Emma was familiar with Barcroft Park, because a stream called Four Mile Run flowed through the park and she sometimes jogged on the trail next to the stream.

Emma drove past the parking lot with Pamela following her. She saw Lynch's car and could see him sitting in it. She called Shandra. "What's Brayden's status?"

"Still the same," Shandra said. "No sign of him."

Emma parked on Chesterfield Road, about three hundred yards from Lynch, and trained night-vision binoculars on his car. As she was doing this, Pamela parked behind her and joined Emma in her car.

"What's he doing?" Pamela asked. "Why's he just sitting there?"

"I'm hoping he's waiting for Brayden," Emma said.

A couple of moments later, Lynch got out of his car and walked out of the parking lot and over to a bus-stop bench where Chesterfield and Columbus intersected. Emma was certain he wasn't waiting for a bus at one in the morning.

Emma said to Pamela, "I wonder if Brayden told him to wait at the bus stop and he'll drive by and pick him up there." But this was not what Emma had wanted. She'd wanted Brayden to talk to Lynch someplace out in the open, so any discussion they had could be recorded. Nonetheless, she had to be prepared in case Brayden—assuming he was coming—decided to speak to Lynch right where he was.

She thought for a second, then said to Pamela, "You see the woods?" Behind the bus stop was a heavily wooded area that was part of Barcroft Park.

"Yeah," Pamela said.

"Leave your car here, circle around the parking lot so Lynch can't see you, and make your way into the woods with the video camera and the parabolic mic. Take up a position where you have a clear line of sight to Lynch and get ready to record Brayden if he shows up."

"Roger that," Pamela said. Her eyes were gleaming with excitement.

Pamela returned to her car, grabbed the recording equipment, and began jogging toward the woods. She was almost invisible in the darkness, dressed all in black, with a black watch cap covering her blond hair. In less than a minute, she'd disappeared from Emma's sight.

Emma's phone vibrated. Shandra said, "Brayden is just pulling out of his parking garage."

Yes! Emma said, "Don't tail him. I don't want to take the chance of him spotting you, and I know where he's going. He's headed to Barcroft Park, to a bus stop on the corner of Columbus and Chesterfield. Do you know where that is?"

"No," Shandra said. "I'm from D.C., not the suburbs where rich white ladies live."

Emma laughed. "Use your phone to locate the park. I'm parked about half a klick southeast of the bus stop, near the Claremont School."

"Copy that," Shandra said.

———◆◆◆———

Brayden's apartment in Arlington was about five miles from Barcroft Park, and Emma figured it would take him no more than ten minutes at this time of night to reach the bus stop.

She texted Pamela: *Are you ready with the camera and the mic? Brayden will be here soon.*

Pamela: *I'm ready.*

Almost exactly ten minutes later, Emma watched Brayden's Lexus drive up and park next to the bus stop. She was still hoping that Brayden would get out of his car and speak to Lynch, so Pamela could record their conversation, but doubted that was going to happen. It seemed more likely that Lynch would join Brayden in his car, and they'd talk while Brayden was driving. If that happened, Emma would have video proof that Lynch had met with Brayden but wouldn't be able to record what they said to each other.

But Brayden didn't join Lynch on the park bench.

Nor did Lynch get into Brayden's car.

Brayden did the last thing Emma had expected.

Through the night-vision binoculars, she saw Brayden extend his arm and then saw two tongues of flame.

Brayden had shot John Lynch where he sat, on the bus-stop bench.

40

Emma's phone vibrated.

Pamela screamed, "Jesus Christ! He just shot him, he fuckin' shot him!"

Emma said, "Did you video it?"

"No. It happened too fast. I had the camera in my hand, and I was ready to start filming when he got out of the car, but then he just shot the guy. I got video of him driving away, but that's all I got."

Damnit! Pamela should have started filming as soon as Brayden drove up.

By now Brayden was two blocks away, and Emma, without turning on her headlights, took off after him. She didn't know what she was going to do, other than follow him. For one thing, she wasn't armed. She hadn't been expecting to confront Brayden or Lynch, and she certainly hadn't expected Brayden to kill Lynch. Nor were Pamela and Shandra armed. No way was Emma going to give those two troubled young women weapons and put them in any position where they might be forced to shoot someone.

"What do you want me to do?" Pamela said. She was screaming into the phone. This was the last thing Emma had wanted: to expose Pamela and Shandra to more violence.

As she was driving, Emma said, "Pamela, honey, calm down. Go see if Lynch is alive. Check his pulse. If he's alive, call nine-one-one and try to help him. If he's dead, return to your car and get away from the park as fast as possible."

Pamela said, "Yeah, okay." She sounded as if she was barely functioning.

Emma called Shandra. "Where are you?"

"I'm a block behind you," Shandra said. "I can see your car. What happened?"

"Brayden shot Lynch."

"Oh, shit," Shandra said.

"Follow me," Emma said.

Brayden was still two blocks ahead of Emma. He'd slowed down after he'd sped away right after shooting Lynch. He clearly didn't want to take the chance of getting pulled over by a cop and was now observing the speed limit. Emma matched his pace, hoping he couldn't see her following with her headlights off.

Pamela called. "Lynch is dead. Jesus Christ, he's dead. The guy shot him twice right in the heart."

Emma said, "Pamela, I want you to take a deep breath. Go on, do it. Take a breath." She heard Pamela inhale and exhale over the phone. "Okay," Emma said. "Now go to your car and drive to Neil's office. I want him to look at the video you took and see what it shows."

Emma thought about telling Pamela to remove the tracking device from Lynch's car, but considering Pamela's state of mind, she decided she wanted her away from the crime scene as soon as possible. Plus the police would most likely do only a routine search of the car and the probability of them finding the tracking device hidden on the underside of the vehicle was small.

"Yeah, okay," Pamela said.

Brayden had headed north on Columbus from the bus stop, then turned onto George Mason Drive. Emma, still two blocks behind him, hit her brakes when she saw him stop on the bridge that passed over Four Mile Run. The next thing she saw, barely visible in the streetlights near the bridge, was an object fly out the passenger-side window of Brayden's car.

Emma had been too far away to see what Brayden had tossed from his car—but she knew what it was. She called Shandra, who was a block behind her.

"Brayden just threw a gun into Four Mile Run from the bridge on George Mason Drive."

"I saw his car stop on the bridge," Shandra said.

"Find the gun," Emma said. "Call Pamela. She's on her way to Neil's, but tell her to come back and help you."

"Roger that," Shandra said. "What are you going to do?"

"I'm not sure yet. Just find the gun."

Actually, Emma now had a plan—she just hadn't decided if she was going to follow through with it.

Emma could tell that Brayden was headed back to his apartment in North Arlington. She remained a couple of blocks behind him and watched as he turned into the apartment building's parking garage. After his car had entered the garage, she parked near the garage entrance.

She wasn't sure what had made Brayden decide to kill Lynch. She figured that with Nikita Orlov disappearing, Brayden was already nervous, and then he got a panic call from Lynch right after Emma had threatened him in Rusty's. She didn't know what Lynch had said to Brayden, but it was probably something along the lines of: *Some woman knows I killed Canton.* Or maybe he said: *We got a big problem. We need to meet.* Whatever was said, Brayden had decided that Lynch had become an intolerable liability and had to go.

And she knew exactly what Brayden was doing right now: he was destroying all the evidence linking him to Lynch's murder.

But what was *she* going to do?

41

Bill Brayden was proud that he was a man who never panicked.

He remembered one time in Afghanistan when somebody, either the Taliban or al-Qaeda—you never knew who the hell was trying to kill you over there—started lobbing rocket-propelled grenades into the Bagram air base. While everybody else had been running around, screaming and ducking for cover, he'd calmly assessed the situation and begun directing his security force to take out the attackers. He'd earned the Bronze Star for his actions that night.

He'd also been in a few tight situations while working for Sebastian Spear. With Spear, the risk of being arrested was greater than the risk of being killed, but the job still required that he stay in control and not become unnerved. And he was in control now. He'd never committed murder before, and he was pleased to see that he was focused only on the tasks he needed to perform. He wasn't wasting mental energy second-guessing his decision or worrying that he might be caught for what he'd done.

After he parked in the garage, he popped the trunk lock before getting out of the car. He was wearing gloves and mechanics' coveralls over his street clothes. Inside the trunk were a black garbage bag, a spray bottle of cleaning solution, and a few rags. Also inside were his license plates, which he'd removed in case someone saw his car when he shot Lynch.

He walked a few feet away from his car, carefully stripped off the coveralls and his gloves, never touching the outside of any of the items, then placed everything in the black garbage bag. Next he put the license plates back on his car and, using the cleaning solution and the rags, carefully wiped down the interior of the car, paying particular attention to the frame around the passenger-side front window. He was fairly confident that no one had seen him shoot Lynch—it had been after one o'clock in the morning, and there'd been no one on the street near the bus stop—but if by some fluke someone had seen him, he had to make sure there was no gunshot residue in the car.

After he'd wiped down the car, he deposited the rags in the same garbage bag that contained his coveralls. Then he stood for a moment, thinking, to see whether there was anything he'd overlooked.

He'd gotten rid of the gun, so that wasn't a concern, and he knew he hadn't left his fingerprints on it. He'd found the shell casings ejected from the gun on the passenger seat of his car, and he'd dropped them onto the street as he'd been driving back to his place. He knew his fingerprints weren't on the shell casings, either, as he'd worn gloves when he'd loaded the magazine.

The only thing to do now was dispose of the clothes he'd worn and the cell phone he'd used to communicate with Lynch and Hector Montoya. Unfortunately, he hadn't had time after he shot Lynch to remove Lynch's cell phone, and the police would find it after they found the body. But what they *wouldn't* be able to find was the phone that Lynch had been texting and calling—Brayden's burner phone.

Brayden left the parking garage gripping the black garbage bag with a rag to make sure he didn't leave fingerprints on it. Instead of going up to his apartment on the third floor, he took the elevator to the lobby and left the building via the main entrance, which was on the opposite side of the building from the parking garage.

He walked at a normal pace to a restaurant two blocks from his apartment; he didn't see a soul while he was walking. There were three large dumpsters behind the restaurant, overflowing with trash, and he shoved his garbage bag into one of them. On the way back to his apartment, he removed the battery from the burner phone and dumped the battery and the phone down a storm drain.

Back inside his apartment, the first thing Brayden did was pour himself a scotch. A double. It was now almost three a.m., and he was tired, but his mind was spinning and he knew he wouldn't be able to fall asleep.

When Lynch had called him earlier in the evening while he was eating dinner, Lynch had screamed into the phone that some woman had just accused him of murdering Lyle Canton. His actual words were: *Some bitch knows I killed Canton.* Brayden had immediately told the idiot to shut up and disconnected the call before he could say anything more. Killing a United States congressman was not something you discussed over a fucking radio where some eavesdropping federal agency could snatch your words right out of the air.

After he disconnected the call he thought about who the woman could be. He was positive that she wasn't an FBI agent, because the FBI didn't work that way. If the FBI had evidence that Lynch had killed Canton, they would have arrested him. If they didn't have enough evidence for an arrest but suspected him, they wouldn't have told him that he was a suspect. What they would have done was throw a surveillance net around him—and Brayden knew that hadn't happened or he would have been arrested when he shot Lynch. He figured the woman was most likely someone who worked in the Capitol and maybe saw Lynch the night Canton was killed. She might even be another Capitol cop. He also figured that she really had no interest in having Lynch arrested.

If she'd wanted that to happen she would have called the FBI. Maybe she'd been thinking about blackmailing Lynch.

Whatever the case, and regardless of who the woman was, he'd decided less than ten minutes after Lynch called him that Lynch had to die. Lynch had always been the weakest link in the operation because he wasn't terribly bright, and he needed to be killed before he did something stupid that could tie Brayden to Canton's death. As far as Brayden knew, the only connection between him and Lynch that the cops would be able to find would be a text message on Lynch's phone telling Lynch to meet him at Barcroft Park at one a.m.—and the phone that had sent the text message was gone, as was all the other evidence that could tie him to Lynch's murder. Yes, with Lynch gone he should be safe.

Lynch. He couldn't believe it when he saw the damn guy at the Capitol one day. This had been over a year ago, when Brayden, along with a couple of Spear's lawyers, had been forced to testify in a House hearing that lasted two days. A congressman had been outraged that Spear Industries had been awarded a contract that should have gone to a company that contributed heavily to the congressman. So the outraged congressman, along with a few of his cronies who wanted to get their mugs on television, had futilely grilled Brayden and the lawyers for hours on end. The second morning of the hearing, when Brayden walked into the Capitol, he was astounded to see Lynch there, wearing the uniform of a Capitol cop.

Brayden remembered Lynch well from his days in the air force because he'd had Lynch arrested and court-martialed for stealing ten laptops that Lynch most likely had been planning to sell to college kids on a campus near the base. The problem was that although Brayden knew Lynch was guilty, he wasn't able to prove it, not beyond a reasonable doubt, and Lynch had been acquitted. Lynch had been a slug while in the air force: lazy, undisciplined, a shirker, a drinker. Twice MPs had had to be called to his house when he was slapping his wife around. Yet here the damn guy was protecting the Capitol. If that didn't say everything there was to say about hiring standards for federal employees, he didn't know what did.

When Sebastian Spear had ordered him to kill Canton, one of the ideas Brayden came up with was framing someone for Canton's murder so the investigation could be closed quickly and not traced back to him. And that's when it occurred to him that John Lynch, with his access to the Capitol, might be the perfect person to use. He had Nikki Orlov research Lynch, and he discovered that Lynch was practically broke, living in a dump, and had no prospects for advancement with the Capitol Police. So one day he waited until Lynch left work and approached him as he was trudging to the Metro station.

He said, "John, I'd like to talk to you." Naturally, because of their past, Lynch had been belligerent.

He said, "I don't give a damn what you want, *Colonel*. I'm not in the air force, and you're not my boss."

That's when Brayden said, "John, how would you like to earn half a million dollars?"

It took some time to convince Lynch to do what he wanted—but not that much time. Lynch's character hadn't improved since his discharge from the air force. What really took the time—almost four months— was finding someone to frame for killing Canton and preparing Lynch to do the job.

Nikki Orlov had hacked into personnel files and found a number of men who might be suitable to frame. They'd finally settled on DeMarco, this mysterious lawyer who worked in the subbasement and had a mob hit man for a father and ties to John Mahoney, a man known to despise Canton. Nikki discovered the Mahoney-DeMarco connection when he started monitoring DeMarco's cell phone. (Nikki, Brayden recalled, had a wonderful time helping frame DeMarco. For him it was like being back in the GRU.)

Brayden had then set to work figuring out all the details: the fake insignia patch, how to make sure DeMarco would be in the Capitol the night Canton was killed, the locations of surveillance cameras, and how Lynch would get to Canton's office without being identified. Military operations have been planned with less precision. He'd had Lynch make a copy of DeMarco's office key—the Capitol Police had keys for every room in the building—and had Lynch take pictures of DeMarco's office. When Brayden saw DeMarco's rain hat hanging on a coatrack, he told Lynch to remove as many hairs as he could from the hat, hoping to use DeMarco's DNA to tie him conclusively to Canton's murder.

Another thing that had taken so long was training Lynch. With Nikki's help, Lynch had mapped out all the surveillance cameras on the various routes to Canton's office. Then, using three-dimensional computer modeling, Nikki had selected the exact route Lynch would take and determined how he would hide his features from the cameras. They actually laid out Lynch's route to Canton's office by spray-painting it on the floor of a Spear Industries' warehouse and then had Lynch practice for days, walking the route and turning his head and holding up his hands to cover his face when he was supposed to.

Brayden, with Orlov's help, also began monitoring Canton's schedule, and he knew that on the Friday night they killed him, Canton would be in his office working late. It helped that Canton almost always worked late. They also knew where DeMarco was going to be that Friday night, because Nikki had learned about DeMarco's date at 701 from monitoring his phone calls. The day of the murder, Nikki transferred a hundred grand into DeMarco's bank account, sent a text message from Mahoney's cell phone to DeMarco's phone ordering DeMarco to the Capitol, and then—. Well, then everything went exactly as planned. That is, everything went as planned until this unknown woman came along who claimed to know that Lynch had killed Canton.

But now that Lynch was dead, there should be no way for anyone to tie Brayden to Canton's murder. However, he still had two problems—which was another reason he'd poured a drink to help him sleep.

One problem was DeMarco—the fact that the lucky son of a bitch was still alive. But that was a problem that should be rectified shortly by Hector Montoya.

The second problem was Nikki Orlov.

Brayden had no idea where Orlov was or why he'd disappeared or why he wasn't answering his phone. Maybe Orlov, an incorrigible womanizer, had met a bimbo and was having some sort of sexual marathon. That seemed unlikely, however. Orlov had taken a few days off in the past when he was enamored with a woman, but he'd always remained in touch.

Another possibility was that Orlov had convinced himself that he was going to be caught for his role in Canton's murder and had decided to run so he wouldn't be arrested. But that too seemed unlikely. Orlov hadn't shown any concern that he might be caught after Canton was killed; in fact, he'd acted as if framing DeMarco for the murder was some sort of elaborate video game.

A third possibility that Brayden could think of when it came to Orlov's disappearance was that maybe the Russians had spotted him and decided to snatch him. Or kill him. For his first few months of working for Brayden, Orlov had been extremely nervous that the Russians might locate him in the United States, and he'd maintained a low profile. But then, for whatever reason, he suddenly stopped worrying about the Russians and began to live a normal life. Even a flamboyant life. Whatever the case, if Orlov ever showed up again, Brayden might kill him, too, to make sure that Canton's death could never be traced back to himself. That would really be a shame, as Orlov was extremely valuable.

Brayden finished his drink and decided to go to bed. He hoped he'd be able to sleep.

42

As Emma sat in her car near the entrance to Bill Brayden's parking garage, her phone rang. It was Shandra.

"We found the gun."

Emma had been pretty sure they would. Four Mile Run, particularly in the summer, wasn't that deep or that fast moving.

"What do you want us to do with it?" Shandra said.

Emma had been thinking about the answer to that question for the last hour. She said, "Strip it down and dry it off completely." A couple of ex-soldiers would know how to field-strip a weapon. "But Shandra, make sure you don't leave your fingerprints on any part of the gun. Do you understand?"

Shandra hesitated. "Yeah."

"Then bring the gun to me. I'm in my car, near Brayden's apartment building."

"Roger that," Shandra said. Emma noticed that Shandra sounded more subdued than she had at the beginning of the operation.

Half an hour later Shandra drove up, parked behind Emma, and joined Emma in her car. Holding the gun with a cloth, she handed it to Emma. It was a Beretta 92 with a silencer.

"Are your prints on any part of this weapon?" Emma asked.

"No way," Shandra said.

"Good. Now I want you and Pamela to wait for me at Neil's place. I don't know how long I'll be, probably several hours."

"Man, I need a drink," Shandra said.

"No, you don't," Emma said. "You're stronger that, and so is Pamela. You need to be strong for each other."

Emma really regretted having involved Pamela and Shandra in the operation. But there was nothing to be done about that now—other than make sure that Bill Brayden was arrested for murder.

———◆◆◆———

After Shandra left, Emma waited for five minutes. It was almost three a.m., and she was sure that by now Brayden had done everything he could to destroy any evidence tying him to Lynch's murder.

Emma removed a small case from her glove compartment. The case contained her lock picks, the ones she'd used to break into John Lynch's apartment. She verified there were no security cameras near the parking garage entrance and then approached it. The garage had a roll-up metal gate that required a key card to open, but there was also a side door to the garage. Emma picked the side door lock.

She found Brayden's Lexus, picked the lock on his trunk, lifted the carpet concealing the spare tire, and put the Beretta next to the tire.

As she walked back to her car, she thought: *Let's see how you like being framed, Mr. Brayden.*

43

About the time Emma was planting evidence in Bill Brayden's car, Brian Moore and Steve Chin were watching the little Muslim nurse get off the elevator with her clipboard and begin her rounds. This was the third night they'd seen her; she obviously wasn't a threat.

***

Anita Ramirez entered the room of an old man hooked up to all the hospital shit. It seemed he would take a breath about every five minutes, taking so long between breaths that Anita wondered if he was ever going to breathe again. She just hoped the old bastard didn't croak while she was in the room. That would probably set off some fucking alarm, and a real nurse would hustle down to check on him.

After a few minutes passed, she left the room, closing the door quietly, and went to another room down the hall. She'd been in this room before, too; it contained an old lady balder than a cue ball from cancer treatments. As luck would have it, the old bitch woke up when Anita walked in. She said, "Are you here to give me more medication?"

"No," Anita said, "I just came to check on you, but I'll let the nurse know you're hurting. She's busy now but will be here soon. You want some water or something?"

Of course the old bitch wanted water, so Anita filled up one of the tiny cups by the sink and held it to her scabby lips as she slurped, the water dribbling down her chin. It was disgusting. "Thank you," the woman croaked.

"Not a problem," Anita said. "And like I said, the nurse will be here soon, but don't be surprised if it takes a few minutes."

In other words, don't go pressing the fucking button to call the nurse.

Anita left the old lady's room and proceeded toward DeMarco's room.

Tonight was the night.

In the pocket of her nurse's smock was a syringe filled with 100 percent pure heroin, enough to kill three small junkies or one large horse.

What Anita wasn't aware of was an event that had started two days earlier and was still ongoing.

44

Mike Leary had told Emma he had an idea for how to keep MS-13 from killing DeMarco, and—Leary being a military man—his plan was aggressive and direct. He was going to persuade the yahoo in charge of the gang to leave DeMarco alone.

Mike could be very persuasive.

He contacted the gang units in several police departments in northern Virginia—Arlington, Alexandria, Fairfax—and asked who ran MS-13 in their jurisdictions. The cops cooperated with Mike because he was in the security business, and some of them did so because they figured his company might hire them after they retired from the force. The answer he got to his question was always the same: the guy he was looking for was a smart, vicious prick named Hector Montoya.

But then Mike couldn't find Hector. Fairfax and Arlington had two different addresses for him, and the Virginia DMV had a third one, but Hector wasn't at any of those addresses. He'd been evicted from all three for failing to pay his rent. Mike talked to Hector's parole officer, who had a fourth address that turned out to be an abandoned building. He called the cops back and asked for the names of former gang members who might talk to him, guys who had turned their lives around and were now working straight jobs. He knew talking to active gang members would not only be a waste of time but that they would warn Hector that he was hunting for him. Most of the former gangsters, however, either wouldn't talk to him or had no idea where Hector might be, but one of them suggested he go to see Hector's grandmother. He said Hector sometimes stayed with her when he had no other place else to stay. But the guy didn't know the grandmother's name—Hector just called her Grandma—and he didn't know where she lived, so Mike wasted more time identifying the woman and getting an address for her.

Accompanying Mike in his search for Hector were two of his men, selected for their size and appearance. Mike Leary himself was in good shape, he was strong and quick, and could hike twenty miles carrying a hundred-pound pack, but he was only five foot nine and your first impression—which would be completely wrong—was that he didn't pose much of a threat. The two guys accompanying him—one black, one white—were both about six foot four and looked strong enough to pick up the back end of a dump trunk. Their size, however, wasn't their only redeeming quality: they both had the ability to smile at a potential adversary in such a way that the adversary would have no doubt that they would enjoy tearing him limb from limb and eating his heart afterward. The black man could also speak fluent Spanish.

Mike and his guys drove to Grandma's house in Fairfax. Hector wasn't there, and when Mike asked Grandma, through his giant interpreter, where her grandson might be, she said, "What's that fool done now?"

"He hasn't done anything that I'm aware of," Mike said. "And we're not the police. I just need to talk to him."

"You're lying," Grandma said. Before Mike could say that he really wasn't lying, Grandma added, "He's an animal. I don't care what you do to him."

Mike couldn't help thinking that when your own grandmother didn't like you, you had to be one nasty piece of work.

"But I don't know where he is," Grandma said. "You should go talk to Rhonda."

"Who's Rhonda?" Mike said.

"The mother of his two kids."

Grandma didn't know Rhonda's address, but she knew the street where Rhonda lived and was able to provide a description of her house.

By the time Mike spoke to Rhonda it was ten p.m. on his second day of hunting for Hector.

Mike had no idea he was up against the clock.

Rhonda said, "I don't let him stay with me no more. The last time he was here, he—. Never mind what he did, but I told him he came here again, I'd cut his throat while he was sleeping, and he knew I meant it."

Mike could hardly wait to meet this guy. He thanked Rhonda and turned to leave, having no idea what he was going to do next, when Rhonda said, "This time of night he's probably at Zanta's, drinking with his homies." Then she added, "When you find him, I hope you kill the son of a bitch."

———————◆◆◆———————

Around one a.m.—about the time Bill Brayden was shooting John Lynch—Mike and his guys were sitting in Mike's SUV outside Zanta's waiting for Hector to leave the bar. Hector was inside with six or seven other MS-13 guys, playing pool and tossing down endless shots of tequila. Mike knew if he tried to take Hector in Zanta's there'd be a gunfight, for sure, and he didn't want to shoot anyone.

At two, Hector came out of the bar alone, but instead of going to his car he staggered across the street to an all-night convenience store. Mike parked the SUV directly in front of the store, and he and his large companions followed Hector inside. There were no other customers, just a young Korean man behind the counter. As Hector was ordering a pack of Marlboros, Mike walked up to him and said, "Hector Montoya, you're under arrest. You're coming with us."

Before Hector could say anything, Mike's guys slammed him against the counter and handcuffed him.

"Hey, I didn't do anything," Hector said.

They hauled Hector outside and tossed him into Mike's SUV, then Mike's guys joined Hector in the back seat, crushing his body between them. Mike got behind the wheel and took off fast, before any of Hector's men noticed what was happening and decided to get involved.

Hector said, "What are you arresting me for?"

Mike said, "Shut up. We'll talk in a minute."

Hector said, "Hey, I got a right to—"

Mike heard Hector grunt—as if someone had just driven an elbow into his ribs.

Mike drove around until he spotted an elementary school. He said out loud, "This will do," and drove to the unlit parking lot behind the school.

"Where the hell are you taking me?" Hector said—and another elbow hit his ribs.

It was now two forty-five in the morning, and unbeknownst to Mike, Anita Ramirez, in her Muslim headdress, was walking down the hall toward DeMarco's hospital room.

Mike parked, and his men pulled Hector from the car.

Mike looked at Hector—the soul patch beneath his lip, the teardrop tattoos near his left eye, the words *Mara Salvatrucha* inked below his collarbone—and thought: *You pathetic punk. You want to belong to a real gang, you should join* my *old gang, the U.S. Army.*

"Pat him down," Mike said, and one of his guys did. Hector wasn't armed, not even with a knife.

"Take off the handcuffs," Mike said.

"Hey, I got rights," Hector said, still under the impression that Mike was a cop.

Hector was a tough guy, but Mike could tell he was terrified, standing there in a dark parking lot with Mike's oversize pals looming over him. Cops don't take you out behind a school at night if they want to question you. They do that when they've decided that beating the shit out of you is more sensible than an arrest.

Mike said, "Hector, we're not cops, and you don't have any rights. I've been told you're the head of MS-13 in this area."

"So what? It's just a social club."

Mike couldn't help smiling at that. He said, "Your social club has tried three times to kill a man named Joe DeMarco. You tried twice in the Alexandria jail and once in the hospital where he's recovering from being poisoned. What I'm here to tell you is that if DeMarco is killed—"

"Hey, I don't even know who this fuckin' DeMarco guy is," Hector said.

Mike sighed. "Like I told you, Hector, we're not cops. You could say we belong to a gang just like you do, and we look out for the guys in our gang. Well, DeMarco's one of us. So I'm not bullshitting you, Hector. If DeMarco is killed, nobody is going to arrest you. What's going to happen is that I'm going to kill you. I'm going to find you—just like I found you tonight—then me and my friends here are going to take you into the woods, and I'm going to put a bullet in your head. Do you understand?"

"Yeah," Hector said. "I understand."

Mike looked into Hector's eyes. "I don't believe you, Hector."

Mike reached behind his back and pulled out the .357 revolver he carried in a holster on his belt. He placed the muzzle of the gun against Hector's forehead.

"Hey!" Hector said. "I'm telling you, nobody's going to bother this DeMarco guy. I swear."

Mike didn't say anything. He pulled back the hammer on the .357, and it made an ominous *click*.

"I swear!" Hector screamed.

Mike kept the .357 pressed hard against Hector's forehead head for a long five seconds before he finally lowered the gun. "All right," he said. "But, Hector, I'm a man who always keeps his word, and if anything happens to DeMarco, you're a dead man."

Hector swallowed, then nodded his head.

Mike said to his men, "Let's go. I think Hector got the message."

Mike hadn't asked Hector why he was trying to kill DeMarco or who was paying him to do so as Emma had indicated that she already knew the answers to those questions. And knowing Emma, Mike had no doubt she was dealing with the people responsible. His job tonight had only been to make sure Hector didn't keep trying—and he was certain that he'd succeeded.

———◆———

Hector's heart was hammering in his chest. Those sons a bitches, whoever they were, were *serious* dudes. No way did he want them coming after him.

He looked at his watch.

Oh, shit. It was three a.m.

He hoped like hell that he wasn't too late.

45

Anita Ramirez was pretty sure she could make it work. The two body-guards were used to her. She'd smile at them as she'd done the last two nights, go into DeMarco's room, and pretend to check on things—and in particular she'd check to make sure the IV was still dripping.

The plastic tube that went from the IV bag to a vein in DeMarco's forearm had a place where a syringe could be inserted if the staff had to inject something extra into DeMarco's bloodstream—and that's what Anita was going to do: inject something extra, a syringe full of pure heroin. By the time DeMarco's body reacted to the heroin and all the monitors went off like fucking fire alarms, she'd be off the floor, sprinting down the stairs, running to her car. She'd lose the Muslim head scarf on the way.

She reached the door to DeMarco's room and smiled at the guards. One of them said, "How you doin' tonight?" Anita had never spoken to the guards, afraid if she did they'd notice her Spanish accent. When they talked to her, she just smiled and nodded, the way people do when they can't speak English well. And that's what she did when the body-guard said hello tonight: she nodded and smiled like a grinning monkey and went into DeMarco's room.

She checked the clipboard at the end of the bed, the one containing the doctors' orders and the medications DeMarco had been prescribed. As she moved over to look at the IV bag, DeMarco opened his eyes.

Oh, shit! She stood there, unable to move, unsure what she should do. She noticed that his eyes were unfocused, and although he was looking at her, she wondered if he was really seeing her. It was as if he was sleeping with his eyes open. Then, thank God, he shut his eyes and seemed to go back to sleep.

She waited a couple of seconds and moved again toward the IV bag—at that moment one of the damn bodyguards glanced into the room and over at her. She nodded and smiled and pretended to check the catheter bag, as she'd done the previous two nights, and the bodyguard turned away and started bullshitting with his buddy again.

It was time. She had to do it now, and she had to do it fast, before anything else happened.

She pulled the syringe out of the pocket of her nursing smock, removed the protective cap over the needle, and reached for the IV line—and her phone rang.

Son of a bitch! The ringing phone made her jump, just scaring the shit out of her, and when it rang the bodyguards looked into the room.

She pulled the phone from her pocket, intending to silence it, then saw it was Hector calling. She turned her back to the guards, hit the ACCEPT button, and whispered into her phone, "What is it?"

"Get the hell out of the hospital. Don't do anything. Go right now. Now!"

Anita closed the phone and put the syringe back in her pocket, hoping the needle wouldn't stick her. She took a last look at DeMarco as she was leaving the room, thinking: *You are one lucky motherfucker.*

46

After Emma hid the gun in the trunk of Bill Brayden's car, she drove to the nearest twenty-four-hour store for a cup of coffee. She needed the caffeine, as she had hours to go before she'd be able to sleep. Back in her car, sipping the coffee, she called Special Agent Russell Peyton. The fact that it was three in the morning didn't bother her in the least.

Peyton answered his phone, sounding understandably groggy. "Peyton," he said. "Who is this?"

"It's Emma."

"Why are you calling me at this time of night?"

"Listen carefully, Agent Peyton. Sitting on a bus-stop bench near Barcroft Park in Arlington, at the corner of Columbus and Chesterfield, is a man named John Lynch. John Lynch is—or was—a Capitol policeman. He's dead."

"What?" Peyton said, no longer sounding groggy.

"Lynch is the man who murdered Lyle Canton, and I know who murdered John Lynch, because I was a witness."

"What in the hell are you talking about?"

Emma forged ahead. "The first thing you need to do is call the Arlington cops. If they haven't found Lynch's body yet, tell them where it is and to preserve the crime scene until your people can get there."

"What in the hell have you done?" Peyton shrieked.

"Just do what I'm telling you, Mr. Peyton. Call Arlington and tell them about Lynch. I'll meet you at the Hoover Building in one hour and explain everything. I'll be bringing my lawyer with me. I'd suggest you bring a DOJ lawyer but only one. I don't want to see a conference room full of bureaucrats."

Emma hung up before Peyton could say anything else. When her phone immediately rang again—the screen showing the caller was Peyton—she sent the call to voice mail.

Emma's next call was to her lawyer, Janet Evans.

She said, "I'm sorry to do this to you, Janet, but I need you to meet me at the Hoover Building in one hour. I want a witness to a meeting I'm going to have with the FBI. I also want you there to keep me from being arrested."

Peyton and a DOJ lawyer—a sharp-eyed black woman in her forties— were seated on one side of a conference table that could accommodate twenty people. Emma and Janet Evans were seated on the other side. Peyton looked as if he felt like killing something; the lawyer looked as if she'd enjoy skinning whatever he killed.

Emma said, "Have the cops found John Lynch's body?"

"Yeah, and my guys are on the scene right now."

Emma said, "Good. Now here's what happened."

Emma explained that from the beginning she'd been convinced that DeMarco was being framed. She reminded Peyton that she'd told him this; she still didn't admit, however, to knowing DeMarco. She said that because the FBI appeared to be doing nothing to look for another suspect, she'd looked for one on her own.

Using the Capitol Police personnel files that Peyton had provided, she looked for Capitol cops about DeMarco's size with some connection to Sebastian Spear—and she found John Lynch, a man who'd been in the air force at the same time as Spear's head of security, Bill Brayden. She also learned that Brayden was the guy Sebastian Spear used when Spear needed somebody to get his hands dirty. She didn't mention that Neil had helped her.

Emma said, "I also learned in the course of my investigation that Lynch had a large amount of cash hidden in his apartment."

"Wait a goddamn minute," Peyton said. "How did you learn this?"

"It doesn't matter," Emma said. "I know it's there." She could see no reason to tell Peyton that she'd broken into Lynch's apartment and ripped out a wall. Before Peyton could say that it sure as hell *did* matter, Emma said, "Because John Lynch is now a murder victim, you'll be able to search his apartment without a warrant and I'm sure you'll find the money. I'm certain the money is what Lynch was paid to kill Canton."

Peyton started to say something, but Emma held up a halting hand. "Tonight, I decided to follow Lynch to see what else I might learn. I asked a friend to help me, and my friend and I saw Bill Brayden shoot Lynch while Lynch was sitting at the bus stop in Arlington. I have video footage of Brayden driving away from the shooting scene, but unfortunately wasn't able to video him in the act of shooting Lynch."

Emma decided not to tell Peyton that she'd panicked Lynch into meeting with Brayden. Why dig the hole she'd dug for herself any deeper?

"Can you believe this woman?" Peyton said to the DOJ lawyer.

The lawyer didn't respond. She was beginning to appreciate that Emma was not your average witness/criminal.

Emma said, "While my friend confirmed that Lynch was dead—she would have called for an ambulance if he hadn't been—I followed Brayden. I witnessed him put the murder weapon in the trunk of his car."

That was actually the only lie that Emma told.

"In summary, Agent Peyton, what you have are two eyewitnesses who saw Brayden kill John Lynch and a video showing Brayden's car leave the scene. Based on my testimony, you'll be able to get a warrant to search Brayden's car and find the weapon he used to kill Lynch."

As might be expected, Peyton wanted to know a lot more than Emma had told him, and he was bright enough to know that she wasn't telling him everything. So for the next several minutes Peyton bombarded her with questions. Among them was: Who was Emma's friend that had witnessed the killing?

"A distinguished war veteran named Pamela Stewart," Emma said. She didn't see any reason to mention Pamela's issues with PTSD.

When Peyton ran out of questions about Lynch's murder, he said, "Can you prove Lynch killed Canton?"

"No," Emma said. "But you'll have enough evidence to convict Brayden of the first-degree murder of John Lynch. And unlike the District of Columbia, the state of Virginia still has the death penalty on the books, and killing a cop is a death-penalty offense. Therefore, you can threaten Brayden with lethal injection unless he agrees to confess to his and Sebastian Spear's role in killing Lyle Canton."

Emma decided not to mention Nikki Orlov at this point. Orlov's part in framing DeMarco would most likely come out in the future, but Emma wanted to give her NSA friend, Olivia Prescott, a heads-up that the FBI might soon be talking to her about Orlov. Olivia wouldn't be happy, but there was nothing Emma could do about that.

The meeting digressed for a while, as Peyton felt compelled to rant about what Emma had done, and the DOJ lawyer wasted some time threatening Emma with obstruction of justice, interfering in a federal investigation, and violations of a few obscure federal statutes.

When they finished ranting and threatening, Emma said, "Right now the wrong man is in jail for killing Lyle Canton. Agent Peyton, I'm a person who dislikes speaking to the media, but I'm willing to make an exception in this case. I'd suggest that instead of getting your nose out of joint because I caught the killers and you didn't, you should just thank me. I have no desire to take any credit. I'm willing to give all the credit to you. And what that means is that instead of looking like a complete fool for arresting the wrong man, you'll get all the glory for arresting the right one."

Emma left the Hoover Building sans handcuffs and immediately broke her promise not to tell anyone about the imminent arrest of Bill Brayden.

She woke up John Mahoney.

After calling Mahoney, Emma drove to Neil's office, where Pamela and Shandra were waiting for her.

Neil looked unhappy, because Shandra and Pamela had tracked mud—picked up on their shoes while they were hunting for Brayden's gun in Four Mile Run—all over his office. He was also unhappy that in response to the stress, they'd both been smoking in his office—but he'd been afraid to tell them to stop. He could tell they were agitated, and either one of them could have bent his overweight frame into the shape of a pretzel.

"I'm so sorry this happened," Emma said to the two veterans. "I just wanted you to help me prove that Brayden and Lynch knew each other. If I had known that Brayden was going to kill Lynch, I never would have involved you." Speaking to Pamela, she said, "The last thing I ever wanted was for you to see that man killed. The good news, thanks to you, is that the FBI will be able to get Brayden for killing Lynch, and Brayden will confess to conspiring with Lynch to kill Canton, which means my friend, DeMarco, will be freed."

"Am I going to have to testify in court that I saw Brayden kill Lynch?" Pamela asked.

"Maybe, but I don't think so," Emma said. "I think Brayden will cut a deal with the FBI, and there won't be a trial. But you will have to give a statement to the FBI and the Virginia cops that you saw Brayden kill him."

"What do I say?"

"The truth, but no more than necessary. Basically, you'll just say that you were with me in the park when Brayden drove up and shot Lynch, and you videotaped him driving away. We'll figure out the exact wording of your statement later, and my lawyer will be with you when you give it."

"What about finding the gun in the creek?" Shandra asked.

"You say nothing about that. Neither of you. Ever. And Shandra, the police don't know that you helped me tonight, and I don't intend to tell them that you did."

Emma smiled at them. "You two performed *marvelously*, and I'm so proud of you. And you should be very proud of yourselves for taking part in something that will free an innocent man."

"What about me?" Neil said.

"Shut up, Neil," Emma said.

47

Bill Brayden was awakened at six a.m. by what he thought was an explosion. What he'd actually heard was the sound of his apartment door being bashed open by a big cop with a battering ram. Seconds later Brayden, still in somewhat of a dream state, saw two guys in body armor pointing M4 rifles at his head, screaming at him to show his hands. This wasn't a dream; it was a wide-awake nightmare.

And the nightmare continued. He was informed that he was being arrested for the murder of John Lynch. Papers were waved in his face: warrants to search his apartment and his car. He was taken, as DeMarco had been, to the Alexandria city jail. The irony of this never occurred to him, as he had other things on his mind, the most prominent of which was: *How in the hell did they catch me only five hours after I killed Lynch?*

He was told he had the right to an attorney, and he exercised that right immediately by contacting one of the lawyers who worked at Spear Industries. Two hours after he was arrested, he and his attorney met with FBI agent Russell Peyton and a DOJ lawyer. Brayden's lawyer asked why the FBI was involved, since the crime his client had allegedly committed should be under the jurisdiction of some Virginia state law enforcement agency.

To this Peyton said, "Oh, your client will be prosecuted by the state of Virginia. We *want* him prosecuted by Virginia, because Virginia ranks number four in states that have the most executions. In fact, did you know that in Virginia, they actually let you pick your preferred method of execution, either lethal injection or electrocution?"

Brayden's lawyer snapped, "Why are you telling my client this? Are you trying to intimidate him?"

Peyton ignored what he considered to be a rhetorical question. "Mr. Brayden, let me tell you where things stand right now. We have two eyewitnesses who saw you shoot John Lynch, a U.S. Capitol policeman. You killed a cop. We also have a video of your Lexus driving away from the murder scene. The video doesn't show your face, but the time the video was taken matches the time the eyewitnesses saw you shoot Brayden."

"I don't know any John Lynch," Brayden said.

"Shut up, Bill," Brayden's lawyer said.

Peyton wagged a finger at Brayden and said, "No, no, Bill. That lie won't fly. We know that you knew Lynch from your time in the air force."

Brayden started to say something else, but his lawyer again said, "Shut up, Bill."

"We also have the gun you used to shoot Lynch. Ballistics tests prove it was the gun." Peyton paused before saying, "We found the gun hidden in the trunk of your Lexus."

Brayden came straight up out of his chair. "That's impossible," he screamed.

"Not impossible, Bill. It's a fact," Peyton said.

Brayden couldn't tell Peyton that it sure as shit was impossible for the gun to have been found in his car because he'd thrown it into Four Mile Run. So instead he said, "I'm being framed."

Peyton laughed. "You know, it seems like every guy I arrest lately tells me he's being framed."

Peyton continued. "Anyway, we found the gun in your car and have two eyewitnesses to the shooting and a video of you fleeing the scene. So you're pretty much assured a place on a death-row gurney or in the electric chair. Your choice, like I said."

Brayden's lawyer said, "What motive would my client have for shooting this Lynch person?"

"His motive doesn't matter," Peyton said. "That is, it won't matter to the state of Virginia. The state doesn't need a motive to convict him." Before the lawyer could say anything else, Peyton said, "Now for the good news, Bill. I believe that you shot John Lynch because he helped you kill Congressman Lyle Canton."

"What are you talking about?" the lawyer said, genuinely confused. The lawyer may have worked for Spear Industries, but he hadn't been involved at all in Canton's murder.

Again ignoring the lawyer, Peyton said, "I'll be frank with you, Bill. I can't prove that you conspired with Lynch to kill Canton. I did find a hundred grand in cash hidden in Lynch's apartment, which I believe was part of what he was paid to kill Canton, but I can't prove you gave him the money."

What Peyton didn't tell Brayden was that his people hadn't been able to find the money in Canton's apartment without some help from Emma. After Emma had told Peyton that she knew the money was there, he'd dispatched four agents to search for it, and the first search came up dry.

Peyton called Emma and said, "There is no money in Lynch's apartment."

To which Emma had responded, "Yes, there is. Think 'Cask of Amontillado.'"

"What?" Peyton said, but the damn woman had already hung up. Then Peyton thought, *"Cask of Amontillado"? The Poe story? The guy stuck behind a brick wall while still alive?* An hour later, his agents found the money behind the wall in Lynch's closet.

"Bill," Peyton said to Brayden, "you've got one chance here and only one. You may be able to avoid the death penalty, but only if you admit that you paid Lynch to kill Canton and if you name the other people involved in the conspiracy to frame Joe DeMarco. And I'm talking about Sebastian Spear."

"I'm terminating this interview right now," Brayden's lawyer said.

"That's your call," Peyton said. "Your client will be arraigned tomorrow, returned to this jail, and then Virginia is going to convict him of the first-degree murder of a cop. His one and only opportunity for a deal is to tell the truth about Canton."

<hr />

After Peyton left the room, Brayden expected his lawyer to ask him if he knew anything about Lyle Canton's murder. But that didn't happen. Instead, his lawyer said, "Bill, I need to make a phone call."

Fifteen minutes later, the lawyer was back. He said, "You're going to have to retain your own counsel, Mr. Brayden. I can no longer represent you."

That was when Brayden realized that Sebastian Spear's lawyers, to avoid a conflict of interest insofar as protecting their primary client, was throwing him to the wolves.

48

<hr/>

As he usually did, Mahoney added a shot of bourbon to his morning coffee. This morning, however, the bourbon wasn't the old remedy called hair of the dog nor was it simply the daily ritual of a committed alcoholic. This morning's dollop of bourbon in his coffee was instead an act of celebration.

Mahoney had grown sick of the media continuing to imply that he had somehow conspired with DeMarco to kill Lyle Canton. Given the opportunity, he would have mowed down all the so-called journalists with a machine gun as they screamed questions at him every time he ventured outside his office. Well, as soon as Brayden was arrested and Canton's death was pinned on that Capitol cop, Mahoney was going to give the jackals an ass-chewing of epic proportions.

He would say: *This is what happens when you dumb shits start making up the news based on nothing but guesswork. You not only tried to smear my sterling reputation, but that poor lawyer, DeMarco—who I barely knew—was demonized by your irresponsible reporting.* He'd polish the words later—maybe he wouldn't use the word *sterling* when it came to his reputation—but he'd make sure the media looked like the incompetent bunglers they were for trying to tie him to Canton's death.

Yes, Mahoney felt content as the laced coffee went down his gullet; he'd weathered the Lyle Canton storm with no more than a couple of small rips in his political sails. The sad part was that DeMarco was not going to be so fortunate.

DeMarco was going to lose his job.

When Mahoney had set up DeMarco's position all those years ago, he'd been the Speaker and had enough clout to do damn near anything he pleased. Knowing the nature of the things he wanted to use DeMarco for, he'd given him an office down in the subbasement, and there had been no official, documented connection between him and DeMarco. The main reason he had done this was, if DeMarco did something stupid and was caught, Mahoney would be able to say—just as he'd been able to say in the case of Lyle Canton—that he wasn't responsible for any sins DeMarco may have committed. The reason he'd set DeMarco up in a standard civil service position was so that he wouldn't have to waste his budget paying the guy.

And for years everything had worked just fine, until that prick Canton was killed. There were at least twenty thousand people employed by the legislative branch, and about a third of them had law degrees. Mahoney even had one. So DeMarco had been nothing more than a single, tarnished legal needle in a bureaucratic haystack filled with dull and tarnished needles. A couple of times over the course of DeMarco's career, some anal bean counter in OPM had questioned the need for his civil service position, but Mahoney had always been able to bat down any questions with a swipe of his mighty, meaty hand. As time passed, the long-established position of Counsel Pro Tem for Liaison Affairs—a meaningless title that Mahoney had invented—became nothing more than a barely discernible small box on the immense, sprawling organizational chart of the Capitol's bureaucracy.

Moreover, DeMarco had always stayed out of the limelight and never discussed his connection to Mahoney. He certainly couldn't say he was Mahoney's bagman, nor could he talk about the things Mahoney asked him to do when he needed the law bent ever so slightly. When asked what he did, DeMarco would always say that he provided legal services on an ad hoc basis for members of the House and then would say that, due to the need for client confidentiality, he couldn't discuss exactly what those services were. Until he was arrested for killing Lyle Canton, DeMarco's picture had never been in a newspaper.

Now every journalist in America knew who DeMarco was, and as soon as he was released from prison he'd be hounded relentlessly. The host of some morning show—a twenty-five-year-old with a super-model's cheekbones—would ask DeMarco to appear on her show so she could ask how he "felt" about almost going to jail for first-degree murder. As for DeMarco's civil service position, a spotlight had been shone on it by the media, and since the Republican majority in the House now suspected that DeMarco's position was in some way con-nected to Mahoney, they would insist that it be lopped off like a gan-grenous limb on an otherwise unhealthy body.

So DeMarco was probably out of a job, and there was nothing Mahoney could think to do about it. Assuming DeMarco fully recov-ered from being poisoned, he would be unemployed and most likely unemployable, as he'd never practiced law and couldn't put down on a résumé the things he'd done for John Mahoney.

49

It took a couple of days for reality to settle in, but after it did, Bill Brayden sang like the Vienna Boys' Choir.

His new lawyer explained to him that the case against him was rock-solid, in part because the witnesses appeared to be of unimpeachable character. One was a decorated veteran; the other was a wealthy woman respected in government circles and known for her generosity to various charitable causes. Then there was the video of a car identical to his leaving the scene.

His new lawyer said, "I could argue that the video doesn't prove conclusively that it was your car. They didn't get a license plate. I could also argue that the lighting near the bus stop at one in the morning would have made it impossible for the witnesses to positively identify you, but . . . well, it's the gun, Bill. I just can't get around that gun being found in your car."

Brayden just couldn't get *over* the gun. He was obviously being framed, although he supposed *framed* wasn't the right word. All he knew for sure was that he'd thrown the fucking gun into Four Mile Run, which meant that somebody had seen him toss the gun, found the gun, and then planted it in the trunk of his car. That, however, was hardly an argument that could be made in his defense. *I know someone put the gun in my car because I threw it away after I shot Lynch.* Nope, that wasn't going to work.

Knowing he was screwed, Brayden took the FBI's deal: in return for pleading guilty and telling the FBI all he knew about Canton's death, he'd get thirty years instead of a needle in the arm.

He told Peyton how Sebastian Spear had ordered him to kill Canton. He admitted that he'd committed crimes for Spear in the past—crimes he wouldn't discuss in detail. He didn't need to confess to more crimes so he could spend more time in prison. He admitted that he had paid John Lynch to kill Canton and frame DeMarco for the crime. When asked how he went about framing DeMarco, he said that it was with the help of Spear Industries' top computer guy, a guy named Nick Fox. An accomplished hacker, Fox had searched databases to find the perfect person to frame, and DeMarco fit the bill. Then it was just a matter of having Lynch kill Canton and placing all the evidence in DeMarco's office.

"Where's Fox now?" Peyton asked.

"I don't know," Brayden said. Seeing the expression of disbelief on Peyton's face, he said, "I'm telling you the truth. The damn guy disappeared a few days before I shot Lynch. I don't know where he is. If I did, I'd tell you."

Brayden could see no point in telling Peyton that Nick Fox was really Nikki Orlov, a former employee of the GRU, and that he'd helped Orlov enter the United States illegally. Again, he didn't need more crimes to add to the list of the ones they already knew about.

"Back to Sebastian Spear," Peyton said. "Can you prove that he ordered you to kill Canton? Are there witnesses who heard him give the order? Did he send you an e-mail?"

Peyton was being facetious, but Brayden, at this point, had no sense of humor. He said, "Send me an e-mail? Are you shitting me?"

"So what happened?" Peyton said.

"He called me to his office one day, two weeks after Jean Canton died, and said, 'I want Canton gone.'"

"That's it? That's all he said? 'I want Canton gone'?"

"Yeah, but I knew what he meant. He'd said at Jean's funeral that he was going to kill Canton, and I had no doubt whatsoever that he wanted me to kill the man. What else could he have meant?"

Peyton didn't bother to say that "I want him gone" could be interpreted as "I *wish* he were gone."

Peyton said, "Was Spear involved in the planning of Canton's murder?"

"No, he doesn't work that way. He left all the details to me. I did tell him that I was going to frame someone for Canton's murder so the crime wouldn't lead back to us."

"And what did Spear say when you told him this?"

"He didn't say anything. He just looked at me and went back to work. I mean, you have to understand how Spear does things. Like he'd say to me, 'You have to convince Mr. Smith to award us the contract.' Well, I knew that meant that I was supposed to bribe Mr. Smith. But Spear never said to bribe him, not directly. And it was the same way with Canton."

Peyton asked, "What about the money you paid Lynch? Did Spear authorize the payment?"

"No. I had my own operating budget. You know, for doing things like bribing Mr. Smith. So the money came out of my budget, and I didn't need Spear's approval to spend it."

"Were you paid for killing Canton?"

"No, but I would have been. Every year I get a bonus if I've done something for the company that was . . . well, let's say, out of the ordinary. I knew this year I'd get an enormous bonus for taking care of Canton."

"I see," Peyton said.

Peyton was starting to think that there was no way Sebastian Spear would be even indicted, much less convicted, for conspiracy to murder Canton. Nonetheless, he'd go talk to Spear and threaten him, then take it from there.

50

Don Short didn't know what to do.

Don was the project manager for an upcoming job in Uruguay that would start in a month, and he'd assembled twenty people in a conference room to brief Spear, as they usually did before a big job began. For the last hour engineers had been giving PowerPoint presentations on the modifications that would be made to an outdated distribution system; accountants had talked about financial risks and potential profit margins; and a guy from Uruguay, some kind of lawyer, had discussed in accented English political issues that the company might face—and Spear hadn't said a single word. The presenters had stopped several times to see if he agreed with them or had any questions for them, and when he hadn't acknowledged their questions, they'd looked over at Don for guidance. All Don could do was shrug, so they cleared their throats and kept on talking.

Don could tell that although Spear was sitting at the head of the conference table, he wasn't really in the room. Don, like everyone else at headquarters, had heard about Spear's breakdown and his behavior following Jean Canton's death—how he barely spoke and appeared to be oblivious to his surroundings, sleepwalking through the day—but unlike most of his coworkers, Don was somewhat familiar with what Spear was experiencing. He'd had a sister who was a manic-depressive, and when she was off her meds she'd behaved just like Spear: sitting for hours without moving, staring off into space, living in a cocoon of her own making. His sister had eventually committed suicide, and Don knew if someone didn't force Spear to see a doctor, he was liable to end up the same way.

Don was about to end the meeting—there was no point in continuing—when Spear's chief legal counsel walked into the conference room, looking worried.

⸻ ◆ ⸻

Sebastian felt someone or something tap him on the shoulder; he had no idea what or who it could be.

He had been standing alone on a vast, icy plain. He didn't know where the plain was—Siberia? the Arctic, maybe?—but wherever he was, there was snow as far as he could see, the wind was howling, and ice particles slashed his face. Why he was there, he had no idea. The only thing that occurred to him was that he'd been abandoned by God in this bleak, forever-winter place because of the way he'd failed Jean—and he knew he would never find his way to sunshine and warmth again.

The tapping continued and his mind shifted to a different reality. Now he was in a roomful of people, all them staring at him. Why he was in the room he didn't know, but the person who'd been tapping on his shoulder was his lawyer.

The man said, "Sir, I need to speak with you privately. It's urgent. There's an FBI agent here who wants to talk to you about Bill Brayden."

Brayden? Where was Brayden? He couldn't recall the last time he'd seen him.

Sebastian Spear rose from his chair and said to the lawyer, "Deal with it," and walked out of the room.

———◆◆◆———

Don Short wondered if that was the last time he'd ever see Sebastian Spear.

It turned out it was.

51

Spear's lawyer told Peyton that unless Peyton had a warrant for his arrest, Mr. Spear refused to meet with him. The lawyer was the supervisor of the lawyer who'd initially represented Brayden after he was arrested and then dropped him like a hot rock when it appeared that Peyton might come after Sebastian Spear.

The lawyer said, "Mr. Spear had nothing to do with nor any knowledge of the circumstances surrounding Lyle Canton's death. Therefore, he has no reason to talk to you."

Peyton countered: "He threatened to kill Lyle Canton in front of two hundred people at Jean Canton's funeral. Then he ordered Brayden to kill him."

"Really?" The lawyer said. "Do you have proof of this, Agent Peyton? Are there witnesses who heard Mr. Spear order Brayden to kill Canton? Do you have any evidence that he paid Brayden to kill Canton?"

As the answer to all those questions was *no*, Peyton said, "Brayden will testify—and a jury will believe him—that Spear said, 'I want Canton gone.'"

The lawyer frowned as if mightily perplexed. "*I want Canton gone*? I have no idea what that means. Mr. Spear was obviously distraught over Jean Canton's death. There's no denying that. And in a state of grief and under the influence of alcohol, he said he was going to kill Canton at Jean's funeral. But he never did. Nor would he ever do something like that. As for saying to a coworker that he wanted Canton 'gone' . . ."

"Brayden wasn't a *coworker*. He was Spear's go-to guy, his fixer, his bagman. The guy he used to bribe people to get contracts."

As if Peyton hadn't spoken, the lawyer said, "As for saying to a coworker that he wanted Canton 'gone,' that may be true, although you only have Brayden's word that Mr. Spear said any such thing. I mean, Mr. Spear has never said such a thing to me, but I know he despised Lyle Canton because he believed that Canton had been abusive toward Jean. But saying he wanted the man 'gone' . . . That's like saying, 'I wish Canton would drop dead.' If Mr. Spear actually said what Brayden claims, that hardly constitutes an order for Brayden to murder the man."

The lawyer shook his head, as if the whole situation was heartbreaking. He said, "Mr. Spear has no idea why Bill Brayden would have conspired with John Lynch to kill Canton. The only thing I can figure out—which is the same thing I'll tell a jury—is that Brayden may have done this out of some misguided sense of loyalty. And it's tragic that Bill did such a thing, but Mr. Spear certainly didn't order him to commit murder."

In other words, *Go fuck yourself, Agent Peyton.*

52

There was a brief battle between the FBI and the Justice Department, as they argued over which of them would tell the media that it had screwed up by arresting DeMarco. The FBI lost, of course. Its agents were the ones who'd arrested DeMarco and presented a supposedly airtight case to Justice that he was a murderer. If someone was going to end up looking incompetent, it was going to be Russell Peyton or his boss, not the attorney general.

The bureau didn't allow Peyton to speak to the media about DeMarco. For one thing, if Peyton spoke to reporters he wouldn't be able to dodge their questions by saying he didn't know things he obviously knew or should have known. The other reason was that Peyton had a way of making it clear that he had no respect for the media; he was in the company of those who thought reporters should be treated like mushrooms: kept completely in the dark and fed nothing but bullshit. So an FBI spokesperson named Adele Masters was trotted out to appear before the cameras. Masters was a matronly-looking woman with a soft southern accent who looked incapable of lying. The truth was that she was very capable.

The only thing the media had been told prior to the press conference was that the bureau had an announcement related to the death of Lyle Canton.

Without any preamble, Masters said, "The FBI has arrested a man named Bill Brayden for conspiring to kill Congressman Lyle Canton. Brayden has also been arrested for killing a Capitol policeman named John Lynch. Brayden, who works for Sebastian Spear, has confessed that he paid John Lynch to kill Canton and frame Joseph DeMarco for the congressman's murder. He has also confessed to killing John Lynch. Therefore, charges against Mr. DeMarco will be dropped."

It took the gaggle of journalists about two seconds to absorb what they'd just been told—and then they went berserk and started screaming questions at Masters.

How did Brayden frame Joe DeMarco?

Why did he frame DeMarco?

Why did Brayden kill John Lynch?

What's the connection between John Lynch and Bill Brayden?

How did the FBI tumble to Lynch and Brayden being involved?

Was Sebastian Spear involved in anything Brayden did?

And so forth. And to almost every question, Masters said some version of, *I can't answer that question as it's part of an ongoing criminal prosecution.*

After the press conference—which the media, as was made clear in subsequent broadcasts, found completely unsatisfying—the reporters darted off like a flock of angry hummingbirds in different directions. Some went to call sources in the FBI, hoping they'd be willing to leak additional information. Some tried to interview Sebastian Spear; he refused. Some tried to interview Bill Brayden and his lawyer; they refused. More than a few wanted to talk to Joe DeMarco to see how he "felt" about almost spending his life in prison, but when they arrived at the hospital, where DeMarco was still recuperating, his bodyguards refused to allow the press near his room.

Hardly anyone noticed that the FBI didn't apologize for having arrested DeMarco in the first place.

53

When DeMarco opened his eyes, he saw Emma sitting beside his bed. "Hey," he said, "what are you doing here?"

DeMarco hadn't shaved in days, and he needed a haircut, but he looked 200 percent better than he had the last time she had seen him. Thank God.

"How are you feeling?" she said.

"Weak as a day-old kitten but otherwise okay."

"I've talked to your doctor—I've told him I'm your big sister, by the way—and he said you're going to be fine. There's no permanent damage to any major organ. Any brain damage you may have was most likely alcohol-induced and occurred long before you were poisoned."

"Good one," DeMarco said.

Emma said, "They want to keep you here for another day or two, then you'll be free to go."

"You mean free to go back to prison."

DeMarco hadn't noticed that his right ankle was no longer cuffed to the bed.

Pointing at the television above DeMarco's bed, Emma said, "Haven't you been watching the news?"

"No. I keep the TV tuned to the Golf Channel."

That figured. "Joe, you'll be going home when you leave here. The charges against you have been dropped."

Emma told DeMarco everything she'd done, including the few crimes she may have committed, such as tearing out the wall in Lynch's apartment and planting the gun in Brayden's car. Emma didn't ever brag about her accomplishments; people who had done the kinds of things she had done during her lifetime felt no need to brag. Nor did she normally admit to anyone that she'd done something illegal. But in this case, and considering that DeMarco had almost died, she felt he deserved to hear the whole story.

"Jesus, Emma," DeMarco said, "I don't know how I'll ever repay you."

"Oh, I'll find a way," Emma said. That was both a promise and a threat.

It turned out to be a good thing that Emma shared everything with him, because it was DeMarco who eventually realized something she hadn't thought of—an occasion rarer than a Sasquatch sighting.

54

DeMarco met a final time with one of the doctors who'd treated him, an Indonesian woman with a sixteen-syllable name that he couldn't pronounce. She seemed distracted and impatient—as if she didn't have time to waste on healthy people. She told him he was good to go and to check back in a month for some blood tests, and then she was off to see someone who really needed her help.

A couple of Mike Leary's guys, the ones who'd been guarding him on the day shift, offered to give him a ride home. All agreed that with Brayden in jail, Lynch dead, and Hector Montoya terrified into compliance, DeMarco no longer needed expensive armed mercenaries to watch over him. One of Mike's guys went to get the car while the other escorted him to the hospital's main entrance. It never occurred to DeMarco that he should have sneaked out of the hospital wearing a bag over his head.

As soon as he stepped through the door, twenty reporters surged toward him like a stampeding herd of cattle and started screaming questions at him.

Joe! Joe! How do you feel about almost going to jail for Lyle Canton's murder?

Joe, are you planning to sue the FBI?

Joe, do you think Sebastian Spear tried to have you killed while you were in jail?

To his bodyguard, DeMarco said, "Get me the fuck outta here."

Leary's boys drove him to his home in Georgetown, but when they arrived there, DeMarco saw three TV vans parked in front of his house. He told the driver not to stop and to go around the block. They dropped him off at a neighbor's house whose backyard abutted DeMarco's. Fortunately, the neighbor was at work, so DeMarco crept through his backyard and scaled the six-foot cedar fence that separated his own yard from his neighbor's. He entered his house through the back door—and got another surprise.

It looked as if someone had broken into his house and trashed the place—and someone had, the culprit in this case being the FBI. The FBI had just *ripped* his house apart, searching for more evidence to convict him of Canton's murder, and they hadn't bothered to put anything back in its proper place. Cereal and rice and pasta boxes were sitting on the kitchen counter, and he knew that agents had stuck their big hands into each box to see if something was hidden there. All the drawers in the house—bedroom drawers, kitchen drawers, bathroom drawers, desk drawers—were open, the contents removed and not replaced. The clothes from his bedroom closet were lying on the box spring of his bed. The mattress had been flipped off the bed to reveal whether he'd stashed anything beneath it. And that was just the first floor of his house; he knew the second floor and the basement would be in similar states of disarray. Fucking FBI. The only good news was that the blinds were closed, so the reporters outside couldn't see that he was home.

He noticed that the telephone answering machine was blinking with about twenty messages—or as many messages as the machine could hold. Almost all the messages were from newspaper and television reporters asking for interviews. One of the callers was Scott Pelley asking if he'd like the opportunity to tell his story on *60 Minutes. Fuck you, Scott.*

Up to this point in DeMarco's life, no one outside a small inner circle that included Mahoney, Mahoney's secretary, Emma, and Neil really knew what he'd been doing for a living since graduating from college. His neighbors and his friends knew only that he was a lawyer and had some boring job at the Capitol that he never discussed. His photograph, to the best of his knowledge, had never appeared in a newspaper. Now he knew if he googled himself, he'd get about a zillion hits.

They'd photographed him at his arraignment, and he'd seen the photos on the front page of the *Washington Post* and how they'd made him look like the murderer he was accused of being: his hard, unshaven face; his hair in disarray; the intense, jittery eyes of a maniac. The photos had somehow made him look brutal and guilty, as opposed to terrified, which he had been at the time. Now there would be photos of him leaving the hospital, looking gaunt and haggard, as he'd lost about ten pounds, and there would be a startled, wary expression in his eyes, like the eyes of a road-crossing animal caught in the headlights. And the Internet would retain forever everything the media had managed to learn about him: why the FBI had arrested him for Canton's murder; stories dredged up from the past about his Mafia hit man father; and—the worst thing, when it came to his future—all the speculation that he worked for John Mahoney.

DeMarco was almost positive that he couldn't continue to work for Mahoney, at least not in the way he'd done in the past. The whole point of DeMarco's job had always been that it gave Mahoney *deniability*. That is, if DeMarco had been caught doing something shady, Mahoney would have been able to claim he had no connection to DeMarco— which is exactly what he'd done when DeMarco was arrested. But now things had changed dramatically, because the press had shone a spotlight on his civil service position—the one that failed to define exactly what he did and whom he worked for. All the rumors, however— rumors Mahoney had vigorously and repeatedly disavowed—were that DeMarco worked for him.

What this all meant was that the Republicans, who almost certainly didn't believe Mahoney and would enjoy causing him pain—just as Mahoney would enjoy it if the shoe were on the other foot—would insist that DeMarco's job be eliminated. That is, they'd eliminate it unless Mahoney could stop them, and DeMarco doubted that Mahoney would make any attempt to do so, even if he could. How could he after all the denials?

DeMarco didn't like his job, but he *needed* his job. And what he really needed was that golden federal pension he'd get if he survived long enough to get it. If he'd had a normal civil service position, he wouldn't have been so concerned. The way civil service worked was that if a position was abolished, the person who held the position would be placed in some similar, vacant position for which he or she was qualified. The problem, in DeMarco's case, was that there *was* no similar position. *Political fixer/bagman* was actually a very common occupation in the U.S. Capitol—but it was not an accepted federal job title.

DeMarco was about to join the ranks of the unemployed.

———— ◆◆◆ ————

DeMarco couldn't think surrounded by all the clutter, and he spent the next two hours putting the first floor of his house back in order. He didn't have the energy at the moment to tackle the second floor and the basement, so he poured himself a shot of bourbon and took a seat in his den. As he sat sipping bourbon in the dark room—he couldn't open the blinds because of the lurking reporters—he continued to ponder his future. His landline phone rang several times. He ignored the calls, certain they were more interview requests.

He checked his watch: four p.m. Mahoney should still be at work. He pulled out his cell phone and called Mahoney's office. He needed to find out where things stood.

When Mavis answered, he said, "I have to talk to him." He didn't have to identify himself. She knew his voice and had probably been expecting the call.

Mavis hesitated before saying, "Joe, don't call here again. But the congressman will get back to you. Be patient. Oh, and he told me to tell you to stay away from the Capitol."

"I wasn't planning to go there until after I talked to him," DeMarco said. "And I'm going to have to find someplace to stay. I have reporters camping on my front lawn. So tell him to call me on my cell."

Again Mavis hesitated; then she said, "He won't be calling you on your cell, Joe. But just . . . just hang in there for a while."

"Hang in there?" DeMarco said. But Mavis had hung up.

An hour later DeMarco, now on his second bourbon, was still contemplating his options when it came to finding another job. He wondered whether Walmart still hired greeters. *You'll find toasters in aisle ten, ma'am, and they're on sale today.*

His cell phone rang. He didn't recognize the number on the caller ID. So far no reporters had called him on his cell; they apparently hadn't been able to wheedle the number out of Verizon yet, but he was sure they'd get it before long. He decided to answer the call in case it was Mahoney calling from a phone in the Capitol. It wasn't.

The caller said, "Joe, my name is Melissa Monroe. A mutual friend asked me to call you."

DeMarco knew who Melissa Monroe was. She was a famous Washington socialite, and if you weren't invited to a Melissa Monroe dinner party, it meant that you were a nonentity, unworthy of her attention. People's careers had actually been ended by a snub from Melissa Monroe.

Melissa was in her fifties but didn't look a day over forty. Think Zsa Zsa Gabor: a woman who never appeared to age until one day she just died of old age. Melissa was now a widow and a rich one, her last husband, a man thirty years her senior, having left her with about four hundred million dollars. DeMarco suspected that sometime in the past, Mahoney had had an affair with her.

"I have a beach place near Lewisetta," Melissa said, "and you can use it for a while. Get a pen, darling, and I'll give you the address and the security code and tell you where I hide the keys."

DeMarco waited until it grew dark outside, then peeked through the blinds. The reporters were still on his lawn, streetlights shining down on them. They were all eating pizza and drinking beer, yukking it up, having a good old time as they laid siege to his house. It was like watching vultures at a block party. His car was in the garage, but if he tried to use it the reporters would certainly follow him. His mind flashed to Princess Diana and her tragic flight from the paparazzi. Okay, comparing himself to Diana might be a stretch, but he could still see himself sharing her fate.

DeMarco packed clothes and a toilet kit into a knapsack, slipped out his back door, climbed the fence, and scurried through his neighbor's backyard like a cat burglar. From there he walked a couple of blocks, and then Ubered his way to Reagan National, where he rented a car.

55

DeMarco was sitting beneath a poolside umbrella, wearing nothing but swim trunks and holding a cold beer in his hand. He was on the vast deck of a house with a two-million-dollar view of Chesapeake Bay. As it was July, the temperature was about a hundred degrees, but there was a breeze coming off the bay that made sitting outside tolerable. In addition to the deck and the view, Melissa Monroe's beach house had an Olympic-size swimming pool, a Jacuzzi, a refrigerator stocked with enough food to last through Armageddon, and a rec room with a pool table and the largest television he'd ever seen.

He'd been at the house for a week, eating Melissa's food, drinking her booze, and sitting on her deck soaking up the sun. He was tanned and well rested—and miserable.

He still hadn't heard from Mahoney.

He still didn't know whether he had a job or not.

DeMarco heard—then saw—a helicopter pass right over the deck where he was sitting, stirring up the water in the pool. It was a U.S. Navy helicopter, and it landed on the beach in front of the house. *What the hell?*

A moment later, Mahoney walked down the chopper's steps, dressed in a navy flight jacket. On his head was a baseball cap that said USS

Gerald R. Ford. The *Gerald R. Ford* was the latest nuclear aircraft carrier built by Newport News Shipbuilding. DeMarco figured that Mahoney had been visiting the shipyard, and the navy had given him the flight jacket and ball cap after giving him a tour of the carrier. And when he asked for a lift in a chopper to Melissa's place, what could anyone say? You didn't tell the highest-ranking Democrat in the House that the navy didn't give rides to hitchhikers.

Mahoney strolled up to the deck. DeMarco didn't rise to greet him. A normal person would have asked DeMarco how he was feeling; Mahoney was too self-centered to care. Mahoney's opening remark was, "It's fuckin' hot out here." He stripped off the flight jacket and cap, exposing his white hair and a blue polo shirt stretched tight by his big gut. He flopped down in a lounge chair next to DeMarco's and said, "Well, are you gonna be polite and offer me a beer?"

DeMarco took a beer out of a nearby cooler and handed it to Mahoney—then got right to the point. He was in no mood for beating around the bush.

"Do I still have a job?" he asked.

Before answering his question, Mahoney drained half the beer in the can and belched. "Right now, you're on paid administrative leave. You'll remain on paid administrative leave until the end of November."

"How did you manage that?" DeMarco asked.

"I didn't. Your lawyer did, although she got a little advice from me. She talked to the Speaker—that little fuckin' weasel—and to OPM. She said if they abolished your job or tried to fire you, she's gonna sue everybody she can think of. The House of Representatives, OPM, the FBI, the Alexandria jail. But if they keep you on until after November, then she won't raise a ruckus. And, by the way, the hundred thousand that was stuck in your bank account? She's told everybody that they're not to touch that money. Everybody knows it came from Sebastian Spear to set you up, so it's yours as partial compensation for all your mental anguish and suffering. But she said if they fire you or take the money, then you're gonna go on every TV show that wants you and complain about everything the government's done to screw you over, and she's gonna start suing people, asking for millions in damages."

"Maybe I should just let her sue," DeMarco said. If he could win a few million in a lawsuit he wouldn't need a job.

"You could," Mahoney said, "but she might not win, and the lawsuits will drag on for years, and during that time you'll be out of work. It's not easy to sue the federal government."

"But what happens after November?" DeMarco said.

"It's not what happens *after* November," Mahoney said. "It's what happens *in* November."

"What do you mean?" DeMarco said.

"In November there's a midterm election, and the way things are going, with this idiot we have for a president, there's a chance the Democrats might take back the House. And that means I'll be the Speaker again and can do any fuckin' thing I want. But if we don't take back the House . . . Well, you could be in the shits."

"You're telling me that my future depends on the Democrats winning about thirty seats in the House?"

"You remember what O'Donnell said right after the president was elected?" O'Donnell was the Republican Senate majority leader. "He said, 'Elections have consequences.'"

"Are you shitting me?" DeMarco screamed. "'Elections have consequences'!"

"Aw, calm down. Think of this as a vacation. Play some golf, keep your head down, stay out of sight, and come November, we'll go from there."

Before DeMarco could respond, Mahoney said, "You got something besides beer in that cooler? Maybe you could go up to the house and make me a rum and Coke."

"And maybe you could kiss my—"

"Watch your mouth."

56

Melissa Monroe informed DeMarco that it was time for him to find new lodgings. She would soon be holding her annual summer gala at the beach house, and attending would be witty people, Hollywood personalities, politicians (not so witty), and superstar athletes. Had DeMarco actually murdered Lyle Canton she might have wanted him on the guest list, but since he was now just a common innocent man—the key word being *common*—she didn't want him lurking around.

DeMarco had no idea where to go. He doubted that after two weeks the press was still camped outside his house, but he was sure that enough time hadn't yet passed for reporters to have completely forgotten about him. They'd be keeping tabs on his place, and as soon as he showed up they'd start asking question again. He figured it would take at least a month or some enormous scandal—like maybe the president getting impeached—before DeMarco became a story too old to bother with.

He couldn't even stay with his mother in Queens. He'd called his mom three times since Canton's death: once from the jail after he'd been arrested, to assure her that he hadn't killed anyone; a second time from the hospital, to assure her that he was going to live; and a third time after he was exonerated, to tell her he was doing fine but couldn't stay in his house because of the media. That's when she informed him that the jackals had been hounding her, too, wanting to ask about his dad, the hit man; and her son, the man almost framed for murder. The media had been so persistent that she'd fled to Albany to stay with DeMarco's godmother.

The only good news, as far as DeMarco was concerned, was that he still had Sebastian Spear's hundred grand in his bank account. So far the government appeared to be taking his lawyer's threats seriously and hadn't absconded with the money. He thought about flying to some-place where the summer temperature was tolerable, renting a place on a golf course, and spending a month or two playing golf. Normally, if he'd had the opportunity to take a vacation like that, he would have been ecstatic.

Not now. Now he was too angry and worried to enjoy himself. The thing he was worried about was, of course, that he had no idea what lay on the road ahead when it came to a job. But more than the anxiety over his future, he was pissed because the guy who had ruined his life had gotten off scot-free. The FBI might not be able to prove that Sebastian Spear had ordered Canton's death, but DeMarco knew that he had, just as Bill Brayden had said.

DeMarco had done a lot of thinking about Spear and about every-thing else Emma had told him, and he had zeroed in on something that Emma, as smart as she was, apparently hadn't considered.

———◆◆◆———

"How are you doing?" Emma said, when she answered DeMarco's call.

"Good," he said. "Healthwise, anyway. But we need to meet."

"Why?"

"Not over the phone."

Emma laughed. "You think someone might be monitoring your phone?"

"I think someone might be monitoring *your* phone."

"What?"

"You remember that place where Christine almost got bit by a snake? I had a date, and we met you and her there and had a picnic."

DeMarco was talking about Wolf Trap, a center for the performing arts located on over a hundred acres of national park land in Fairfax County. Part of the facility included an outdoor amphitheater, and Emma's musician girlfriend had wanted to see an opera being performed there. DeMarco had no interest in the opera whatsoever, but at the time he had been dating a woman he was trying to impress by pretending he cared about something other than golf and baseball. During the picnic that he'd mentioned to Emma, a copperhead had slithered out of some nearby bushes, scaring the shit out of everyone, but particularly Christine, who'd almost put her wineglass on its head.

"Yes, I remember," Emma said. "I'll meet you there at nine p.m."

"Leave your cell at home and make sure you're not followed."

DeMarco did everything he could think of to make sure he wasn't followed from Melissa Monroe's place to Wolf Trap.

He wrapped his cell phone in six layers of aluminum foil to keep anyone from tracking him with the phone. He had no idea whether the foil would do any good; it was something he'd seen a guy do in a movie. He wasn't worried about the car he was driving having a tracking device on it, as it was a rental and had been parked in Melissa's three-car garage ever since he'd arrived. During the two-and-a-half-hour drive from the beach house to Wolf Trap, he made frequent, erratic turns, constantly checking behind him, stopping twice to see if there was a helicopter or a drone flying overhead. He suspected that none of these measures were really necessary and that he was being paranoid—but in this case, paranoia was good.

He arrived at the main entrance to Wolf Trap at 8:50 p.m., and ten minutes later a motorcycle stopped behind his car. The motorcycle was a black Harley Davidson V-Rod that looked as if it was going a hundred miles an hour standing still. The driver was wearing a helmet that made it impossible for DeMarco to see any facial features, and he wondered who in the hell it could be, until the driver took off the helmet. It was Emma.

When she joined him in his car, DeMarco said, "I didn't know you owned a motorcycle."

"I don't. I think they're rolling death traps. But they are kind of fun. I borrowed it from a friend. I figured if somebody had overheard our conversation and tried to follow me, a bike was going to be harder to follow. I didn't bring my phone."

"Good."

"Now what's going on?" Emma said.

"What was the name of that woman at the NSA, the one who helped you snatch Nikki Orlov?"

"Olivia Prescott."

"Would you call her a close friend?"

"No. But I worked with her several times, especially after 9/11, and I like her. She's dedicated and competent."

"Competent?"

"Yes. Very."

"How come if she's so competent the Russians were able to take Orlov away from her?" DeMarco could tell Emma was getting impatient with the questions.

"I already told you what I think happened," Emma said. "Olivia's men failed to remove Orlov's cell phone when they grabbed him at his apartment building, and he set off a distress signal to the Russians, and they tracked him to the NSA safe house. The GRU is a formidable adversary."

"Right," DeMarco said. "And then, when the NSA finds Orlov, instead of recapturing him, they let the Russians kill him."

"The Russians couldn't afford to let the NSA get their hands on Orlov. I told you that."

"I know, but doesn't it bother you that this woman manages to fuck up everything that has to do with Orlov?"

"Yes, it bothers me, but—"

"I think your buddy, Prescott, screwed you, Emma."

"What are you talking about?"

"I think the NSA wanted Orlov all to itself and didn't want the Russians to know they had him. I think your pal, Olivia, knew that if she allowed you to use Orlov to get Brayden and Spear, then the whole world would know about him, and she'd get into a tug-of-war with the FBI, who would want to arrest him for Canton's murder. So I don't think the Russians killed him. I think he's alive and well and singing to the NSA."

Emma's pale blue eyes bored a hole into DeMarco for a moment, then she closed those remarkable eyes, and they stayed closed for a long time, as she thought over what he'd said. When she opened her eyes, she said something DeMarco, in a million years, never thought he'd hear her say: "I feel like a fool."

———◆◆◆———

"So this was why you were worried about my phone being monitored and me being followed," Emma said.

"Yeah. I figured that maybe the NSA was keeping tabs on you to make sure you didn't screw things up when it came to Orlov.

"Look," DeMarco said, "I want to talk to Orlov."

"Why?"

"Because Sebastian Spear has ruined my life."

DeMarco told her about the discussion he'd had with Mahoney, about how come November he might have a job or he might not. His fate was in the hands of the American public, more than half of whom didn't even bother to vote in midterm elections.

"Even if the Democrats take back the House," DeMarco said, "I'll be screwed. I can't do the stuff Mahoney had me doing if everybody knows who I am."

"Maybe that's a good thing," Emma said. "Make Mahoney get you a job where you don't have to do things you can't talk about. Make him get you a real job, an honest job."

"I might do that," DeMarco said. He'd actually given some thought to blackmailing Mahoney into using his connections to get him something better, something where he didn't have to work out of the sub-basement of the Capitol. And Lord knows he knew things about Mahoney that would make blackmail feasible.

"But if at all possible," DeMarco said, "and no matter what happens to me in the future, I want Sebastian Spear. That son of a bitch is sitting somewhere laughing his ass off. Canton's dead, Lynch is dead, Brayden's going to prison for life, and I'm out of a job while Spear's free as a bird."

"You think Orlov may know something that can be used to get Spear?" Emma said. "Based on what Brayden told the FBI, Spear didn't have anything to do with the operation against Canton other than give the order to kill him."

"So maybe we can't get him for Canton. Maybe we can get him for something else."

57

Emma sent a text message to Olivia Prescott: *Be at my house at six p.m. or I'm going to talk to the FBI about Orlov.*

Emma didn't want to speak to Olivia over the phone. She wanted to look her in the eye when she talked to her.

Five minutes passed before Olivia responded. It probably took her that long to decide exactly what she wanted to say and what she wanted on record. She finally texted: *Threatening me is not wise.*

Emma texted back: *Six o'clock.*

Emma watched through her front window as a black SUV with tinted windows pulled into her driveway at six p.m. sharp. Olivia may have been a devious bitch, but she was a punctual one.

The front passenger door of the SUV opened, and a man stepped out. He was one of the men who'd snatched Nikki Orlov from the parking garage—one of the men who'd been tased by the Russians and was supposed to have been banished to Somalia.

He opened the rear passenger door, and Olivia Prescott emerged from the car. Emma suspected the driver was the other man who'd snatched Orlov, and she couldn't help wondering whether Olivia was thinking about snatching *her* if things didn't go the way Olivia wanted. The stakes were very high for Olivia personally and for the NSA as an organization, and taking Emma off the playing field was not an unrealistic possibility. Emma was glad she'd decided to include DeMarco in the meeting. Killing or kidnapping two people would make things a bit harder for Olivia's thugs—though not impossible.

Olivia stood for a moment, apparently admiring Emma's house, then walked up to the front door alone and rang the bell.

Emma answered the door, and Olivia decided to immediately take the offensive. "I hope you've given a considerable amount of thought to what you're doing, Emma. I like you, I truly do, but as I said, threatening me is not a wise course of action."

Emma closed the door and without saying anything, walked away, leaving Olivia no choice but to follow her. Emma led her to her backyard patio, where DeMarco was sitting.

Olivia stopped abruptly when she saw DeMarco. She said to Emma, "We're not going to talk about anything with this man here. I'm not about to discuss classified matters with a, a *civilian*."

"Sit down, Olivia," Emma said. "And we're going to talk about whatever I want."

Olivia took a seat, and DeMarco smiled at her. He was drinking a beer, and he raised the bottle and said, "You wanna beer?"

"No, I don't want a damn beer," Olivia said. "I want—"

Emma interrupted. "First, we're going to skip past the part where I tell you how angry I am and how foolish I feel for having been duped by you."

"Duped by me?"

"And you're not going to waste my time denying that it was your people, pretending to be Russians, who took Orlov from the safe house."

"*My* people?" Olivia said. "I have no idea what you're—"

"Like I said, Olivia, we're going to skip past the lies and the denials, and I'm going to tell you what's going to happen next. Right now you're holding Orlov someplace and—"

"Orlov's dead. I told you that. We buried him at sea."

"No, he's not. You've got him stashed somewhere and you're bleeding him dry, and I'm sure he's telling you all sorts of useful things about the Russian cyber-warfare program. Which is fine with me. But if you don't do what I want, I'm going to the FBI and the president's chief of staff—a guy who owes me—and tell them what you've done. I might even go to the media, and the next thing you know, you'll be testifying in front of the Senate Intelligence Committee." Emma treated Olivia to a wintry smile. "I'll bet your boss doesn't even know what you've done, and by the time all is said and done the NSA will be humiliated and you'll be out of a job. Or maybe in jail."

Olivia Prescott had the face of a world-class poker player, but Emma noticed that her jaw had clenched when she'd mentioned Olivia's boss.

The head of the NSA was always military—an admiral or a general. These officers usually played things by the book and didn't commit acts that might be considered illegal and might jeopardize their careers. But the high-ranking civilian old-timers in the NSA, people like Olivia Prescott, often kept their military masters in the dark in order to better play the games they played. And that's what Emma was saying: she doubted that the officer who ran the NSA had any idea that Olivia had snatched Orlov, not once but twice, and was now grilling him in an NSA sweatbox.

"What do you want?" Olivia said. Her tone wasn't one of capitulation. She just wanted to know Emma's price so she could decide whether she was willing to pay it. Emma and DeMarco, on their own, were no match for the National Security Agency.

"What I and DeMarco want," Emma said, "is for Sebastian Spear to pay for what he's done, and I think it's possible that Nikki Orlov can help us. So we're going to spend some time talking to Orlov to see what he knows. If he gives us something we can use, and if we can get Spear without exposing the fact that you have Orlov, then we won't expose Orlov. But if necessary, for example if Orlov has to testify in court against Spear . . . Well, then, you give up Orlov."

Now Olivia smiled. "What makes you think I'll allow you to force me to do anything? Enemies of the NSA have a tendency to, I guess you'd say, *evaporate*."

DeMarco came out of his chair, pointed a finger at Olivia's face, and said, "Hey! Let me tell you something, lady."

Emma cut him off. "Olivia, please, don't embarrass yourself. You know that I've already taken steps to expose you if anything happens to us."

Actually, Emma hadn't done any such thing.

Emma was a better poker player than Olivia Prescott.

58

Nikki Orlov was being interrogated by the National Security Agency in a farmhouse west of Havre de Grace, Maryland.

The house was a large, two-story structure with a palpable air of neglect. The white paint was peeling off the siding, the front porch sagged, the windows were opaque with grime. Near the house was a once-red barn with listing walls and a swaybacked roof that had faded to a rusty brown. Surrounding the house and the barn were fallow fields. Closer observation, however, would have revealed barely visible surveillance cameras, floodlights activated by motion detectors, and the realization that the fallow fields provided an unobstructed 360-degree field of fire and view of anyone approaching the place.

Parked near the house was an ancient Ford pickup that could have belonged to a debt-laden farmer. Emma parked her Mercedes next to the pickup. As she and DeMarco were walking up the front steps, the door opened and a compact man wearing a tan T-shirt and jeans appeared in the doorway. Because the T-shirt was the type worn by soldiers in sandy places like Iraq, Emma suspected he was ex-military. He didn't ask who they were—he'd obviously been told they were coming—but gestured for them to enter the house. When he turned, they could see the Beretta stuck in the back of his jeans.

The interior of the house bore no resemblance to its shabby exterior. The living room had the appearance of a high-tech office. There were three workstations with an array of computer equipment, and on one wall were monitors showing the live feed from surveillance cameras. What appeared from the outside to be dirt on the windows was instead a thin foil mesh that prevented electronic eavesdropping. At one of the workstations was an overweight white kid in his twenties wearing a Star Wars T-shirt and drinking Red Bull. Sitting at a chair in front of the security monitors was the same stocky woman who'd pretended to be Russian when she supposedly took Nikki Orlov away from Olivia Prescott. She, too, had a Beretta, hers in a military-style thigh holster. She smiled at Emma and said, "Za zdorovie."

Emma knew that was a Russian drinking toast, but in this case it probably meant: *No hard feelings, lady. I was just doing my job.*

Another young guy walked into the room and took a seat in front of the other workstation. He was tall and beanpole-thin and might as well have worn a sign around his neck that said *Geek.* It was apparent that there were two types of people at the farmhouse: muscle and brains. The muscle was providing protection and guarding Orlov. The brains were doing something related to whatever information Nikki was giving the NSA.

"Where's Orlov?" Emma said to the man who'd let them into the house.

At that moment, a man walked down the stairs from the second floor. He was older than the others, in his sixties. Wire-rimmed glasses covered granite-gray eyes.

"My name's Harris," he said to Emma. "I'm in charge here. Orlov's in the kitchen. You can talk to him in there until noon. At noon we'll need the kitchen for an hour to feed my crew, but after lunch, we'll give you the room again. Or, if you prefer, you can sit with him in one of the bedrooms upstairs or in the barn, which is serving as a bunkhouse, but the kitchen will be more comfortable."

Emma knew immediately that Harris was the one debriefing or interrogating Orlov. The difference between a debriefing and an interrogation was simple. A debriefing meant that Orlov was cooperating and voluntarily telling what he knew. An interrogation meant that he wasn't cooperating and . . .

Emma had met people like Harris before and knew that sleep deprivation, drugs, and waterboarding were the tools of his trade.

Emma said, "The kitchen will be fine, as long as we're not disturbed."

She suspected that no matter where they questioned Orlov, their conversation would be recorded.

———————◆◆◆———————

Nikki was sitting at a table made from rough wooden planks and designed to seat a farm family of eight. He was eating a bowl of Cheerios. He was wearing cargo shorts, a blue T-shirt that matched his eyes, and flip-flops. His dark hair was still wet from his morning shower, and he looked well rested and perfectly healthy; no one had been using a rubber hose on him.

"Hi," he said. "I was told you'd be coming by to talk to me, but I don't know what you want."

DeMarco and Emma took seats at the table. When Nikki dipped his spoon into the cereal bowl, DeMarco yanked the bowl away from him, slopping milk on the table.

"Hey!" Nikki said, empty spoon in his hand.

"You can eat later," DeMarco said. "As for what we want, we want information that will put Spear in jail. So let's start with you telling us what you did for him."

Nikki smiled. "Oh, you know. A little of this, a little of that."

DeMarco moved so fast that Emma wasn't able to stop him. He cuffed Orlov on the side of the head with his open hand, knocking him out of his chair. Standing over him, DeMarco said, "Do I look like I'm in the mood for a little of this, a little of that? I was almost killed because of what you did."

Nikki, now in the proper frame of mind, said that mostly what he did for Spear was hack into computers and steal information that would give Spear Industries a leg up on the competition, like estimates his competitors were developing for bids on upcoming projects and technical information that could give Spear an edge.

"One time," he said, "Spear was looking for proprietary information on a device called a flux capacitor made by Siemens, a German company that does some of the same stuff Spear does. So I got into Siemens machines and pulled out everything I could about it."

Sometimes Orlov would be asked to find information that could be used to bribe or blackmail a person. The person could be someone in a government, foreign or domestic, who would be in charge of awarding a contract. It could be a regulator who was making Spear's life difficult. It could be a competitor who was breathing too hard down the back of Spear's neck.

"There was this one creep," Nikki said, "an OSHA inspector who was driving Spear nuts on this job in Alaska. The guy had two laptops. One of them he used for normal work stuff, but the other, it was filled with disgusting child porn. After I passed this on to Brayden, Brayden told the creep that if he didn't back off, he was going to contact the FBI. I mean, it made me sick. I thought we should have given him to the FBI after the job was done, but Brayden didn't want to, figuring he might be able to use him sometime in the future."

In less than two hours, they had a list of twenty crimes that Orlov had committed for Spear Industries, including extortion, bribery, theft of proprietary information, violations of various financial regulations, contract fixing, and corruption of public officials. This was exactly the sort of information that DeMarco had been hoping to obtain:

information that could be used to land Sebastian Spear in jail for twenty or thirty years.

But there was one major problem: Nikki Orlov had never worked directly with or for Sebastian Spear. All his orders had come from Brayden.

Seeing that DeMarco was not delighted to hear this and looked as if he might knock him out of his chair again, Nikki said, "I'm sorry, but the whole time I worked for Spear, I never spoke to him. Not once. Hell, I hardly ever saw him. Every once in a while, I'd get a glimpse of him in the building in Reston, but he was like a, a ghost wandering around a haunted house."

Emma asked Orlov how he came to work for Spear Industries in the first place. She knew from what Neil had told her that Orlov had fled Russia to keep from getting killed by a GRU general whose wife he'd been screwing.

Nikki, clearly proud of his skills, explained how he'd applied for a job with Bill Brayden by hacking into Spear's computers and gumming up the works on a job Spear was doing on Volga River hydroelectric plants. He laughed. "The first job Brayden gave me was giving a kickback to Vladimir Putin."

"What are you talking about?" Emma said.

Nikki said that in addition to stealing information, he was also the guy who helped Spear move money when it had to be moved in an untraceable manner. This came as no surprise to DeMarco, since he knew Orlov was the one who'd moved the hundred thousand into his bank account.

First Nikki had to explain how business worked in the new Russia. That is, in order for Spear to get the Russian contract, he had to kick back money to various folks, such as the oligarch who ran the electrical distribution system; local criminals who would screw things up if they weren't paid; and of course, the Boss, Vladimir Putin, who got a little slice of everything.

He said that for the Volga River job, the kickback was twenty million. The money originated from two Spear shell companies, one in Qatar and one in Panama, and then Orlov sent it on a meandering journey through half a dozen banks, and as it left each bank, its origin became murkier and murkier. Finally, the money was laundered through a Russian-owned factory in Thailand that made lawn furniture and another Russian company in Mexico that made soccer equipment. Five million eventually ended up in a Liechtenstein hedge fund called Hassler Frick and fifteen million went to the Vontobel bank in Zurich.

Nikki smiled. "Hassler Frick is one of Vladmir's little offshore piggy banks. The account in Vontobel belonged to Fedorov's sister, meaning it really belonged to Fedorov."

Emma, who'd been getting a cup of coffee when Orlov said this, turned and asked, "Are you talking about Evgeni Fedorov?"

"Yeah, Evgeni," Nikki said.

"Who's Evgeni Fedorov?" DeMarco said.

"A Russian oligarch," Emma said. "He controls a number of power companies in Russia, as well as a few other things." To Nikki, she said, "And you're saying that Fedorov ended up with two-thirds of the kickback?"

Nikki shrugged. "I guess, but I don't know what he did with his share. Maybe he made payments to other people involved, like whoever in Russia is supposed to look out for money laundering. Maybe he sent more to Putin out of the Vontobel account. I don't know."

"How does this help when it comes to Spear?" DeMarco asked.

Emma said, "I don't think it does. I was just curious. But we need to talk. Let's go for a walk."

Emma and DeMarco left the kitchen. They found Harris, the NSA inquisitor, sitting at one of the computer workstations. He was wearing a headset, and Emma was about 99 percent certain that he'd heard every word that Orlov had said to her and DeMarco.

"Are you finished?" he asked Emma.

"No. We're just going out for some fresh air."

"Ms. Prescott would prefer that you remain in the house. We don't want the locals to see people over here and decide to drop by for a visit."

"I don't really care what Ms. Prescott prefers," Emma said.

59

Emma and DeMarco left the house and walked over to the barn. Near a side door were four folding lawn chairs and a small pile of beer cans. Harris had said the barn was being used as a bunkhouse. Emma figured that in addition to Harris and the two geeks they'd seen inside at the computer stations, there were four to six NSA agents providing security around the clock. It looked as if the chairs were used by Harris's team to sit outside after the sun went down and enjoy an after-work beer or two.

Emma took a seat in one of the chairs and gestured for DeMarco, who seemed too agitated to sit, to plant himself in another one.

Emma said, "I think the only way to get Sebastian Spear is on a RICO charge. But that's going to be problematic for a couple of reasons."

RICO—the Racketeer Influenced and Corrupt Organizations Act—was originally intended to get Mafia bosses, and it allowed the leaders of a syndicate to be tried for crimes they might not have committed personally but had ordered others to do.

Emma said, "DOJ will offer Orlov and Brayden deals to testify to all the crimes Orlov just told us about, arguing that there's no way that Spear could not have been aware of or complicit in those crimes. If the prosecutor is any good, he'll subtly encourage Brayden to commit perjury and claim that Spear directly ordered him to commit these criminal acts, whether Spear did or not."

"Why would Brayden agree to testify, much less commit perjury?" DeMarco said. "He's already going to jail for life."

"Because the government will agree to knock some time off his sentence or put him in a better prison. Or put him in a worse prison. I don't know, but they'll come up with something to get him to testify. As for Orlov, because he's valuable to the NSA, he'll be offered immunity."

"So what's the bad news?" DeMarco said.

"The bad news is that Spear will hire the best law firm in the world to defend him, the case will drag on for years, and in the end Spear may not be tried much less convicted. His lawyers will argue, just as they did when it came to Canton's murder, that Brayden did all these things without Spear's knowledge and that there's no proof that Spear ordered Brayden to do anything. But there may be a bigger problem."

"Which is?" DeMarco said.

"Olivia Prescott is not going to want Nikki Orlov to testify against Spear. Right now, no one knows she has Orlov, and she wants to keep it that way. He's not only telling her what he's been doing for the Russians since he's been in this country, he's also providing her with a treasure trove on the Russian cyber-warfare program. The last thing she wants is for the Russians to know she has him."

"Well, I don't give a damn what Prescott wants," DeMarco said. "I want Spear in jail. Let's go talk to the FBI. We'll tell the bureau about Orlov being out here, they'll arrest him, and things will proceed from there."

"Joe, there are significant national security implications here."

Before DeMarco could tell her that he didn't give a rat's ass about the national security implications, Emma said, "We should get out of here and go talk about this somewhere else."

"Sounds good to me," DeMarco said. "I'm starving."

As Emma opened the driver's-side door of her Mercedes, DeMarco said, "Shouldn't we tell Harris we're leaving?"

"No. Get in the car. And hurry."

They were too slow. Harris, the guy in the tan T-shirt who'd let them into the house, and the faux Russian woman came out of the farmhouse. Harris said, "I'm afraid I can't let you leave yet. Ms. Prescott is on her way here to talk to you."

DeMarco heard a sound behind him, and saw two more men come out of the barn and walk in their direction. They were both armed.

"Please come back into the house," Harris said.

"Hey, fuck you," DeMarco said. "We're leaving. We don't work for Prescott."

The woman who'd pretended to be Russian smiled and drew her Beretta.

"What are you going to do? Shoot me?" DeMarco said.

"No, not you," the woman said.

She shot the right front tire of Emma's Mercedes.

DeMarco said, "Jesus! Are you people nuts?"

"We have our orders," Harris said. "We don't want to hurt you, but we can't let you leave."

Emma saw DeMarco's hands fold into fists, and he took a step toward Harris. DeMarco, after everything he'd been through, *wanted* a fight— he wanted to hit *something*. But Emma knew that he was no match for the three security men, all ex-soldiers and probably Special Forces. For that matter, he might not have been a match for the woman, who was most likely an ex-soldier herself. If DeMarco started something he was going to get his ass kicked.

"Joe," Emma said, stopping DeMarco before he could take another step. "Let's wait to hear what Olivia has to say." To Harris she said, "Have your goons change my tire."

Harris took them back to the kitchen. Nikki Orlov was no longer there.

Harris said, "Would you like an iced tea? A Coke?"

Before DeMarco could say something rude, Emma said, "Iced tea would be good."

Harris poured them glasses of tea and said, "Ms. Prescott will be here soon."

60

Olivia Prescott walked into the kitchen. She was dressed in a dark blue pantsuit, most likely her office attire at the NSA's headquarters at Fort Meade. DeMarco was amazed by how much she resembled Emma, and not only physically. She had the same aura of command that Emma did.

Emma had suspected that Harris had eavesdropped on the conversation she and DeMarco had had with Nikki Orlov in the kitchen. He may have even eavesdropped on their conversation outside the barn, using a parabolic mic. Whatever the case, Emma was pretty sure that Harris had told Olivia what they'd discussed with Orlov; he may have even been transmitting the conversation directly to her at Fort Meade, and at some point, she'd told Harris to keep them at the farm.

Olivia sat down at the table with Emma and DeMarco. The first words out of her mouth were, "Do you know how the next world war is going to start?

"In Hollywood's version of Armageddon," Olivia said, "it usually shows the doors of the missile silos opening and the ICBMs being launched. Well, it won't start that way. What will happen first is that every vital system controlled by a computer—which is *every* vital system—will shut down: communication systems, power grids, systems for controlling satellites. Everything will crash, and we'll be totally blind and unable to communicate. That is, everything will crash unless we can protect those systems."

Speaking to Emma, Olivia said, "Nikki Orlov is the most significant Russian asset this country has gotten its hands on since the Cold War. Not only did he work for the Russian cyber-warfare program, he was the best they had, and we've already learned things about their capabilities that we were totally unaware of. And since he's been in this country, he's continued to work for the Russians, as you suspected. The main thing he's been doing is inserting back doors into systems that will allow the Russians to cripple the East Coast power distribution network, and working for Spear Industries gave him a particular advantage in this regard. If he'd had time to complete his task, the Russians could have created a power blackout any time they wanted that would have included the Pentagon, the White House, NORAD installations, and the National Reconnaissance Office."

Prescott looked directly at DeMarco, stabbing him with her eyes. "I cannot allow you to do anything that will compromise the information we're getting from Orlov. Right now the Russians think he's dead, because we leaked a story to them via a Russian agent we've known about for years. So I cannot, under any circumstances, permit Orlov to testify against Sebastian Spear, as that will tell the Russians he's alive, and they might be able to do things to counter the information we're obtaining from him."

Turning back to Emma, she said, "I'm sure, with your background, you understand this."

"I do," Emma said.

"What about you?" she asked DeMarco.

"Yeah," DeMarco said.

"What I will allow you to do—"

"Hey! I don't work for you, Olivia," DeMarco said. "I'll do anything I damn well please."

"Mr. DeMarco, I guess you really don't understand the significance of what I've just told you. Before you leave here today you are going to sign a document that says you agree to never disclose what you know about Orlov and what you learned here today. If you violate the agreement, you will be prosecuted for treason and go to prison for a very long time."

DeMarco looked over at Emma. Emma said, "She's serious, Joe. And what she's not saying is that she might have us killed, because our deaths are unimportant compared with the national security value of Nikki Orlov."

As if Emma hadn't said anything about having them killed, Olivia said, "What I will allow is Brayden to testify against Sebastian Spear to see if you can bring him down with a RICO charge. However, I believe Emma is correct and that the likelihood of convicting Spear is low."

There was now no doubt that Prescott's elves had eavesdropped on their conversation near the barn.

"There is, however, another way to get Spear," Olivia said.

"Oh, yeah. What's that?" DeMarco asked.

61

"What do you know about Russian oligarchs?" Olivia said to DeMarco.

"About as much as I know about flux capacitors," DeMarco said.

"Well, let me tell you about 'em."

According to Olivia, most Russian oligarchs were businessmen in the same way that Vito Corleone had been a businessman, and they ran Russia's major industries and financial institutions.

She rattled off a few names DeMarco couldn't pronounce of people he had never heard of: Alexander Grigoryevich Abramov, who controlled Russia's largest steel manufacturer. Roman Arkadyevich Abramovich, majority owner of the private investment company Millhouse LLC; he also owned the Chelsea Football Club. Oleg Vladimirovich Deripaska, founder of an industrial group with stakes in energy, aluminum, machinery, and financial services. Mikhail Dmitrievitch Prokhorov, chairman of a company that was the world's largest producer of nickel and palladium.

The lavish lifestyles of the oligarchs were well documented and photographed: the yachts, the Lear jets, the private islands, the dachas on the Black Sea. They were protected by private security firms and shielded from the law by battalions of cagey lawyers. The biggest thing they had going for them was that they all had personal and financial relationships with the most influential Russian since Joe Stalin: Vladimir Putin.

Olivia smiled. "These guys make Sebastian Spear look like somebody who bakes cupcakes for a living, and a few of them aren't above killing people to solve their problems."

"Okay," DeMarco said, "but I don't see how this helps when it comes to Spear."

"I'm getting there," Olivia said. "You see, there have been a number of instances where oligarchs have gotten on Putin's bad side, and the consequences are never good for the oligarch."

She gave a couple of examples. One was a man named Mikhail Khodorkovsky. He made his fortune by gaining control of Siberian oil fields and at one time was reportedly worth about fifteen billion dollars. In 2003, however, Khodorkovsky got cross-wired with Putin, and the next thing you know, he was convicted for tax evasion, money laundering, and embezzlement. He spent ten years in prison and lost most of his fortune.

Another was Vladimir Petrovich Yevtushenkov, a man involved in telecommunications, who managed to accumulate eight billion dollars. Like Khodorkovsky, he was also arrested for money laundering, and his company was nationalized and taken over by the state—the state being, of course, Vladimir Putin.

Olivia said, "Putin gets concerned when these guys get too much power and too much money and start to act too independently. In the case of Mikhail Khodorkovsky, he veered into Putin's lane politically, talking about the need for reforms, reforms that might result in Russia having a real democracy. As for Yevtushenkov, Putin accused him of plotting some sort of palace coup."

DeMarco was way past impatient. "But how the hell does this help me get Spear?"

"It helps because Evgeni Fedorov, the guy that Spear kicked back fifteen million dollars to, is currently in Putin's crosshairs."

Olivia said that Fedorov had a mansion the size of a medieval castle and a yacht about as long as a naval destroyer. His current mistress was a Victoria's Secret model, and he'd recently bought a pair of Lipizzaner stallions for his five-year-old daughter because one night she said she liked "horsies." However, according to sources inside Russia—of which the CIA had several—Fedorov had recently fallen out of favor with Putin for reasons that were not totally clear. It may have been as simple as Fedorov not showing sufficient respect or reacting too slowly to one of Putin's royal commands. Whatever the case, Fedorov learned that Putin was considering having him arrested, and he was currently in self-imposed exile on a Greek island he owned, hoping to negotiate his way back into Putin's favor.

Olivia said "The last thing that Fedorov would want is for it to become public knowledge that Spear made a kickback to him, because Putin could use that as an excuse for having Fedorov arrested on corruption charges."

DeMarco said, "I still don't see how that would affect Spear."

"Fedorov is a killer, DeMarco," Olivia said. "Like Putin, he's ex-KGB, and he has a reputation for assassinating people who get in his way. There's a story about a journalist who was writing an exposé about him. The journalist's body was dropped off on his editor's porch, minus the head, which was never found."

"But what the hell does this have to do with—"

Olivia looked at DeMarco as if he were the slowest student in the class. She said, "DeMarco, if it got back to Fedorov that Sebastian Spear was about to talk about the kickback he made to Fedorov, Fedorov might very well kill Spear."

"But what would make Spear talk about the kickback?" DeMarco said, completely exasperated.

"He wouldn't, but Fedorov wouldn't know that." Seeing the confusion on DeMarco's face, she said, "Don't you understand? We'd make up a story that Spear was going to testify to a grand jury or a congressional committee about the job he did in Russia, then we'd leak the story in a way that would get back to Fedorov."

Olivia smiled—a smile that would have given small children nightmares. "I believe that when Fedorov hears that Spear might talk about him, he'll send in a team to take him out. Then Spear will be gone, you'll be happy, and you and Emma can stop meddling in my affairs."

DeMarco couldn't believe the way Olivia Prescott's mind worked, but he figured this was a typical intelligence agency maneuver. Instead of doing the correct thing, the legal thing, the straightforward thing, she was going to maneuver a corrupt Russian megalomaniac into killing Spear by telling the Russian a lie.

"So that's my offer," Olivia said. "Just say the word and I'll do my best to get Fedorov to take care of Spear for you."

DeMarco didn't even hesitate. "No," he said. "I want the man in jail. I don't want him assassinated, for Christ's sake. This isn't Russia."

Although he was really thinking that with people like Olivia Prescott running intelligence agencies, maybe that wasn't exactly true.

Olivia shrugged. "Well, it's your call, DeMarco. I don't care what happens to Sebastian Spear. All I care about is Nikki Orlov."

62

As they were driving back to Washington, DeMarco was silent, staring out at the Maryland landscape, brooding.

Emma said, "You did the right thing, Joe. Orlov's more important than getting Spear. And as for being part of some NSA game for killing Spear, you don't want that on your conscience."

DeMarco didn't respond.

Emma said, "I am concerned, however, that Olivia still might use Fedorov to kill Spear, even though she said she didn't care about him."

Now DeMarco looked over at her. "Why would she do that?"

"Because she wants this whole thing with Spear and Brayden and Canton finished. She doesn't want the FBI investigating Spear Industries. She doesn't want any trials. She doesn't want anything that might cause the FBI to learn that Nick Fox is really Nikki Orlov."

"Well, I'm going to talk to Brayden anyway," DeMarco said, "to see if a RICO case can be made against Spear. But I won't say anything about Orlov or anything Orlov told us." Then DeMarco shouted into the car radio, "Did you hear me, Olivia? I'm not going to talk about Orlov, you twisted bitch."

Emma laughed—although she didn't consider it outside the realm of possibility that Olivia had bugged her car.

———◆◆◆———

DeMarco met with Brayden in the Alexandria city jail. Brayden had initially refused to meet with him, seeing no good reason he should, until a guard passed him a note that said: *I'm trying to find a way to get Sebastian Spear. Talk to me.*

Brayden would not be a resident of the jail much longer. He was waiting for the paperwork to be completed to transfer him to a federal prison. In return for pleading guilty to the first-degree murder of John Lynch and conspiring with Lynch to kill Canton, he was given thirty to life as opposed to the death penalty. The FBI had particularly wanted his plea for Canton's death so they could clear that one off their books. He'd be eligible for parole in thirty years, at which time he'd be eighty-four years old. In other words, he was fairly sure he'd die in prison.

Brayden and DeMarco were separated by a two-inch-thick Plexiglas window; they would use phones to communicate. This was the first time Brayden had seen DeMarco in the flesh—it was somewhat ironic that the man he'd try to frame for murder and then have killed by MS-13 was practically a stranger to him.

Brayden picked up his phone to hear what DeMarco had to say. He figured the guy would rant for a bit, but he didn't. DeMarco calmly said, "I want Spear to pay for what he did to me. He's pretty much ruined my life."

Brayden shrugged. He didn't care about DeMarco's problems.

DeMarco continued. "I also figure that you'd like to see Spear pay, too, considering how he hung you out to dry. Well, the only way I can think of to get him is on a RICO charge. You know what that is?"

Brayden nodded.

DeMarco said, "I think—in fact, I'm positive—that you committed a lot of crimes on Spear's behalf. You bribed and blackmailed people for him and did a lot of other illegal shit to help him beat his competitors."

Another shrug. Not a denial shrug but a "So what?" shrug.

DeMarco said, "You need to come up with a list of those crimes, crimes that can be verified when the FBI subpoenas Spear's records, and then you need to testify that he ordered you to commit them." DeMarco paused. "Do you understand what I'm saying, Brayden? If necessary, you lie and say that he personally ordered you to do things, because that's the only way we'll get him, and a jury will believe you because they'll figure there's no way he could not have been complicit in those crimes."

Brayden shook his head and spoke for the first time. "There are no records, DeMarco, because I made sure there were no records. I have no proof whatsoever that Spear ordered me to do anything. If the FBI could find Nick Fox that would help, because then he could back me up, but they tell me Fox has disappeared."

"He has," DeMarco said. No way was DeMarco going to say anything about Nick Fox, aka Nikki Orlov, just in case Olivia Prescott had bugged the jail. Olivia Prescott could bug the whole wide world.

"Plus," Brayden said, "with Spear's money and his legal team, I think no matter what I said, and even if Fox could corroborate my testimony, he'd still get off. The guy went off the deep end after his girlfriend died, but he's not stupid."

DeMarco stared at Brayden for several seconds before finally saying, "Well, then, fuck you." He hung up the phone on his side of the glass.

Brayden rapped hard on the Plexiglas. DeMarco picked the phone back up.

"Tell me one thing," Brayden said. "Who put the gun in the trunk of my car?"

"Beats me," DeMarco said, and started to hang up the phone again, and again Brayden smacked the glass.

Brayden said, "DeMarco, because I figure I sort of owe you for what happened to you—"

"*Sort of*?" DeMarco said.

"—I'm going to tell you something." Brayden paused. "Sebastian Spear's a dead man."

"What are you talking about?" DeMarco said.

Brayden smiled, hung up his phone, and walked away.

———◆———

What DeMarco didn't know was that yesterday Bill Brayden had met with Hector Montoya.

Brayden told the inmate who ran MS-13 inside the Alexandria jail— the man who'd planned the attack on DeMarco in the jail cafeteria— that he needed to meet with Hector.

"Why?" the guy asked.

"Just tell him that it'll be worth a lot of money to him, some of which I'm sure he'll pass on to you."

The next day Hector was on the other side of the Plexiglas, and Brayden couldn't help seeing the humor in the situation. A fucking criminal like Hector, for maybe the first time in his life, was on the *right* side of the glass—the right side being the side where you got to leave afterward.

Brayden said, "I've got a lot of money, money that I'm never going to be able to spend."

"Okay," Hector said, not having any idea where Brayden was going with this.

"I want you to do something for me," Brayden said. "And I'll pay you half a million dollars.'

"Half a million?" Hector said. "Is this some kind of a joke?"

"No. The money's in a bank in Nassau, and all you need is the account number and a password to transfer the money to any bank you want. For a fee, like ten percent, the guy who runs the bank will help you move the money so you won't get caught for income tax evasion."

"But half a million?" Hector said. If you added up all the money that Hector had made in his thirty-two years on earth it probably wouldn't come close to half a million.

Brayden said, "Yeah. And if it was a million, it wouldn't matter to me. I'm never going to be able to spend the money I have in Nassau, so I might as well put it to work."

"What do you want me to do?"

"I'll get to that in a minute. But first you need to know that I won't give you the password to get the money until you finish the job. I think you know I'll pay you, but if I don't, you can always get people inside the prison to take care of me."

"You got that right," Hector said. "So what's the job?"

Brayden figured there was a good chance the phones he and Hector were using were monitored, so he took a piece of paper out of his pocket and held the paper against the glass. After Hector had time to read the note, Brayden stuffed the paper into his mouth, chewed a few times, and swallowed.

The note had said: *Kill Sebastian Spear.*

63

A helpful nurse directed DeMarco down a long corridor to Lazlo's room.

DeMarco wanted to see Lazlo and thank him for saving his life. It had taken him half a dozen phone calls to learn that he was at the MedStar Washington Hospital Center in D.C., a place that had a lot of experience when it came to knife and gunshot wounds. He had been told that Lazlo was in stable condition, after having been stabbed four times, but that he'd lost a kidney; it was a good thing the good Lord designed folks with a spare.

He found Lazlo in a private room, sitting up in bed, reading a John Grisham paperback, looking perfectly healthy. The guy was so tall his feet extended beyond the end of the bed. With his shaved head, brutal features, and the eight-pointed stars tattooed on his neck, the reading glasses perched on the end of his nose seemed incongruous. DeMarco had expected to see a guard sitting outside Lazlo's door, but there was no guard, nor was Lazlo cuffed to the bed.

DeMarco stepped into the room and said, "Hey," and Lazlo looked at him over the top of the glasses.

"Ah, it's you," Lazlo said, then surprised him with a broad smile. Considering that Lazlo had almost died saving his life, DeMarco had not been expecting a warm greeting.

"I've been reading about you," Lazlo said. "You know, you're the only guy I know who was actually framed for a crime. Everybody else I know, including me, deserved to be in jail."

"Yeah, well, I just came by to see how you were doing and to tell you thank you. You saved my life. So how are you doing?"

"Doin' great," Lazlo said. "I'll be going home tomorrow."

"Home?" DeMarco said.

"Yeah. I got a lawyer, told her how the sheriff assigned me to be your bodyguard and how I was almost killed. The lawyer started talking about a lawsuit, and by the time everything was all said and done, they decided it would be best to let me off for time served. So I'm free man, thanks, I guess, to you."

DeMarco never had found out what crime Lazlo had committed to be in jail in the first place—and now, frankly, he didn't care.

———◆◆◆———

After seeing Lazlo, DeMarco turned in the rental car he'd been driving and took a cab to his place in Georgetown.

Ever since being evicted from Melissa Monroe's beach house, he'd been staying in a rental property that Neil owned in Springfield, Virginia, because he hadn't wanted to take the chance of running into any relentless journalists who might still be staking out his own house. The last thing he wanted was to get his picture in the paper again; he wanted the media to forget all about him.

But now he was headed home, not to move back in, but to pack.

He was planning on leaving town the next day.

DeMarco had decided that he couldn't just sit around for the next four months stewing about what might happen in the midterm elections, and the way he looked at it, he had two choices when it came to how he should spend his time.

One: Take the hundred grand in his bank account, pay off his mortgage, and spend the time until November looking for a new job. Yep, choice one would be the smart, prudent, practical, grown-up thing to do.

Two: Throw his golf clubs into the trunk of his car and spend the next four months playing every golf course he'd ever wanted to play—greens fees be damned—and seeing America.

It didn't really take him too long to make up his mind.

He sneaked into his house after first checking to make sure no strangers with cameras were lurking about. He cleaned out of his refrigerator the food that would spoil—and the food that had already spoiled—turned off the air conditioner, and set the timers for the lights. He then tossed his golf clubs, golf shoes, and a suitcase packed with casual clothes into the trunk of his car. Tomorrow, on his way out of town, he'd drop off at the post office the form that would forward his mail to Emma. He'd also call the neighbors across the street, a guy and his wife he'd known for years, and ask them to watch his house until he returned.

But there was one more thing he had to do before he took off to see the U.S. of A.

He just had to.

He had to look Sebastian Spear in the eye and say, *I'm going to be watching you for the rest of my life, and if I ever get a chance to get you, I'm gonna get you.*

64

Boris Kasso and Yuri Kamenev were parked in front of Sebastian Spear's home in McLean.

They were exhausted. They hadn't slept in a day and a half.

They'd flown from Evgeni Fedorov's private island off the coast of Greece to New York. From JFK, they took a cab to Brighton Beach and bought guns and a car from a guy who used to be a gangster in Moscow and was now a gangster in Brooklyn. They couldn't borrow the car, because there was a good chance they wouldn't be bringing it back. From New York, they drove to Sebastian Spear's headquarters in Reston, Virginia, hoping to pick up Spear when he left work.

Evgeni Fedorov had told them that Spear had to die. All they knew was that Evgeni had gotten a phone call, and after the call he'd stomped around for a while cursing, yelled at his girlfriend, made her cry, and then told Boris and Yuri to get their fat asses to Virginia and kill this guy Spear, whoever he was. Evgeni told them, if possible, to make it look like an accident—a car accident, a hit and run, a house fire, whatever—but if faking an accident wasn't possible, then just shoot the son of a bitch.

Boris and Yuri had done this sort of thing for Evgeni several times before so they weren't surprised by the assignment. When an oligarch like Evgeni had a significant problem with a person, one that couldn't be solved with money, he had the person killed. What they didn't like was killing the guy in the United States. The cops actually caught killers in the States, and it would take more than a bribe to get them out of jail.

So yesterday they'd watched when Spear left his office, driving as if he might be drunk, slowly, under the speed limit, yet oblivious to other drivers and traffic signals. He rolled through two intersections without stopping, and it was a miracle he wasn't T-boned by another car. Boris said to Yuri that it might not be necessary for them to do anything, as it looked as if Spear might arrange his own fatal accident.

Oddly, Spear ended up at a cemetery, where he parked his car and walked over to a headstone. Then the damn guy lay down in the suit he was wearing, curled into a fetal position, and appeared to go to sleep on top of a grave. He didn't move for an hour.

What the fuck?

Yuri, who was younger than Boris, and had been hired for his muscles, not his brain, said they ought to just walk into the cemetery and put a bullet in Spear's head while he was lying there. Boris said no. He pointed out that they'd be completely visible, standing in the middle of the cemetery shooting the guy, and if someone should drive into the cemetery—

Just as Boris was making this rational argument, a twenty-car funeral procession, led by a black hearse, drove into the cemetery. Boris gave Yuri a now-you-see-why-I'm-in-charge look.

Spear must have heard the funeral procession—the doors slamming as people got out of their cars—because he got up. But then, instead of leaving, he looked down at the grave for another couple of minutes, talking to himself. Or maybe he was talking to the person in the grave. After he finished his speech, his prayer, whatever it was, he staggered back to his car, and Yuri thought the way he moved made him look like one of those *Walking Dead* zombie guys. Yuri loved that show.

From the cemetery, Spear drove to his house in McLean, again driving as if he were the only driver on the road, and again Boris thought a fatal accident might be a lucky possibility. When he reached his house, he opened the big driveway gate with a remote, drove halfway into his garage, then zombie-walked into the house. He didn't close the gate, and his car was only halfway in the garage, and the garage door was wide open. If someone shut that garage door it was going to bounce right off the roof of a very expensive car.

Yuri said, "There's nobody on the street. Let's just go shoot him. Please. We go in through the garage, walk into the house, shoot his ass, and make it look like a robbery."

Boris pointed. "You see the camera over the door, dummy? The way he parked, it looks like he's going out again. We'll just wait. When he leaves, we follow him. With some luck, he'll park someplace, cross a street, and I can run over him."

Hours later, they were still waiting in front of Spear's house as the sun disappeared over the horizon. The neighborhood was a wealthy one, and well lighted with streetlamps, and Boris was afraid that one of Spear's rich neighbors might call the cops and tell them two strange men were parked on the street. Boris knew that he and Yuri looked like the kind of guys the cops would roust and search, and then they'd find the weapons they were packing. As he was thinking this, lights went on in Spear's front yard, like lights on timers, and Boris thought, *So much for a nighttime assault.*

Boris said, "Okay. We'll go buy some ski masks, find a motel, have some dinner, and get some sleep. Tomorrow morning we'll come back early, and if the gate is still open, we'll just whack him."

"Sounds like a plan to me," Yuri said, the idiot not realizing it wasn't a plan at all.

The next morning—a Saturday—they arrived back at Spear's house and saw that the gate was still open and Spear's car was still parked halfway in the garage.

Boris said, "Let's wait a bit, see if he leaves."

"Aw, come on," Yuri said.

At that moment, a battered black Camaro parked on the street about fifty yards in front of them. Whoever was driving, however, didn't immediately get out of the car.

"Now we're going to have to wait for this asshole to leave," Yuri said.

A long five minutes later, the driver got out of the Camaro: a short, tough-looking Muslim woman wearing a blue hijab, jeans, and a T-shirt. She stood there next to her car, appearing to study Spear's house, then turned to get back in her car.

"Holy shit!" Yuri said. "She's got a gun."

Yuri was right. The woman hadn't pulled her T-shirt over the Glock stuck in the back of her jeans.

Anita Ramirez had been amazed when Hector Montoya came to her mother's house yesterday and said he'd pay her twenty grand to kill a guy.

"That DeMarco guy?" she said.

"No, not him. Stay the hell away from him," Hector said. "It's another guy, this rich guy named Sebastian Spear. I'm paying you so much because he might have guards and shit."

"Why do you want him dead?" Anita asked.

"What do you care?" Hector said.

Anita decided that she really didn't care, and for twenty grand—hell, she'd probably be willing to kill her mother. If Anita had known how much Brayden was paying Hector, she would have asked for more, but she didn't know, and twenty grand was a *lot* of money, enough so she could afford to move out of her mother's house and get a place of her own again. And there was something else: she was really pleased that Hector had come to her again to kill someone. She'd become, like, his *designated hitter*. If there was any outfit that had a glass ceiling when it came to women, it was MS-13—but Hector had somehow become enlightened.

Anita drove to Spear's house in McLean the next morning, not knowing what she was going to do, but figured as it was a Saturday, the guy might be home. Once she got to the house she'd decide what her next step would be—like maybe just knock on the door and shoot the fucker.

She parked in front of Spear's place, studied the house for a while, then got out of the car, thinking she might walk around and see what the place looked like from the back. She was happy to see that the big wrought-iron gate for the driveway was open. Then she noticed the security camera over the front door. She was glad she'd decided to wear her Muslim disguise, the blue hijab. If she decided to go into the yard, she'd wrap the hijab around her face like a mask, let the cameras see her, and after she killed Spear, the cops would go crazy looking for a terrorist.

She turned to get back into her car to think things over, when she noticed the car parked down the block from her and the two big guys sitting in it. Who the hell were they? Spear's security? She'd just sit awhile and see what they did.

Then, she couldn't believe it. *Another* car arrives, and this one drives right through Spear's open gate and parks in front of his garage. When the driver got out of the car, Anita said out loud, "What the hell?"

It was that guy DeMarco. What was he doing here?

65

―――――◆◆◆――――――

Sebastian Spear was sitting in a dew-damp Adirondack chair near his swimming pool.

He was wearing a white bathrobe, the robe open, and white boxer shorts. He didn't remember getting undressed and putting on the robe. He had no idea how long he'd been sitting by the pool. He suspected he'd been there all night. He was vaguely aware that there was something heavy in the right-hand pocket of the robe.

He remembered talking to Jean yesterday. At least he thought it was yesterday. He'd gone to the cemetery to say good-bye to her, as the last time he'd been there he'd been arrested before he could do so. Then he had decided to lie down on her grave so he could be as close to her as possible. As he lay there he had vivid memories of her, so vivid it was as if a movie had been playing inside his head. He remembered the way she'd looked at the senior prom in high school, wearing a blue dress with spaghetti straps that had transformed her from a girl into a woman. He recalled her on a cold day at the stadium at UVA watching the Cavaliers play, her cheeks red, her eyes shining with excitement, her hair blowing behind her in the wind. He remembered the last time he saw her, two days before she died, lying next to her in bed, mesmerized by the heart-shaped birthmark on the back of her neck.

He remembered everything.

Including the last thing he'd said to her: *We'll be together soon.*

His right hand moved slowly toward the heavy object in the pocket of his robe.

———◆◆◆———

DeMarco knew it was possible that Sebastian Spear wouldn't talk to him, but he was going to try. As it was early on a Saturday morning, he drove to Spear's house thinking Spear might be there, unless he was out of the country. When he arrived at Spear's place, he was surprised to see that the wrought-iron driveway gate was open.

DeMarco drove through the gate and parked, noticing that the garage door was also open. A Mercedes SUV with snow tires was parked in one bay; in the other bay was a Tesla, but the Tesla was only halfway in the garage. He couldn't imagine why the driver wouldn't have driven the car all the way in.

He rang the doorbell, but no one came to the door. He pressed the bell again, holding it down long enough to be irritating to anyone inside, but still no one came. He walked away from the door and looked in through the front windows. With the gate and the garage door open, someone had to be there.

He walked toward the rear of the house, looking into windows as he walked, until he came to the backyard and a low fence surrounding a patio and a swimming pool. Spear was sitting in a chair next to the pool, dressed in a white terrycloth bathrobe, looking down at the water.

DeMarco opened the gate to the pool area, figuring Spear would hear him and turn to face him, but he didn't. He just continued to sit there, oblivious to the world.

DeMarco walked up to him and said, "Spear."

Spear didn't appear to hear him. He seemed captivated by the blue tiles at the bottom of the pool. It was as if he was in a hypnotic trance.

"Spear!" DeMarco said again, this time yelling the name.

Spear slowly turned his head and looked up at him. His eyes seemed to have a hard time focusing, as if he'd been awakened from a dream.

"Go away," Spear said.

"Do you know who I am?" DeMarco said.

"No, and I don't care. Go away."

He wondered if Spear was telling him the truth, and he really didn't know who he was.

"Well, you should care," DeMarco said. "I'm Joe DeMarco. The guy you tried to frame for Canton's murder."

Before DeMarco could say another word, Spear came out of his chair—he popped up like a jack-in-the-box—and pulled an ancient-looking revolver from the pocket of his bathrobe. He pointed the muzzle at DeMarco's chest.

Oh, shit! DeMarco thought. *I'm going to die.*

But Spear didn't pull the trigger. He said, "Are you here to kill me?"

"What? No," DeMarco said. "I just wanted you to know that—"

Spear took a step toward him, still pointing the gun at him—then he reversed the weapon in his hand, now holding it by the barrel, and thrust it at DeMarco.

"Take it," Spear said. "Go on, take it. Kill me."

He's insane.

DeMarco backed away, holding his hands up. "I don't want to kill you. I just wanted to tell you that—"

"Take it," Spear said, advancing closer, thrusting the gun at him. "Go on, take it. Kill me."

"You're fucking nuts," DeMarco said. "I just came here today to tell you that I may be out of a job thanks to you, and if I ever get the chance, I'm going to make sure you go to jail. But I didn't come here to kill you."

"Why not?" Spear said.

Jesus! DeMarco knew he had to leave, and he had to leave *now*. At any moment Spear might change his mind and shoot him. Or he might kill himself, and DeMarco sure as hell didn't want to be there if that occurred. He could just see himself trying to explain Spear's death to a bunch of cops who might not believe him and would most likely think that he'd killed Spear.

He backed away from Spear, toward the patio gate, watching Spear as he did, and Spear finally stopped moving forward with the proffered gun. Then, as if nothing had happened, Spear put the gun back in the pocket of his robe, sat back down, and resumed staring into the pool.

DeMarco began walking rapidly away, toward the front of the house and his car, his heart still hammering in his chest.

DeMarco had been expecting to confront the diabolical mastermind who'd ordered Bill Brayden to frame him, but it was obvious that Spear had had some sort of mental meltdown and hadn't even known who he was. To Sebastian Spear, he'd been nothing more than a nameless pawn that had to be sacrificed to avenge the queen that Spear had lost. It was as if everything that had happened to him—almost going to prison for life, almost dying—had been as random and as senseless as being struck by lightning.

DeMarco could understand Spear hating Lyle Canton and wanting him dead, because he blamed Lyle for taking Jean away from him. He could also understand the man plunging into a deep, suicidal depression after Jean died. DeMarco had known a man personally who had become so depressed after his son died that he'd killed himself. But what he couldn't understand was the son of bitch being willing to frame an innocent man for murder so he could satisfy his need for revenge.

He took a breath.

It was time to get on with his life. He was going to enjoy the next four months with Sebastian Spear's money, and come November he'd see if he still had a job. And if Spear was still around after he returned, he might do as he'd promised and see if he could find some way to put Spear in a cell. But he was starting to think that he might not have to do anything, because it looked as if Spear could end up spending the rest of his miserable life in a loony bin. That is, if he didn't kill himself first.

66

DeMarco started to get back in his car, when he noticed, parked across the street, two guys in a Caddy with New York plates. They were big guys, hard-looking guys—and although he didn't know them, he knew them.

DeMarco's father had worked for a mob boss in Queens named Carmine Teliaferro. The men in the Caddy looked like the type of men Carmine had employed: large muscles, small brains, no scruples. They were the ones Carmine sent when he wanted someone maimed. DeMarco's father was the one Carmine sent when he wanted someone killed.

It was then that he remembered Emma saying that Olivia Prescott might leak it to that Russian oligarch—DeMarco couldn't remember his name—that Sebastian Spear posed a threat to him. Could these two thugs have been sent by the Russian?

He realized he was staring at the two men in the car and looked away. That was when he noticed a second car, an old black Camaro with Bondo on one fender. It was parked about fifty yards in front of the car containing the thugs.

A woman was in the driver's seat, apparently a Muslim, as she was wearing a blue hijab. She was looking over at him, just like the guys in the Caddy. Then he thought: *Blue hijab?* He remembered when he was in the hospital, a brown-skinned woman in a blue hijab leaning over him. He thought he'd been having a dream, but why would the woman in his dream be here and why was she just sitting in her car?

Anita thought: *What is it with this son of a bitch? Why is he just standing there?* First the goddamn guys in the Caddy behind her and now this yahoo, DeMarco.

She hadn't known what to do about the guys in the Caddy. She'd been thinking she'd wait awhile and see if they left, and after they left, she'd use the hijab to cover her face and walk into Spear's house and shoot the asshole. If the guys in the Caddy didn't leave, then she had a plan B—and plan B would be really bad for them. She'd walk over to their car, all smiley, looking all little and humble and harmless, and say, "Hey, I'm lost. Can you tell me where Elm Street is?" When they relaxed, she'd whip out the Glock and shoot them both—*then* she'd go shoot Spear.

But now, goddamnit, DeMarco was standing there, first looking at the guys in the Caddy, now looking at her. Why didn't he just get in his car and drive away?

Yuri said, "What the hell's he doing? Why's he standing there?"

"How the hell would I know?" Boris said.

Until this guy, whoever he was, had shown up, Boris had had a plan. His plan, although he didn't know it, was pretty much the same as Anita Ramirez's plan. They would wait a few minutes to see if she left, and if she didn't, he and Yuri would put on the ski masks they'd bought last night and walk toward her car, holding their guns in their hands. She'd sure as shit leave then. After she'd split, they'd kill Spear, drive to Dulles, and catch the first plane out of the country.

But now this damn guy was standing there, looking at him and Yuri. Maybe he should modify the plan. Yeah, they'd put on the ski masks, Yuri would scare off the Muslim while he shot this asshole who was screwing things up, *then* they'd kill Spear.

Aw, shit. The guy just took out his phone.

———◆◆◆——

DeMarco's inclination was to get in his car and leave—but he couldn't do that.

There was something wrong with this situation, these people all parked on the street in front of Spear's house. And although he didn't know who the Muslim woman could be, it did seem possible that the guys in the Caddy were Russians sent to deal with Spear. He'd told Olivia Prescott that he wasn't going to play any part in some underhanded NSA plan to execute Spear, and he'd meant what he said.

He thought for another second or two about what to do, then did the simplest, most straightforward thing he could think of: he pulled out his phone and called 911.

He told the 911 operator that he was at the home of Sebastian Spear, gave her Spear's address, and said that Spear was armed and appeared to be suicidal. He said, "You need to send a cop here to disarm him before he kills himself. And maybe you ought to send a suicide counselor to talk him down."

As he'd been talking to the 911 operator, he'd been watching the people in the cars on the street, particularly the car with the two men in it. He noticed they were looking intently back at him while he was on the phone.

Then he did something that maybe he shouldn't have. He used his phone to take photos of the men in the Caddy and the woman in the Camaro.

———◆◆◆———

"You motherfucker!" Anita screamed.

"Fuck me!" Boris yelled.

Yuri said, "Let's do it. I'll go shoot that fuckin' woman. You go shoot that asshole and take his phone."

"He called someone," Boris said.

"So what?" Yuri said. "He doesn't know who we are."

"Okay. That's it," Anita said out loud. These sons of bitches were costing her twenty grand. She was going to kill them all. She wrapped the lower part of the hijab around her face, pulled the Glock out of the back of her jeans, and started to open the door when . . .

"Yeah, let's do it," Boris said. He started to pull the ski mask down over his face when . . .

A Fairfax County Sheriff's cruiser turned the corner, its light bar flashing blue and red, and came directly down the street toward Spear's house.

———◆◆◆———

Thank God, DeMarco thought.

When the deputy parked in Spear's driveway, the two guys in the Caddy and the woman in the Camaro took off, leaving like a two-car Shriner parade.

The deputy who stepped out of the cruiser was an irritated-looking guy in his forties with a buzz cut. His nose was peeling from a recent sunburn, and his gut flopped over his gun belt. DeMarco got the immediate impression that he was one of those arrogant small-town cops who reveled in the authority a badge gave them.

The deputy said, "You the one who called nine-one-one?"

"Yeah," DeMarco said.

"You look familiar."

Oh, great.

"What's your name?" the deputy asked. "Where have I seen you before?"

"Look, forget about me," DeMarco said. "I came here this morning to talk to Mr. Spear and—"

"Why?"

"It doesn't matter. Anyway, I went to talk to him—he's in the backyard sitting by the pool—and he pulled out a gun and pointed it at me. But then he tried to give me the gun and told me to kill him."

"He did?"

"Yeah. He's obviously got some kind of mental problem, and I think he might be suicidal. Which is why I called nine-one-one." DeMarco decided not to mention the two thugs and the woman in the Camaro.

"Okay," the deputy said. He started toward Spear's backyard.

"Hold on," DeMarco said. "You need to get someone here who can talk to him, like a hostage negotiator, a suicide shrink, someone like that."

"Hey, I'm not going to call a bunch of people until I've assessed the situation. You just stand back and stay out of my way."

"I'm telling you, the guy's dangerous, to both you and himself. If you go back there—"

"Just stay out of my way," the deputy said.

Less than a minute later, DeMarco heard the deputy yell something he couldn't understand.

The next thing he heard was a gunshot.

Aw, shit.

DeMarco ran toward the backyard, already knowing what he was going to find. He turned the corner where he could see the swimming pool, and there was the deputy standing over Spear's body. Spear was on his back, looking skyward, the expression on his face oddly peaceful. His bathrobe was open and there was a small black hole in the center of his chest. The old revolver was clutched in his right hand.

The deputy turned to face DeMarco, the arrogant putz now ashen and shaken looking. He said, "He pointed his gun at me. He wouldn't put it down. I didn't have a choice."

Four hours later, after giving statements to three different cops, DeMarco was headed west, golf bag in the trunk of his car.

In his rearview mirror was Washington, D.C.

Ahead of him was . . .

He had no idea.

Acknowledgments

House Arrest is the eleventh novel I've published with Grove Atlantic. I consider myself extremely fortunate to have had such a long relationship with such an outstanding publishing company and I want to thank Morgan Entrekin, Brenna McDuffie, Deb Seager, Allison Malecha, Justina Batchelor, Bill Weinberg, Peter Blackstock, Julia Berner-Tobin, and Amy Hughes for their work on this book as well as on others over the years.